THE
HOPE OF JANUS

The Hope of Janus

The Third Novel in the Janus Chronicles

Patrick David Daley

THE HOPE OF JANUS
THE THIRD NOVEL IN THE JANUS CHRONICLES

Copyright © 2017 Patrick David Daley.

All rights reserved. No part of this book may be used or reproduced by any means, graphic, electronic, or mechanical, including photocopying, recording, taping or by any information storage retrieval system without the written permission of the publisher except in the case of brief quotations embodied in critical articles and reviews.

iUniverse books may be ordered through booksellers or by contacting:

iUniverse
1663 Liberty Drive
Bloomington, IN 47403
www.iuniverse.com
1-800-Authors (1-800-288-4677)

Because of the dynamic nature of the Internet, any web addresses or links contained in this book may have changed since publication and may no longer be valid. The views expressed in this work are solely those of the author and do not necessarily reflect the views of the publisher, and the publisher hereby disclaims any responsibility for them.

Any people depicted in stock imagery provided by Thinkstock are models, and such images are being used for illustrative purposes only.
Certain stock imagery © Thinkstock.

ISBN: 978-1-5320-3555-5 (sc)
ISBN: 978-1-5320-3557-9 (hc)
ISBN: 978-1-5320-3556-2 (e)

Library of Congress Control Number: 2017916272

Print information available on the last page.

iUniverse rev. date: 11/07/2017

The Janus Chronicles

The Hope of Janus is the third book in the four-novel Janus Chronicles. The first books, *The Mark of Janus* and *The Word of Janus*, are available at online booksellers. The final novel, *The Time of Janus*, will be published in late Spring, 2019.

For Wendy, who has always shared and cherished the dream. You are the light that shows the way along the path of life and the one for whom the words are written.

Acknowledgments

With much thanks to Stephen Brouitt for his insightful and valuable editorial contribution. To David Brouitt and Dorothy Brouitt for their encouragement. A special note of appreciation to John Ferguson and Susan Derby for your friendship and continuing support.

Janus

※

In Roman mythology, Janus is the god of gates, doors, doorways, and all beginnings. The month of January is named for him. Depicted as having two faces on opposite sides of his head, Janus is able to gaze into the past with one, while the other allows him to look to the future.

In *The Hope of Janus*, the island's eponymous name reflects the ancestors' belief that all those who followed should always remember the past and use it to shape the present and the future.

Chapter One

The doctors had given him six months to a year. But the disease ravaging his brain possessed no knowledge of human timetables or medical opinions. The dementia had moved with the speed of a rampaging army, destroying every cell and nerve it encountered.

It had taken slightly less than four months for him to be rendered incapable of continuing with his responsibilities.

And now he was alone with his fears and anxiety, stumbling through that dark tunnel of desolation as he realized the life he had known would soon be forever beyond his reach. Unable to remember the names of longtime friends, once cherished memories now hardly visible through a dense fog of remorse, and incapable of performing simple tasks he once took for granted, Pope Paul VII knelt at his private altar and prayed for the strength to carry out his one final official act with dignity and grace.

Soon, he wasn't sure when—the measurement of hours had become too complex for his deteriorating brain—his principal secretary, Nicholas Fata, would knock on the door of the papal apartment. At that point, the official end to this part of his life would begin. He would be escorted by Fata, a Jesuit priest, to a suite of offices the pope had once labored in with constant humility for the grave responsibility the papacy entailed.

Life was about to dramatically change for the man who would soon sign away all accountability for the world's more than 1.2 billion Roman Catholics. With what remained of his mind left to him by the dementia, Paul knew that his final task as pontiff would leave him feeling he had somehow failed in his duty. Popes were supposed to die in office. But he was preparing to abdicate.

Fortunately, if one could call it that, with the dementia being diagnosed several months before the disease had stolen most of his mind, it had given him time, that most precious of all earth's wonders, to bring his official duties to a close. The one who followed him would have many issues to deal with, but they were problems that constantly bedeviled the Church as it tried to impose old-world values on a globe too distracted to listen as it raced toward an uncertain future.

None of it mattered anymore to Paul. He stumbled through the days mostly unaware that his life's road had taken this turn. But Paul never let his faith in God waver. The pope fiercely believed that, if this was his god's will, then he would accept the sentence with understanding and humility.

There was a light knock on the door, and then it slowly swung open, revealing Fata. The pope was confused. He recognized his secretary, but why was the priest standing in his doorway?

Paul stood up from the altar and took a seat on the edge of his bed.

The man was saying something, but Paul couldn't make out the words. He could hear, but couldn't understand. Somewhere deep inside his befuddled mind there was the realization that something important was about to happen. But as if trying to capture a ray of sunlight with his hands, it kept slipping through the shadows of his thoughts.

The pontiff watched with some curiosity as Fata went to his clothes cupboard and took out a white robe. For some reason, Paul remembered that it was called a cassock. The priest crossed the room, gave the garment to Paul, and told him to put it on.

The pope sat motionless, unaware of what to do next. And then, like flashes of lightning on a rain-filled afternoon, a multitude of synapses in his brain began firing. He remembered.

This was going to be an event unlike any other in his life. He had to hurry, for there was no way of knowing how long this grasp on reality would last. Paul allowed himself only a momentary feeling of embarrassment at being found in his underwear. Since the dementia's onset and the resulting loss of self-awareness, he had been forced to wear a diaper. With relief, he noted it was clean.

Paul stood and, with the assistance of Fata, shouldered himself into his cassock. Fata tied the white fascia, or sash, around his waist and handed him his pectoral cross. Paul slipped the gold cord holding the cross over his head and felt the comforting weight of the symbol for Christ as it rested against his chest. Next came the red cape, and Fata diligently adjusted the material so that it sat securely on the pope's bent shoulders.

Finally there was the small, white skullcap—a zucchetto. Fata smoothed Paul's wisps of white hair and placed it on his head.

The priest guided Paul to a chair.

The pontiff stared at Fata, bewildered. What was he supposed to do? Fata softly told him to sit. Paul did as he was asked. The priest knelt and slipped a pair of red shoes onto the pope's feet.

The men had so far said very little to each other. There was the request for Paul to sit, but apart from that, Fata's brief comments had focused on helping the pope get dressed.

For his part, Paul had observed the proceedings with a silent sense of detachment. He vaguely understood what was happening yet felt powerless to affect the outcome. He knew enough to be frustrated at his inability to think clearly so that he could put words to his thoughts. But well beyond that, he couldn't seem to will his mind into having his body perform even the most menial task of getting dressed.

And yet he recognized that this was now his life. It was confusing and terrifying.

Paul had forgotten the priest's name, but for now he was glad to have someone with him. And then Paul noticed that the priest wasn't in the room. Waves of panic swept over the pontiff. He felt his chest tighten, there was moisture on his face, and his hands were shaking. He was trying desperately not to soil himself.

From somewhere behind him, he heard footsteps. He swung his head around, and there was the priest. A feeling of such relief swept over Paul that tears came unbidden to his eyes and began to roll down his cheeks. The priest came and stood in front of him, arms outstretched.

In one hand was a glass filled with water. In the other, a collection of what Paul remembered were pills. The priest indicated he was supposed to take them with the water. Paul did as he was instructed. The pills burned his throat and settled uneasily on his stomach. He handed the glass back to the man standing in front of him. Had he done this before? It was too difficult to remember. Better to ask the priest his name.

It was Nicholas.

Paul rolled the name around in his fractured mind. It was a good name for a priest.

Something was intruding on his thoughts. Nicholas was taking him by the hand, telling him to get up and that it was time they were going. He followed willingly. The priest took his arm and guided him carefully out of the apartment. They were in a long hallway, and Paul noticed that he had trouble walking, but the priest wasn't rushing. He didn't recognize the corridor, but Nicholas seemed to know where they were going.

He felt the steady pressure on his arm as the priest guided him down another hallway and into a large room. Paul was immediately intimidated. The surroundings were vaguely familiar, but who were these men? He whispered the question in Nicholas's ear. The priest replied that they were important men of the Church.

What did that mean? wondered Paul.

And then, like fog before a strong wind, the mist in Paul's mind cleared, and he grasped the event's significance. He was abdicating as pope.

These men were cardinal bishops, the highest-ranking members of the College of Cardinals—the Church's most powerful body next to the papacy. They were here to watch him sign and affix the papal seal to a series of documents that would make his abdication official.

Each man moved forward, took Paul's right hand, bowed, and kissed the gold band that he hadn't noticed was on his ring finger. He looked to Nicholas, pointed to the band, and asked what it meant. The priest explained that it was the ring of the fisherman, denoting his rank as pope.

Paul experienced a great weight of sadness. Although not sure what he was giving up, the pontiff sensed that he had enjoyed his time in this office. Nicholas steered him toward a desk and a large, leather chair. Sitting down, Paul looked at the five men who had come to witness his departure and realized he couldn't pull their names from his broken memory.

They were all standing in front of the desk. Each face bore a solemn expression. In a fleeting moment of awareness, he wondered if the look in their eyes was pity for his condition or fear that what had befallen him might one day be their fate.

He looked at the papers neatly arranged on the desk. The priest—Paul had again forgotten his name—placed one of the sheets in front of him, gave him a pen, and indicated where he should sign. Once more, panic overtook Paul like an onrushing wave. What was his signature? He stared at the paper and felt the paralysis of fear.

The priest took his hand and steered it in long, looping letters. They did that for all six pages. After each was completed, it was passed across the desk, where the red-robed men lined up and placed their marks on the documents.

Once it was done, the priest told him that the papal seal would later be affixed to each document. Paul had no idea what the priest meant but instinctively knew that a fundamental part of his life was over. One of the men walked around the desk and stood next to Paul. He took his right hand and gently removed the ring.

The priest moved to his side and guided Paul out of the chair. The former pontiff looked around the room. He recognized nothing. He asked the priest his name. The man said it was Nicholas, and Paul wondered why that had been kept from him.

Nicholas took his arm and escorted him through the hallways. They walked in silence. Arriving at a door, Nicholas opened it and ushered Paul into a room that he only vaguely recognized. He asked the priest where they were and was told it was his apartment. The answer gave Paul some comfort.

After helping him undress, Nicholas assisted the former pontiff with a nightshirt and a bathrobe. Rays of sunlight were filtering into the room. Paul asked if he could sit where the light would flow over him. Nicholas moved a chair, and Paul slowly sat down, bathed in the midafternoon brightness.

Paul didn't hear the priest say that he would soon be back or notice him leave. His mind had flowed like the sea into a space where memories were orphans and thoughts nothing more than pieces of driftwood.

Chapter Two

It was one of those days where the heat is so intense the air seems to shimmer like mist rising off a waterfall. Janus hadn't experienced anything like these temperatures in years. The warmth and humidity had hovered for the past three days. And for an island located in the North Atlantic, just south of the Faroe Islands, the unusual weather was something to be enjoyed.

The islanders were used to mid-May days where heavy, dark clouds played hide-and-seek with the sun and the thermometer warned that a jacket or sweater was required. But as Sean Brennan walked along the sand-covered Ring Road—so named because it encircled the island—he could see there wasn't a cloud in the azure sky. Puffs of dirt were kicked up as he strolled toward Elijah's farm.

At thirty-seven years old, Sean was lean and well toned. Standing a couple of inches over six feet with medium-length brown hair that flowed in tight curls, he possessed an easygoing grace that made others comfortable in his presence. Not a natural-born islander, Sean was here on his second visit to Janus. He had come to the island two years ago and stayed for a couple of months before returning to his job as a columnist at a London newspaper. He had not anticipated revisiting, but an ongoing issue with the island's Spirit had brought him back.

The Spirit believed that humanity was on the verge of collapse unless all nations, societies, and cultures could find a way to live in peace. A large part of the plan for bringing unity to the globe had the islanders, based on Janus's 2,000 year history of non-violence, leading the movement. And the Spirit wanted Sean to spearhead the crusade. The Spirit, however, was refusing to be directly involved. For Sean this meant the entire mission was so idealistic that it would never succeed.

He wondered if that's why Elijah had insisted on seeing him today. Sean already knew his answer would be the same as it had been since he'd first heard of the Spirit's initiative. If the Spirit's plan, and specifically Sean's involvement in it, did turn out to be the reason for today's meeting, Sean would settle the issue with a definitive explanation of why it didn't interest him. Elijah had to understand that he wanted the subject put to rest.

Sean entered the path that led to a front gallery, which fronted the one-story stone and wood farmhouse. Clearing the six steps two at a time, he made his way over to where Elijah was sitting on a slung back, wooden chair with wide arms. There were six chairs on the gallery, and the man known as the Prophet because he was the island's spiritual leader motioned Sean into the one beside him. A jug of lemonade, along with a couple of glasses, rested on a small, wrought iron table within easy reach of Elijah.

"It's freshly made," greeted the Prophet, pointing at the jug. "Would you like some?"

The words were uttered with a finality that was out of character for Elijah. Sean knew the Prophet was putting up a brave front, but a recent event had caused him much distress.

Sean nodded his acceptance.

Taking his seat, he watched as Elijah poured lemonade into the two tumblers. The Prophet handed one to Sean, who took a long pull from his glass. The chilled liquid felt good in his dry mouth and parched throat. Elijah took several swallows, before cradling the tumbler in the palms of his rawboned hands.

"I know you're avoiding a meeting with the Spirit," noted the Prophet. "You have your reasons, but you're expected at the cave."

Societies throughout the world had different names for what the 1,900 islanders referred to as the Spirit. Regardless of what the countless religions called their Supreme Being, there was an understanding among all believers that the deity existed in a realm that could only be truly experienced upon the believer's death. This was one of the fundamental tenets of religious faith.

That was not the case governing the islanders' relationship with their Spirit, or God as the divinity was known within many Western and Middle Eastern religions. In a cave on the island's rocky northern coast, the islanders conversed with the Spirit. This had been a part of their lives since the initial group of settlers landed on Janus late in the first century.

Sean distinctly remembered when Elijah first told him about the islanders' relationship with the Spirit and let a wry chuckle escape his full lips. He had been staggered and had believed that everyone on the island was delusional at best or belonged to some bizarre cult at worst. However, as he'd discovered, reality came in many guises.

Elijah raised a quizzical, thick eyebrow at the sound of Sean's low laugh.

Noticing the Prophet's look, Sean said, "I was just thinking back to when I had my first conversation in the cave. It was unbelievable to find that everyone on Janus was right and you do speak with the Spirit."

"And that is what brought you back to Janus," offered Elijah. "Have you given any more consideration to what you're going to tell the Spirit?"

Leaning back in the chair, Sean looked over at Elijah. The Prophet's almond-colored eyes behind round, rimless glasses were staring intently at him. Sean noted the sadness that had replaced Elijah's usually impish gaze but decided now was not the time to make a comment.

"I've thought of little else," said Sean. "And my answer is still the same. I'm not willing to participate."

The Prophet put his tumbler on the table and pulled a bandanna from his shorts pocket. Taking off his glasses, he used the cloth to wipe the moisture from his weathered face and across his tanned bald pate, bordered by a receding horseshoe of short, gray hair. He tucked the bandanna in his pocket and slipped on the glasses.

"The Spirit has decided to work with you," Elijah told his guest. "For the sake of the world, you can't reject its plan."

The Spirit's insistence on being referred to as "it" had always intrigued Sean. He knew from Elijah that the unusual pronoun had been in use since the first settlers. The Prophet explained that, as an amorphous entity overseeing the universe, the Spirit refused to be categorized as either masculine or feminine, saying these were earthly and confining words that did not represent the being's true essence.

Sean ran a hand wearily over his face and could feel the sweat on his forehead that stood watch over dark, brown eyes; prominent cheekbones; and a strong chin. The resignation was not from physical fatigue. Although he and Elijah were good friends, the Prophet's inability to accept Sean's position had begun to mentally wear on him. "As we've already discussed," Sean said, "if the Spirit won't participate directly, then what it wants for earth is impossible. Not only that, but there are other things I want to do with my life. I still have a job in London, and that's important to me."

"How can anything, even a job you like, be more significant than working with the Spirit to make the world a better place?" asked the Prophet.

Sean sighed inwardly. "If Jesus had not had a son with Mary Magdalene, none of this would be happening," noted Sean.

"But he did," said Elijah. "And through the birthmark on your thigh, you are directly related to Jesus and, through him, to the Spirit. You can't deny your heritage or your destiny. You have the mark of Janus."

The raised, bloodred mark in the shape of a triangle had been given to Jesus's son, Daniel, by the Spirit. Passed through the centuries from father to eldest son, the birthmark was a reminder that a time would come when the Spirit would call upon the one who bore the nevus to work with it in leading the world to global unity.

"You've been told by the Spirit that the point has been reached where earth must find peace if the human race is to endure," Elijah reminded him. "It has chosen you to be at the forefront of this mission."

Sean thought about his initial meeting with the Spirit and how it had blamed humanity's headlong rush to self-destruction on such factors as war, ecological devastation, and a growing inequality among all people. Humanity's survival had never been at a more critical stage.

But the Spirit had also revealed that, while it would be there to guide him, it would not interfere with what the Spirit believed was humanity's right to free will. If earth was to survive, the task would be accomplished through a self-imposed commitment to peace by every individual.

"When I last visited the Spirit, it still wasn't prepared to become directly involved," said Sean. "And if that's the case, the plan will fail. I don't understand why it's so hard for you and the Spirit to understand this simple fact."

"We've had this discussion before, and nothing has changed. If you asked me over to see whether I now thought differently, I'm sorry for wasting your time. Just because I have the birthmark doesn't mean I'm interested in leading a quixotic movement for peace. I really want this to end."

"I thought that's what you might say," observed the Prophet. "Therefore I've decided to become involved."

So this was why Elijah wanted to meet, thought Sean.

"What are you intending to do?" he asked.

"It came to me yesterday that I've been looking at this all wrong," said Elijah. "My concern has been with you and the Spirit. On Janus, we've always viewed the world as something outside the island. We are unknown to the globe, and the Spirit has ensured we stayed that way. I assumed this was an issue between you and the Spirit that didn't involve me or the islanders.

"But I believe it's time to change my thinking. Whatever happens in the world will eventually impact Janus. Already we can smell the pollution from Europe. And how long will fish remain a staple for our tables if the world's oceans continue to be overfished?"

The Prophet placed his glass on the table and abruptly stood. He leaned back against the gallery railing, facing Sean. For the first time in a couple of weeks, Elijah was animated. The recent tragedy seemed to have been put aside, at least for the moment. "I now realize that you're right," he said, excitement infusing his voice. "The Spirit has to be directly engaged. I'm going to start discussing this during my next visit to the cave. Perhaps if the two of us work at convincing it, the Spirit may come around to our way of thinking."

Sean knew that, as the island's spiritual advisor, Elijah's opinion was deeply valued by the Spirit. The Prophet's contribution might just get the Spirit to change its view about participating. If that happened, he would have to take a long look at his future. He couldn't very well say no to the Spirit if it offered to directly intervene. This was, after all, the Supreme Being.

"Do you really think the Spirit will change its mind if you get involved?" asked Sean.

"It will take time and numerous conversations," responded Elijah. "But we've known each other for many years. It will listen to what I have to say. And we mustn't forget that the Spirit has already announced its concern for earth by involving you. You're the chosen one.

"I'm going to work on convincing the Spirit. And I'll get every islander involved. This is bigger than just you. I've only begun to realize how important the next few years could be for Janus and the world. We need the Spirit's full participation."

Elijah's reference to including the islanders was something Sean hadn't expected. It was becoming an afternoon full of surprises.

"I don't think everyone on the island would support you," he said. "What you're proposing would change a way of life that has existed for centuries. There isn't one islander who doesn't cherish the island's anonymity."

"It will take some convincing," admitted Elijah. "But once everyone understands the magnitude of what we're undertaking, I'm sure they'll want to participate."

The Prophet's eyes were gleaming with excitement. He moved away from the gallery's railing and began to pace back and forth. "You and I can do this," he said. "We can lead the world to a better place. I suspect it will be quite the discussion once I let the Spirit know of my desire to get it involved. But can you think of anything more important to do with our lives? Imagine what it will be like once the world realizes the Spirit is participating in our quest for peace."

The Prophet's zeal washed over Sean like a rising tide. He smiled at Elijah's passion and felt the first stirrings of enthusiasm for the Spirit's proposal. It was an incredible project, but imagine what could be accomplished if the Spirit decided to participate.

Should that happen the islanders' commitment would be the next hurdle. It promised to be a struggle convincing everyone that it was worth sacrificing Janus's independence for a chance at saving the world. Even with the Spirit's involvement, there would be holdouts, and nothing could move forward until there was unanimous agreement.

But that was an issue for the future. And for the moment, Sean was quite prepared to share Elijah's eagerness.

Having arrived with the intention of telling Elijah he still wasn't interested unless the Spirit was fully engaged, Sean realized that the Prophet's participation had completely changed the ground rules. Sean wasn't sure what the future held, but he did know that his next session with the Spirit would be unlike any they'd shared in the past.

"I want to visit the cave before nightfall," said the Prophet. "It's never too early for our project to get started."

Sean saw that the sun had already begun its descent in the late afternoon sky. It was time to be on his way. "In that case I should be going," he told Elijah.

Placing his half-empty glass on the table, Sean stood, towering over Elijah who stood just a few inches over five feet. Although having entered his late sixties, the Prophet still worked his farm, leaving him with a finely muscled frame.

He gripped Sean's arm with his right hand. For several seconds, there was silence between the two. Sweat glistened just above the Prophet's pronounced upper lip. "We can do this," he said, his voice charged with emotion. "By working together, we can get the Spirit and the islanders on our side. Are we partners?"

Taken aback by Elijah's intensity, Sean took several seconds to respond. When he did, his voice was slow and measured. "For the moment, let's just say I'm more optimistic about the Spirit's participation now that you're involved. So yes, in that sense, we have a partnership."

The men shook hands, and Sean descended the steps. He headed toward Diane's place, his mind a jumble of possibilities. Just as important, it seemed as though Elijah had shaken off his bout of melancholy. For Sean, that was another positive to take from the session.

But as with most things in life, there were undercurrents below the water's surface that could easily sink a boat filled with dreams and good intentions. Sean and Elijah would soon find that events far from Janus would wreak havoc on their plans.

Chapter Three

He could see the surprise in Diane's eyes. Normally the color of cinnamon, they had hardened to almost black. Her back had gone rigid; another indication his words had come as a revelation. For just a moment, Sean felt uncomfortable. He hadn't expected this reaction.

"Why is the news such a shock?" he asked.

"Because the Prophet has never interfered with the bond between an islander and the Spirit," responded Diane. "This is completely out of character."

"Well my situation with the Spirit isn't exactly normal," countered Sean. "I don't think the island's usual rules apply to our relationship. I wasn't expecting Elijah's involvement, and I can't stop him from trying to get the Spirit's direct participation."

"If the Spirit does get involved in this movement for global peace, it will change everything on Janus," noted Diane. "Our whole way of life will be affected."

"I mentioned that, but Elijah seemed to feel the islanders would understand, given the project's magnitude," said Sean. "And not only Janus will be impacted. Can you imagine what it will do to the world?"

Running the fingers of her right hand through auburn hair that fell in waves to just below her shoulders, Diane wondered, "How do you feel about that?"

"I don't know," admitted Sean. "Elijah seems to believe that, if he can get the Spirit onside, my participation in its plan will be guaranteed."

"And will it?"

Sean looked across the table at Diane. The sun had bronzed her angular face with its high cheekbones; petite nose; and full, red lips. She was wearing a snug, white T-shirt that emphasized the swell of her breasts and tanned arms.

They were seated in the kitchen. Sean had made coffee in anticipation of a lengthy discussion.

"That's not a choice I'm prepared to make on my own," Sean answered. "You and I have committed to sharing our lives, and that means making joint decisions, especially when it involves working with the Spirit."

The couple had been engaged for two months. They had met during Sean's first visit to Janus. Both had come out of difficult marriages, and the relationship had proceeded cautiously. Neither was looking for a rebound romance. She had visited him a couple of times in London, and the understanding, love, and commitment had grown slowly. Now they were living in Diane's ancestral home. An islander, she could trace her heritage back to the first settlers. Diane farmed the land her family had tilled for two millennia. She was also the island's nurse and midwife.

"What do you think are Elijah's chances of getting the Spirit to participate?" asked Diane.

Shrugging his shoulders, Sean replied, "I don't honestly know. But I haven't seen him this excited since we returned from Inverness."

"That's good news," said Diane. "He wants everyone to believe he's fine, but there's been a sadness about him since the codex's theft."

"That was the case when I first got to his house," noted Sean. "But the more he talked about getting involved with the Spirit and me, his mood improved. I don't know if it will completely take his mind off what's happened with the manuscript, but it has given him something else to think about."

"I'm glad," said Diane. "I know it has been hard on him. But he shouldn't be taking it so badly. No one is holding Elijah responsible for the loss."

Sean noticed that Diane's eyes had softened and were returning to their normal color. The sympathy she felt for the Prophet seemed to have relaxed her. Sean wondered if Elijah truly understood that none of the islanders were blaming him for what had happened to the codex, a two thousand-year-old collection of parchments. Written by Jesus's son, Daniel, the codex detailed how Christ did not die on the cross as the Bible and Christian writings claimed. Having survived his crucifixion, Jesus, along with his wife, Mary Magdalene, raised two children—Daniel and a daughter, Rachel.

Known as the Word of Janus, the codex was brought ashore during the latter part of the first century by the initial settlers—Israelites escaping the Roman occupation of Palestine. It established a foundation for how the islanders should live with each other. The catechism of understanding, tolerance, equality, and peace had governed the island's population through the centuries. Daniel's writings explained that the tenets were given to him by Jesus, who had received them from the Spirit.

There were three copies of the codex. The original was written in Aramaic, an ancient Middle Eastern language. What followed was a Hebrew translation created in the sixteenth century by the islanders and an English version produced by the Prophet's great-great-grandfather.

Over the centuries, the Aramaic and Hebrew copies had become so worn and damaged through constant use by the islanders that the decision had been made to have them repaired. While undergoing restoration in Inverness—a port city in northern Scotland—the codex, along with its Hebrew translation, was stolen by the Praetorian Order, an adjunct of the Roman Catholic Church.

The theft had devastated the islanders, but no one more than Elijah. He believed that, as the island's spiritual leader, he shouldered the responsibility of safeguarding the documents.

"Although it isn't the case, I believe Elijah feels that, since it was his idea to send the codex to Inverness, he bears some accountability for what happened," said Sean. "But that's not my concern at the moment."

Diane gave him a puzzled look. "What's bothering you?" she asked.

"There are a couple of issues at play here," he began. "The first is, if Elijah is successful at getting the Spirit and the islanders to buy into the project, I have to finally determine whether working toward a peaceful world is something I want to spend the rest of my life doing."

"And the second?" wondered Diane.

"We've always agreed that any talk regarding your participation shouldn't happen until events necessitated a decision. Well, I think that time is now."

"This is because of what's written in the parchments," said Diane, leaning back in her chair.

"That's right."

Daniel chronicled how the Spirit had told Jesus that the person who would one day work with it for peace "will have a partner equal in every respect, and all decisions are to be made by mutual understanding."

"I think it's a good idea to take a look at what we're going to do," said Diane. "With Elijah intent on getting the Spirit's direct participation, we should be prepared with an answer. I know you haven't considered it, but perhaps we should rethink our plans. It would be entirely our decision, but leading a global peace movement with the Spirit's involvement seems exciting and would be tremendously fulfilling."

Diane's words caught Sean by surprise. They had often discussed her love of farming and nursing, along with her desire to remain on Janus. This was the first time she had indicated any thought of working with the Spirit.

"Have you changed your mind?" he asked. "I thought we'd agreed that taking part in the Spirit's plan was a non-starter."

"That was when the Spirit said it would advise but not help you implement its initiatives for peace," responded Diane. "But if the Spirit is willing to take part, it puts everything in a different light. We should be discussing what happens if Elijah is successful. That could be our future."

"Have you thought this through?" questioned Sean. "If we did work with the Spirit, everything about our lives would change. Is that what you want?"

Diane frowned and was silent for several moments.

"I realize it would mean a different way of life," she began slowly. "Obviously it would impact our relationship. But this could be an opportunity to do something that's never been attempted. I can't think of anything better than working for peace across the world. And the Spirit would be with us. That's a powerful ally earth has never seen."

It was Sean's turn to let quiet overtake their conversation. He knew that Diane was right. Working with the Spirit would be greater than anything humanity had experienced. They would be ambassadors for peace in a deeply troubled world. But was it a life he was truly seeking? Elijah was taking it upon himself to get the Spirit involved, and Diane was indicating how much she wanted to work with it.

Yet it was Sean who bore the birthmark—the mark of Janus. Ultimately, it was his decision. But the Janus philosophy was compromise. The island's society had survived for two thousand years based on its ability to understand that, regardless of how divergent two positions may be, there is always room in the center for a fair settlement to be achieved.

The moon's light was beginning to steal through the open kitchen window. Sean was surprised. They'd been sitting at the table longer than he thought. Then again, it was an important issue they were discussing, and it needed to be resolved.

"We're still a long way from having the Spirit agree to be involved," noted Sean. "And even if it does, I haven't decided what I'm going to do."

"You have to make a decision," responded Diane, a note of gentle persuasion in her voice. "I want to know what you think of us working with the Spirit."

Once again, Sean lapsed into silence. He couldn't help but think how bizarre his life had become. He was sitting on an uncharted island in the middle of the North Atlantic having a rational discussion about working with the Supreme Being who had decided humanity needed saving from itself.

"It would be the adventure of a lifetime," he finally said, directing a large smile toward Diane. "And we would be in it together."

"Does that mean you're ready to work with Elijah in persuading the Spirit to participate?" Diane asked, a ripple of excitement coursing through her voice. "And if the Spirit does agree, will you and I then meet with it to determine how we go about changing the world?" Diane laughed, and her happiness was contagious.

"Yes." Sean chuckled, caught up in her enthusiasm. "I'll do my part in getting the Spirit to see that the only way a peace plan can work is if it directly participates. I don't know about bringing peace to earth, but if the Spirit is fully with us, we can at least give it a try."

"Since we're in this together, I'll also talk to the Spirit and do my best to persuade it into becoming part of the adventure," said Diane. "This is now our project, and I want to do my share from the beginning."

"Let's not be naïve about this," cautioned Sean. "We are trying to change the course of human history. Ever since the first tribes were formed, there have been armed battles over water and other resources. The only thing that's changed is the magnitude of the many conflicts."

"I realize that," answered Diane. "But if we don't start now, what is earth's future? The by-product of peace will be a concentration on the environment and human equality. And that's where humanity really needs to become engaged."

Although Sean sensed the mood change from cheerful to somber, he wasn't prepared for Diane's next question.

"With our plans about the Spirit, does this mean you're committed to staying on Janus and not returning to London?"

The query surprised him—not because they hadn't talked about the possibility of his relocating to the island permanently, but that it was, in Diane's mind, tied directly into their relationship with the Spirit.

His original plan had been to marry Diane on Janus, and then they'd move to London. He had his job at the newspaper and a small apartment. She could work as a nurse at one of the city's many hospitals. But the longer he stayed on the island, the less alluring the plan seemed.

Having worked the farm with Diane for several weeks, Sean was surprised at how much he enjoyed the various tasks associated with her land. Whether it was baling hay or feeding the sheep, goats, and chickens, he found a satisfaction in doing manual work that left him fulfilled at the end of the day. While he liked being a journalist, working with Diane gave him far more satisfaction than did his life in London.

He knew Diane wanted to remain on Janus. Regardless of what happened with the Spirit, it was time to cut ties with his old life. His thoughts couldn't be in two places. And his heart was on the island.

"Let's plan our future for Janus," he said. "We can always visit the city, but we don't have to live there. I'm happy here with you."

The radiant look that spread across Diane's face was all he needed to know it was the right decision. She leaped up from the table, walked quickly over to where he was sitting, pulled him to his feet, and smothered him in a hug. They kissed with passion.

The Hope of Janus

"We'll make this work," she promised, once they'd disentangled. "We may end up traveling the world for the Spirit, but Janus will always be our home."

After a lifetime of searching, Sean experienced a deep sense of inner peace. No longer did he feel like a stranger in his life. The decisions he'd shared with Diane had made both of them happy. He knew their lives wouldn't stretch out in an unbroken ribbon of joy and success. But he had a partner now, and Sean had the wonderful belief that together they could conquer whatever mountains rose up in their path.

Chapter Four

It was evening, and the tourists, along with the locals, were strolling through the streets of Valencia, a port city in southeastern Spain. The atmosphere was relaxed and casual as people searched for a restaurant to enjoy a quiet dinner or a café to wile away the hours with pleasant company.

Approximately twenty miles northwest of the city, a Mercedes Benz slowly glided along the quarter-mile, winding driveway that led from the imposing front security gate to the large, oaken doors of the Chateau Valencia. As night began to fall, the air was still and slightly muggy from a heavy morning rain that had only let the chateau out of its grip around noon.

None of this made an impression on the passenger in the air-conditioned limousine's rear seat. He had been away from the chateau for three weeks, and there was much on his mind.

Dante Sabatini was the head or prelate of the Praetorian Order, one of the Roman Catholic Church's most closely guarded secrets. Also known by the code name Fraternity, the clandestine group's existence was known only by the pope, his closest advisors, and the College of Cardinals.

The order had been formed in 957 through a papal decree from Pope John XII. Its mandate then, which continued to this day, was to swiftly and effectively confront whatever negative challenges were encountered by the Church. Whether it was removing from their parishes wayward priests involved with drugs or negotiating with the government of a non-Christian country to have churches remain open for the faithful, the Fraternity carried out its tasks efficiently and with no publicity. The principle governing every mission undertaken by the order was to be successful while ensuring that no activity could be traced back to Rome.

However, while the order, throughout its history, has not generated controversy beyond the Vatican, the same could not be said for its dealings within the Church.In 1583, a group of nine cardinals, fearing that the order was becoming too powerful, staged an attempt at having the prelate removed and the Fraternity report directly to the College of Cardinals.

This meant bypassing the pope, who they contended was too busy to oversee the order's activities. However, the move so angered the pontiff at the time, Gregory XIII, that he banished the implicated cardinals from the college. Of more importance to the order, though, was a decree signed into canon law several months later by Gregory guaranteeing the Fraternity's virtual independence.

The decree stated that, in perpetuity, the order would report only to the pope. Additionally, no one, including cardinals, was permitted to visit the order's headquarters at the Chateau Valencia unless specifically invited by the prelate. The only exception was the reigning pontiff. The last pope to visit the chateau was Clement XIV in 1770.

This provided a unique situation for the order's prelates. Operating in the shadows and answerable only to the pontiff, the Fraternity gradually evolved into an all-powerful force, where any action—including abductions, tortures, and assassinations—was considered viable if conducted in the interests of strengthening and expanding the Church's influence.

The Fraternity had carried out killings on behalf of African dictators, as well as kidnappings for rival factions in the South American drug wars, and had brutalized prisoners on behalf of several Eastern Bloc tyrants. This had all been done on a quid pro quo basis for allowing the Church, with its priests, nuns, and missionaries, to continue preaching the Catholic gospel throughout these regions.

Despite the order's growing propensity for solving issues through violence, the Fraternity's prelates always considered their organization an instrument of Church policy. The order was funded through the Church and received its operating instructions from the Vatican. No mission was undertaken without first receiving approval from Rome. Loyalty to the pope was a fundamental directive for all those who guided the order.

Over the centuries, this allegiance had been repaid in various ways, including land holdings throughout the Roman Catholic world; mineral and mining rights, particularly in South America; and pieces of art, antiquities, and historical documents valued in the millions of dollars and collected by the Church. However, what troubled many of the prelates was that these rewards did not officially belong to the order. They could be withdrawn or confiscated at any time according to the whim of whatever pope was on the papal throne.

This perceived wrong was rectified following the First World War and set the stage for the Fraternity's massive growth in power. During the conflict, the order had worked efficiently and covertly in protecting many of the Church's holdings throughout Europe. In 1920, Pope Benedict XV, who had toiled alongside the Fraternity during the war and recognized the value of its work, issued a decree on behalf of the order. It declared that all of the Fraternity's holdings were the sole property of the order. There was also an appendix that stated whatever artifacts and documents were at the chateau could only be removed at the discretion of the prelate.

The Hope of Janus

At the time, it was thought to be a needless codicil meant to placate the then prelate, who had acquired some stolen German art that he wanted for the chateau's collection. Time would prove, though, that the addendum would play an important role in the relationship between the order and the Vatican less than a hundred years later.

In return for the decree, it was expected that each prelate would swear undying allegiance to the sitting pontiff and carry out whatever mission he requested. It was a reaffirmation of the order's centuries-old pledge that viewed loyalty to the pope as a fundamental part of its existence.

That code had changed dramatically with Dante Carlos Sabatini.

Rescued from a Palestinian refugee camp when he was barely eighteen months old, Dante had grown up as a ward of the order. His education and road to manhood had been guided by the Fraternity's Jesuit priests. His extraordinary intelligence, drive to excel, and ruthless need for control had been noted early, and by his late teens, he was being groomed to, one day, head the order.

That became a reality on his twenty-third birthday, making him the youngest prelate in the Fraternity's history. His predecessor, in apparent good health, had died suddenly of a heart attack at fifty-one years old. A lethal dose of sodium thiopental, Pavulon, and potassium chloride had been injected into the man's arm while he slept. He was dead within three minutes of the needle entering his vein. Dante had left the room immediately after ensuring the man was no longer breathing. The body had been discovered that morning.

Dante had a vision for the order, and he was in a hurry to begin its implementation. The killing of his predecessor was easily rationalized—it was for the greater good of the Fraternity. Time was a precious commodity and should not be wasted on waiting for events to naturally unfold. Success went to those who controlled their lives, and power was to be taken, not given.

No one had suspected Dante, and as was the custom at the chateau, an autopsy was not performed. The death was considered God's will, and a new era was born for the Fraternity.

The young prelate immediately set the order on a road that would, over several years, bring about immense change. He brought two longstanding practices – a monthly reporting to the pope and the sanctioning by the Vatican of all the order's activities – to an immediate end. The transformation was made possible through the prelate's overarching commitment to having the order operate financially independent of Rome. He was driven by one goal—the need to make the Fraternity a self-sufficient and autonomous force.

Guided by a single-mindedness that only the highly intelligent zealots possess, Dante had built the Fraternity into a global enterprise that comprised twenty-seven privately held, multinational companies and four independent banks. The massive organization operated throughout Asia, Europe, and the Americas. The order's involvement was kept virtually hidden in the international half-light through a complex web of cross-ownership, numbered companies, asset manipulation, and money laundering.

The Fraternity employed more than 195,000 people. However, the only ones who knew of Dante's involvement were the president and chief executive officer within each corporate entity. These men and women, raised and schooled by the order, had been placed in their positions through Dante's direction. As such, their allegiance was not to the Church, but to the Fraternity. And while Dante did not necessarily evoke affection, he generated tremendous loyalty and respect, which was what he truly preferred.

This virtual invisibility afforded the prelate a luxury few global leaders could claim—the ability to conduct whatever action he desired without the need to have it sanctioned by shareholders, interest groups, or governments. And in the order's case, there was now the added factor of not having to be concerned with Rome. Although the Fraternity was still an adjunct of the Church, Dante's actions benefited the order first and the Vatican second.

The corporate giant was a reflection of Dante's unwavering work ethic, an obsessive devotion to secrecy, and a passionate commitment to detail, along with a ruthless drive for power that was about to garner him a prize he had sought for more than four decades.

Building his corporate empire was not an end in itself. Nor was it designed solely to be independent of Rome. Dante was intent on taking over the Vatican by installing his own pope. It was an audacious plan, but one the prelate was intent on making a reality. Control the papacy, and every aspect of the Vatican's government would be his to command. Once that was accomplished, he would be able to impact the lives of the world's Roman Catholics, who represented more than one-seventh of the globe's population. Along with his vast corporate empire, Dante could effectively influence global policy on everything from the environment to international banking.

Dante was also seeking control of the Vatican because he had a distinct view of how the world should be structured. The prelate considered Roman Catholicism as the one true religion, and all others were blasphemy. His global vision was to spread the Catholic creed throughout the planet. Dante was dismayed that, while the pope had influence, the papacy did not have the power to guide world events.

He was continually troubled at how his Church had become an afterthought in many countries. Dante believed that a powerful Church was needed for sound governance. It mattered little to him that societal change was a major factor in his Church's faded relevance.

The prelate held fast to the belief that a strong Church, which showed tangible benefits for its followers, would bring people back to Roman Catholicism. And that would be accomplished by having faith-based governments. In democracies, he would use his companies and the power inherent in the Vatican to support and promote politicians who adhered to Catholicism. In nations where autocrats and dictators ruled, his aim was to fund Christian-leaning rebel groups that would take over the ruling institutions.

At the same time, the prelate was not some wild-eyed fanatic. Dante had been working on his strategy since before becoming head of the order. He had developed contacts throughout the world who believed as he did. Being a compulsive and detailed organizer, he had spent countless hours crafting his plan. The order's computer hard drive housed a vast collection of files that spelled out exactly how the global campaign would unfold. It had started with ensuring the order's financial strength, would move to controlling the Vatican, and would escalate to an international uprising led by his devotees.

The prelate knew his plan to restore the Church's global domination with the order as its head would take years and might not be accomplished in his lifetime. But he was laying the groundwork, and those who followed would complete the mission. He viewed himself as a religious warrior—a Christian soldier—who was creating a legacy that would live on long after he had secured his rightful place in heaven.

Dante often prayed in the order's chapel. He had discussed his intentions with his god and knew there was an understanding from the Lord. He based his rationale on the fact that his companies continued to expand and that control of the Vatican would soon be in his hands. Dante rationalized that God wouldn't have allowed all this to happen if he wasn't pleased and that he was prepared to see other religions pushed aside.

Although Dante had not expected to make his move on the Vatican until some time at the end of the decade, Pope Paul VII's dementia and need to abdicate had provided the prelate with the perfect opportunity to move his plan forward. And the man he had chosen to be his designate was Cardinal Bishop Charles Emile Ambrosia.

As one of six cardinal bishops within the current 126-member Roman Catholic College of Cardinals, Ambrosia wielded enormous power. Next to the pope and his personal counselors, the college comprised the most important group of men within the Church's hierarchy. The cardinals advised the pope on all matters relating to the Church. Cardinal bishops were the senior ranking members of the college. Their influence extended well beyond the Vatican and was a principal dynamic throughout the considerable expanse of the Roman Catholic Church.

When a pope died or, as was the case with Paul, abdicated, his successor was chosen from among the College of Cardinals. The cardinals gathered in what was called a conclave within the Vatican's Sistine Chapel and remained secluded until a pope was elected.

Inclusion in the college was administered by the pope. He chose new members from a carefully reviewed group of ordained bishops. Although there were several avenues through which a bishop could be considered by the pope, including the work he had done representing the Church throughout his archdiocese, it was a committee comprised of the pope's personal advisors, along with the cardinal bishops, that decided whether the candidate's name would be placed before the pontiff.

What was known only to the pope and his personal secretary was that, once this process had been completed, the list was then passed to the order for vetting by its prelate. The order's review was designed to uncover any transgressions that had been committed by the candidates. Dante was particularly adept at using the order's resources to delve deeply into a candidate's background. What not even the pope knew, however, was that Dante didn't end his surveillance with a bishop's acceptance into the College.

The order maintained an ongoing and secret observation of every cardinal. It included telephone taps, video and photo documentation, and computer hacking. For more than forty years, the prelate had built a considerable file on every cardinal. Not all were guilty of stepping outside the bounds of their priestly vows. Many were good and decent men who worked exceedingly hard on behalf of their Church. However, Dante had information on twenty-seven cardinals whose lives would be forever ruined if he decided to reveal what was in his files.

One of those cardinals was Ambrosia. Prior to Ambrosia being named to the College in 1997 by Pope John Paul II, Dante had performed his usual due diligence. Even then, Ambrosia had been viewed as a man who would one day be considered for the papacy. He was intelligent, steeped in Church doctrine, and an able diplomat. He was progressive and committed to bringing the Church into the twenty-first century. However, Dante had discovered a secret about Ambrosia that he chose not to reveal.

The cardinal had committed a grievous sin when he was the archbishop of Vienna. He'd had a long-term sexual relationship with a married woman. Dante had acquired film and audiotapes of the affair from a detective hired by the woman's husband. To ensure that he was the only one who knew of Ambrosia's failing, the prelate had the detective and the woman, along with her husband, killed soon after he'd acquired the taped evidence.

In a sign of Dante's long-range planning ability, he earmarked Ambrosia for further consideration. And in 2004, the prelate's prescience was validated. That year, Pope John Paul II once again rewarded Ambrosia by naming him a cardinal bishop. It was at this point that Dante began to use his considerable influence to ensure Ambrosia was given key tasks within the Vatican that made certain his name was well known throughout the Church. Dante also highlighted the cardinal's achievements when he was in Rome and speaking with various Vatican leaders.

However, Dante's emphasis on Ambrosia's accomplishments was far from altruistic. In planning to take over the papacy, the prelate's overriding consideration was having a pope he could use to implement the foundation for his mission. With his rising profile at the Vatican, along with the prelate's evidence of his affair, Ambrosia was the perfect choice for Dante.

And when the pope's dementia became known to the order, the prelate was positioned to strike with maximum power.

A pope does not generally indicate who he thinks should succeed him upon his death. Traditionally, the decision has been left entirely with the college members, as it was believed their deliberations were guided by God. However, in Paul's case, he knew well in advance that he was abdicating and possessed a strong sense that God was leaving him enough time to decide who should be his successor. He had forcefully conveyed his views to the college, and there was a general agreement among the members that Paul's wishes would be respected.

After a thorough review of several candidates and on the recommendation of Dante, the pope had chosen Ambrosia to succeed him. In endorsing Ambrosia, Dante had selected a man he knew could be controlled. Some men may have relinquished the opportunity to be pope rather than be blackmailed. However, Dante understood how much Ambrosia lusted after the papacy. The cardinal was vain and egotistical.

He would sacrifice everything, including his pride, to sit on the papal throne.

Although Ambrosia was the primary factor in Dante's drive to control the Vatican, there was much more involved—so many levers that had to be pulled at the right time, and with just the correct amount of force. As the limousine wound its way through the chateau's grounds Dante was in deep thought about the many elements he was controlling.

Chapter Five

✤

The prelate's executive assistant, Juan, was waiting at the bottom of the nine beautifully crafted marble and stone steps that led up to the chateau's front entrance. He opened the car's rear door, and Dante uncoiled his lean and tightly muscled frame from the seat. The prelate stood for several moments, his deep-set, dark brown eyes scanning the chateau's grounds. Dante was back on familiar territory, and he felt good to be home.

"I trust you had a satisfactory trip," said Juan.

"It met my expectations," responded the prelate.

Dante and Juan always spoke English. Although his first language was Spanish, the prelate prided himself on being able to fluently converse in what he considered the language of business throughout the world. All of the order's executives used English in their daily dealings, and it was the common language throughout the Fraternity's vast holdings.

Juan collected Dante's briefcase and suit jacket from the vehicle's interior. The prelate's luggage, residing in the limousine's trunk, would be brought in later and unpacked by Juan. The assistant closed the door. Knowing he would no longer be needed, the vehicle's driver put the limousine in gear and began the trip that would take him to the rear of the chateau, where the order's four Mercedes were kept.

As they walked up the stairs, Dante, who stood a couple of inches under six feet, nevertheless towered over his diminutive executive assistant. In his late sixties, Dante looked and had the lithe appearance of a man fifteen years younger. A regular exercise program and carefully controlled diet were not only responsible for his elegant appearance but once again characterized the prelate's overriding commitment to controlling every aspect of his life and, by extension, the order.

Reaching the doors, Juan swung the right one open, and both men passed into the building. Together, they climbed the sweeping mahogany staircase to the second floor. The men walked in silence down the thickly carpeted corridor. At the end of the hall was Dante's suite of rooms, which contained his office, a galley kitchen, a meeting room, a dining room, a bedroom with a large en suite bathroom, and a small office for Juan. It was a self-contained stronghold from which the prelate guided his empire.

While Juan went into the kitchen to make an espresso, Dante slid behind his desk. The assistant had already powered up the computer, and Dante immediately began reviewing the daily financial results of the order's corporations. Juan came in with the espresso and silently left the demitasse, along with a plate containing a sliced apple, on the corner of Dante's desk, before withdrawing into his office.

Absently chewing on pieces of apple and sipping his espresso Dante reviewed reams of figures that enunciated the order's financial health. He had recently extended a salt-and-pepper moustache into a full, closely cropped beard that, along with his thick, gray hair, worn short and parted on the left, gave him the appearance of a dignified university professor. But there was nothing professorial about the prelate. He was a ruthless and driven man who fully believed he was on a mission from God.

Satisfied with his review of the order's daily operational and financial results, Dante got up from behind the desk and walked over to where Juan had placed his briefcase on a coffee table that fronted a comfortable leather sofa. Popping the latches, he opened the case and pulled out a leather sleeve with twenty-seven individual pockets, each containing a memory stick.

The memory sticks had been an integral part of Dante's travels through Europe, Asia, and South America. The sleeve contained damaging video images, computer data, and audio files collected by Dante over the course of his tenure as prelate on the twenty-seven cardinals under his control. While it had always been recorded that the voting for a pope is done in secret within the walls of the Sistine Chapel, Dante had cultivated enough men over the years that he knew exactly what took place during the conclave.

Ambrosia would carry with him the pope's blessing into the conclave. The cardinals believed piously that God directed the pope's thoughts, and if Paul had chosen Ambrosia, then Ambrosia's selection must also be God's will. Dante did not expect the vote to be close. But in his meetings with each of the implicated cardinals, the prelate not only directed them to vote for Ambrosia, but also indicated they were expected to convince anyone who was against Ambrosia becoming pope that he was the one the college should support.

Through his contacts within the Sistine Chapel, Dante would know if any of his chosen cardinals did not perform to his satisfaction. No cardinal would be willing to sacrifice his position within the church by failing to carry out Dante's instructions. They all knew that Dante's threat to release the material to the world's media if they didn't comply was grounded in harsh reality.

Dante walked behind his desk. Shifting a painting of a biblical feast created in 1527 by the Italian artist Paolo Veronese, he exposed a wall safe. After undergoing a retina scan, he pulled back the safe's door and deposited the leather sleeve with the memory sticks. Closing the door and moving the artwork back to its original position, the prelate turned and punched the intercom on his desk. Juan answered within a heartbeat. Dante instructed his assistant to locate Ambrosia.

A date would soon be set for the conclave. There were plans to be finalized with Ambrosia. Almost six weeks had passed since he'd seen the cardinal. It was time for Ambrosia to visit the chateau. The cardinal didn't yet know what plans Dante had in store for the Vatican. Ambrosia needed to understand the role he was going to play in Dante's blitzkrieg and capture of Rome and, by extension, the Roman Catholic Church.

Chapter Six

They had collected in a non-descript conference room at the Guardians' headquarters in Inverness. The fluorescent lights cast a pale glow over the barren, white walls; worn, gray carpet; stained, long, brown wooden meeting table; and hard-backed chairs.

The calendar was coming up on seven weeks since the codex had been stolen. Although it was known that the Word of Janus theft had been engineered by the Praetorian Order, the Guardians were no closer to determining where the codex was being held. The air was spitting anxiety among those gathered around the table.

The Guardians served two primary functions. The first was to shield Janus from the world. Comprising 1,400 people and dedicated to the islanders' welfare, the group supplied whatever commodities and services were required by the island's residents.

Equally important, the Guardians were a crucial link between Janus and its 18,000-member diaspora. Having expanded to each of the globe's regions, every follower was committed to extending the Janus mantra of forgiveness, understanding, tolerance, equality, and peace throughout the planet.

Critical to the Guardians' mandate was the over-riding directive that all actions undertaken by the group must first be approved through a general meeting of the islanders. It was a sacrosanct understanding that had never been broken in the Guardians four hundred-year history—until now.

Seated at the table were the Guardians' four key personnel. Chairing the meeting was Andrew, the head of security and senior Guardian in terms of authority. With him were Leyland, responsible for communications with the diaspora; Olga, the group's technology chief; and Bella, its financial director.

It was this management team that had secretly guided the Guardians into the uncharted territory of ignoring a firm directive from the islanders. As with many disagreements over abiding by established rules, the causes for the Guardians action were based on a simplicity of facts yet embroiled in the complexity of human emotions.

Under the heading of facts were the following realities: The Word of Janus had been sent to Inverness for restoration; the work was being done in a specially constructed laboratory on land owned by Andrew and Leyland; and the theft had occurred despite round-the-clock security.

On the emotional side, Andrew had taken the codex's loss personally and, during a meeting with the islanders on Janus, had been forced to weather the brunt of their initial displeasure. Although Elijah had attempted to deflect the criticism by assuming responsibility, Andrew believed he was being blamed for the loss. It was a low point for a man who possessed a steely pride in being able to control all situations.

In keeping with the Janus philosophy of understanding and peace, the islanders had decided not to confront the order and Sabatini. An English copy of the codex remained on the island, and Elijah had volunteered to translate the Word of Janus into Aramaic and Hebrew. Andrew had lobbied hard

The Hope of Janus

for aggressively pursuing the order and retrieving the original parchments, but the Guardians were explicitly instructed to stand down and accept that the codex was lost.

That was where the issue should have remained. But being exonerated by the islanders wasn't good enough for Andrew. Seething with resentment that he'd been made to look incompetent by the order, Andrew returned to Inverness intent on seeking revenge.

It meant defying the centuries-old edict, but the Guardian wasn't prepared to let that fact stand in his way. His pride was non-negotiable. A brooding and taciturn personality, he was driven by the constant need to succeed, regardless of the endeavor.

On this morning as he looked around the table, Andrew was impatient at the slow pace it was taking to discover where the codex was being held. Of average height, he took pride in a body that was trim and conditioned by daily workouts in the Guardians' gym. Topped with short, black hair and sporting a well-groomed beard, his angular face was unremarkable except for deep-set, coal black eyes that resembled two bottomless pools of Indian ink.

Those eyes were now fixed on Olga, whose team had been tasked with hacking the order's Internet and telephone networks.

"What progress have you made?" he asked. "We could use some good news."

Olga was excellent at her job. The Guardians' computer operation ran with an efficiency which rivaled that of any major corporation or government facility. Along with her technological expertise, Olga possessed the important ability to decipher complex computer terms and phraseology into a language that was easily understood by those she was briefing. The tall, slim, elegant woman treasured results, not the ability to spew computer jargon.

"I believe we're getting close," Olga responded. "As we know, the order's network is incredibly sophisticated and complex. But we also have good people. With our twenty-four-hour monitoring and probing, we've been able to break through on a couple of occasions. Unfortunately, our searches were soon discovered, and we were shut down before anything could be found.

"Nevertheless, no system is without its weaknesses. And the more we probe, the more we're learning about their operation. It's a bit of a cat-and-mouse game. While we're scanning their network to determine a flaw, they're constantly upgrading their firewalls and routers. What we need to do is keep probing without being detected."

"Is it possible they know what we're doing and have established systems that are impossible for us to penetrate?" asked Andrew.

Hooding her cobalt blue eyes, which were complemented by high cheekbones and short, blond hair, Olga took a moment to frame the answer. "We're working through the independent server at our Edinburgh office," she said slowly. "There are no ties to the operation here in Inverness. We've managed to obscure our IP address, and that should hopefully hold us until we find where the codex is being kept.

"The order's firewall and routers are not designed to hold off a specific, long-term, and dedicated attack. They're meant to guard against random hackers. But we have to acknowledge that they must suspect we wouldn't let the codex's theft pass without some kind of response.

"That's why we've also stepped up our phone monitoring. I've allocated extra personnel and resources to track whatever conversations are taking place that involve Sabatini and his key people. I'm hoping the order will believe all our efforts are focused on hacking its computer network and not be so diligent when it comes to guarding their phones.

"Having said that, we're all aware they know who we are. The order has been scanning us for years. It was how they found out about the codex and where it was being restored. I'm anxious for the opportunity to pay them back."

"We've been at this for almost two months," voiced Bella, breaking into the conversation. "How do we know they haven't destroyed the codex, and there's nothing to find with all our probing and monitoring? Given the threat it poses to the Vatican, I can't see them keeping it around."

"We don't know that," Andrew retorted sharply.

"I understand you want to get it back, but we have to be realistic," said Bella. "A lot of our technology personnel have been taken away from other projects they should be doing. We can't carry on like this indefinitely."

A petite woman, Bella made up for her lack of stature with a bulldog personality that was now on full display. Her eyes, the color of hazel, were flashing in frustration behind tinted designer glasses.

"I don't have to remind all of you that I was against defying the islanders' instructions," she said. "I only came on board because we agreed this would be a short-term mission. We should start planning how we're going to wrap it up. That's what we need to discuss," she concluded, angrily tossing her long, auburn hair.

"Do you feel the same way?" asked Andrew, looking over at Olga and Leyland.

"Definitely not," said Olga. "We keep going until we either find the codex or have concrete proof that it's been destroyed."

Everyone's eyes swung toward Leyland, whose easygoing nature often kept the other three, with their intense personalities, from clashing. Tall and rail thin, with ginger hair, emerald green eyes, and fair skin, it was in his nature to always seek compromise.

"I agree with Andrew and Olga," he stated, his voice quiet and calm. "The codex is a fundamental part of our history. We must focus all our energy on retrieving it. Everyone associated with Janus deserves that from us. If it has been destroyed, that would be a disaster. But an even greater tragedy would be if we gave up without knowing what had happened to our codex."

"It looks as though I'm outvoted," Bella noted. "So we keep looking. But I have a question."

"And what's that?" asked Andrew, his tone wary.

"Even if we discover where the Word of Janus is being kept, we haven't given any thought about how we're going to get it back."

Andrew surveyed the room, his eyes resting briefly on each of the others. He was about to deliver news he realized would upset the group, but he believed initially withholding the information was justified. If he had previously discussed the undertaking with them, Andrew knew there would be resistance. However, now that the plan was fully under way, he could argue that it was too late to call a halt.

"I have put together a four-person team of young Guardians," he told them. "They are in London being trained by a former member of the elite British commando unit, the SAS. He has a reputation of being one of the best in the business. The moment we know where the codex is being held, our squad will be sent to retrieve it."

There was a momentary stunned silence among the meeting's other participants.

Bella was the first to speak. "And when were you going to tell us this?" she asked, outrage evident in her voice's unyielding tone.

"I didn't know these types of decisions had to be approved by all of you," retorted Andrew. "It's an operational plan and falls completely within my mandate as head of security."

"You didn't believe this decision was important enough to share with us?" Bella challenged. "What were you thinking? This is not a case of business as usual. I realize some plan had to be put in place to salvage the codex if we found it. But we should have been involved. All of us have committed our futures to the success of bringing the Word of Janus back to the island."

"Bella makes a good point," said Leyland. "We all agreed to share the risk. That also means keeping each other informed of what's happening in our respective areas regarding the codex."

The words were said calmly and without any hint of reproach, but they had an immediate impact on Andrew. The Guardian now realized that Bella and Leyland were right. He had taken the codex's theft personally and acted as though he was the only one affected by the loss. But the other three had backed him when he'd called on them to defy the islanders' directive. For the future, he had to respect their support and include them in whatever he was planning.

"You're right," Andrew said quietly. "I should have told you what I was doing. It's not something that will happen again.

Moving forward, I'll run all my plans through the group before acting on them."

It was a rare concession from Andrew, who, as the senior Guardian, was used to a large degree of decision-making independence. However, Bella was only partially satisfied.

"The question that has to be asked," she began, "is where do we go from here? We are an organization dedicated to supporting the Janus commitment to peace. If the team is being trained by a former SAS commando, does that mean you expect a confrontation should we find the codex and attempt its retrieval? If that's the case, it goes against all our principles. How do you expect the rest of us to support a mission that may include violence?"

Before Andrew could respond, Olga said, "We all knew finding the codex's location was only part of the equation. At some point, we would have faced the decision of how to retrieve it. Andrew is dealing with the issue. Let's hear what he has planned before determining what we're going to do next."

The admonition had the effect of dampening Bella's indignation. She stared glumly around the table.

"I think it's time we were updated on what's happening in London," said Olga.

Andrew spent the next five minutes explaining that the team was going through an intense regimen meant to meld the two men and two women into a cohesive unit that would be prepared to travel the moment the codex was located. Their preparation involved, among other skills, a focus on advance planning; hand-to-hand combat; the intricacies of surveillance; break-and-enter techniques, including rappelling and determining escape avenues; and finally, a grueling physical and mental training program.

"We're also assuming that, wherever the codex is located, there will be guards. And they'll probably be armed."

Andrew could tell the news had startled the other three. Olga and Bella looked at each other, their arching eyes telling Andrew all he needed to know. Leyland, meanwhile, shifted uncomfortably in his chair.

"What does that mean for our people?" asked Bella. "They won't be carrying any weapons. That places them in danger."

"We are conducting the type of mission that has never been undertaken in our history," said Andrew, more forcefully than he'd intended. "The rules governing how we conduct ourselves don't apply in this situation. The squad is also receiving weapons training."

Andrew knew there would be opposition, but he wasn't prepared for the force it generated among the other three. Everyone began talking at once. Holding up his hands for quiet, the senior Guardian said that he needed the opportunity to explain. It took several moments but finally the noise gave way to a restless silence.

"The team that stole the codex was armed with AK-47 automatic assault rifles," began the Guardian. "Those are lethal weapons. Our guards, in keeping with the Janus principle of peace, carried low-wattage Tasers. If a firefight had developed, they wouldn't have stood a chance.

"The squad going after the parchments will be involved in a situation that carries a large amount of risk and danger. They have to be prepared for any eventuality. And that means being armed with more than Tasers."

Andrew was about to detail the weapons recommended by the SAS instructor, when Bella cut him off. "We've already gone off the grid in disregarding the islanders' strict instructions not to confront the order," she said. "And now you want to break the most sacred principle that has guided Janus for two thousand years by openly preparing for violence. Have you forgotten that, throughout our history, peace has been the foundation for everything we do?

"This is not a decision you get to make alone. I fundamentally believe that all issues, including getting the codex back, can be brought to a peaceful resolution. I am an islander and will not allow you to disregard or jeopardize my values."

Andrew had never seen Bella so upset. A deep flush had mottled her face, and while she tried to hide it by clasping her hands together, it was obvious they were shaking.

"We are all islanders," noted Andrew, trying to bring some calm to the discussion. "But I don't see how else we can protect our people. Olga, what do you think?"

"I support Bella," stated the technology chief. "The only weapons I will agree to are Tasers. If this SAS agent is so good, he can instruct our team how to rescue the codex through stealth and cunning. I've agreed to this mission because I have faith that my people can find out where the codex is being held. But I won't stand by and see you make a mockery of all that Janus represents."

The words said calmly and with little emotion, were nevertheless harsh. Andrew felt their sting.

Focusing his gaze on Leyland, he asked, "Do you agree with Olga and Bella that Tasers will be good enough for the squad if they encounter any trouble?"

"I believe it's the best course for equipping the team," responded Leyland.

The Hope of Janus

In a culture where compromise and understanding were features of all discussions, the senior Guardian realized it was time to concede that he'd been wrong in advocating for lethal weapons. "Well, it looks as though the three of you are in agreement," he said. "I'll contact my SAS agent, and he can begin preparing the team according to a new set of instructions."

There was a noticeable lessening of tension. Breaking the silence that had momentarily overtaken the room, Andrew asked if the issue had been settled. Everyone nodded their heads in agreement.

"Good," said the senior Guardian. "I believe we have one more agenda point, and that's a report from Bella."

"There are a several items I'd like us to review," said the diminutive financial officer.

As Bella was passing out a small binder of papers containing spreadsheets and flowcharts, there was a knock on the meeting room door, and in walked a young man, dressed in sneakers, jeans, and a gray sweatshirt.

He looked at Olga and stated, "Sorry to interrupt, but we've found something you need to see immediately."

"Is it important?" the technology chief asked. "We're in the middle of a meeting."

"It's crucial," was the response.

Olga got up from her chair, apologized to the group, and said, "I shouldn't be more than a few minutes."

"That's fine," acknowledged Andrew. "We won't focus on your area until you get back."

Chapter Seven

The unmistakable sense of anticipation was rippling through the room. The Guardians' technology section was noted for the steady and somewhat unspectacular way the division conducted its business. Having Olga called out of a meeting was rare and usually involved some sort of technical malfunction. However, Andrew knew that everyone was thinking the same thing, but no one dared voice their thoughts.

Could this be the breakthrough they'd all been hoping would happen?

While they waited for Olga's return, Andrew, Bella, and Leyland reviewed aspects of the Guardians' financial operation that didn't impact the technology division. The conversation was sporadic, for it was a case of doing something to occupy their minds. Bella asked Andrew to provide a cost breakdown for the team in London, along with the SAS trainer. He had just agreed to the request when from the corridor came the rapid staccato sound of a woman's heels hitting the floor. Olga was in a hurry, and the three Guardians tensed.

She burst into the room, red-faced, fighting to catch her breath. There was no sign of the calm, composed technology chief that everyone was used to seeing.

"We have a location," she exclaimed, gulping for air.

A jolt of energy shot through the room. Andrew could feel his pulse begin to race.

"Where's the codex?" he demanded. "Is it at the order's chateau in Valencia?"

"It's a bit more complicated than that," responded Olga, taking her seat and gradually regaining her composure.

"Don't say it's at the Vatican," said Andrew. "Trying to get it back from inside that place would be next to impossible. All of our preparations have assumed it would be at the chateau."

Olga held up her hand. "Just let me explain what we've discovered. It's not at the Vatican; nor is it at the chateau."

"Then where is it?"

"We intercepted a couple of e-mails between Sabatini and a Luigi Monte, who heads an order facility in Zaragoza. It appears to be an archival restoration center. Monte was reporting on the progress for repairing both the manuscript's Aramaic and Hebrew versions."

"They're restoring the Word of Janus," said Andrew, confusion evident in his voice. "It doesn't make sense. Why is the order working on preserving a document that could wreck the Catholic Church's foundation?"

"Whatever the reason, it has to be considered good news for us," noted Bella.

Andrew nodded his head in agreement. "You're right," he said. "They obviously have no intention of destroying the manuscript. Still, I'd like to know what Sabatini has in mind."

And then another thought struck the senior Guardian. "Where is Zaragoza?"

"It's in Spain's Aragon region, about two hundred miles northeast of Madrid," responded Leyland, surprising everyone with his knowledge.

"Do we know where in Zaragoza this archival restoration building is located?" asked Andrew.

"Not yet," responded Olga. "But my technicians are going through every bit of information related to the Vatican museums. It won't be long before I have an answer for you."

"The sooner the better," noted Andrew. "In the meantime, I'm going to put our team in London on notice that the chateau is no longer the target. Once we discover the building's location, we'll send the squad to Zaragoza. Our people will need time to reconnoiter the place before determining the best way of getting in and recovering the manuscript. But that's fine. We can deal with the change of site.

"What's important is that the Word of Janus is being restored. It will be there when we carry out the retrieval mission."

"Will your SAS agent be with the team?" asked Bella.

"That has always been the plan."

"And you'll tell the squad that the only weapons will be Tasers," Bella reminded him.

Andrew knew it would be difficult to convince his SAS trainer that the crew was to carry out the mission armed only with Tasers. But that was the commitment he'd made. "They will be told," he said. "It won't make them happy, but I'll make sure everyone understands this is an operational rule that can't be broken. There's no need for concern."

"It's not the Guardians I'm worried about," said Bella. "They've lived the Janus principle of peace all their lives.

The Hope of Janus

Carrying out the mission with Tasers won't be a problem for them. The one who's giving me anxiety is your SAS agent. He's used to dealing with weapons. Will he agree with your instructions?"

The question caught Andrew unprepared. It was something he hadn't considered.

"He's part of the team," the senior Guardian finally answered. "Once I deliver the mandate, he'll fall in line."

The last sentence was spoken with more confidence than Andrew felt. However, no one disputed his claim.

"I should be getting back to the tech center," announced Olga, standing up. "With apologies to Bella, this is too important for me to be in a meeting room talking about financials and looking at spreadsheets. We can do this another time."

"No offense taken." Bella chuckled, gathering up the binders. "You're right. You should be with your people."

She suddenly turned and looked directly at Andrew. "By the way, what's your SAS man's name?"

"It's Ray Shepherd."

"Good to know," responded Bella as she and Olga departed the conference room, leaving the two men alone.

"Do you really think Shepherd can be trusted to agree with your directive?" asked Leyland. "After all, he's used to going into dangerous situations with something more than a Taser."

Andrew had already answered Bella. But this was Leyland. The men had worked closely together for the better part of two decades and shared living quarters in a house on the Inverness outskirts.

"I don't know," he admitted. "From his training, I assume Ray is used to following orders. But this is a different case. He's now an independent contractor. He may believe that, in carrying a gun, he's able to offer the team protection in case things fall apart. The best I can do is give the order. Since Ray's not a Guardian, he technically isn't bound by our principles."

"You're walking close to the line," Leyland quietly admonished. "He's working for us and leading Guardians on a mission. Perhaps when you talk, those are things you should impress on him."

Andrew understood why Leyland was making the point. The Guardian was a gentle and caring man. He was devoted to the Janus tenets of peace and understanding. However, this was a situation that had never been experienced by the Guardians.

Andrew realized he was fully responsible for creating the current reality by persuading his management team to defy the islanders' directive. And he was pragmatic enough to recognize that all would be forgiven once the manuscript was returned to Janus. With this in mind, and knowing the Guardians would carry Tasers, he was comfortable telling Ray to do the same but ready to accept that the SAS agent might not comply. The endgame was retrieving both the Aramaic and Hebrew versions of the Word of Janus. That thought alone was driving Andrew, and if some Janus principles had to be bent, he was prepared to live with the consequences.

"I'll be firm in my instructions to Ray," said Andrew, breaking the silence that had settled over the men. "I know that, from the beginning, he has planned this as a covert mission rather than an open confrontation."

"So all we need now is for Olga's team to determine the exact location in Zaragoza," observed Leyland.

"That's right," responded Andrew. "Once we have the information, the mission is initiated, and everything should go according to plan. It may take a few more weeks, but I'm confident the codex will be recovered."

"Something tells me we may need more than confidence to pull this off," noted Leyland as the men got to their feet and slowly walked out of the room.

Chapter Eight

---✢---

The Zaragoza museum's recent history was a mirror of the uneasy alliance that had developed between the Vatican and the order during Dante's time as prelate. The nine hundred-year-old property was originally a large abbey, comprising several buildings. Franciscan monks devoted their lives to working with rare parchments, paintings, and sculptures, along with priceless gold, silver, and bronze works of art.

Although the monks labored over their work, the abbey's main mission remained a place where the men led quiet lives of prayer, reflection, and penitence.

All that changed with the First World War. Pope Benedict XV, fearing an attack on the Vatican by the German Army, secretly transferred some of the Church's most treasured art pieces to Zaragoza for safekeeping. The pope also decreed that the order would be responsible for the facility's protection until the war ended. However, in the confusing aftermath of the conflict, the original document detailing the understanding had been lost. Although still legally a part of the Vatican, Zaragoza had effectively remained under the Fraternity's control.

During the early part of Dante's tenure as prelate, he'd brought more change to Zaragoza. The monks were relocated to a newly built monastery on the outskirts of Madrid, where they were no longer responsible for working on the Vatican's artifacts. Dante had then razed the monastery and subsequently built a modern facility on the original site that was more than quadruple the abbey's size.

Over the years, further additions included state-of-the-art equipment, improved lighting, upgraded tools, and university-trained specialists. All of the technicians were members of the order. Dante had created a museum that rivaled such famous institutions as the State Hermitage Museum in Russia and Washington's Smithsonian Institution.

Under Dante's direction, the order's control of Zaragoza was strengthened. The museum had become virtually independent of the Vatican. All decisions regarding the facility's operation were routed through the chateau.

That was, until Cardinal Wolfgang Reinhart's appointment as director of the Vatican Museums—a collection of fifty-four galleries spread over nineteen buildings—and the subsequent agreement in which Dante gave up control of the artifacts, equipment, and supply purchases but retained responsibility for security, restoration projects, ownership, and costs associated with the building, along with personnel management.

It was rare for Dante to compromise. He believed in total control over anything impacting the order. However, the prelate knew that once he had taken over the papacy, every aspect of the Vatican, including the museums, would be under the order's jurisdiction. It was a clear demonstration of Dante's greatest strength—a profound belief in his ability to control events that affected the order through intense planning, extreme patience, and ruthless implementation.

The Janus codex represented one part of Dante's plan for complete domination of the Vatican. Although Dante had earlier indicated to Ambrosia that he would destroy the document, the prelate had no such intention. He planned to have the parchments restored and kept at the chateau.

The codex would be used as another instrument to ensure Ambrosia and succeeding popes followed the order's dictates. If one of them considered rebelling against the order's hold over the papacy, the threat of releasing the manuscript to the world would quickly negate any thrust for independence. No pope would want to be responsible for the demise of the Roman Catholic Church. And that's what would happen if it were shown that Christianity was built on a fabrication.

The key, though, lay in ensuring the codex was carbon and X-ray date tested, restored, and then maintained in pristine condition. And thus far, everything was proceeding as planned. Preliminary date testing had shown the parchments were from the first century. Repairing the manuscript was underway at Zaragoza. Within four to five years, the codex would be ready for transfer to the chateau. In the meantime, Dante had the dossier and film on Ambrosia that would keep the soon-to-be-elected pope under his control.

Dante's drive to take over the papacy was not an extremist's grab for power. It was a calculated business decision. He was seeking the capability to influence how Rome's followers perceived their world. Having built the order into one of the world's largest conglomerates through start-ups, buyouts, and hostile acquisitions, he was using the same operating philosophy to acquire the Vatican.

Blackmail, intimidation, and occasional violence, along with sound corporate decisions, were at the heart of his success. A pragmatist, he found nothing ironic in using these same devices in taking over one of the world's great religions. Dante believed he was a religious purist when it came to his faith.

Dante had planned on controlling the papacy since before becoming prelate. Now, forty-five years later, he was on the cusp of enacting his plan. The looming success neither satisfied nor excited him. Instead, his mind was focused on the knowledge that, once Ambrosia became pope, the work would begin on truly bringing every aspect of the Vatican under his power.

And that was Dante. His triumphs merely led to more goals. This is what made him such a dangerous adversary. Success was not an emotional release for him. It was merely a completed objective on the never-ending road to make the order a global conglomerate.

Chapter Nine

✣

As Dante sat in the chapel communing with his god on this late-May morning, he could hear the melodic drumbeat of raindrops throbbing against the building's beautiful stained glass windows.

It was a week since Dante's return from his travels and nine days after Pope Paul's abdication notice had been released to the world. The date of the conclave for the College of Cardinals had been set. It meant Ambrosia would be the new pope within six weeks if everything transpired as Dante had planned. And that was something the prelate had no doubt would happen.

Sitting in the pew, Dante allowed himself a few minutes to reflect on his upcoming meeting with Ambrosia. The cardinal would be at the chateau in a couple of hours. Dante was going to use the meeting to detail for Ambrosia how the Vatican was to be controlled through the order. The prelate had already chosen the advisors who would surround the new pope. During Dante's travels, he had met with seven cardinals, whose intense loyalty to the Fraternity was unquestioned. They were to form Ambrosia's inner circle. Another position, the Cardinal Secretary of State, the most senior posting in the Vatican's hierarchy, would also be revealed during the session.

And a Franciscan monk, who for years had worked diligently with the order's Bolivian enterprises, would be Ambrosia's executive assistant. From this group would flow the senior personnel changes within every department of the Roman Curia, the central body through which the pope conducted the Church's affairs. It included such areas as banking, diplomacy, human resources, communications, and security. Dante was going to leave no area untouched. It was a massive undertaking, but he was more than prepared for the task.

And as with everything Dante did, there was a specific reason for being in the chapel today. While his thoughts were focused on the coup d'état he was about to stage, the prelate was also driven by how his god would view the upcoming operation.

Usually, Dante prayed while kneeling in his pew. But the events that were about to unfold required a different form of communication with God. He got to his feet, shuffled out to the central aisle, and walked up to the small altar. Kneeling at the communion railing, he looked up at the crucifix that dominated the pulpit. Dante knew deep within his heart that God had blessed this takeover of the Vatican. For him, the logic was inescapable. His god would not have provided him this opportunity unless it was what he wanted.

But there was another part of the plan that was even greater in its scope. Hence the visit to the altar, the chapel's most sacred area. This was more than the Fraternity increasing its dominance over the Church. While that would be the case, the prelate believed he was on a mission to not only save the Roman Catholic Church, but to expand its power throughout the world. Satisfied that he had communicated his objective of world domination to God, Dante rose to his feet.

Ambrosia would become the pope, but it was Dante who truly had his god's blessing. A man of intense precision, the prelate always allowed himself fifteen minutes in the chapel. His time was at an end. He walked quickly to the side entrance, his steps echoing on the marble floor. The door opened, and he was met by Juan, who was holding an unfurled umbrella. The two men walked in silence back to the chateau.

Chapter Ten

✣

Although engrossed in reviewing a series of financial reports for the order's Monaco-based bank, Dante clearly heard Juan's soft voice over the intercom. Ambrosia had landed at Valencia's airport and was en route to the chateau in one of the Fraternity's limousines. A GPS tracker, located in the car's trunk, provided Juan with an unerringly accurate computer readout of where the Mercedes was in relation to the chateau.

After informing Dante that the cardinal would be arriving in ten minutes, Juan entered the prelate's office and shifted two Queen Anne chairs, along with the beautifully carved cherry wood coffee table to in front of the fireplace. The small, pale man with a thick waist; thin, wispy, gray hair; light brown eyes; and a prominent Adam's apple waited as Dante closed the computer. The prelate slipped on the jacket of a beautifully tailored blue, pin-striped suit and, along with Juan, proceeded along the hallway and descended the curving stairway to the chateau's front door.

The limousine slid gracefully to a stop just as the men walked outside and down the granite steps. Focused as he had been on the Monaco operation, Dante was surprised to see that the rain had stopped. Although the sky was clearing and patches of blue could be seen, the humidity still hung heavy. While it didn't bother Dante, the prelate could see that beads of sweat had already popped onto Juan's upper lip. The assistant opened the car's back door. Ambrosia unwound his large frame from the seat and handed a calf's leather briefcase to Juan.

Dante noticed that, as usual, the cardinal had opted for a business suit rather than his red church robes. Ambrosia enjoyed luxury and that included flying corporate class. In a rare unguarded moment between the two men, Ambrosia had told Dante that traveling as a businessman afforded him the opportunity to fly in relative comfort that would be unavailable if he wore the red cassock of a cardinal.

"Can you imagine how it would look if a man of the Church, regardless of my position, opted not to fly economy," he had told the prelate. "I have earned the right to enjoy the privilege that comes with power."

For Dante, the admission had been one more insight into the personality of the man he was using to wrest control of the Vatican. The sixty-nine-year-old cardinal's vanity was matched only by his sense of entitlement. He was not alone among many of his fellow cardinals who reveled in their position within the Church, but for Dante it confirmed what he believed about the man. It was another facet of Ambrosia's character that could be exploited. Dante continually played to the cardinal's vanity by subtly assuring Ambrosia that, of all the cardinals, he was best suited to sit on the papal throne.

Standing well over six feet and weighing approximately 215 pounds, Ambrosia was an imposing presence. He carried himself with a stately grace that made his appearance all the more powerful. As they shook hands, the two men briefly scanned each other's face and Dante looked into one of the cardinal's more striking features. His eyes were a mismatched color—one a deep brown, the other sapphire blue. Sitting above prominent cheekbones that framed a thick nose, their cold stare reflected what Dante knew was Ambrosia's anger at being summoned to the chateau.

"This meeting should be taking place in my office," the cardinal grumbled as they walked up the steps and through the large oak doors with Juan leading the way. "I have scheduled two hours for this meeting, and my return flight is booked for four o'clock. It is not wise for me to be away from Rome so close to the conclave."

"The vote is a mere formality," replied Dante, his tone conciliatory. "I asked you here because I thought it best we're not seen together in Rome. It is well known throughout the college that I was responsible for evaluating you and the three other candidates to replace Paul. Therefore, it's important no one knows I am directly responsible for you receiving his blessing to be the next pope.

"How would it look if it was known you met with the head of the Fraternity before you and your fellow cardinals are locked in the Sistine Chapel? People might suspect there was some form of collusion between us. Although the result is a foregone conclusion, it is still vital, at least for the sake of appearances that our plans remain in the darkness where they can't be seen."

Dante believed it was important to reiterate that the cardinal was certain to succeed Paul only because of the order's recommendation. More importantly, it was a way of emphasizing that this meeting was not a casual get-together between the soon-to-be pope and the order's prelate. It was going to be a session where Ambrosia would quickly learn exactly how far Dante was prepared to go in gaining control of the papacy.

Juan continued to walk in front as the men ascended the staircase and walked down the corridor.

Ambrosia had been silent as he labored up the stairs and was breathing heavily while they followed Juan along the hallway. His first utterance came as they entered the prelate's office.

"There should be an elevator in this building," he complained to Dante. "We're not all as fit as you."

The prelate turned and noted Ambrosia's flushed face, the sheen of sweat on his forehead, and the tortured breathing. It confirmed what he suspected about the cardinal's physical condition.

"You'll need to be in better shape if you're going to be an effective pope," admonished Dante. "We're going to begin with what you eat and drink. I've assigned a dietician and chef to your personal staff. They'll handle all your meals."

The prelate wasn't about to let the possibility of Ambrosia's early death from overexertion ruin his well-crafted campaign. The cardinal was the key, and Dante was about to begin controlling almost every aspect of the man's life.

Juan took their jackets and slipped out of the room. Dante slid into the Queen Anne chair at the left of the fireplace, while the cardinal, knowing the steps to this well-choreographed dance instinctively took the chair to the right.

The assistant silently reappeared, carrying a silver tray containing bone china cups and saucers, cloth napkins, and a coffee urn on a metal stand. Juan poured the java; both men took it black. The assistant plugged the urn's electric cord into a wall socket, ensuring the men would have hot coffee for the meeting and, just as quietly, left the room.

"So you've decided I need help with my meals," said Ambrosia, the bitterness evident in his voice. "What else do you have planned for me?"

Dante took a sip from his cup and placed it back on the saucer. He then proceeded to outline for the cardinal who would be his advisors. Under Pope Paul's administration, all members within the College of Cardinals had performed the vital task of consulting with the pope and guiding the decisions that came from the papal office. Dante was still involving members of the college, but the seven cardinals handpicked by the prelate would form an administrative group between the pope and the college.

"This means every decision I make will come from this select assembly that reports directly to you," said Ambrosia, his tone caustic. "Will I be able to initiate anything without your approval, have my own opinions, or even seek advice from members of the college not included in your council?"

"You can have as much freedom as you like," shot back Dante. "Of course you can have thoughts about changes you want to introduce and meet with as many cardinals as you want. The only difference is that, before you implement a decision, it must first be approved by the group of cardinals I have chosen."

Ambrosia nodded his head, deep in thought.

"Will I be able to keep my assistant?" asked the cardinal. "He has been with me for years and knows my habits. I want him to stay."

"I have selected someone new for you," offered Dante. "He is a young Franciscan monk who will handle all your needs. His name is Georgio Casavante."

Ambrosia leaned forward and scowled. "I'm not going to let you control me," he said defiantly, his voice rising. "You seem to have forgotten that the order comes under the Church's rule, not the other way around. I will administer my Papacy in the way I believe is best for the Church, not for you and the Fraternity."

Dante had expected this reaction and was prepared. It was not the first time the cardinal had chafed at the impending yoke being placed on him and conveniently overlooked the reality of his position. The prelate waited several seconds, letting the cardinal's outburst hang heavy in the air between them. Ambrosia settled back in his chair.

When Dante did finally speak his voice was low and calm. "This is not a matter of power," he began. "It is simply enacting the terms of our partnership. I am directly responsible for Paul blessing you to be his successor. The order also controls enough votes in the conclave that your ascendency to the papal chair is guaranteed."

"But the voting is by secret ballot," countered Ambrosia. "How can you be so sure the election will fall my way?"

"Do you think you're the only cardinal I have files on?" Dante said, spreading his arms wide. "I have personally met each of these errant men of the cloth and was very specific that they will not only vote for you but will also lobby for your election. Coupled with the papal blessing, this guarantees you will become the next pope."

"And these cardinals know you have sources within the college that will tell you how the voting transpired," said Ambrosia.

"That's right," confirmed Dante, resting his hands on the chair's arms. "Not one of the cardinals I have incriminating files on will dare go against my wishes. So I have kept my part of our agreement. In a few short weeks, you will be pope because I engineered your ascension.

"Which brings me to your file. I was hoping not to raise this subject, but you have brought it upon yourself. No one has to ever know about your affair in Vienna. But it is something I am prepared to use if you don't fully cooperate. You will occupy the highest office within our Church. Your pronouncements will be reported on by the world's press. You will hold the rank and have the privileges of a head of state. Just understand that, from the moment you become pope, you will follow my instructions. This is non-negotiable."

"Are you threatening me?" challenged Ambrosia.

"There is no need to be melodramatic," chastised the prelate. "This is a partnership that offers each of us what we want. You'll become pope, while the order will be able to put in place changes to strengthen our Church."

"A partnership." Ambrosia laughed. "This is no such thing. True, you are helping me succeed our Holy Father, but at a steep price. I can't help but wonder if I have made a pact with Satan."

Chapter Eleven

The acrid air of tension filled the room. Dante picked up his cup, drained it, and poured himself more coffee. He offered Ambrosia a refill, but the cardinal declined with an abrupt shake of his head. Although Ambrosia's defiance was to be expected, Dante had detected something else in the man's words. There was a note of confidence the prelate hadn't expected. Was it just bravado? Or was Ambrosia trying to demonstrate that he would hold some power in this arrangement?

While building the Fraternity into a global empire, Dante had learned and completely understood the many nuances of negotiation and compromise. The prelate believed the time had come to take a more conciliatory approach with Ambrosia.

"You're the best man at the right time to take our Church into the future," he began. "As I have said before, we need a strong and charismatic pope to lead us from the wilderness to being the dominant force we must be in the world. There is no doubt you will bring a new and transparent image to the Church.

"We are not here to follow the dictates and changes that evolve through societies. The Church must be seen as a leader in initiating change. I would not have worked so hard in ensuring you become the next pope unless I believed in your strength and courage to take our Church where it rightfully belongs.

Roman Catholicism will not only become the dominant religion; it will become a guide for all those seeking hope and salvation."

"I didn't realize you were so fanatical about your faith," Ambrosia said, his words laced with sarcasm.

"It is realism, not fanaticism," responded the prelate. "What we will be doing is bringing the world to the realization that Roman Catholicism is the one true religion and that, only by following our faith, will people everywhere find their rightful place in heaven. All other beliefs are corrupt, and their followers will never know the joy of meeting God when they die. This is what we must convince every man and woman, because it is the truth."

As usual, Dante had spoken in an even and measured tone. The words might convey a passion for his faith, but the prelate was incapable of emotion. He took several sips of coffee waiting for the cardinal's response. In the silence that followed, Ambrosia refilled his cup.

"I find it somewhat curious," said the cardinal, breaking the quiet. "You preach a devotion to our religion, yet you're blackmailing me. I can't help but wonder why you don't find that hypocritical."

"Because I am doing what has to be done so that our faith triumphs."

"Is it our religion or the order that you want to see victorious in the battle for the soul of every human?"

The question didn't bother Dante. He calmly answered, "The order's mandate is to protect the Vatican. That's what I'm doing by ensuring the Fraternity takes the Church into a secure future."

Once again silence, like the menacing stillness before a devastating storm, stole across the room. It was a clash of wills to see who would be the first in succumbing to the need for conversation. Dante sipped his coffee, watching carefully as Ambrosia avoided making eye contact while placing his cup on the table.

"Suppose I don't agree to being blackmailed," challenged Ambrosia, aggressively ending the psychological game.

There it was again, thought Dante. This was something else besides the cardinal straining against the constraints being placed on him. It seemed as though Ambrosia believed he could negotiate a more favorable arrangement. That wasn't possible, and Dante was about to detail the reasons why.

"If you at any time go against my wishes, I'll reveal to the world the file I have on you," said Dante in a tone so matter-of-fact he could have been discussing the gardens that dotted the chateau's grounds. "Anyway, we are well past that. Everything that happens to you from this day forward, including the not-insignificant task of ensuring you become pope is under my control."

The cardinal shifted his bulk in the chair. "Would you really expose my past?" he asked, his voice showing the confidence Dante had previously detected. "Think of the damage it would cause the Church. And if the Vatican were wounded, the Fraternity would also suffer. You couldn't possibly escape the chaos. If you harm me, you cripple the order.

"And while your influence is necessary if I am to become pope, you also need me. I don't have to tell you how much talk there has been throughout the Vatican of making the order more accountable to Rome. Some have even questioned your leadership, saying you've become too independent. And there are calls among a number of quarters for you to be replaced. I will provide the necessary safeguards for the order to continue expanding with you as its prelate.

"So you see, I believe we have a stalemate on two fronts."

Ambrosia leaned back in his chair, a self-assured smile showing how much he believed Dante's plan had been thwarted.

Dante responded with a relaxed shrug. Throughout this quest for dominance, the prelate knew he held the upper hand. In a calm, soft voice he said, "You believe I need your protection to keep the order shielded from those who would strip the Fraternity of its power and have me removed as prelate?"

The cardinal nodded in agreement, but his eyes had taken on a wary look.

"Let me explain something," continued Dante. "My people are spread throughout Rome. There may be talk in some quarters of my replacement as you claim, but there is nothing to it. No one would dare move against the order. I have too many incriminating dossiers and know all the buried secrets.

"Do you think I began my campaign when I heard of Paul's illness? I have worked at this for almost half a century. The only ties remaining between the Vatican and the order are those I have chosen to maintain. And they can be cut the moment I decide.

"Now to your point about the Fraternity's exposure should the Church falter. I have built the order for just such a situation. My organization is one of the world's most powerful and secret corporations. We are strong enough and so far removed from the Church that the Fraternity can withstand any scandal that would swamp the Vatican. If you refuse to work with me after becoming pope, I will release your file. It would take years, if ever, for the Church to recover. Your place in history would be as the man who destroyed people's faith in Roman Catholicism. Are you prepared for that eventuality?

"Of course you could withdraw your candidacy. In that case, I will make your file public, and you would be ruined. No, you will become pope, and I will control the papacy."

The lethal attack on Ambrosia had been delivered with quiet and emotionless efficiency. Although the cardinal averted his eyes, the troubled look on his face led Dante to believe the brief insurgency was almost over. All that remained was for Ambrosia to confirm his acquiescence.

"Are we agreed that my plan is the one we're going to follow?" asked the prelate.

The beads of sweat had returned to Ambrosia's forehead, and his mouth was set in an angry grimace. Lifting his eyes, he impaled the prelate with a look of naked distain. The cardinal's outrage was riveting, and Dante saw that his hands were gripping the chair's arms so tightly the knuckles were white. The seconds ticked by, and neither man spoke.

The prelate stared directly into Ambrosia's eyes, refusing to let the cardinal claim victory in this intense and emotionally charged encounter. For the prelate, it had little to do with control of the papacy. In his mind, that was a foregone conclusion. Rather, this was a battle for the psychological domination of the cardinal. Dante wanted no more discussions about whether Ambrosia was going to comply with the order's commands when he was pope. The prelate needed the focus to be on his objective of taking over the Vatican.

Dante saw Ambrosia's eyes shift, breaking the lock they'd had on the prelate. But his posture was not that of a defeated man. The cardinal was sitting up straight in the chair, his face a fierce mask of resolve.

"Fine. We'll do it as you've planned, with one exception," said the cardinal. "I have something that needs to be considered. You can surround me with whomever you want, but the Cardinal Secretary of State shall be my selection."

This was the major point Dante had wanted discussed. It was the one position that would be central to Ambrosia's Papacy. That the cardinal had raised it without any prodding made the prelate wonder if this was the reason for Ambrosia's self-assurance.

But something wasn't right. Ambrosia had no power to negotiate for any position, especially the Secretary of State. Yet the cardinal's continued confidence indicated Ambrosia believed differently. He was demanding control over who would be appointed to the most important post within the Roman Curia.

The Secretariat of State was responsible for both internal Church affairs and the Vatican's relationship with nations and with international organizations. The Secretary of State was the pope's senior advisor and usually his most trusted confidant. It was vital to Dante's plan that this position be filled with someone loyal to the order.

The post was currently vacant because the Cardinal Secretary of State resigned upon the pope's death or abdication. It allowed the new pope to choose the man who would be responsible for implementing, through the Curia, decisions made by the pope and his advisory group of cardinals. Dante's plan called for his seven chosen cardinals and the Secretary of State being the ones to ensure the order's agenda was implemented.

The prelate had researched what he believed were all the possible ramifications regarding Ambrosia becoming pope. There wasn't anything the cardinal could do to derail the plan. Still, Dante was curious.

The Hope of Janus

He got up and moved over to the credenza behind his desk. Dante picked up a laptop, looked through several neatly arranged and labeled memory sticks, chose the one he wanted, walked to his chair, and sat down. Placing the laptop on the coffee table, he opened it and shifted the unit so that the screen was visible to both men. He then plugged the memory stick into the laptop's USB port. The display folded from black to white, as though turning in on itself. Dante noted the cardinal was intently watching the screen.

Rolling the mouse, the prelate brought up a page with the words "Cardinal Secretary of State."

Ambrosia took his eyes off the screen and focused them on Dante.

"You've already selected my executive group of cardinals and my assistant. I assume you have someone in mind for the Secretary of State. Well, that won't be necessary. I'm going to choose Cardinal Wolfgang Reinhart for the position. He has been my most loyal friend for more than twenty years. Not only that, he is a strong and progressive leader within the College of Cardinals. He is a wise and thoughtful man who possesses all the qualifications for the position.

"I also believe you have had some dealings with Wolfgang in the not-too-distant past. I'm sure you found him to be a capable negotiator and administrator during your discussions regarding Zaragoza."

Reinhart was the Vatican Museums director, a relatively low level function within Rome's bureaucracy. He reported to Ambrosia through the byzantine labyrinth that was the Vatican's hierarchy. Although Reinhart was the museums director, it was well known throughout the Vatican that Ambrosia controlled most of what happened within the museums.

Reinhart was not part of the prelate's collection of captive cardinals. And even if he was, Dante did not share Ambrosia's view of the man's capabilities. He was a mere functionary and had already achieved his level of competence.

The relationship between the two men since the intense negotiations for control of the Zaragoza museum had left the head of the Vatican Museums a bitter and vocal critic of Dante. Reinhart, not satisfied with the Vatican having control over only the artwork and artifacts, continued to lobby for full control of the Zaragoza operation.

"Reinhart will not fill the position," Dante declared emphatically. "Not only is he unqualified for the post, I have assigned someone else to fill the role."

Ambrosia's eyes widened. The prelate saw raw anger as the cardinal's face quickly turned a splotchy red.

"Is this because Wolfgang forced you to compromise over the Zaragoza museum?" said Ambrosia. "Is this your petty way of getting back at him and at me?"

"This has nothing to do with Zaragoza," Dante responded calmly, mildly shocked that Ambrosia would have such a thought. "I have simply chosen the best man to assist you."

"Next to the pope, this is the most important position within the Vatican," declared the cardinal through clenched teeth. "It has to be Reinhart, for I trust him. He will be my one confidant among the nest of vipers you are building around me."

Dante was unmoved. It was precisely because of the secretary's vital role that the prelate would not allow Ambrosia to appoint Reinhart. The time had come to end this debate.

"This is no longer a discussion," said the prelate. "We will proceed with the plan as it has been designed. Your Secretary

The Hope of Janus

of State will be Cardinal Antonio Giambese. I am presently preparing his briefing papers for when you become pope."

"I have known Giambese for fifteen years and never realized he was one of your people," the cardinal said quietly. "But that's beside the point. I will have Reinhart. Let me explain why he is going to be my Secretary of State."

"Yes, please enlighten me," said Dante, his voice colder than an arctic wind.

"You sometimes forget I am one of the very few who know about the Janus codex," began the cardinal. "I am also aware that, despite your claims of having it destroyed, the parchments are being secretly restored in Zaragoza. You see, Dante, the order is not the only one with spies throughout the Vatican. I can only surmise that your plan is to have it as another weapon to keep me under your control.

"We both know the disastrous impact it would have on the Church and all Christian faiths if it was proven that Christ survived his time on the cross. Not only that but he had children and a life lived with Mary Magdalene. The Church would be ruined, for it would take away one of the basic tenets of our faith.

"And it would happen while I was pope. You would leave me to preside over a fallen empire. But as you have already explained, the order would experience no ill effects if you were to ruin one of the world's foremost institutions and my life along with it."

It took a great deal to surprise the prelate, but Ambrosia had succeeded. Although Dante showed no outward sign of the shock he was feeling, his mind was racing. How had the cardinal found out about the restoration? Who was the spy and how had Ambrosia discovered him? He needed to formulate a response. The cardinal saved him the immediate trouble by continuing.

"So let us discuss Cardinal Reinhart," said Ambrosia. "Either he becomes my Secretary of State, or I will tell him about the work being undertaken on the parchments at Zaragoza.

"I realize that, apart from the team at Zaragoza, only our departed pope, his assistant, you, and I know about these parchments. We have all taken a vow of silence before God. But I am going to break that commitment. It may come as a surprise, but you are not the only one who can use our faith as a convenience.

"And just as important, I will have Reinhart demand that the codex be returned to one of the museums within the Vatican. There is nothing you can do to stop this from happening. Under the current agreement, the Vatican is responsible for all the artifacts in Zaragoza. Not only will it provide me with immense pleasure at having handed you a defeat, it will also take away one important element in your bid to control my Papacy."

"That's quite the supposition you've made," responded Dante. "What makes you think I'm having the parchments restored?"

"I assure you it's not speculation. And Reinhart will verify that I'm right. After that, it's just a short matter of time before we move them to the Vatican and out of your control.

"I am therefore proposing an understanding. Reinhart becomes my Secretary of State, and you get to keep the codex, along with all the power it holds over me. If you do not agree, I will have the parchments removed from Zaragoza and shipped to the Vatican. They are too dangerous in your hands."

Dante leaned back in his chair. He had not built a global empire without the ability to adapt quickly when required by the

The Hope of Janus

blustery winds of change. Completely immersed in the order's relationship with the Vatican, the prelate believed he knew something that had been overlooked by Ambrosia. This was the decree signed in 1920 by Pope Benedict XV that declared all artifacts and documents at the chateau could only be removed with the prelate's permission.

Dante wasn't sure what was physically and technically involved, but he was determined to have the parchments removed from Zaragoza and transferred to the chateau before Reinhart could take them to the Vatican. He would not tell the cardinal of his plan. It was best that Ambrosia believe time was on his side in moving the codex. In the meantime, however, Dante had the cardinal to deal with.

"You seem to have forgotten something," the prelate said quietly. "I hold the tape of your infidelity in Vienna. I can make it public at any time. The codex is merely added insurance."

"You wouldn't dare release the tape over something as inconsequential as having the codex taken to the Vatican."

"I wouldn't," said Dante, confident in his plan to have the parchments removed to the chateau. "But if you make a move to install Reinhart it will be the last thing you do as a newly crowned pope."

The words were spoken with a steely purpose that Dante saw had the desired impact on Ambrosia. The cardinal's hand was shaking as he picked up his coffee cup and took a deep drink. His eyes were wide, and red splotches again dotted his face. He no longer displayed the confidence shown earlier.

"So you are allowing me no say in this decision." The frustration was evident in every word. Ambrosia was a proud man who was about to assume the Church's most powerful position. Yet he was being forced to stand by while a major coup with international implications was carried out during his Papacy.

"Your view is always valuable and will be requested in the future," Dante said. "But for now, let's proceed with the plan as it has been designed."

Ambrosia sighed, shifted forward, and placed the cup on its saucer. "Giambese is a good man, and I believe we can work well together." Ambrosia gave Dante a thin smile. "It is important, though, that you understand I will share no secrets with him. We will have a business relationship, and that is all. You will learn nothing about my thoughts.

"But I will confide in Reinhart and others like him who don't belong to you. They will be the ones I'll trust. And where it can be done, I will have my people work to ensure that there is prolonged resistance to the moves you want to make. You may have a plan, but I will make it difficult to implement.

"And that will begin the moment I return to Rome and tell Reinhart of the parchments."

The final words were uttered with a cutting edge of defiance, which Dante pointedly ignored.

Nothing had fundamentally changed in Dante's power over the cardinal. Yet the prelate was disappointed in Ambrosia's clumsy attempted insurrection. It was not because the cardinal had tried to seize some form of power but because the move had obviously been badly planned and poorly executed.

Given all the years of knowing each other, Dante was surprised that Ambrosia failed to realize he was no match for the prelate's intelligence, business acumen, and vision. Still, a close watch would have to be kept over Ambrosia. Dante accepted that his choice for pope was a man who obviously failed to fully appreciate the situation's reality. Experience told the prelate there would other attempts to loosen the limitations.

Of immediate concern, however, were Reinhart and the codex. The parchments had to stay under his control. Equally important was determining how Ambrosia had discovered the restoration project. There was obviously a leak at Zaragoza. It had to be quickly located and immediately sealed.

Dante glanced at his watch and saw with some relief that, if Ambrosia was to catch his flight, it was time to bring the session to a close. The prelate had achieved what he wanted, and there was no point in further discussions.

"I believe we've accomplished much today," said Dante. "We know exactly what is going to happen in the conclave. And the Church will be on a firm footing with the agreements we have reached. The future looks bright, and I know you will be a strong pope."

"I'm glad you have so much faith in my abilities," said Ambrosia, the cynicism evident with every word.

While the cardinal was speaking, Dante had pressed a button located on the underside of his chair's right arm. This was the signal for Juan to have Ambrosia's car brought around to the front.

Moments later, the assistant walked into the office carrying Ambrosia's suit jacket.

"And so our meeting comes to a close," said Ambrosia, standing up and stretching to his full, imposing height. "Similar to all my times with you, it has been interesting but not enjoyable. As I said earlier, once I claim the papacy, things will be different between us. You can't control everything, and I'll show you exactly what that means when the codex is at the Vatican. It will only be the beginning."

Dante was once again unimpressed with the cardinal's overemotional words. For the prelate, this was a business deal, and he failed to understand how someone who was going to become pope could be so unappreciative of the work done by the order.

After Juan had helped the cardinal into his jacket, Ambrosia beckoned for the assistant to hand him the briefcase. Dante noted that the cardinal had not once glanced at it during their talk and wondered if it was carried merely to enhance Ambrosia's illusion of being a businessman.

Juan positioned himself by the door, waiting to accompany Ambrosia to the car. As the cardinal was walking past Dante, the prelate reached out to shake his hand. Ambrosia made a point of ignoring the gesture and, without a word to Dante, told the assistant he was ready to leave.

Several minutes later, Dante stood by the window and watched as the limousine made its way down the driveway toward the property's gates. He was no longer thinking about his meeting with Ambrosia. That was in the past. Rather his focus had turned to unearthing the leak in his organization. While most people in Dante's position would have been furious at the security lapse, the prelate viewed it impassively. It was a problem to be solved, and he would approach it the way he did every issue—with ruthless efficiency.

Leaving the window, Dante walked several steps and took the seat behind his desk. He pushed the intercom button. When Juan answered, the prelate indicated he didn't want to be disturbed for the next two hours. Dante pulled the keyboard toward him and, within several seconds, was immersed in reviewing all facets of the Zaragoza operation.

The prelate failed to acknowledge Juan's presence when he came in to take away the used cups and coffee urn.

Chapter Twelve

✥

Dante sat back in his chair and stared at the computer screen. He had just completed a thorough combing of the Zaragoza files. What no one at the museum knew, including its director, Luigi Monte, was that every aspect of their internal and external communications were monitored by the order. The prelate had pored over computer data, personnel records, and telephone traffic of everyone at the facility and initially could find no link to the Vatican.

But the knowledge that there was a traitor within the order's ranks meant Dante would not stop until he discovered who had told Ambrosia about restoring the parchments. He was feeling neither frustrated nor vindictive. It was a problem that needed to be solved, and Dante's lack of emotional investment stood him well. He approached the task of uncovering the traitor in the cold, analytical way he brought to every situation, whether it was a suspected computer hack, a million-dollar accounting error, or plotting the assassination of a troublesome business competitor.

Having been unsuccessful at finding the spy, he assessed the situation and decided it was time to enlist technical support. Juan answered moments after Dante had pushed the intercom button. The prelate told his assistant that he wanted to see Anna, the order's head of technology for the past thirty years.

Minutes later, there was a light tap on Dante's office door, followed by Anna's entrance.

The number of people Dante trusted could be counted on the fingers of one hand. Anna was among the sacred group. Her unquestioned loyalty, forged over years of working with the prelate, was deeply treasured by Dante. Tall and slim, Anna had pitch-black hair worn straight, which caressed her shoulders when she walked. Deep-set, dusky eyes were in stark contrast to her abnormally pale skin that served to highlight prominent cheekbones and full, red lips. Raised and schooled at the chateau, the order was the only way of life Anna had ever known. She shared living quarters with seven other women in a house on the property and seldom ventured off the grounds.

When Dante had initially called for the creation of a technology department in the late 1970s, Anna had been the first participant. As a forward-thinking and visionary technician, she had impressed the prelate with her ability to instinctively understand, implement, and capitalize on the many advantages offered by technology. She had immersed herself in all phases of the discipline. Under her guidance, the division had grown to become one of the most sophisticated in the world and was integral to the order's operations. With a staff of more than a thousand, it functioned on a 24-7 basis.

As she took a seat in front of his desk, Dante began without preamble, "Someone at Zaragoza has betrayed us. The person has to be found before any more damage can be created."

Dante proceeded to give Anna all the background information, including his unsuccessful attempt at discovering where the leak had occurred. Anna was wise enough and fully familiar with the prelate's operating methods that she knew this was a task only she was expected to handle. All data would be kept on a memory stick, with nothing being transferred to the order's main hard drive. It was also a mission to be initiated the moment she returned to her office. There would be little sleep until the answer was found. All of her other projects were to be put on hold.

Involving Anna did not mean Dante had decided to withdraw from the search. They agreed he would run a parallel operation and the two would share information through the night, or for however long it took to find the traitor.

As Dante ended his briefing, Anna quickly rose from her chair. "I'll report back the moment I have something," she said, walking toward the door.

Within seconds of the technology chief's departure, Dante was back on the computer.

Close to an hour after Anna had left, Dante glanced up from the screen and saw on his ornate desk clock that it was time for dinner. He wasn't hungry—the chase through computer files was satiating him—but the prelate was a man of precision. He hit the intercom button, and the ever-faithful Juan answered.

Dante ordered a light meal of poached salmon with a side salad and mineral water. His mind was still laser focused, and in the twenty-five minutes before Juan laid out the meal in the prelate's dining room, Dante came to the conclusion that the answer lay in determining what Ambrosia could offer someone in return for the information on the parchments. He relayed the thought to Anna, then got up from behind his desk and walked into the dining room, where Juan was already pouring the mineral water into a glass.

*****

The meal was over, Juan had cleared the dishes, and Dante was at his desk when Anna called.

"I think I've begun to connect the dots," the technology director said. "The technicians in Zaragoza are not part of the Vatican Museums' personnel corps. They are locked into their jobs without any hope of advancement. For most of them, that's quite satisfactory. They love the work and are well paid by the order. But suppose one of them had ambitions that go beyond Zaragoza. Ambrosia, through Reinhart, can offer someone a top position within the Vatican Museums that would carry great prestige and far more money. It could be a tremendous enticement."

"But how would Ambrosia find such a person?" asked Dante. "Outside museums have sometimes tried to hire our people, and they've always reported it to Monte. No one can offer what we provide our technicians in terms of money and benefits."

"You're assuming Ambrosia did the approaching," countered Anna. "What if the contact was initiated by one of our people?"

Dante didn't waste time on being surprised. His time in the corporate world had taught him that power and money were prime motivators. "There are only two people who have the experience and the technical knowledge to initiate that sort of conversation with Ambrosia," reasoned Dante. "They are Monte and his lead technician Alberto Salazar. I'll drill down deep on Monte; you do the same with Salazar."

Cutting the connection, the prelate returned to his computer. For the next five hours, Dante again pursued every aspect of Monte's world. He used the order's technical resources to hack into Monte's computer files, pulled readouts of his phone calls, went over his corporate correspondence, and checked through his banking history. There was nothing that tied him to Ambrosia. All of his dealings outside the order, as they should be, were with Reinhart. The result pointed toward Salazar being the traitor. Dante wondered if Anna was reaching the same conclusion.

Lifting his eyes from the keyboard, Dante looked through his window and saw the sun rising in a fiery ball of majestic red, yellow, and orange flames spanning the horizon. Sadly, the beauty stirred nothing within the prelate.

His intercom buzzed. It was Anna. He opened the line, and she asked to see him. Dante told her about his result with Monte, and she replied, "I have our answer, but you should see the facts and the trail."

After telling Anna to come through, Dante tapped the intercom for his assistant. When Juan answered, the prelate requested two cups of coffee and a basket of croissants. Dante never thought to wonder why his assistant was available at such an early hour. Juan had spent the night in his office knowing a call would come. His life revolved around the prelate—something Dante assumed but was unable to appreciate.

Several minutes later, the door opened, and Anna, carrying a laptop, entered, followed by Juan. Dante had moved to his usual Queen Anne chair by the fireplace. The technology director sat in the chair opposite the prelate. On the table separating the two, Juan put down a silver tray. It contained two cups of black coffee, along with a basket of croissants, a pair of small plates, and napkins. He quietly closed the door as he left.

Anna picked up a mug and took several long swallows. Her eyes were hooded and looked weary, but there was a sense of accomplishment in her demeanor that Dante fully understood. She had been successful, and Dante didn't mind the brief wait.

Anna put her cup on the tray. "The person we've been looking for is Salazar," she said in the direct manner the prelate valued. "His contact is Cardinal Ambrosia. They must have suspected their communications were being monitored. The calls never mentioned the codex, and if I didn't know what we were looking for, the references would have been easy to miss.

"Someone from the Vatican's tech department must have been working with Ambrosia because the e-mails were encrypted. It was a rudimentary mask, and once I narrowed down what we were looking for, it was fairly simple to break."

The technology chief opened the laptop, plugged in a memory stick, and walked Dante through the facts she had uncovered.

"Monte had sent out an in-house e-mail telling everybody that the only outside person the project was to be discussed with was you," she began. "He emphasized the project's secrecy and indicated that no one at the Vatican knew about the codex's repair. The restoration team has worked on some parchments where this is standard operating procedure. But when Salazar saw the codex's contents, he realized this was an opportunity to trade his knowledge for a major position in the Vatican Museums."

As Anna detailed the evidence from e-mails and telephone logs between Salazar and Ambrosia, Dante listened and watched the screen impassively. It was all there. From the first e-mail where Salazar indicated he had information that would greatly interest the cardinal to the phone discussions about what the information would be worth to the Vatican. And finally, there was Ambrosia's offer of a museum directorship in return for photographic proof that this was the Janus codex undergoing restoration.

It was obvious Salazar had no knowledge of the arrangement between Dante and Ambrosia but was, instead, trading on how the parchments would impact Christianity if ever revealed.

When Anna pulled up several photos of the parchments with Salazar's notation that the section indicated how Jesus had survived the cross, Dante leaned forward and saw for himself that his technician had traded the order's secrecy for an influential position in Rome.

Dante picked up his cup and took several sips. Next, he took a croissant and thoughtfully chewed until it was finished. Although he hadn't found any evidence to the contrary, Dante wanted to know if Anna had discovered anything that would also implicate Monte.

"From what I can determine," she replied, "the only person Ambrosia has communicated with about the parchments is Salazar. There's no connection between Monte and the cardinal."

"Have they set a date for when Salazar would leave?"

"There's nothing firm. Everything will take place several weeks after the conclave for the new pope."

"Is there anything else?" asked Dante.

Anna shook her head, pulled the memory stick from the computer's USB port, and handed it to Dante. He got up and walked behind his desk, while Anna made her way to the door with the laptop under her arm.

Shortly afterward, Juan entered the office, cleared the dishes, and left the prelate in quiet contemplation.

Dante plugged the memory stick into his computer. He carefully scrolled through everything as he thought about what to do with Salazar.

The lead technician was a world-recognized restoration expert. He was also one of the few who had a fundamental grasp of the Aramaic language. His loss would set the project back by at least a year. Dante decided the practical course was to keep Salazar working on the parchments. He needed the technician's expertise while he had Monte review the files of the Zaragoza personnel for someone who could take over for Salazar.

There was no doubt in his mind that Ambrosia would tell Reinhart about the parchments. There would then be a demand for the codex to be shipped to the Vatican. The next step was to prevent that occurring by having the Word of Janus moved to the chateau.

In the meantime, there was Salazar. It mattered little to Dante if Ambrosia carried through on his commitment to the technician and gave him a prestigious position at the Vatican Museums. Whether Salazar stayed or left, Dante had already sentenced the man. Within six months, he would be dead from an assassin's bullet. His death would also serve as a graphic message to Ambrosia and Reinhart that no one betrayed the order.

Chapter Thirteen

The Prophet stopped by while Sean and Diane were eating a late dinner. Although invited to stay for coffee, Elijah declined. He suggested only that Sean drop by sometime the next day. When asked what he wanted to talk about, the Prophet merely said it was related to Sean's connection with the Spirit.

"That seems to be the focus for most of our recent conversations," noted Sean as he and Diane walked with Elijah toward the front door. "I still haven't made up my mind about undertaking its mission. And until that happens, what more is there to consider?"

"This is important," responded Elijah. "It might shed a new light on your relationship with the Spirit. Just come over to the house. I'll explain everything."

Intrigued by Elijah's uncharacteristically mysterious request, Sean agreed to be at the Prophet's home shortly after dawn broke.

"I'll see you then," said the Prophet, before saying good night and striding out to the Ring Road

The couple watched Elijah go, and he was soon lost from sight in the fading light. Walking down the hallway to the kitchen, Sean and Diane returned to their meal of roast lamb and scalloped potatoes. There was little use in discussing what Elijah wanted to see Sean about, so the couple quickly dropped the subject. Only when they were in bed and Diane was asleep did Sean's mind return to the Prophet's invitation.

I hope he doesn't want to again discuss how close I am to deciding about working with the Spirit, thought Sean. Nothing was going to happen until he met with it. And that would be at a time of his choosing.

This wasn't new ground. Sean's position had framed his most recent discussions with the Prophet. If that was what Elijah wanted to talk about, Sean wouldn't hesitate to cut the conversation short. Not even the Prophet was going to force him into making a decision until he was ready. Feeling confident about his continuing resolve, Sean let the wispy strands of sleep slowly wrap themselves around his mind. His thoughts gradually floated free and he was soon in the land of the dreamless.

*****

A cold front sweeping in from the Norwegian Sea had broken the heat wave that had blanketed Janus for the past week. Walking toward Elijah's house, Sean noticed the dawn's air was pleasantly warm, without being stifling.

Janus was a familiar world that had become comfortable for Sean. He felt at home working with Diane on her farm. Sean knew he could reject the Spirit's request and spend the rest of his life on the island. But there was a part of him that recognized he wanted more from life than being isolated on Janus. From pollution to unchecked violence and from inequality to rampant poverty, the world was gradually sinking into a morass from which it might never escape unless firm action was taken.

People—that vast multitude of global citizens—had to decide; if they wanted a future with hope, a commitment to peace had to be made. That's what the Spirit was offering him. He was being given the chance to make a difference—to make his world a better and more humane globe. And now that Elijah had committed to being involved, the aspiration seemed more feasible.

Journeying back to the thoughts he'd had during the night, Sean accepted that the time for making a decision was coming close. It was not just his life that was being affected. Ever since they had learned from the Word of Janus that Diane would play an equal role in the Spirit's campaign for peace, Sean's decision was no longer his own. And now that he and Diane were engaged, resolving their future had taken on a greater urgency.

But there still remained the issue of the Spirit's participation. In their last meeting, Sean had felt the Spirit was at least willing to consider some form of intervention. However, what that meant was still an unanswered question. It had never indicated an inclination to participate directly in resolving earth's growing list of issues. And without that, Sean wondered if any campaign for peace was doomed to failure.

His plan had always been to work with the Spirit but not to lead a peace initiative. And the more Sean thought about his preference, the greater his determination became. When he next met with the Spirit, Sean would put forth two proposals. The first was that, if he was to be involved, the Spirit must commit to some form of participation. What that contribution would entail could be negotiated. And second, if the Spirit chose not to participate, Sean would be free to walk away.

Sean could not help but realize the enormity of his plan. He was entering a discussion with the Spirit not as a subservient man before God, but with a hard and fast negotiating position.

It was incongruous, yet it was also his reality. The birthmark on his thigh meant he was a direct descendent of Jesus. Just as important, he was a human with free will. And since those two facts were indisputable, Sean fully believed he had the right to discuss and plan his journey through life. Whether it meant working with the Spirit or walking away from its plan and living a quiet life on Janus, the ultimate decision would be made in discussions with Diane. The Spirit represented part of the equation, but it would not determine the answer.

From what seemed like a long distance away, Sean heard his name being called. He slowly, and with some difficulty, brought his mind back to the present. It was then he realized with a measure of embarrassment that it was Elijah's voice. Lost in his thoughts, he had walked several yards past the Prophet's front gate.

Doubling back, he strode into the Prophet's front garden and up the steps to the gallery. With a sheepish grin, he said, "I would've walked to the other end of the island if you hadn't called me."

"What were you thinking about?" wondered Elijah, an inquisitive crease furrowing his brow.

Sean told him what he'd decided, concluding with, "Either I partner with the Spirit or I don't, but it's time for my indecision to end. I owe it to you and to Diane."

Elijah slowly nodded his head. "You're right. I believe, for your peace of mind, knowing sooner rather than later whether you and the Spirit will work together is a good thing. But this is something to be decided between you and Diane. I can only offer my guidance. You owe me nothing except your friendship, which you have freely given."

Sean smiled and looked at the Prophet with affection. "And what advice would you give me? Is that why you wanted to see me this morning?"

Elijah, who had gotten up from his chair with Sean's arrival, proposed coffee for both of them before continuing with their talk. As Sean took a seat, the Prophet disappeared inside. He returned a few minutes later with a polished metal tray containing two steaming mugs of black java and a small, wooden box with Hebrew writing on the top. Handing a cup to Sean, who immediately took a long drink, the Prophet sat, leaving one of the large wooden chairs between them. Taking his mug, he placed the tray, along with the box, on the empty chair.

Sean was curious but said nothing. He knew from experience that Elijah would divulge in his own time what the box contained and the reason for bringing it out. He was idly wondering what it had to do with the Prophet inviting him over this morning, when his thoughts were interrupted by a question from Elijah.

"Will you definitely abandon the Spirit's plan if it refuses to be directly involved?"

"Without a doubt," responded Sean, taking a sip of coffee.

"I have something that I hope will make you reconsider," voiced Elijah. "Even if the Spirit is not directly involved, working with it would provide you with the ability to do so much good for the world. No one has ever been provided this opportunity."

For the first time since he'd known the Prophet, Sean experienced a slight feeling of frustration. "It's my life," Sean noted, not attempting to hide his annoyance. "And I'm going to live it the best way I can for Diane and me."

If Elijah noticed Sean's irritation he gave no indication. Instead, he took a drink of coffee, then leaned over and picked up the wooden box. Smiling, he said, "I've been waiting for the right moment to give this to you."

With that, the Prophet reached out and handed the small, highly polished, oblong case with rounded corners to Sean.

Taking it from Elijah, the first question Sean asked was, "What does the Hebrew writing mean?"

"It says, 'For the one who gives us hope.'"

Sean was puzzled. "Does this have something to do with the Spirit and me?"

"I wouldn't be giving it to you at this time if it didn't," was the response. Elijah sat back and drank some more coffee.

Holding the box in his left hand, Sean used his right forefinger to trace the writing that had been burned into the wood. Even though he didn't understand Hebrew, Sean experienced a feeling of intimacy with the words. It was as though they were meant for him alone, which didn't seem possible. But this was Janus, he reminded himself. And from what he'd experienced with the Spirit, the improbable didn't always apply.

There was a silver clasp on the front of the box. Sean carefully undid the hook and gently opened the lid. Revealed inside was a small, leather pouch with a drawstring. Removing the satchel, Sean placed the box on the chair's armrest. As he cradled the pouch in his right hand, a wave of familiarity swept over him. His senses were pulsating; the world had narrowed to these few minutes. The smell of cured leather was intense.

Sean pulled at the drawstring, opening the satchel. Turning the pouch over, he felt something smooth and round drop onto his left palm. It was a wide-band silver ring with Hebrew engraving on the inside. Sean held it up to take a better look.

"Is this for me?" whispered Sean.

"Yes," responded Elijah in an equally subdued voice. "It is known as the *hope of Janus* and was crafted by my great-grandfather on instructions from the Spirit."

"And the words?"

"Translating them into today's English, they read, 'Hope is the first step toward peace.'"

Elijah suggested that Sean try the ring on.

"I can't until I know how this impacts my relationship with the Spirit. It's obviously important because the Spirit was involved in its creation. But if this is meant to signify that I'm ready to lead a movement for peace, then I'll ask you to keep it until my decision is made."

A look of disappointment flashed across Elijah's face. It was fleeting, but Sean caught the revealing signs of a creased brow and hooded eyes. Instead of replying, the Prophet suggested he refill their coffee mugs.

Sean waited until Elijah was inside before examining the *hope of Janus*. It was a beautiful piece of jewelry. Sean held it up and admired the workmanship. The exterior was knurled and burnished in such a way that, when the sun's rays struck it, the ring glistened as though covered in diamonds. But there was something else. Sean was filled with the strange sensation that the ring was meant for him. It had nothing to do with the band's beauty. Rather, it was a feeling of physical well-being that began in his belly and spread throughout his chest.

Sean slipped the *hope of Janus* on his right-hand ring finger. It was more an act of curiosity than any thought of working with the Spirit. The fit was perfect, and the ring rested around his finger as though it had been there for years. Momentarily dumbfounded at the flawless sizing, Sean didn't notice Elijah's return until the Prophet placed the tray with the two filled cups on the armrest of the chair between them. Taking his mug, Elijah sat down and took two deep swallows of the coffee.

Silence existed between the men for almost a minute before Sean, feeling somewhat awkward, stated "I can't explain what happened, but despite the fact I said I wouldn't try the ring on something came over me and I felt comfortably compelled to put it on my finger. What's even more strange and undeniable is that the ring feels as though it was made for me."

"It was," responded Elijah.

"That's not possible," said Sean, as he slipped the ring from his finger. "It was crafted by your great-grandfather. Obviously, he couldn't have predicted my arrival on Janus."

"Of course he didn't," said the Prophet. "But don't forget the Spirit was involved, and none of us can really understand what it knows about the future."

Sean picked up his mug and took a couple of sips. The coffee was hot and tasted smooth. He had never contemplated what role, if any, the Spirit played in deciding the future. Every human had free will. Therefore, it stood to reason that, with the amount of decisions made daily over every region of earth, the future was unpredictable.

And yet, the ring was a perfect size. At the same time, he had also been born with the mark of Janus. In that moment, Sean had a revelation. The Spirit didn't determine the future. His birthmark was the legacy linking him to the ring. That it fit was convenient but immaterial. What truly mattered was that it had been crafted for the one who bore the mark of Janus and would be called upon by the Spirit to lead the world toward peace.

The Hope of Janus

The Spirit had never interfered with humanity's journey through time. It was only doing so now because it believed earth was at a crucial point. And Sean knew it was just because of circumstance that he'd been chosen. The Spirit did not control the future. If it did, earth would not be at such a desperate juncture.

Sean heard Elijah's voice calling him. "What are you thinking?" wondered the Prophet. "You seemed to have disappeared into a world of your own."

After telling Elijah what he'd been contemplating, Sean took another sip of coffee. The Prophet stared over the gallery railing before turning back to face Sean. He quietly said, "I believe that, even for the Spirit, the future is unknown territory. The *hope of Janus* is meant to symbolize the Spirit's desire for peace. But the fact it is calling upon you to lead the movement shows me that the ultimate decision to live in harmony will be made by every human on this planet."

Putting his mug on the armrest, Sean asked, "What's the ring's history? And how did it become known as the *hope of Janus*?"

"The answers to both questions are intertwined," began the Prophet.

Elijah explained the story passed through the years was that his great-grandfather, the island's silversmith, one day returned from visiting the Spirit with a mission to craft a ring that would be worn by the man who bore the mark of Janus and was prepared to take the island's message of understanding and peace to the world.

"It was the Spirit that called it the *hope of Janus*," continued the Prophet. "It's meant to signify the belief that the way we live on Janus can serve as a beacon of hope for a world that has truly reached a crisis stage. We may only be an island in the

North Sea, but we are also an example of how a diverse group of people can live together in harmony.

"It's more than a ring," emphasized Elijah as he leaned forward in his chair. "The band represents the ideal of what hope can mean to the world and to every person. It is cultures, societies, and nations reaching across real and imagined borders and working together for peace through a commitment to understanding that, while we may have different beliefs and customs, we are all part of the global family. Every individual is the face of our collective humanity.

"No one needs to be told the world is facing unprecedented problems. What's needed is someone who can bring hope that, through forgiveness, understanding, tolerance, and equality, we can arrive at a destination called peace."

"Do the islanders know that's what the ring means?" asked Sean.

"Everyone is aware of its significance," responded the Prophet. "It is shown to every islander as part of the ceremony that surrounds their first meeting with the Sprit. They learn the story and that we are waiting for the one who will wear the ring."

"And you believe I'm that person," said Sean.

"I do," replied Elijah. "You've been asked by the Spirit to take the Janus message to the world. The ring rightfully belongs to you."

Sean shifted in his chair. The fingers of his right hand drummed a steady tattoo on its flat, wooden arm. "The *hope of Janus* is just a dream," he finally said. "Despite the harsh realities of death and misery that war brings, the world continues to see open conflict as the ultimate answer for resolving its differences. And the further we advance technologically, the greater our descent into warring tribal communities."

The Hope of Janus

"But that's exactly the point," challenged Elijah. "We seem to have forgotten that collective hope is driven by every individual dreaming for a safe and secure life. What I'm talking about is born in the heart but lives in the soul. It is striving to achieve what is best in oneself. Most people want the same thing, and that's a present filled with plans for a future they believe is attainable. By providing equality in education, meaningful employment, and adequate housing the possibility of a better tomorrow can become a reality.

"And because of that, the *hope of Janus* represents more than nations committing to living together in peace," noted Elijah. "It is also the ability of individuals from every global community to build a society whose strength lies in treating each other with respect, understanding, and compassion.

"Unfortunately, we live in a world where too many societies define themselves by their differences with other cultures, rather than celebrating and cherishing our common humanity. We somehow have to move into a reality where diversity is seen as a global strength not a weakness."

"But hope is such a nebulous quality," offered Sean. "One can live in hope without anything being achieved. There has to be more to accomplishing something of value than having faith it will happen."

"I agree, to a point," responded Elijah. "Hope is one of the most intrinsic of all our human qualities. It sets us apart from every other creature in that we can envision what is ahead in our lives. It has fueled humanity's progress through the centuries. Hope is what generates medical and technological advances. It makes us chase the possibility of life on other planets.

"Hope is using past experiences, along with present realities to forge a life you control. And if hope is to be a meaningful part of our lives, it must contain goals that can be achieved.

"Wishful thinking or dreaming for a better life should never be confused with hope. I believe hope is a tangible expression of how a person wants to live their life. It is looking at both the long- and short-term future and plotting a course that can bring us to what we want to accomplish. It requires a commitment and a plan that is flexible enough to withstand day-to-day realities but possesses a boldness that allows for an attainable goal to always be in sight.

"Hope ought to be a practical expression of our wants and desires. And so long as we don't hinder or hurt others, all of us should have the right to pursue a future where hope can become reality. At the same time, we must view hope in pragmatic terms, or we may lose sight of the present. Our lives become a wish for the future, rather than intensely living the day we have been given."

"What about people who work for a better world?" offered Sean. "Based on your criteria, it cannot be defined as hope. So what would you call it?"

"It is hope," responded Elijah, with emphasis. "Very few people can directly influence global events, but if everyone truly strives for a better world, there are a myriad of things that can be done. Trees can be planted, garbage recycled, and the less fortunate can be assisted through volunteering; these are all individual acts among many that can make our world a more livable place."

"But what is achieved?" asked Sean. "If the world continues down its destructive path, then that form of faith can lead to disillusionment."

"That's where I believe hope has to be viewed in a light that is manageable," answered the Prophet. "What is wrong in taking satisfaction by saying you plan to plant a hundred trees and then achieving that goal."

"On Janus," noted Sean, "everyone has faith in the Spirit. Is that what's needed out in the world? Must there be some form of religious belief that grounds everybody to continually treat their neighbors with respect and understanding?"

"Not at all," responded Elijah. "For one thing, as you know, we have no religion on Janus. And we believe religion is not a prerequisite for having faith. Without religion, we have built a peaceful and understanding society. Faith can just as easily be defined as having a strong belief in being the person you want to be. At the same time, faith is about believing in the inherent goodness of your fellow human beings. It is each of us striving for a better world. And it is that world in which our hopes can be realized."

"And how does one deal with disappointment?" wondered Sean.

"There are frustrations and defeats in life," acknowledged the Prophet. "But isn't that the essence of hope? One has to move beyond the hurt and the sadness and let the belief in something better make this day and the ones to come be a place where you want to live."

"But there are events that shape our lives and that can take away our dreams," offered Sean. "The loss of a child or a spouse can be devastating."

"I am not disagreeing with you," responded Elijah. "Instead, my belief is that, since we are all in possession of free will, we have a choice to journey through today and plan for the future with hope and courage or let the weight of past and present tragedies, failures, and disappointments crush us.

"Hope is an intensely personal emotion. How people choose to look at the world and the future is for them alone to decide. The hope of Janus, as symbolized by your ring, is the dream of a better world, through our island's principles of forgiveness, understanding, tolerance, equality and peace. It is people realizing that everyone's passage through life should be guided by the hope of a life worth living.

"Equally important, the ring embodies the Spirit's belief for the world's future."

"And that's where I come in," stated Sean. "If I do decide to wear the *hope of Janus*, that's a physical demonstration of my commitment to the Spirit's cause."

"That's right. Along with your birthmark, it will be a tangible link to the Spirit."

"And what happens if I elect not to participate?"

Once again, a cloud of concern furrowed Elijah's brow, and his lips compressed into a thin, red line that looked to Sean like an uneven scar across his face. But it was only fleeting, and moments later the Prophet was saying, "Why don't we wait until you visit with the Spirit to determine whether you'll participate? You will be negotiating with it, and your involvement could take many forms. What's important is that you and the Spirit come to an agreement, whatever that may be."

"To be honest, I'm not sure what to expect," noted Sean. "In the meantime, you've given me a lot to think about."

"That's why I wanted to meet before you visited the cave. What do you want to do with the ring?"

Sean realized with surprise that he'd been holding it during their conversation. The box still rested on the arm of his chair. He picked it up and placed the ring inside the leather pouch before securing them in the case by closing the lid and fastening the clasp.

"I'll keep it," said Sean. "But before wearing the ring, I'll talk with Diane. My future is still unclear, and she'll play an important role in how it unfolds. After Diane and I decide the direction we want to take, I'll visit with the Spirit. Hopefully we can arrive at an understanding that aligns with what I want to do. But, as we both know, that's still undecided. And if I'm not going to participate in the Spirit's plan, I'll return the ring. You may have to acknowledge that I was never predestined to embody all that is meant by wearing the *hope of Janus.*"

Sean knew Elijah would accept his proposal. It was a compromise in which both their positions were honored. And that was the essence of Janus.

"That's a fair arrangement," said the Prophet, confirming Sean's thought. "I believe you and the Spirit will come to an understanding. There is plenty of room for negotiating an agreement you both can be comfortable with."

"That remains to be seen," responded Sean. "In the meantime I should be getting home. There's work to do on the farm, and Diane will have already started. One of the stalls for the sheep requires repairing and it needs to be done today."

Sean stood and put his mug on the tray. Elijah followed suit.

"I'll let you know when I'm going to visit the Spirit," said Sean. "It will be sometime over the next month."

Elijah nodded his head and noted, "That will be one of the more interesting sessions in our island's history."

Sean descended the steps and made his way along the path to the Road, where he turned and headed toward Diane's house. The box felt light in his hand, but the expectations that were an integral part of the band's history and its future weighed heavily on his mind. There was so much about the ring that related to a world far beyond the Janus shores. Was he really meant to work with the Spirit?

His birthmark, the prophecy contained in Daniel's codex, and now the *hope of Janus* all seemed to be pointing him in that direction. At Sean's request, he and Diane had purposely refrained from discussing his next move with the Spirit. But the time was fast approaching when a decision needed to be made.

He would show the ring to Diane, and they'd have the conversation he'd been avoiding. Their relationship had always been a partnership of equals. He already knew Diane was excited about working directly with the Spirit. He was the one holding out for negotiating a role that would have them participate but not lead.

Somewhere between those positions was a compromise.

Only when he'd been walking for several minutes and was going over the conversation in his mind did Sean realize he had called Diane's place home. It was the first time he could remember thinking that way. He had always thought of it as Diane's house. It made him recognize that his job and apartment in London had faded into the background of his life. Home was Diane and Janus.

Chapter Fourteen

─────────────✣─────────────

The night sky, with all its cosmic beauty, was beginning to descend on Janus. Sean and Diane were sitting on the home's front gallery. For a few minutes they sat quietly, drinking their after-dinner coffee. The only sound breaking the silence was the rhythmic pulsation of ocean waves flowing against the island's rocky shoreline. It was deeply peaceful and, as Sean thought, an ongoing personification of the islanders' commitment to living in harmony with one another.

After arriving home following his visit with Elijah, he had shown the box to Diane. They had agreed to hold off any talk about the ring until their nightly time spent discussing the day's events. It was something they both enjoyed—a time of calm reflection and thoughtful conversation.

Sean had brought the oblong case outside and put it on the arm of his chair. After they'd reviewed the work done on the sheep pen, Diane reached over, took the wooden box, and rotated it slowly. It was obvious to Sean that she was captivated by the case's significance.

"Isn't it beautiful," she said. "These Hebrew words about the one who gives us hope are deeply meaningful to everyone. It is part of our history that only the one who has the mark of Janus and has been called by the Spirit will wear the ring. This must mean that Elijah truly believes you're the person to take our message of peace and hope throughout the world."

Sean nodded his head. "You're right. Elijah considers it my birthright. Why don't you open the box."

Diane undid the silver clasp, lifted the lid, and took out the leather pouch. Once again, the powerful scent of cured leather hung in the air. She loosened the drawstring and tilted the pouch. The silver ring dropped gently into the palm of her right hand. Holding it up so she could get a better look, the ring's pulsating radiance was evident even in the half-light cast by the rising moon and burgeoning umbrella of stars.

"This is exquisite," responded Diane, turning the band over several times. "It must have been an incredible experience for Elijah's great-grandfather. Working with the Spirit to craft something that would one day call on our island to provide an example for the world gives the ring an earthly spirituality that is almost beyond comprehension."

"I was surprised the Spirit got involved in its creation," said Sean. "In my conversations, the Spirit has said it doesn't and will not directly interfere in the affairs of humans. And yet I've been given a ring in whose formation the Spirit played an integral role. I'm having difficulty balancing these two conflicting impressions."

Diane responded with a light laugh. "You know the Spirit is a vital part of every islander's life. We can have conversations with it anytime we go to the cave. While the Spirit doesn't intrude in our lives, Elijah's family is different. It has had a special relationship with the Spirit since we landed on this island. The role of spiritual advisor has been passed through Elijah's ancestors from generation to generation. The fact Elijah's great-grandfather would be called upon to do something like this for the Spirit is entirely in keeping with our knowledge of the Prophet's family history.

"But this ring is not the only case of the Spirit's involvement in something that impacts you. Everything that's happened to you since being born with the mark of Janus and your ties to the Word of Janus has intersected here on the island. The ring is just one more example that your future lies in carrying out the Spirit's hope for earth."

Sean was quiet for several moments.

"I can't deny my ties to the Spirit," he slowly began. "And while I remain willing to work with it, my initial response hasn't changed. I will not be in the forefront of a global movement for peace."

Diane frowned. "You haven't spoken with the Spirit in several weeks. Why not wait until you meet with it before making up your mind. This isn't a business plan that can be altered to fit your specifications. We're talking about a relationship with the Spirit. What can be nobler than using your life to work for world peace?"

Sean responded that, regardless of what the Spirit said, his position was firm. "It isn't a question of not wanting to work for some form of global harmony. It's simply that, if I'm going to take on this project, I want to have some say in how I'll participate."

Smiling, Diane said, "This ring tells me the Spirit will have a lot to say about your decision."

She held up the band for emphasis, allowing it to catch the moon's light. While the reflection was muted, the Hebrew words carved on the inside were clearly visible. Pointing them out to Sean, she said, "I suppose Elijah not only translated these words but also explained what 'hope being the first step toward peace' signifies."

Sean nodded his head. "According to Elijah, the Spirit told his great-grandfather that the day would come when the world's future hinged on the need for everyone to accept the humanity in each other."

"But it's no longer a day in the future," said Diane. "The Spirit believes you hold the key to earth's destiny and the future it spoke about has become the present. The way Janus's different races and cultures live together will show the world that everyone can be part of a peaceful human family.

"We have built a society where everyone is equal and shares the same rights. The islanders are able to demonstrate that, by working together, by recognizing we are all one people, and by striving to make our society livable for every person, there can be peace. We will offer the globe hope that a world without systemic violence is possible."

Sean grinned at Diane's enthusiasm. "If every islander shares your passion and they work as one with the Spirit, it will definitely create a global force to be reckoned with."

"That's exactly what we'll be," she said, laughing.

Diane was about to hand the band back to Sean, when she stopped and said, "Wait. Why aren't you wearing the ring? It's supposed to go on the ring finger of your right hand. Doesn't it fit?"

As an answer, Sean took the band from Diane and slipped the ring on. "It fits perfectly," he said.

"And was obviously made for you," said Diane, a hint of awe in her voice. "You really are the Spirit's messenger. Doesn't that change how you feel about working with it?"

"I know you understand and appreciate how strange this is for me. Everyone associated with Janus has grown up with

The Hope of Janus

the Spirit in their lives. Until I came here, the existence or nonexistence of a Supreme Being had no bearing on my life. And now I'm confronted with the expectation that I'll work with it in bringing peace to the world.

"I've been given a ring that was carved more than a hundred years ago and fits as though a jeweler crafted it for me. While it's true this ties me even closer to the Spirit, I don't believe a global peace plan will succeed without its participation.

"At the same time, there has to be more than hope," continued Sean. "Hope is only valuable if it is bolstered with a concrete drive to achieve the goal of peace. The Spirit has to somehow take this individual yearning for an end to violence and use it to create a world where there is personal and societal peace.

"Elijah is confident he can get the Spirit directly involved. From my conversations with it, I believe that may be difficult. But I'm willing to concede that the Spirit and Elijah have a special relationship. My hope is that Elijah can get the Spirit to participate."

Diane nodded her head in agreement. "This may come as a surprise, but I believe you're the Spirit's way of becoming involved. It brought you to Janus at this time because it realizes the world's situation is critical. And by working through you, along with the islanders, the Spirit may just be preparing the way for an incredible plan that will bring global violence to an end."

The words struck Sean like a hard blow to the chest. He had never thought of himself in those terms. "You're saying the Spirit will work with me to put in place a plan that will accomplish its hopes for earth. That's completely out of the realm of anything I'd ever imagined."

"It shouldn't be," offered Diane. "All we're doing is offering a rational reason as to why you've been chosen by the Spirit."

Sean gave his eyes a brief massage with both hands. Could Diane's supposition be accurate? Was he fated to be the Spirit's chosen emissary for peace?

"But how can one person influence the world?" he asked. "Many corners of earth have become dark and dangerous places, where hope and optimism for a life well lived are snuffed out by the realities of war, ethnic cleansing, discrimination, and a host of other ills meant to disenfranchise and, in some cases destroy large groups of the world's population.

"The practical aspects of peace do not apply in these regions. These societies have been dysfunctional for generations. It is foolish to believe that, within cultures where violence is the norm, change can occur without concrete actions. Politicians and diplomats can talk in lofty terms about peace, but unless individuals are provided equal opportunities through innovative social programs, progressive economic reforms, inclusive educational institutions, and balanced justice systems, there will be no peace.

"Even in the most progressive countries, it is difficult to reinforce an appreciation for the humanity of those who surround you and to understand that, while a group of people may have different beliefs and customs, it does not make that group or the people within it your enemy.

"And that doesn't begin to look at how nations can learn to cooperate with each other. There has to be a global acceptance of tolerance, equality, and justice between all peoples both domestically and internationally.

"Do we have the will for all that to take place? Or has earth devolved to the point where peace and inclusion are merely illusions? If that's the case, my involvement with the Spirit won't matter, because we'll soon run out of time to save our planet."

"But you're missing the Spirit's point in asking you to work with it," said Diane. "You've been given an opportunity that goes far beyond anything that has ever been provided another human being. Whether or not the Spirit is directly involved doesn't matter because it will be there to guide you. And you won't be alone. You and I will share equally in this incredible mission. Can you think of anything better we can do with our lives?"

"The question is," said Sean, holding up his ring, "how does the *hope of Janus* translate into a world at peace?"

"It begins with every islander becoming a global ambassador for an end to violence," responded Diane. "Once it starts, others throughout the world will take up the cause."

"And that opens up a new question," noted Sean. "If the Spirit becomes involved through me, our next task will be getting the islanders onside. The island's isolation has allowed everyone to live in peace. Getting them to share Janus with the world will be difficult. That alone could take several years."

"Does Elijah have any suggestions about how that could be accomplished?" Diane asked.

Sean leaned back in his chair. Diane's question had sparked a thought he'd been contemplating for several weeks. The idea had slowly taken shape. He had never wanted to lead a worldwide movement for peace. But he now saw that his mission could be to persuade the islanders this was their vocation. He didn't have to be the one to go into the world promoting and advancing the ideal. There were many strong and accomplished people on Janus. Several of them could become leaders for the movement.

It would allow him to live quietly on the island with Diane. He could carry out the Spirit's mission by working with those on Janus. The idea needed more thought, and for the time being, he would share it only with Diane. Between the two of them, the concept could be molded into a plan that would be taken to Elijah and the Spirit.

"Well, does he have any ideas?" asked Diane, breaking through his thoughts. "If anyone knows what the Prophet is thinking, it would be you."

"I don't know if that's the case." Sean chuckled. "But from what I can tell, Elijah has been so focused on my working with the Spirit he hasn't given much thought to how the practical application of bringing peace to the world would be accomplished. And that includes the islanders' response to being suddenly thrust into the globe's spotlight.

"But I have an idea that could solve the problem."

Diane looked at him expectantly, and laughed. "Don't keep me in suspense."

Sean sat back and explained his plan for the islanders to become peace ambassadors. He finished by saying, "I can contribute by being a leader for the islanders as they confront a world that has billions of moving parts, but global peace isn't one of them."

"It seems as though you've given this a lot of thought," noted Diane.

"To a certain extent that's true. But it's an idea that's still forming, and I'm hoping we can work on it together."

"I'll gladly join with you," replied Diane. "We can be the engine that powers the movement to get the islanders onboard."

"We have an equal partnership," said Sean. "Are you sure this is what you want?"

"It's something I've also been thinking about," she said.

"You've never said anything," Sean noted.

"This is your issue with the Spirit," Diane responded. "Knowing you as I do, my sense was that this would be your proposal when you met with it. I just felt it was important for you to arrive at your own conclusion without any interference from me. How do you think the Spirit will react?"

"The Janus way is for opposing sides to make concessions in order to reach an agreement. I'm proposing to work with the Spirit in preparing the islanders to act as messengers of peace. That is my compromise."

"What happens if the Spirit offers a counter compromise?" asked Diane quietly. "The Spirit could say it will disengage if you don't agree to personally take the peace message global. How would you respond to that situation?"

The question caught Sean by surprise.

"That's not a compromise," he finally said. "It would be blackmail, and I don't believe the Spirit wants to go down that route. How can you succeed at advancing peace with an unwilling advocate?"

It was getting harder to see now that darkness was fully engaged in capturing the gallery. But Diane's smile still lit up the night.

"That makes a lot of sense," she said. "It will take time, but together I believe we'll get the islanders to participate."

Sean focused his eyes on Diane. She noticed and gave him what he knew from experience was a gentle look of reassurance. They would face whatever the future might bring locked arm in arm. He stood and took her hand in his, gently bringing Diane to her feet. They hugged in silent confirmation of their love for each other.

As they walked inside and down the hallway to the bedroom, Sean noticed the *hope of Janus* was still on his finger. He contemplated removing the band but then decided against it. The ring was, after all, part of his legacy.

Chapter Fifteen

It had been three days since Ambrosia's visit and the subsequent discovery of Salazar's treachery. Dante had wanted to focus on Zaragoza, but liquidity problems with one of the order's Venezuelan banks had occupied his time. Through the order's finance department, the issue had finally been settled and the prelate quickly turned his attention to the museum.

Dante didn't believe in waiting for events to overtake him. Ambrosia's anger would drive the cardinal to break his vow of silence and tell Reinhart about the codex. The question was when, not if, Reinhart would visit Zaragoza to see the parchments for himself. The prelate wanted to have an action plan ready for when that occurred.

Leaning forward in his chair, Dante placed a hand over the computer mouse, jockeyed it, and brought the screen to life. He punched several keys, and the first page of Reinhart's file appeared.

A section of the order's technology division, known as the Rome Protocol, was devoted to continually updating the dossiers on everyone in power at the Vatican. Every rumor and innuendo was tracked. Bribes for information from disaffected priests and bishops were routinely paid, and no claim was too small to be ignored. Dante dealt in secrets and blackmail. His endgame was power. He was at once feared and loathed at the

Vatican for his relentless drive to uncover facts that, if revealed, would ruin well-crafted lives. It was a fine balancing act. The prelate knew his enemies were many, but so were the secrets he held. There would never be a successful move against the order while he was alive.

For now, though, there was nothing occupying his mind other than solving the current situation. He began the slow, methodical, and predatory process of reviewing Reinhart's dossier in detail. While his knowledge of every cardinal was immense, his trip through Reinhart's life was more than familiarizing himself with what he already knew. It was an opportunity to seek even a small advantage over a man he realized was going to be a part of a problem Ambrosia was about to create.

Reinhart was a cardinal deacon, the lowest rung within the College of Cardinals. His Vatican past was dotted with several minor positions of influence until being appointed director of the Vatican Museums sixteen years ago. The low-level post was not normally held by a cardinal. However, it had been given to Reinhart as a reward for his dogged dedication to expanding the Church's role throughout the globe.

Unlike some of his fellow cardinals, he lived an austere life. His small, unadorned apartment was in a tattered, three-story walk-up on Via Germanico. He never took vacations and seldom ventured beyond Rome. The man was a paragon of celibacy and virtue, had never mismanaged funds, and possessed a sterling record as caretaker of the museums' treasures.

Reinhart's demeanor and his views were rigid. He was an old-fashioned Church conservative who believed all Catholic religious power should be concentrated at the Vatican. This had brought him into sharp conflict with the Fraternity. Reinhart had, for several years, lobbied his fellow cardinals to have Dante replaced and the order brought firmly under Rome's control. The prelate had never worried about the threat, given the incriminating files he had on many of the Vatican's senior personnel.

Dante came to the dossier's last page. The prelate released the mouse and absently drummed the fingers of his right hand on the desk. A plan had taken shape, but he needed more time to finalize the details.

The amber light on Dante's telephone console began flashing, showing that an external call had come through.

Moments later, the intercom buzzed, and Juan's soft voice floated into the room. "One of our Venezuelan lawyers is on the phone. There appears to be a problem concerning the arrangement with the government that requires clarifying."

Dante had Juan put the call through. For the next six hours, rescuing the Venezuelan situation fully occupied the prelate. It was close to midnight when Dante finally sent the last e-mail required to get the deal back on sound footing. He was about to close the computer when the intercom sounded.

"Luigi Monte needs to speak with you urgently," said Juan. "He's phoned several times already and is waiting at his office for your call."

The prelate knew Monte was calling about Reinhart and, rather than delay the conversation until morning, told Juan to get the Zaragoza facility's head and chief curator on the phone. When Dante opened the line, Monte didn't bother with any of the usual pleasantries, instead immediately launching into, "We have a problem."

"And what's that?" asked Dante, his voice calm and reasoned, confident he knew the answer.

"Late this afternoon, I received an e-mail from Cardinal Reinhart's office. He's coming for an inspection of our facilities on Friday. That's only three days from now. He specifically wants to see the parchments and how we are proceeding with their restoration. The cardinal hasn't visited us in more than four years. How could he have found out about our work?"

The prelate was direct when dealing with an issue. It was not a conscious decision but instinctual. Quickly define the problem and then focus on the next steps. "Your lead technician, Alberto Salazar, betrayed us to Ambrosia, who then told Reinhart."

There was silence from Monte. Dante could hear his rapid breathing over the phone connection.

"Are you sure?" Monte finally asked. "Alberto has been with us for several years and has always been loyal and conscientious."

"We have the evidence."

"Why would he do such a thing?"

"That's not important," responded Dante. "What matters is that he has betrayed the order."

"This is terrible news," said an obviously distraught Monte. "What are we going to do? Should I fire him?"

"You will do absolutely nothing. This is not a problem for you to handle. I'll take care of Salazar when the timing is right. For now, we need his expertise on the folios. And how much more damage can he cause? He has already let the Vatican know what we are doing."

"But how can I work with someone who's no longer trustworthy?"

"Not only will you continue working with him, you'll act as though everything is normal. Change nothing about his assignment with the codex. Salazar must never realize we're aware of his treachery. I don't want the Vatican to know we've discovered their spy."

"I can do that if it's what you believe is best," said Monte. "Actually, it's a problem I'm glad you're handling. I've always liked Salazar. He's a good worker who seemed happy here. I'm shocked he would betray us."

For Dante the problem had been discussed, and he had no intention of deliberating it further with the curator. "Salazar is not your concern," he told Monte. "Our immediate issue is handling Reinhart and his interest in the parchments."

"Is there any way you can stop him from coming?" asked the curator. "Once he sees the parchments and understands their value, he'll want to have them at the Vatican. We'll lose them forever."

There was nothing Dante could do to prevent the visit. As head of the Vatican Museums, it was not only within Reinhart's mandate to tour Zaragoza but also, and more importantly, to inspect the parchments' restoration.

After Dante explained the situation's reality, Monte asked, "What are we going to do?"

During the time working on the Venezuelan issue, Dante had fully fleshed out his plan for Reinhart. But the prelate wanted time to review it and ensure there was nothing he had overlooked. Dante told Monte to expect a call within thirty minutes.

If the curator was concerned about the late hour, he gave no indication. Instead he responded with a "thank you," and Dante could detect the relief in the man's voice.

Immediately closing the line, the prelate tapped on the console opening the intercom. Juan answered, and Dante told his assistant when to place a call to Monte. In the meantime, he wasn't to be disturbed. Signing off, Dante leaned forward in his chair, resting his forearms on the desk. He went over the plan in his mind, probing to determine if there were any weaknesses.

The basic objective was to keep the parchments from being transferred to Rome. If that happened, they would be buried in the Vatican vaults, and Dante would lose a tool vital to controlling the Vatican.

There was no doubt, based on Ambrosia's words, that Reinhart was traveling to Zaragoza with instructions to prepare the way for stripping the museum of the codex. Given Reinhart's animosity toward the order, it was an assignment the deacon would obviously enjoy. But there was more to Reinhart's mission than just following Ambrosia's demands. Dante knew from the deacon's file that his commitment to the Church was unwavering. The codex threatened his faith, and he would not offer any resistance to Ambrosia's order that it be transferred to Rome.

Dante had briefly examined the idea of having the codex and its explosive secret removed from Zaragoza before Reinhart arrived. It would detonate a volatile confrontation between Reinhart and Ambrosia on one side and Dante on the other. Although the prelate did not fear a battle, he knew there wasn't time to have the codex sent to the chateau prior to the director's visit. The logistics of having them prepared and shipped for storage in Valencia weren't practical in such a short space of time.

But it could be done within the near term.

Dante estimated it would take approximately three months before Reinhart was in a position to have the codex transported to the Vatican. With the conclave scheduled to meet for the election of a new pope, every cardinal, including Reinhart, would be busy with the preparation.

Following that, there would be the ceremonies surrounding the papal coronation and then at least four to six weeks while Ambrosia settled into his new role. Once again, the College of Cardinals would be heavily involved. Only then would Reinhart, backed by Ambrosia, be in a position to demand the codex's shipment to the Vatican.

That gave Dante approximately ninety days to slip the codex away from Zaragoza before Reinhart had a chance to move it. And once at the chateau, the codex was there to stay. The 1920 decree by Pope Benedict XV declaring that all artifacts and documents held at the chateau were the sole property of the order and could only be removed at the prelate's discretion had never been cited during Dante's lengthy tenure. But he was ready to invoke the condition by having the parchments shipped to Valencia, should Reinhart or Ambrosia, as he expected, stipulate they be sent to the Vatican.

There was an empty storage facility at the back of the chateau's grounds that provided ample space for the construction of a small laboratory. With all of the order's resources at his disposal Dante realized he could build a facility that would house the parchments, along with enough technicians to complete the codex's restoration.

More importantly, the prelate believed the laboratory could be built during the ninety-day window he had given himself. It wouldn't have all the refinements found in the Zaragoza lab, and Salazar would not be on the team. But those issues could be solved after the codex's shift to the chateau. The important element of the plan was that the parchments would be safe from the clutches of Reinhart and Ambrosia.

There was an engineering and architectural firm in Lyons, France, the Fraternity had owned for more than a decade.

Dante would give them a call in the morning and begin the process.

The prelate realized that much of his plan depended on the adroit handling of Reinhart. The deacon had to believe he was being treated with the respect and humility that was always accorded a cardinal. For Dante, the immediate issue was finding a way that made it appear he was attempting to build a bridge of understanding with Reinhart. Dante needed a passive cardinal in order to buy the time required for his planned extraction of the codex.

He would send an e-mail saying he was pleased the deacon was visiting the Zaragoza facility. Dante would be there to personally show Reinhart through the building and highlight the changes that had taken place over the last four years. It was well known throughout the Vatican that Dante seldom paid attention to the phalanx of cardinals populating Rome. Reinhart would consider it quite the victory in having the Fraternity's prelate at his disposal for a day.

For Dante, the apparent concession was a price worth paying. He wasn't going to leave the parchments' future in Monte's hands. The only time the curator would be needed was to provide a detailed explanation of the codex's restoration.

Next, Dante turned his attention to Reinhart's impending arrival. Flying with a commercial airline between Rome and Zaragoza was a nightmare. There were few flights, and all featured stopovers. The traveling time could take anywhere from four to six hours. As a result, it was standard practice for the order to provide its Learjet for anyone journeying between the Vatican and the facility. The trip, made in the comfort of a private aircraft, took less than ninety minutes, as the route was straight over the Tyrrhenian Sea. One of the Fraternity's fleet of Mercedes limousines would meet the plane and then drive the visitor into Zaragoza.

Although the men hadn't spoken in several years—a combination of Dante's infrequent visits to the Vatican and Reinhart's dislike for the order's leader—the prelate believed that even the austere deacon would accept the use of a private plane, along with a limousine, rather than endure a mind-numbing and physically punishing journey of interminable hours. Reinhart was well into his seventies, and the obvious comfort would be accepted, albeit grudgingly and with some wariness. But Dante would put the distrust to rest with the next part of his plan.

The prelate knew that Reinhart would be expecting him to lobby for the parchments remaining in Zaragoza. It would arouse suspicion if neither Dante nor Monte made a case for having the restoration completed at the facility.

The contact from the deacon had been through Monte. Dante would have the curator make the initial response and then follow up with his offer of the aircraft and the limousine. The prelate wasn't going to tell Monte about the plan for shifting the codex until after Reinhart's visit. Instead, Dante would instruct the curator to strongly make the case for not moving the codex to Rome.

This would be done through the e-mails and phone calls that would flow between Zaragoza and the deacon's office to establish the tour's schedule. The curator's lack of knowledge about the codex's relocation to the chateau would bring passion to his request and, therefore, render it completely believable.

With meticulous care, Dante continued to plot out the day's campaign. Following the general tour, Reinhart and the prelate, accompanied by Monte, would visit the laboratory where the restoration work was being conducted. While Monte was reviewing with Reinhart the process for restoring the codex, the curator would emphasize the procedure's complexity, the Zaragoza technicians' knowledge, and the parchments' fragility. It was meant to impress upon the deacon that moving the codex to one of the museums within the Vatican would be a mistake—at least until the restoration had been completed.

The plan firmly in mind, Dante refocused his gaze. He looked at the communication console and saw the outside line was flashing. Hitting the speaker button, he heard Monte's voice cascade throughout the room. When the prelate finished explaining what was to be written in the initial Reinhart e-mail, he ended the conversation by telling the curator that Juan would be in touch with further instructions for the day's visit.

Moments after Dante closed the line, he tapped the intercom. When Juan answered, the prelate issued his instructions. It would require a lengthy series of e-mails between the chateau, the Vatican, and the Zaragoza facility. But that wasn't the prelate's concern. Juan would handle the arrangements and organize the required schedule.

Juan said he'd begin the process immediately and told the prelate his breakfast would be ready in fifteen minutes. The time didn't surprise Dante. He was used to working through the night. While he waited for his meal, the prelate mentally poked and prodded his scheme. There was a weakness in that Reinhart might opt for immediately taking the parchments back to the Vatican. But Dante believed that, with all the preparation and time required for electing the new pope, Reinhart would follow the script—fully believing the parchments would be in Zaragoza when he wanted them.

The parchments are mine, and I'll do whatever is needed to keep them, even if it means catering to a low-level cardinal, Dante thought.

Chapter Sixteen

———————————— ✣ ————————————

Dante watched as the order's Mercedes transporting Cardinal Reinhart made its way across the wide expanse of asphalt that fronted the Zaragoza museum. Standing beside the prelate was Monte. The short, rotund man with unruly gray hair, a fleshy face, and dark eyes was nervously shifting his weight from one foot to the other.

Glancing away from the approaching car for a moment, Dante noted the sweaty gloss on the curator's forehead, along with the dampness that stained the armpits of his snug lab coat. While he intellectually understood Monte's discomfort, the prelate was unable to empathize with the curator's uneasiness.

"You should calm yourself," the prelate said, with no emotion. "Reinhart is here on an inspection tour. He may be a cardinal and head of the Vatican Museums, but I am responsible for what happens at Zaragoza."

"This is a difficult situation for me," noted Monte, trying to explain his anxiety. "I know you are directly in charge of this facility, and we report to you as prelate of the order. But the Fraternity is part of the Vatican, and Cardinal Reinhart still has the last word when it comes to the work done here. It hasn't happened in the past, but today I feel as though I'm serving two masters."

"Let me make one thing very clear," rasped Dante. "You and everyone at Zaragoza report to me. Your job is to show Reinhart the parchments and explain the restoration process. That is all you have to be concerned about. I will handle Reinhart. Is that understood?"

The middle-aged curator nodded so intensely his jowls jiggled in unison. "What happens if Reinhart wants the codex taken back to Rome? Neither of us can prevent that from happening."

"Why don't you let me worry about that," said Dante, in a more even tone. "Just stay with what you know and give him detailed answers to whatever questions he asks. As we discussed, I suspect the deacon is here to make problems for the order. If he does decide to relocate the codex to the Vatican, that isn't your issue. It's mine."

Monte responded with a glum look and let out an air of resignation.

Reinhart's car pulled up in front of the two men, ending the conversation. As the driver stepped out and proceeded to open the back door, a cold blast from the Mercedes's powerful air-conditioning system swept over Dante and the curator. The prelate, noting the chill, thought it was a fitting metaphor for how he and Reinhart viewed each other.

The fact Reinhart was one of the cardinals who had long advocated bringing the order firmly under Vatican control didn't bother Dante. In the corporate world where he conducted the vast majority of the Fraternity's business, the prelate was used to hostile meetings. Dante was so accustomed to the power he wielded that being at a disadvantage in any encounter never occurred to him.

The prelate had a finalized plan he believed would nullify whatever moves Reinhart and Ambrosia might have devised to seize the codex. The only negative was the storm of e-mails it had taken to get everything arranged over the two-day window available for ensuring the necessary elements were in place for the deacon's visit. Dante assumed the Guardians were attempting to hack his phone calls and e-mails. Juan had, as was customary, followed all the cloaking protocols. Phone conversations had been kept short, and e-mails were routed through several offshore servers.

Still, the Guardians' technology division had become increasingly sophisticated over the past few years. But Dante knew the order's security systems were among the best in the world—they had to be in the ongoing battle to thwart industrial and government-sponsored espionage. He felt confident the Guardians had not penetrated his network.

The deacon gathered his red cassock and stepped from the car. The driver got back in, and the limousine slid quietly to the end of the building before turning into a reserved parking space.

A shade under six feet tall, Reinhart was whippet thin, abnormally pale, and carried himself with the erect bearing of a soldier on parade. His scarlet skullcap sat atop a surprisingly full head of bone white hair worn short. A slender nose that flared slightly at the end ran between russet-colored eyes and high cheekbones so etched they appeared able to cut glass. His colorless lips sat above a faintly protruding chin.

After the men executed a less-than-hearty handshake and were walking up the four concrete steps that led to the double glass doors fronting the museum, Dante asked if the flight and limousine ride had been pleasant.

Reinhart gave Dante a humorless smile. "I know what you're attempting to do," he said. "It is agreeable to have a plane and a limousine at my disposal. But do not think these niceties will matter when it comes to deciding what will happen after I examine these parchments you've been hiding from me."

"No one has been hiding anything from you," Dante responded, his voice cold. "As for the parchments' future, I believe they should stay here. The work is progressing well, and to move them would risk irreparable damage."

"We shall see," offered Reinhart as the three men walked into the air-conditioned cool of the windowless lobby and past the security station with its two armed guards.

*****

Following a tour of the facility, which Dante had ensured did not include the area where the parchments were being restored, the prelate and Reinhart had stopped for a late lunch. Juan had made reservations and ordered the meal—pan fried sea bass complemented with freshly picked mushrooms and tomatoes mixed in a garlic sauce—at a restaurant located a short drive from the facility.

During the meal, Dante purposely stayed away from mentioning the codex, and Reinhart didn't bring up the subject. Conversation was sparse, sporadic, and focused on the various changes that had occurred at the museum since Reinhart's last visit.

The men eschewed dessert and had just ordered coffee when, as planned, Monte joined them. Reinhart immediately became more animated. The deacon was a manager, not a specialist. Although his technical expertise was limited, it didn't prevent him from blitzing the curator with a series of questions. It was obvious to Dante the queries were an attempt to determine what progress had been made on the restoration and, more importantly, whether the parchments could be relocated to the Vatican.

Having been coached by Dante, Monte kept his answers short and to the point. He described the repair work in technical terms, delving into how some pieces of parchment were being painstakingly cleaned by his team of specialists using white vinyl erasers. To another question, he responded that several sheets were undergoing a delicate restoration process using a laboratory grade gelatin solution. And when asked about progress he described how some of the folios were still at the initial stage of being flattened and the creases taken out in controlled humidity chambers.

Whether Reinhart understood much of what Monte was describing didn't seem important to the deacon. He kept circling back to the parchments' readiness for transport. It was an interesting tug-of-war. Reinhart persisted while Monte continued with his technical descriptions. Dante stayed quiet, sipping on his coffee and watching the battle unfold. He was pleasantly surprised how well Monte adhered to the script they'd reviewed and was giving away nothing about the codex's state of repair.

Dante waited until he'd finished his coffee before speaking. Interrupting Reinhart as the deacon again asked if the parchments could be transported, the prelate said, "I believe the best way for you to determine that the work on two thousand-year-old parchments is difficult and requires intense dedication from a team of specially trained experts is for you to see where the restoration is being done."

Out of the corner of his eye, the prelate saw Monte give him an intense look, which Dante knew was gratitude that he'd stepped in and effectively ended the questioning.

"That's an excellent idea," said the deacon, immediately rising from his chair. "The lunch has refreshed me. I'm looking forward to seeing these incredible parchments that wrongfully claim God's holy son did not die on the cross."

Monte departed to pay the bill and joined the two men as they climbed into the limousine. During the short drive back, no one spoke, each man lost in his own thoughts. The driver pulled the car up to the front door and the men stepped out into the hot afternoon sun.

Once inside the building, Monte shepherded his guests up a flight of gray, steel-backed stairs and down a long, well-lit, industrial-carpeted corridor. Large windows, spaced every fifteen feet, looked over a series of laboratories that featured various sculptures, paintings, and parchments being worked on by small teams of technicians.

Monte stopped at the last window. "This gives you an overview of the work being done on the codex," he said to Reinhart. "We can stay here for a few minutes, and I'll explain the tasks being carried out in each area of the lab. That way, when you get downstairs, you'll have an understanding of what is happening at each station."

The deacon looked through the glass for a few seconds. "This is interesting," he said, "but I want to see what's actually taking place at the workstations."

Monte appeared nonplussed at Reinhart's response. He looked at Dante, who, sensing the curator's confusion, suggested the group move directly to the lab.

Turning abruptly from the window, Monte led his guests to a large industrial steel door at the end of the hallway. Gripping a pass card that hung from a lanyard around his neck, the curator slid it along the channel in the security pad and then punched in five numbers on the keypad. He waited as the twin locks released and then pulled open the door. The men walked through to a large landing that contained a cupboard with shoe covers, white cotton gloves, lab coats, and hairnets. After donning the gear, everyone descended a metal stairway that wound itself around to the lab's floor.

The Hope of Janus

The lab was windowless, except for the one fronting the hallway. Illumination was provided through a series of muted, ultraviolet blue lights hung low over the workstations. Blue lights along the walls provided general lighting. The low lighting was designed to ensure no bright and direct light was focused on the parchments. The room had its own thermostat and hygrometer to control both temperature and humidity. Instead of carpet, the floor was a gray, painted concrete, so no static electricity could be generated.

Dante hung back as Monte began the tour. The curator started by noting the Aramaic script. He then discussed how the parchments were written on goatskins, where the hair had been removed and the skin had been stretched against a frame, scraped, wetted, and then dried to create a soft and durable writing surface. The Word of Janus was recorded on nineteen pieces of different-sized parchments. Located throughout the lab were sixteen stations. Each represented a different phase in the restoration process. The eight technicians were divided into groups of two, and each team had a specialized skill set.

Dante noted that Salazar was at a light table in deep conversation with one of the specialists. The lead technician paid no attention to the three visitors.

The curator guided Reinhart to the first series of workstations, where a team was working with a humidity chamber to thoroughly moisten several pieces. This was being carried out to flatten and remove curls from the sheets. Once that was completed, the parchments would be meticulously flattened by hand and then shifted to a suction table, where they would be attached with polyester strips and carefully dried.

It was obvious Monte was in his element. The curator slowly explained each procedure as they stopped at the various posts.

One squad was carefully applying gelatin to a series of large tears in two of the sheets. As they moved through the lab, Reinhart took a particular interest at one station, where several small holes in one of the parchment sheets were being infilled with ground up animal hide. He silently watched the process and then turned to Monte, saying, "I've seen enough. Your people are very skilled, and as the museum director, I appreciate the work they are doing. But it's time we address the codex's future."

Briefly caught off guard by Reinhart's desire to suddenly end the tour, the curator stammered, asking the deacon if he would like to see the passage that claimed Jesus had not died on the cross.

"There's no point." Reinhart shrugged. "I don't read Aramaic. And I've seen enough to know the codex's value."

Chapter Seventeen

They walked into Monte's office. It was a small, cluttered room with a large pile of papers and small artifacts occupying two corners of the curator's coffee-stained desk. Monte casually draped his lab coat over a large statue of Apollo that Dante knew had been created by Leonardo da Vinci. On a low credenza behind his desk, Monte was using a centuries-old bust of Julius Caesar as a paperweight for a disorganized collection of documents.

In the room's center were four chairs arranged around a small table. While Dante and Reinhart opted for seats facing each other, Monte took the chair on Dante's right side. On the table was a coffeepot. Three cups, along with two small beakers holding cream and sugar, were arranged around it. Monte distributed the mugs and poured the coffee. Everyone took it black.

Reinhart swallowed a large mouthful and quickly put the cup down. Dante had one sip and found the java weak and barely warm. He looked at Monte, whose eyes pleaded forgiveness. The prelate slightly inclined his head and smiled. Coffee was not the issue at the moment.

A brief silence enveloped the room before Monte asked Reinhart, "So what's your opinion of our operation?"

"I think, as I have always done, that it is efficient, well run, and staffed with excellent technicians. The Vatican has always appreciated the work conducted here at Zaragoza. However, your coffee leaves something to be desired," the deacon finished with a chuckle.

While Monte laughed and then murmured his appreciation for Reinhart's praise of the facility, Dante wordlessly waited. He knew the deacon was about to enunciate his terms for moving the codex. Smoothing out his cassock, Reinhart locked eyes with Dante.

"The conclave will soon be upon us," began Reinhart. "It is a foregone conclusion that my good friend Cardinal Ambrosia will be elected the next pope. The occasion will be momentous and deserves something special to mark this defining point in our Church's history."

Dante returned the stare but stayed silent. If the deacon thought he was going to respond in some way, the prelate wasn't prepared to give him that pleasure.

Dante knew Reinhart was about to demand that the codex be shipped to the Vatican. Once the prelate's thought became fact, the clock would be ticking on the ninety days Dante believed he'd have for moving the parchments to the chateau.

"I have decided that our new pope should have in his possession the codex," the deacon said with a quiet laugh. "What better way to mark the beginning of his reign than to provide the pontiff with such a priceless gift."

There was a momentary silence until an obviously agitated Monte blurted, "These parchments are unique pieces of history. My technicians have been working hard, and they deserve the opportunity to finish what they've started. I fear that if the codex goes to the Vatican, it will be destroyed because of what the manuscript contains. And if that's the case, then why should we keep restoring them?"

Monte leaned back, his chest heaving. Sweat beads were again dotting his forehead.

While Dante was surprised at the curator's off-script words, he was glad they'd been spoken. Monte's obvious passion added authenticity to his position that the codex should remain in Zaragoza.

Dante looked at Reinhart and saw shock reflected in the deacon's eyes.

"Despite my lack of technical knowledge," Reinhart began, his voice low and directed at Monte, "I am deeply committed to preserving religious history. You said earlier that the codex has been carbon and X-ray dated, and from initial results, it appears to be a genuine first-century manuscript. Am I correct?"

Monte slowly nodded his head but said nothing.

"We may be the Vatican Museums, but that does not mean everything in our vaults venerates the Catholic faith," continued the deacon. "While I don't believe what has been written in the codex is the truth, it is still an extremely valuable document for historical purposes. The manuscript adds to our knowledge of life during that period, and while it will never be shown to the public, the parchments will be of immense benefit to our scholars. I also want them in Rome to ensure they don't fall into the hands of those who would use the codex to destabilize our Church."

The last sentence was said while looking directly at Dante. The prelate did not respond.

"Since you both have nothing to say," Reinhart offered, "I'll continue with my instructions.

"Now, every cardinal will be extremely busy before the conclave, and that includes Ambrosia and me. But if this gift is to be truly meaningful, it should be delivered shortly after our new pope is confirmed. I believe seven days would be sufficient. That means the parchments, along with the Hebrew translation, are to be at the Vatican during the week of the twenty-seventh next month."

Dante sat stone-faced, Monte's eyes reflected shock, and Reinhart's lips were curled in a cynical smile.

"I hope this doesn't cause either of you too much upheaval," continued the deacon.

For one of the few times in his career, Dante had been out maneuvered. The three-month window had been shrunk to just over six weeks. But the prelate hadn't built the order into a global empire by accepting any form of defeat. His mind had already seized on a counter-measure. Once Reinhart was put in the Mercedes and on his way back to the airport, Dante would review the details with Monte.

"You're presuming a great deal," said Dante. "There is still a vote to be taken at the conclave. Anything can happen."

"You don't really believe that," countered Reinhart. "Ambrosia has revealed to me the work you've done to ensure he becomes the next pope. I would expect you'd share in my confidence that he will soon sit in the papal chair.

"I am sure you can understand why this gift of the parchments will be especially meaningful for him. We both believe it will signify the beginning of a return to the time when the order's prelate did not act so independently of Rome. I could have delivered the news in an e-mail, but that is terribly impersonal. It is so much better to have this discussion face-to-face."

The Hope of Janus

Dante could easily see that Reinhart was enjoying the moment. The deacon's eyes were wide and radiated a vitality that accompanied his yellow teeth-baring smile.

The prelate was briefly silent, calmly evaluating how to ensure what he said did not give the deacon any hint the codex would never make it to Rome.

"As you saw by your inspection of the parchments, none are ready for travel," said Dante, knowing it was what Reinhart expected to hear.

"That is why I'm giving you time to prepare them. After that, they can be placed in a portable, vacuum-sealed chamber and shipped to our laboratory in Rome. I'll expect you," Reinhart said, looking at Monte, "to accompany the chamber. We have to ensure nothing happens with our precious cargo while it is en route."

Dante chose to ignore that the cardinal was overstepping his bounds by giving instructions to someone directly employed by the order. This battle had already been decided, but Reinhart would soon find it an impotent victory. In the meantime, Dante wanted to demonstrate that he had no quarrel with the incoming papal regime, although that would soon change.

"I'll provide the order's jet to ensure the codex's safe transportation," offered Dante.

The look of surprise on Reinhart's face would have been comical, had the subject not been so serious and filled with treacherous undercurrents.

"That's very generous," observed the deacon, who had recovered quickly from his momentary shock. "I'll gladly accept the offer. Our assistants can work out the details. Is that satisfactory?"

Dante nodded and saw that Monte was slumped in his chair looking defeated and weary. If Reinhart had any suspicions that the prelate was intent on deceiving him, they would be allayed by the curator's demeanor.

"I'm glad we've come to an agreement," voiced the deacon. "We have had our differences in the past, but hopefully this marks the start of a new cooperative era between us."

Dante wasn't surprised by the depth of Reinhart's hypocrisy. The deacon assumed he had dealt a major blow to the prelate's drive of controlling the papacy long into the future. Just as important, Dante knew Reinhart would not rest until the order was stripped of its power and its independence from the Vatican. There would never be peace between the men. It was simply Reinhart's way of indicating that this victory was the beginning of many more for the Vatican over the order.

Dante had purposely let several moments of silence hang in the air until he saw that Reinhart was growing impatient waiting for a reply. "We'll see what the future holds," the prelate finally offered.

"That we will," responded Reinhart. "But my advice is to seek a more collaborative relationship with everyone at the Vatican."

"I'll do my best."

The deacon held Dante's eyes for several moments before breaking contact. "And now I believe we can safely say this meeting has come to an end," Reinhart said, rising to his feet.

Chapter Eighteen

✣

The driver closed the rear door, sealing Reinhart inside the car. Moving to behind the steering wheel, the chauffeur put the vehicle in gear. It slowly exited the compound and turned north onto the road leading toward the airport.

Monte looked at Dante and said, "All our work has been for nothing. We're going to lose the codex."

"No one is taking the parchments away from us," said Dante. "Let's go to your office, and I'll explain."

The men walked with a quiet purpose through the facility's front door, up the steps and along the corridor to Monte's office. As they took their seats around the table, where only minutes before, Dante had agreed to have the codex shipped to Rome, the prelate began explaining his plan. He detailed for Monte that the team working on the parchments would prepare the codex for transportation. However, instead of being shipped to the Vatican, the order's jet would fly the parchments to the chateau.

The plans for the lab on the chateau's property took several minutes to detail, and throughout the explanation the curator's expression gradually evolved from dismay to excitement.

"You're going to keep them in Valencia," said a suddenly confident sounding Monte. "Although the lab won't be ready for three months, we can leave the parchments in a vacuum chamber. Normally, there would be some degradation. The oils and moisture in each piece would gradually dry out making them extremely brittle. But knowing this, I can get our technicians to add oil and mineral water to the pieces before they are placed in the chamber. That should be sufficient to hold them until the lab is prepared. However it is only a short-term solution. We need the lab up and running within your ninety-day time frame.

"In the meantime, I'll have one of my technicians accompany the vacuum chamber, and she can regularly inspect the parchments. Is there somewhere she can stay at the chateau?"

Dante indicated a guest room would be set aside.

The prelate paused and waited for what he knew would be the next question.

"What happens to my team working on the parchments when your lab is operational?" the curator asked.

"We'll have half of them on a two-month rotating schedule," answered the prelate. "There are enough rooms at the chateau where they can stay. I realize most of your group has families here in Zaragoza, but there are times when sacrifices must be made for the order. This is one of those occasions. And I don't see it lasting more than eighteen months. There will obviously be personnel changes with the new pope. I believe Reinhart will not keep his post. Once that happens, we can shift the codex back here."

The men were silent for several moments, until Monte leaned across the table and, in a conspiratorial whisper, said, "The plan is perfect because it will also keep Salazar in check. All that the traitor will see is the parchments being prepared for shipment, which is exactly what Reinhart and Ambrosia have demanded. He will know nothing about your strategy to have the plane fly to Valencia instead of Rome.

"But what are you going to tell Reinhart and Ambrosia? This will mean a war with the Vatican."

"Leave that with me," responded the prelate, once again thinking of the files he had on Ambrosia. However, Reinhart would be a problem. He was a man without faults or vices, so he was beyond Dante's reach. And although he was only a cardinal deacon, he still had enough followers throughout the college and within the Vatican's bureaucracy to mount a focused campaign against the order.

A number of the Fraternity's companies did business with the Vatican in areas that included accounting, food, and medical supplies, along with engineering and architectural work. Reinhart could have the contracts canceled. It would be a loss of corporate revenue and some prestige for the involved corporations, but the effect would be short term.

And when Dante fully moved against the Vatican, Reinhart's brief reign of causing difficulties for the Fraternity would end. Once Ambrosia was in place, Reinhart was going to be shifted into an area where he could do no harm to the order. And his official influence on the new pope would be minimal.

Satisfied that he had the issue under control, Dante returned his attention to Monte, who didn't seem to have noticed that the prelate had mentally slipped away for several seconds.

Dante believed he'd told Monte all that the curator required at this point. "Is there anything else you need to know?" he asked.

Monte shook his head. He had no further questions. "If you think it's the best way to handle the codex, then we'll make it work."

"Of course we'll be successful," said a mildly surprised Dante. "There's no question we're going to keep the codex. All you have to do is follow the plan."

"That's what we'll do," responded the curator.

Dante nodded and looked at his watch. "It's getting late," he said, lifting himself out of his chair. "Please have my car brought around."

After Monte finished with the brief phone call, the men proceeded out of the office and down the corridor.

They arrived at the bottom of the outdoor steps just as the Mercedes pulled up beside them. It was a four-hour drive to the chateau. As usual, Dante had brought files to work on during the return trip. They contained information on the possibility of the order buying out a Silicon Valley tech company to augment the Fraternity's package-delivery system.

Dante shook hands with Monte and said, "The day didn't go exactly as anticipated. But we know what we're going to do. I'll be in touch early next week and we can finalize the details. You did well today."

The prelate turned and got into the car's back seat. Monte closed the door. As the driver put the vehicle in gear, Dante opened his laptop and buried himself in the stored financial and operational information about the tech company.

He didn't notice that Monte was still standing in the driveway, his face flooded with red at the prelate's praise.

Chapter Nineteen

✣

The tension was evident on everyone's drawn faces.

Several minutes earlier, Olga had summoned the three other executive Guardians to the non-descript meeting room with news that the codex's location had been determined.

Holding an iPad in her left hand, Olga was at the room's front, while Andrew and Leyland were seated beside each other several chairs from where the head of technology was standing. Bella was in a chair opposite Leyland.

Andrew cracked the knuckles on his left hand, which drew an irritated look from Bella. She was about to say something when Olga started to speak.

"A couple of days ago, we intercepted several e-mails between a Cardinal Wolfgang Reinhart, who manages the Vatican Museums; Luigi Monte, who we know from earlier hacks is the curator for the Zaragoza facility; and Dante Sabatini's office. They were planning a visit to Zaragoza by the cardinal to look at the parchments. So not only do we know the codex is intact, we also have the building's location.

"But we had a problem." Olga glanced at her iPad, and the passing seconds only deepened the anxiety of the three seated Guardians.

"What was the issue?" asked Bella.

"We were able to verify the Zaragoza facility's e-mail and IP address," explained the technology director. "Unfortunately, that didn't give us the physical location. But one of my tech people was able to pull up a copy of an e-mail sent from Monte to Reinhart.

"The facility has a standardized e-mail form that is used for all its Internet correspondence. Most organizations have the same type of document, and many list a street address. We weren't that fortunate because none of the Vatican museums post an address, which is an interesting fact, but it didn't help us.

"We did get lucky, though. Below Monte's sign-off, the telephone and fax numbers are displayed. And that was golden for us. We used the Internet tool reverse lookup, which allowed us to input the telephone number. And that pulled up the street address. My team found the lab's location a few minutes ago, and through our mapping app, I can show you the exact building.

"The facility is on a street that runs off the Paseo de la Independencia. It's in the same general area as the Museo de Bellas Artes."

Andrew responded with a loud cheer, clapped Leyland on the back, and then reached across the table and gave Bella's hand a firm shake. Olga had moved between Andrew and Leyland. She laid the iPad on the table and showed the group a Google map layout and street views of where the building was located.

It was in a large compound that housed a number of other buildings. At the back of the facility was a small parking lot. Surrounding the enclosed complex was a residential area with what looked to be several small apartment buildings encircled by a number of streets containing medium-sized factories and a few low-level office blocks.

Andrew raised his eyes from viewing the iPad. The relief he felt was reflected in the noisy chatter and smiles of his fellow team members. Although the dangerous work of retrieving the codex was about to begin, Andrew was enjoying the moment. He experienced a strong sense of justification at persuading the group to follow his lead in going after the codex.

However, the satisfaction was short-lived. Bella, who had stood to look at the iPad, sat down and asked the senior Guardian the question he'd been hoping wouldn't be raised.

"When will you be leaving for Janus?" she queried. "We have the location, and your recovery squad is prepared to travel. But this is where my approval ends. We need Elijah and the islanders to give their consent before this thing goes any farther. They have to know what we're doing."

"She's right," voiced Olga. "The obvious next step is to send your squad in to retrieve the codex. This isn't a complicated issue. I'm with Bella. Unless we receive the islanders' authorization, I'll withdraw my support."

Andrew pursed his lips. There was nothing he could do. Violating the islanders' specific instructions to ignore the order and not search for the codex was only possible because Bella and Olga had agreed to the plan. But together they represented half the Guardians' executive management group. Without the assistance of Olga's technology team and Bella's finance department, the project couldn't proceed.

"We've come this far," said the senior Guardian. "Why waste what we've achieved? My vote is to go in, get the codex, and tell the islanders what we've done once the parchments are in our hands. I'm sure we'll be forgiven for breaking the Janus decree of not confronting the order if the mission is a success."

"That's not the point," argued Bella. "The administrative decree clearly states that the Guardians shall undertake no action unless approved by the Islanders. We've already skirted the line by conducting surveillance in looking for the codex. I'm not prepared to go any further."

Leyland, who had said little throughout the presentation and subsequent discussion, asked, "Is it possible to review a compromise?"

"What does that mean?" responded Bella, her voice cautious.

"I think we've been incorrectly looking at the next part of our mission," offered Leyland. "We've grouped reconnaissance and retrieving the codex as one undertaking. But they're really two separate operations. I'm sure Andrew can detail for us what's involved in an exercise of this type."

"And how does this help us?" challenged Bella. "I'm adamant that we don't move forward unless the islanders give us permission. So far, I haven't heard a solution that answers my concern. I can't speak for Olga, but without my approval, this project ends right now."

Andrew got up from his chair and began pacing along one side of the room. "Leyland's right," he said, as the other three closely watched him. "We can send our team in to conduct surveillance on the facility. The mission will take anywhere from seven to nine days, including travel time to Zaragoza, renting cars, setting up hotels, surveillance, and planning. Once that's completed, the squad must wait for further instructions from us.

"That gives Leyland and me time for traveling to Janus, meeting with the islanders, and returning prior to completion of the reconnaissance mission. If we get approval to proceed, the team can act immediately. Should our plan be rejected, there is still time to call everything off and bring the squad home."

The Hope of Janus

The room went quiet as everyone pondered what Andrew had offered. The senior Guardian sat down and waited silently for the group's comments.

"I believe it's the perfect plan," suggested Leyland. "Once again, we are proceeding with the mission without engaging the order."

Olga and Bella looked at each other. The technology director nodded and said, "I agree that, under this plan, there'd be no interaction with the order unless we get approval from the islanders. But can you guarantee that your squad won't come into contact with anyone at the facility?"

"The whole point of surveillance is to conduct it covertly," responded Andrew, trying not to sound patronizing. "The unit has been training since a week after the codex was stolen. Every member has become professionally seasoned. They're prepared and ready. There will be no mistakes."

"Why the rush?" asked Bella. "We should wait to see if there is approval from the islanders. If and when that happens, then a campaign can be mounted."

"Because we don't know how long the codex will remain in Zaragoza. With the cardinal and Dante visiting the site, they could be planning on moving it to the Vatican or to the chateau in Valencia. If that happens, we'll never see the codex again. The security at both sites, not to mention the myriad places they could store the parchments, would make a search-and-find mission impossible. This is our best and only chance."

"That sounds like a fair compromise," offered Olga. "I believe it's a plan Bella and I can accept."

Bella nodded her head in agreement. "When are you planning to contact the team?"

"The moment this meeting is over, I'll phone Shepherd. After that, Leyland and I will prepare to leave for Janus in the morning."

"There's just one more thing," announced Bella, as Andrew prepared to get up.

"And what's that?" responded the senior guardian, his voice tense.

"The only weapons carried by our people will be low-impact Tasers. That was agreed to at our last meeting."

"We've implemented the change. Shepherd wasn't happy when I told him of the directive, but the squad is equipped with Tasers and has been using them on the practice range.

"And now if there is nothing more to discuss," continued Andrew, "Leyland and I have to prepare for our trip to Janus."

Olga and Bella nodded in unison. The four rose from their seats and proceeded out of the meeting room. The two women turned left and proceeded along a hallway that would take them to their respective offices.

"We're going to have a difficult session with the islanders," said Leyland while the men walked down the corridor that brought them to Andrew's office and a telephone call to Shepherd. After that, they'd be heading toward the harbor and readying the Guardians' ship for the voyage to Janus.

"I believe we can pull it off," Andrew responded confidently. "There will be some initial resistance because we went against the decree, but once everyone realizes how close we are to retrieving the codex, they'll give us the approval to proceed.

"We'll talk to Elijah first and get his support. That should make it easier when we go before the islanders."

He picked up his cell phone from the desk and began punching in the numbers for Shepherd.

"I hope you're right," responded Leyland quietly, staring out the window and noting that fog and a light rain had settled over Inverness. It would be wet work for the men loading the Guardians' vessel, *Journey*, with crates of meat, vegetables, and fruit for the islanders.

Chapter Twenty

Sean and Diane had just finished breakfast when they heard Elijah's voice calling from the front door. They invited him in to share some coffee. The Prophet made his way to the kitchen but quickly declined the offer.

Not bothering to take a seat, he told them that *Journey* was about five minutes out from the island's harbor. The ship, a beautiful, 128-foot vessel, generally made the twenty-four-hour run from Inverness to Janus once every two months loaded with supplies. However, the ship had been in Janus a mere three weeks previously.

"Were there any plans for *Journey* to make an early run?" asked Sean.

"Not at all," replied Elijah. "It can only mean that something has either happened within our diaspora or there's a problem with the Guardians."

After Sean washed out the dirty dishes, the three islanders made their way down to the harbor. They arrived just as Andrew, who served as captain, was guiding the ship into its berth. The crew consisted of Leyland, along with identical twins Malcolm and Joseph. The fishing fleet, as usual, had left before dawn.

The Hope of Janus

A concerned and expectant mass of islanders had taken up the entire dock area and spilled up to the Ring Road where they were gathered in pockets of five or six people that stretched far back from the harbor. Every conversation was focused on why *Journey* was returning so far ahead of schedule and the hope that nothing terrible had happened to far-flung relatives. Although the group was large there was no jostling or pushing. Once again, Sean was impressed at the islanders' tolerance and orderliness.

"It looks as though almost everyone, with the exception of our fishing crews, is here," said Elijah to Sean and Diane.

"The only time we see this many islanders in one place is during our Community Center meetings," noted Diane.

"Is *Journey* arriving earlier than expected so unusual?" asked Sean.

"Normally not," said Elijah. "But three weeks is such a short time frame that everyone is wondering what has happened."

After *Journey* was securely tied up against the wharf, Malcolm and Joseph let out the gangplank. Elijah, Sean, and Diane made their way through the throng. They met Andrew and Leyland after the Guardians had descended the walkway and stepped on the dock.

"We weren't expecting you for another five weeks," said Elijah. "Is there a problem?"

"Nothing terrible has happened," offered Andrew. "But we have some news that should be talked through in the privacy of your home."

This represented a shocking departure from the way life was lived on Janus. The islanders prided themselves on being an open society, where secrets were not kept. Elijah's normally weathered visage had gone pale as he absorbed the full impact of what Andrew was proposing.

"If you have something to discuss we should call a meeting for the Community Center," said the Prophet. "Whatever you have to say must be reviewed with everybody."

"I'm not suggesting we should ignore the islanders," the Guardian said hurriedly. "It's just that what I have to say needs to be reviewed with you before we take it to everyone."

Sean looked around and could see that the overflow crowd was focused on the conversation between Elijah and Andrew. While not everybody could hear, the discussion's essence was passed back through the gathering, so that each person understood what was being said. A low rumble of confusion began to make its way along the dock as the islanders tried to puzzle what was so critical that it had to be reviewed with Elijah prior to a general meeting.

"I'll agree to a private talk on one condition," said Elijah. "We will have a general session this evening. There will be no secrets on Janus."

"That's exactly what I want," offered Andrew. "Why don't we walk over to your house, and I'll let you know what's been happening in Inverness."

The news there was going to be an island meeting chased itself through the crowd. This only served to heighten everyone's anticipation that Andrew's news would have a major impact on the island. But living through the constant vagaries inherent with farming, sheep herding, and fishing for their survival, the islanders had learned the value of patience. Satisfied there was to be an evening assembly where the reason for *Journey*'s early arrival would be revealed, people quietly made their way homeward.

Malcolm and Joseph, along with several of the island's young men and women had taken off some of the supplies from the ship. Although provisions had been delivered three weeks earlier, no opportunity was lost when it came to providing the islanders with foodstuffs not available on Janus. The unpredictable North Atlantic weather sometimes delayed *Journey*, and the Guardians did their best to ensure the islanders were always well stocked.

The donkeys were loaded and as the crowd dissipated, the Guardians, along with the securely packed animals, followed. Malcolm and Joseph would spend the day distributing the provisions throughout the island.

Diane decided to leave with the rest of the islanders. "You can tell me this mysterious news when you get home from Elijah's," she told Sean. "I'm interested in what Andrew has to say, but we have sheep and crops needing my attention."

"It would be good to have you there," Sean responded. "But at this time of year, the farm has to take precedence. I expect from the way Andrew wants to meet privately that this evening's session at the Center will be quite interesting."

Soon, the only people left on the dock were Elijah, Sean, Andrew, and Leyland.

As the men departed the harbor and walked along the Road toward the Prophet's house, the conversation ebbed and flowed. It mostly focused on how the growing season was progressing, and both Guardians voiced their satisfaction with the strong crop in the fields. Sean noticed that Andrew purposely kept the conversation focused on Janus. And whenever there was a lull, Leyland quickly took over with questions about the daily fishing catches. Nothing was said about what had brought the men to the island. In this way, they arrived at the Prophet's home.

While Elijah went inside to fix a pot of coffee, Sean and Leyland arranged the balcony chairs in a rough semicircle. Andrew walked to the gallery's far end, and it seemed to Sean that he wanted no distraction until Elijah came outside.

Leyland and Sean took chairs across from each other. Not knowing one another that well, their conversation stumbled from the warm weather being experienced on the island to the rough seas experienced by *Journey* on her trip to Janus. Sean felt an immense relief when Elijah arrived with four mugs and a pot of coffee sitting on a tray. Seeing the Prophet, Andrew made his way to the chairs and took one beside Leyland. As was typical on the island, everyone took his coffee black.

After pouring out the java, Elijah leaned back and said, "Well, Andrew, here we are. What's so important that it had to be discussed in private?"

*****

The news had hit Sean like a pile driver. He looked over at Elijah and saw that the Prophet's reaction was similar. Elijah's hands were tightly gripping the arms of his chair. In a repeat from the harbor, the Prophet's face had gone pale, and his eyes reflected either confusion or frustration; Sean wasn't sure which emotion Elijah was feeling.

The answer wasn't long in coming.

"What were you thinking?" he asked, his voice indicating puzzlement that the Guardians had ignored an administrative decree from the islanders.

Sean reflected that, as was always the case with everyone on Janus, there was no anger from Elijah. The emotion was viewed as counter-productive by the islanders. It achieved nothing, other than to create or prolong divisive situations.

However, that didn't mean Elijah was about to absolve the Guardians for their actions.

"You consciously went against the specific instructions agreed to by everyone during our last general assembly," said Elijah. "And now you're claiming you've done nothing wrong. That's not how I see it. And I'm sure the islanders will feel the same way."

"We haven't disobeyed the decree," claimed Andrew, his voice rising. "It was specific that we were not to confront the order. At no time have we had any contact with it. Our Internet hacking was done without the knowledge of the order and the Vatican. It merely continued, albeit with more intense scrutiny, what we have been doing for the past several years. And the team we have in Zaragoza has specific instructions to conduct surveillance, nothing more.

"It's the final step that might bring us into conflict with the order, and that's why we're here. If you agree, we'll put it before everyone at tonight's meeting."

Elijah picked up his cup, and took several sips. Sean watched the Prophet carefully. He seemed at a loss about what to do or say. Sean decided to intervene.

"We are a pacifistic society," he said to Andrew. "How can you possibly believe the islanders will agree to any action that might result in a confrontation with the order?"

"Because my squad has no intention of using violence," answered Andrew. "We will go in at night. Based on the e-mails we intercepted, all the technicians work a regular day. The team will take the codex, along with the Hebrew translation, and fly them back to Inverness. If there are guards, we'll temporarily disable them with Tasers. This will be a clean and swift operation."

Sean thought for a moment. On the surface, the plan seemed workable. But there was something he believed Andrew was overlooking.

"Even if the operation goes as planned, Sabatini will know it was the Guardians who engineered the theft," Sean said. "I have to believe there will be a response, and thus we have a confrontation."

"You're making an assumption based on conjecture," argued Andrew. "We don't know why the codex was stolen, and therefore, it's only speculation that Dante will again come after it. And if he does, we'll be ready. I believe we could defuse any attempted theft without resorting to violence."

Sean wasn't sure how Andrew could make that claim, but then again, that wasn't the point of this session. They were here to discuss going before the islanders with a proposal to get the codex back.

"I know you don't look at it this way," said Sean, "but you've broken Janus's most sacred trust between the islanders and the Guardians. I think before any decision is made by Elijah, you have to explain your justification for the action you've taken."

Andrew sighed, and it was evident to Sean the Guardian was frustrated.

"My rationale is simple," he began. "First, as I've explained, we did not break the administrative decree. But more importantly the Word of Janus is our most sacred artifact. The codex is a physical representation of our foundation as a society. It is the basis for who we are and how we live. The order is the guilty party for stealing it from us. We are attempting to right that wrong.

"Not only that, but if anyone would want the parchments back, it should be you," continued Andrew, staring directly at

Sean. "It represents your birthright and gives proof that you're a direct descendent of Jesus. And I see you're wearing the *hope of Janus*. That must mean the Spirit has something special planned for you.

"None of us know what the future holds, but along with your birthmark and the ring, the codex could play a vital role in your life."

Not expecting to become directly implicated in the deliberations, Sean was momentarily taken aback. But he knew Andrew was right. For Sean, Janus was no longer just an island in the North Sea. It meant much more. The three signs from the Spirit encapsulated his story. With a passion that surprised him, Sean realized he wanted the parchments back to physically complete the triumvirate. And now that Andrew seemed to have a plan for retrieving the codex, he was ready to support the Guardian.

"What do you think?" asked Sean, looking at Elijah. "I believe the islanders have a right to know what Andrew is proposing. After that, the responsibility is for everyone to make a decision."

Putting his cup on the chair's armrest, Elijah rubbed a right hand that had the appearance of dried leather over his face. Andrew took several sips of java and stared intently at the Prophet. Leyland, who, as usual, had remained quiet, emptied his mug before putting it on the tray. He turned his gaze to Andrew.

Sean watched the tableau and marveled at the silence that had overtaken the group. It was so quiet a farmer several fields away could be heard calling to his sheep. Elijah stirred and then stood. He went behind his chair and grabbed the top with both hands. Looking at everyone in turn, he said, "Sean is right. Andrew should put his proposal before the islanders."

The Guardian smiled and nodded his head at Leyland. The two shifted in their seats, preparing to stand.

"I'm not finished," noted Elijah, and the men settled back in their chairs. "You must also acknowledge that, for the first time in our history, the Guardians have gone against an administrative decree from the islanders. Before your proposal can be voted on, there must first be a decision about whether you will be exonerated for this transgression. We are an understanding people, so I know the islanders will forgive you, especially since it is part of our mantra of forgiveness and understanding. Only then will we decide on your plan."

Sean knew exactly the point Elijah was making, and he marveled at the man's wisdom. Andrew, however, looked confused.

"If it's a forgone conclusion that we'll be vindicated for our actions, why bother going through the exercise?" the Guardian asked.

"Because you have disobeyed the decree, and there should be some penance. Although the two of you are the most senior Guardians, it doesn't mean blanket immunity. The importance is not so much in the act of showing you are contrite, but in understanding that you crossed a boundary. I don't want this to happen again, so I'm calling on the islanders to help you recognize that your success in locating the codex does not justify your actions."

"But you will work with me in asking everyone to accept my plan," argued Andrew. "Doesn't that mean the decision I took was ultimately correct?"

Sean watched the interplay with fascination. It was obvious that Andrew wasn't used to being challenged. Although there might be discussions with his executive management team, Andrew's views were generally the ones implemented. Elijah was holding him to a higher standard, and from the chagrined look on the Guardian's face, it was obvious he didn't appreciate the thought of going before the citizens' assembly and admitting to a mistake.

"Our world is a long way from Janus," continued the Guardian. "And in this case, the common good, which is retrieving the codex, meant we had to adjust our priorities. However, having said that, I still don't believe we went counter to the decree."

"Your method may work in the world, and I realize that is your backdrop," said Elijah. "But you're a Guardian and are sworn to protect the ways of Janus. Accept my offer, and I will support your proposal."

"And if I don't, we will lose the codex," said Andrew truculently.

"Then so be it," said Elijah, his tone soft and gentle. "Nothing is worth sacrificing one of our fundamental principles—not even the Word of Janus."

The air was taut with the strain of wills between the Prophet and the Guardian. Sean watched as Andrew looked over at Leyland, who briefly nodded his head.

"We'll do it your way," said Andrew. "I'll follow your principles."

"It is not my way, and the principles are not mine," offered Elijah. "They belong to Janus, and we are all citizens of the island. No one, not even a Guardian, is more important than any other member of the Janus global community, whether here or throughout the world."

Chapter Twenty-One

The mood in the Community Center was tense. The air was thick with a distinct mixture of disappointment and bewilderment that had settled over the islanders as soon as they'd learned of the Guardians' actions.

Sean was standing at the front, along with Elijah and Andrew. Leyland and Diane were seated together in the front row. Andrew had once again defended the Guardians' activities regarding the decree by declaring they were necessary given the realities that existed beyond Janus.

"We function in a harsh and unforgiving environment where the order is a ruthless enemy. The Guardians always follow the Janus principles but, in this case, we had to accept that we were operating under real world conditions.

"I don't believe we technically went against what was decided in this hall," he had said. "But it is true that we did not directly follow the mandate we were given. However, we know where the codex is located and have a team ready to recover it.

"And while there has been no direct contact with the order I apologize, on behalf of the Guardians, if we strayed slightly outside your instructions. But, I believe the results of our actions justify what has been accomplished."

Andrew had paused, and then in a strong voice declared, "Now that I have explained our actions and expressed my regret, I think we should move to the primary reason for this meeting, and that is to receive your approval for mounting a mission to recover the Word of Janus."

Although Sean believed Andrew's explanation had been half-hearted, Elijah was ready to accept the public act of contrition and asked the islanders to consider retrieving the codex. However, the crowd was not so quick to forgive the Guardian. Several people stood and chastised Andrew for his actions. The most vocal was Pedro Fernandez, the captain of a fishing boat.

"I don't care that you're close to recovering the parchments, the Guardians broke what we all consider as sacrosanct," he said. "You're claiming that this positive outcome excuses your actions. That isn't the Janus way."

The small, wiry man with a gray handlebar moustache, a craggy face, and coal black eyes had been an islander for close to forty years, Strong in both body and opinions, he looked around the Community Center for support. A number of people nodded their heads and voiced agreement.

"We're not really here to criticize the Guardians," offered Elijah. "The question before us is whether we want Andrew's recovery team to raid the Zaragoza facility and bring our parchments home."

"I disagree," said Pedro. "I realize a large part of our creed is forgiveness and understanding. But what the Guardians, led by Andrew, did was to knowingly go against our explicit instructions. How can that be condoned?

"I believe we are looking at two things here—first, the actions of the Guardians and, second, whether we retrieve the codex. We pride ourselves on the ability to compromise. Perhaps the concession we should be looking at is forgiving Andrew but also replacing him as head of the Guardians. After that, we can debate the merits of going after the Word of Janus."

Sean was surprised to hear rumblings of agreement coursing through the crowd. He looked at Andrew, whose clenched fists, pale visage, and straight ahead stare demonstrated his shock at the proposal. Glancing over to Elijah, Sean waited to hear how the Prophet would respond. Instead, Elijah walked over to where Sean was standing and whispered, "This is taking a turn I never anticipated. They're listening to Pedro and not to me. Perhaps you should say something."

Sean had half-expected this would be Elijah's reaction. Ever since being handed the *hope of Janus*, he had noticed that the Prophet had begun asking his advice on many matters concerning the island's governance. More and more, it seemed, he was relying on Sean's counsel.

As Elijah retreated to where he'd been standing, Sean raised his hands for silence. It took a couple of minutes, but gradually an expectant quiet came over the center.

"There is no argument that the Guardians broke one of our most sacred decrees," began Sean. "But in this instance, forgiveness and compromise don't belong together and must not guide us. Our forgiveness should never come with a caveat. How can we absolve Andrew and then replace him? I don't believe the punishment fits the act.

"Our principles are forgiveness, understanding, tolerance, equality, and peace. Compromise results through understanding and tolerance. Forgiveness is an act in which we let go of the angst toward another person."

"And that's exactly what I'm proposing," argued Pedro. "We will forgive the betrayal of our instructions. But there has to be some form of penalty for what's happened. Our directions were explicit: Do not confront the Praetorian Order. The compromise is that we are giving Andrew something, and he must now give us something in return. And that is leadership of the Guardians. We are not asking him to leave, merely to turn the position over to someone else."

Once again, the crowd's agreement with Pedro's position resonated throughout the hall as various islanders stood to voice their support. It wasn't so much anger as disappointment that Andrew had willingly gone against the administrative dictate.

Sean noticed that Andrew was about to speak. Elijah put a hand on the Guardian's arm and suggested, "Silence is your best ally at the moment. Let Sean finish what he started."

The Guardian looked at Sean and said, "I knew my decision would evoke a lot of passion, but I didn't expect this type of response. Unfortunately, none of our islanders live in the real world. They don't know what it's like away from Janus. I made a tough decision on behalf of these people, and I'll stand by it."

So typical of Andrew, thought Sean. The Guardian, having lived in Inverness for so long, had lost sight of the basic truth that, on the island, the collective was more important than the individual. And fundamentally that was what the islanders were responding to, whether they were aware of it or not. It had nothing to do with the Guardians disobeying the administrative decree. Instead, it was all about one person putting himself above the group.

And that, Sean thought, was how he was going to resolve the issue—by appealing to their instincts as a group dedicated to the Janus principles. Pedro and those who supported the captain were not being vindictive. That emotion was no less foreign than anger to the islanders. Instead, they were wrestling with the level of forgiveness that should be accorded Andrew. However, Sean did not believe forgiveness was an emotional act that could be given in partial amounts. Forgiveness was an absolute. You can forgive while not forgetting. But that should not detract from the act of amnesty.

The hall was growing noisier again, and Sean realized the crowd was becoming restless. Now was the time to bring forward whatever final arguments he had for Andrew's defense.

"I'm not disagreeing with Pedro when it comes to the fact Andrew was wrong," he began. "But there should be no half measures with forgiveness. I am asking that you pardon Andrew's actions and, in doing so, allow him to retain his position as lead Guardian.

"This was an extraordinary occurrence that has no comparison throughout our history. The document that forms the essence of our existence on this island was stolen by an incredibly powerful organization. And let us remember that the Guardians have not confronted the order. That will only come if we agree to it during this meeting."

Sean continued by describing his belief that, as one of Janus's core principles, forgiveness meant the islanders either forgave Andrew in full or they did not. It was straightforward, and compromise should play no part in the decision.

"Seeking the middle ground is the result of our principles," he argued. "It is not one of them. We do not compromise when it comes to understanding, tolerance, equality, or living in peace. These are absolutes. The same should be applied to forgiveness."

Finishing his talk, Sean looked to Elijah for opening the floor for debate. The Prophet moved over to where Sean was standing. "This is your meeting," he said. "You should continue to chair it."

In a surprise to Sean, the debate was far more one-sided than he expected. The vast majority of islanders agreed that absolving Andrew should not carry with it the penalty of losing his position. There was a vocal minority, led by Pedro, who felt some form of sanction should be imposed. The debate was intense but always fair and never mean-spirited. However, it soon became apparent that Pedro's small group was not going to persuade the majority to change its collective position.

And in what Sean viewed as one of the wonderful aspects of life on Janus, there was agreement when the vote was called. Pedro asked his supporters to make the vote unanimous—which was the Janus way—and fully absolve Andrew for ignoring the administrative decree.

The vote carried with no dissenters.

Chapter Twenty-Two

"So we have an understanding," Pedro said with a smile as he walked up to Sean. "It wasn't what I envisioned, but we arrived at a unanimous decision, and that's how it should be."

Andrew ambled over, and in another display of the islanders' commitment to a peaceful society, the two men shook hands, with Andrew saying, "That was quite the debate. I thought Sean did a good job of defending my interests. My commitment is always to do what's best for Janus."

"I realize that," countered Pedro. "I was doing the same thing. We just looked at the same objective differently. But the vote is over. And we're all in agreement."

For Sean, it spoke to the ongoing strength of the Janus society that a debate, which could have been divisive, had arrived at a united conclusion. His thoughts gravitated to the Spirit, and once again, he wondered at its belief that humans could live in peace if shown the way through the example of Janus's multicultural and multiracial society. The *hope of Janus* was a tangible link to the Spirit's belief that global peace was possible.

The Spirit might have faith in humans, but does humanity have faith in itself? wondered Sean.

The Hope of Janus

His reflections were interrupted when Elijah came over and said it was time the session's next part got underway.

"This will be a meeting unlike any other," observed the Prophet. "We have never considered being an active aggressor in a situation. I'm not really sure how to handle the debate. You did a good job with the last session. I'd like you to chair this one. Think about it for a couple of minutes and let me know."

Sean knew what Elijah was doing. Giving him the ring along with the Prophet's commitment to discuss with the Spirit that it participate in the campaign for peace, and now having Sean shepherd another groundbreaking meeting were all part of Elijah's plan to have him become so intertwined in the Janus culture that Sean couldn't envision leaving. And having already committed to staying on the island with Diane, Sean felt remarkably comfortable with the prospect of becoming more involved in the island's day-to-day life.

But all that was for another time. Right now he had a session to chair, and he wanted Diane to share it with him.

She was talking with Andrew and Leyland. Sean went over and, after apologizing for taking her away, guided Diane to a position at the front of the hall. After explaining what he intended, Sean asked if Diane would work with him. She accepted with an alacrity that pleased and relieved him. This was going to be a difficult session, and he hadn't wanted to chair it alone.

He looked for Elijah, who was talking to a farmer and his family seated in the third row. Raising his hand to get the Prophet's attention, Sean nodded his head a couple of times. Elijah excused himself, and walked over to where Sean was standing. The moment the Prophet was in earshot, Sean explained that he and Diane would be chairing the meeting.

The Prophet smiled and said, "I hoped that's what the two of you would decide."

Sean moved to the front and, once again, held up his hands. Conversations were ended, people found their seats, and everyone settled in. Opinions were deeply divided about whether to confront the order. Sean was prepared for a contentious and lengthy debate. But he knew that, as always, whatever decision was reached would be through compromise and understanding. It was the way of Janus.

Andrew had joined Sean and Diane. The Guardian would deliver the mission's briefing. Leyland had returned to his front-row seat. The Prophet was at the back of the hall.

Turning to Diane, Sean said, "Here we go."

Chapter Twenty-Three

Hidden by night clouds for much of the debate, the full June moon finally made an appearance. Sean hoped it was an omen the islanders would come out from behind the wall that had developed between the two sides—one arguing for going after the Word of Janus, regardless of the consequences, the other just as strongly believing the mission should be canceled because of a likely confrontation with the order.

Andrew had delivered a detailed account of all that had transpired since the codex's theft. He talked about how intercepted e-mails and telephone calls had led to the discovery of the facility in Zaragoza. The Guardian then detailed the plans for retrieving the parchments. As he completed the presentation, a raft of hands dominated the room.

The possible use of Tasers soon became the flashpoint for both sides. Those supporting their deployment believed that, if Tasers had to be utilized, the fact they would stun and not permanently injure the target justified their use. Countering that argument were those who contended the risk of violence against a fellow human being could not be rationalized within the context of Janus's overriding commitment to peace.

As is usual with group dynamics, each of the opposing sides was led by an individual who managed to take the sometimes confused but similar views of their faction and distill them into a cogent and powerful argument.

A farmer, Carol Ackerman, who traced her history back to the island's first settlers, was a vocal supporter of going after the codex. Tall and thin, with flowing, auburn hair and lively, dancing hazel eyes, she was a fiery and ardent defender of the island's past.

"My family was part of the group that brought the Word of Janus ashore," Carol said. "It is not only part of our history, it has guided how we've developed as a people. Our society and culture are built on the bedrock of those nineteen pieces of parchment. The codex belongs to every islander now and into the future. We not only should, but also need to get it back. It must not be allowed to stay with the order. Hopefully, the Tasers won't have to be used. But if that's the price for getting the codex back, then we should be prepared to use them. After all, they merely stun, and no great harm can come from that."

Equally passionate and using the same argument, only with a different perspective, was Daiki Ito, a crew member on one of the fishing boats. Short and balding, with a weightlifter's build, Daiki had a visage burned a deep bronze by the relentless sea winds. He was a gentle man, whose hands were as adept at skillfully wrestling fishing nets onto a boat deck as they were at carefully cradling his newborn son.

"The word of Janus contains the ideals of our society," maintained Daiki. "It stresses that we live in harmony and that no provocation is worth losing that commitment. Peace defines us as a culture. Even the remote possibility of using weapons is counter to our beliefs. We have the English version. What we are missing is the Aramaic and Hebrew copies. The only person who can read Aramaic is Elijah, and he has committed to translating our English account.

"Therefore we will have an Aramaic copy. It may not be the original. But when compared against the possibility of losing our ideal of peace, I believe it is worth the compromise. Let's pull this recovery team out of Zaragoza before something happens that we'll all regret."

The debate centered on the island's battle with its centuries-old innocence. In the past, Janus had never been impacted by what happened beyond its borders. Its society, a mirror of the globe's many races and cultures, was an oasis of serenity without the specter of violence, long-standing feuds, or religious bigotry.

No form of government or religion existed. All decisions that impacted the island's collective were taken after debate in the center and involved all residents. The result was a society at peace with itself and one in which every Islanders' primary priority was to maintain their egalitarian society. The tenets of peace and understanding had been passed from generation to generation for two thousand years, and every islander was committed to ensuring these principles continued into the future.

However, they were now confronted by something beyond their control. This situation with the order and the Word of Janus was new and uncomfortable. The debate between the sides, although representing two divergent views, was not about winning or losing. Rather, it was focused on seeking a compromise that would satisfy both positions.

As the debate continued, Sean thought about the *hope of Janus* and why Elijah had given him the ring. The Prophet had been prescient in knowing that the world, through the order, would intrude on the islanders.

Hope comes in so many guises, and while the true meaning never alters, its application can change like the rays of light through a rotating prism. What we hope for today might change with the coming of a new dawn. But the relentless longing to believe in something that we desire never leaves the human spirit. Sean understood that, with the ring, Elijah was planning on entrusting him with Janus's future and the faith he would shepherd the islanders through life's vagaries while ensuring they retained every one of the principles that had guided their ancestors through the centuries.

It was a daunting responsibility, especially if he decided to work with the Spirit. But all that was in the future. He would have plenty of time to talk with Diane about what should be done with the coming months and years.

Thinking of Diane brought Sean back to the moment's reality. No progress had been made in the time he had mentally drifted away from the meeting. Turning to Diane and Andrew he asked, "Do either of you have any thoughts how this stalemate can be resolved?"

"I have an idea, but I don't think you'll like it," Diane said, looking at Andrew.

"What is it?" responded the Guardian, his voice wary and filled with concern.

"I think we could reach a compromise if the recovery team isn't equipped with Tasers," Diane began. "The major problem Daiki's group has with this mission is the possible use of force. If we take that away, I believe you'll get an agreement to proceed."

Sean was surprised at Andrew's reaction. He had expected him to vehemently oppose Diane's suggestion. Instead, the Guardian didn't say a word but went directly to where Leyland was sitting. Sean watched as Leyland got up and followed Andrew down the right side aisle to the back of the hall, past Elijah, and then through the twin oaken doors taking them outside.

The Prophet looked at Sean and began walking up the center aisle, puzzlement masking his features. Reaching the couple, he asked, "What was that about?"

Diane explained her proposal, and the Prophet's face turned gloomy. "They'll never accept your suggestion," he said. "Andrew is fixated on getting the codex back and doesn't want his squad at a disadvantage. We've already seen that with his disregard for the administrative decree to not confront the order. He won't want his team going into Zaragoza without any weapons."

Sean understood that the Prophet's concern was based on a realistic assessment of Andrew's temperament. He had known the Guardian since Andrew's birth. Who better to judge the man's character?

Sean, though, believed that, in this unique case, Elijah had misjudged the Guardian. This was a situation unlike any other, and therefore Andrew's response would be pragmatically based on his love for Janus and desire to have the codex returned. Ignoring the islanders' original directive may have been misguided, but it was done out of a desire to right what the Guardian believed was an unacceptable wrong.

"I think you'll be surprised," said Sean. "Andrew has already shown a willingness to do what he believes is necessary to retrieve the parchments. Diane's proposal is a compromise everyone can accept. I'm hopeful Andrew will see it that way and agree to have his team go in without weapons."

"Which brings us to the larger question of whether we should confront the order," said Elijah. "I don't believe possibly sacrificing our commitment to peace is worth the risk."

"I realize the ideals contained in the Word of Janus are what's important and not necessarily the codex itself," responded Sean. "But it is the one remaining artifact we have that links us with the original settlers. It is our tangible history and should be part of the island's heritage."

"And for that you're willing to jeopardize our overriding principle?" questioned the Prophet.

For Sean, all aspects of the center and the ongoing debate among the islanders had faded into the background. The hall was an ever-flowing ebb of noise and conversation. But for the time being, everything had crystalized around his discussion with Elijah.

Nothing intruded as he sought to justify his position. He realized with a sudden surge of self-awareness that his belief in the islanders and their way of life had become vitally important to him. Through the *hope of Janus*, he now identified with them. That fact was influencing his thoughts as Sean grappled with what to do about recovering the codex.

"We aren't sacrificing the Janus dedication to peace," argued Sean. "The compromise we are offering is to recover the codex without the use of weapons. Our instructions to Andrew must be to employ stealth rather than brute force when the team goes into Zaragoza."

"And if he doesn't agree," countered the Prophet.

"Then we leave the codex with the order."

"I know Andrew will truly believe this puts his team at a critical disadvantage," added Diane. "But it has to be this way. Nothing is worth sacrificing our principles. We can live without the codex, but what happens to us as a society if we allow our basic beliefs to erode?"

"We lose the essence that is Janus," said Sean. "That can't be allowed to happen."

"What about the consequences?" Elijah asked. "The order obviously wants the Word of Janus. Suppose Dante decides to come after it again. It may end in a confrontation. If we don't want to risk having our principles being jeopardized, we should leave the codex where it is and not risk a conflict."

"That's a hypothetical situation," countered Sean. "We have to deal with what we know. The Guardians have an opportunity to recover the codex. If the retrieval team is successful, we can then decide our next move, both in terms of further restoration and how to deal with the order."

So engrossed were Diane, Sean, and Elijah in their conversation that they hadn't noticed the arrival of Andrew until he spoke. "What do you mean no weapons?" said the Guardian, surprising the group, his voice strained. "There is no intention of having a confrontation, but if we meet resistance, it will have to be countered. Going in unarmed would be foolish. Doesn't anyone realize that we could be risking the lives of every Guardian involved with this mission? The Janus principles are wonderful, but they won't stop a bullet."

"We understand your view," answered Diane. "But you're forgetting that you came here asking for authorization to recover the codex. I believe that is what everyone wants. But you won't receive an approval if you stay with your stance on the use of Tasers."

"Then I'll pull the team out of Zaragoza."

Sean looked at Diane, who gave him a tight grimace. It was obvious she understood the irony as much as he did. Andrew had gone against the islanders by disregarding the administrative decree and sent in a team to recover the codex. Now he was threatening to again ignore the islanders' instructions, this time by canceling the mission.

"You came close to losing your position as senior Guardian by snubbing the islanders once," said Sean. "I don't believe you can get away with it a second time. You put yourself in this position. If we vote to proceed with the operation without the use of weapons, including Tasers, then that's how the mission must go forward."

"Is that you talking?" challenged the Guardian, his taut voice reflecting the tension that had developed between him and Sean. "Or are you speaking for everyone in this hall? Let's put it to a vote and get this thing settled."

Sean gazed around the hall. It was obvious by the way people were milling about and congregating in small groups that they were waiting for a vote to be called.

"Why don't I speak first and then you can follow with your rationale for arming the squad," Sean suggested to Andrew.

"Fine with me," answered the Guardian.

Once again Sean thrust his arms in the air. It didn't take long for the room to become reasonably quiet. He suggested everyone take their seats in preparation for a vote. Elijah and Diane sat on either side of Leyland in the front row, leaving the hall's podium to Sean and Andrew.

The undercurrent of expectation permeated the room, and Sean could feel the islanders' intensity. This was a decision that would impact the Janus philosophy well into the future. Would they endorse the possibility of violence carried out in their name? And if they did, how would that impact the Janus principles? Was recovering the codex worth the possibility of sacrificing tenets that had stood for two thousand years?

Sean hoped he knew the answer. He desperately wanted Andrew's proposal to be rejected and hoped the islanders felt the same way. As someone from the outside world, Sean understood that violence only brings more hostility. And Sean wanted to protect the islanders from endorsing a move he believed they would soon come to regret.

At the same time, the majority of islanders wanted the codex recovered. He considered the proposal he was about to put forward a sound compromise. Sean scanned the crowd and took a couple of deep breaths to calm himself.

"There are two positions that have been put forward this evening," he began. "Carol's group believes we should stop at nothing to recover the codex. And that includes the use of Tasers. Those associated with Daiki are lobbying for us to leave the codex where it is and pull the recovery team out of Zaragoza.

"The compromise Diane and I are putting before you is that, without the use of Tasers, we go into the facility where the parchments are being kept. The recovery squad will be instructed to come back with a plan that relies on detailed preparation so that the codex can be recovered without the use of weapons.

"As you know, Andrew believes differently. Once he has spoken, there will be a vote to decide the course we'll follow."

An eerie silence, similar to the lull before a storm, overtook the room. For a moment, Sean was unnerved. He had expected the hall to erupt into a wall of noise as spirited discussions took place following his proposal. Instead, the islanders seemed to have taken what he said and were either unimpressed or waiting for Andrew to speak before reviewing the options. Sean fervently hoped it was the latter.

Stepping forward a couple of paces, Andrew opened his arms wide and began with, "Friends, we can't look at this as a smash-and-grab operation. We are dealing with the Praetorian Order. The defenses at Zaragoza will be strong and unyielding.

I believe that we must be prepared for any eventuality, and the best way to ensure the mission's success will be having a Taser in case it's needed."

Sean quickly noted the switch in Andrew's phrasing. Instead of talking about numerous Tasers, he was now proposing the use of just one. Sean thought he knew the compromise the Guardian was about to propose and rapidly began thinking of a way to counter it.

Andrew continued. "The squad is comprised of four Guardians and a trainer who is a former SAS officer. Originally, every team member was to be equipped with Tasers. I realize this is an unsatisfactory proposal for some of you. Instead, we will have only the trainer carry the Taser. The Guardians will be unarmed. If the squad does encounter any problems, the only one deploying the stun gun would not be directly associated with Janus. The SAS trainer is merely under contract."

Although Sean had anticipated this would be Andrew's position, he was still shocked. He found it hard to believe the Guardian would use this type of nuance to gain the islanders' approval.

Andrew was still speaking. "There has been a lot of talk about our principles and values. One aspect, however, hasn't been discussed. Our team is not going into Zaragoza with the intent of using violence to acquire the codex. Our team leader would only deploy the Taser if the need arises. And we are not talking about guns that would inflict lasting damage. The Taser would be used to stun, not injure. The effect will wear off in a few hours.

"The compromise I am seeking is not about conducting the mission without a Taser. That would be foolhardy and could lead to the capture, wounding, or even death of a team member. Instead, my proposal is that we carry out the recovery operation using someone who is not a Guardian to be armed.

The Hope of Janus

And the Taser would only be deployed in a defensive situation. We would not initiate its use."

Andrew turned and smiled at Sean. "Would you like to say something?" he asked.

There was no malice in the grin or contained with the words. It was a though they were playing a friendly game of chess, and the Guardian had just placed Sean's king in check. Sean knew he would have to be extremely creative to stay away from being figuratively checkmated by Andrew's surprise concession. But this wasn't a game. This was a struggle that reached into the island's soul. Janus's legacy was at stake.

Sean focused on the crowd, hoping his words carried the conviction he felt. "Since when have we become a society that uses a mercenary to escape guilt if anything goes wrong? The Taser may only stun, but it is still an act of violence against a fellow human being. No justification can be found for that. The Taser would be used by an individual directly associated with Janus. And there is no rationale to the contrary that can allow us to escape this fact.

"We are a culture that renounces violence of any kind. Attempting to recover the codex with even one Taser is armed aggression. It is not only the act of violence we must guard against but also the intent to use it as a method of achieving what we want."

As Sean concluded his plea, a murmur ran through the crowd like the sound of a fast-moving river. It was impossible for Sean to determine whether it meant his words had met with acceptance or resistance. As he scanned the room, it was easy to see that the islanders were still divided. People had left their seats, and intense conversations were taking place. There was an air of concern throughout the hall. Looking out through the windows positioned along the top of the center's walls, he could see the moon was riding high in the star-dotted sky. It was getting late. Sean believed the time had come to call for a decision.

Turning to Andrew, he asked if the Guardian was ready for a vote to be called. To Sean's surprise, Andrew shook his head. "I have one more point to make," he said. "Would you mind getting everyone settled?"

Sean could tell his surprise was amusing the Guardian. Andrew was smiling and whispered, "What I'm about to say will swing everyone in my favor."

Not sure how to respond, Sean said nothing as he brought the crowd back to their chairs, and the hall settled into a semblance of quiet.

Andrew thrust his arms forward, figuratively reaching out to the islanders. "This is not the first time Tasers would be used in relation to the codex," he said. "When the parchments were stolen by the order from the lab in Inverness, our guards were equipped with the weapons. Sean, Diane, and Elijah visited the lab where the codex was being restored. None of them said anything against their use at the time. My question is this: If having Tasers was fine for safeguarding the parchments, why can't one of them be used in our recovery operation?"

Chapter Twenty-Four

The shock Sean experienced tore through his body and left him sweating. His shirt felt damp, and running a hand across his forehead, he could feel the building moisture. He had forgotten about the guards having Tasers. Looking over at Diane and Elijah, he could tell by their startled looks that Andrew's words had also caught them unprepared. It was obvious neither of them had remembered the guards were armed.

At first, the hall echoed with stunned silence. Then came the sound, reminding Sean of a freight train rumbling over a trestle. It was loud and discordant.

Sensing the possibility of reaching a consensus had become far more difficult with Andrew's revelation, Sean motioned for Elijah to join him. Elijah got up and slowly walked to the front. The sight of him settled the crowd. This was their Prophet, whose relationship with the Spirit was unlike any other. He was someone most of them had known all their lives. Elijah was their guide through the island's cycles of triumphs and tragedies and would help lead them through these rough seas.

Sean watched as the small man, with a look of sadness etched across his features, stood before the islanders. He said nothing for several moments, and the hall gradually fell silent.

"We did have guards with Tasers," Elijah began. "It was a mistake then, and it would be wrong to have them on a recovery mission for the codex. When I was informed Tasers would be used in Inverness, I did not countermand the order. I now realize it went against everything we believe and have always practiced on Janus.

"But because it happened does not make it right. We have a chance to ensure that another error is not committed. It was a personal lapse in judgment. Let's not have my mistake change what every islander is committed to as a way of life. Peace and understanding are the cornerstones of who we are as a people. We must not lose that fact.

"When the vote is taken, it should only be considered on the merits of the question before us. Our past should be used to inspire our decision making, not hinder it."

With that, Elijah moved to stand beside Sean. The hall erupted in a passionate debate between groups of islanders who had become trapped in a collective mind-set of how the use of Tasers affected their centuries-long commitment to non-violence. The discussions ebbed and flowed across the hall with no resolution on the horizon.

Sean sensed the evening's debate was becoming increasingly complicated. What had started as Andrew seeking permission for the Guardians to mount a campaign designed to recover the codex had devolved into an emotional minefield.

It needed to be refocused on the question of whether the Guardians should attempt a recovery of the parchments and, if they did, whether weapons would be used. It was no longer important that Andrew had gone against the administrative decree or that guards had been armed with Tasers while protecting the codex when it was in Inverness.

With those thoughts in mind, Sean decided it was time to take complete control of the session. He called out loudly, asking that everyone return to their chairs. It took a couple of minutes, but soon everyone was seated, and an expectant quiet had seized the hall.

"We have a simple issue," he began. "Do we want to retrieve the codex? And do we want the squad to be armed? That's what you are being asked to decide, so let's get on with it."

From a seat on the left side of the hall, a farmer from the valley began to clap. Soon others joined in. The angst that had pervaded the hall after the issue about armed guards protecting the codex was lost in the relief that everyone now had a clear mandate. It was getting late, and people wanted the question resolved.

Sean began by asking who was in favor of leaving the codex with the order. Not one hand was raised. When he called for a show of hands on recovering the word of Janus, but without weapons, the vote was virtually unanimous. Only three people did not support the motion—Carol, Andrew, and Leyland.

Given the island's commitment to egalitarianism, in which cooperation was the basis for unanimity, while Carol, Andrew, and Leyland represented just three votes out of 1,900, they had the right to discuss some form of compromise. The practice's strength rested in the long-held belief that having a policy which everyone felt they'd contributed to was far better than a minority feeling its voice hadn't been heard.

The question was, in the face of such an overwhelming vote against their position, would the three want to negotiate? A sense of weariness pervaded the hall, and Sean knew that, while the islanders viewed this principle as sacred, everyone was hoping the three outliers would accept the vote.

Focusing on Andrew, Sean asked if the Guardians, along with Carol, would unite behind the decision. The senior Guardian looked at Leyland and Carol. Both nodded their heads.

And suddenly a long night of discussion had come to a unified closing. Sean sensed a collective sigh of relief travel through the hall.

But Andrew held up his hand, and Sean tensed. "I have something to say," the Guardian began. "We've made it unanimous, and I'll abide by the vote. I warn you, though, that this is a dangerous mission. Sending in an unarmed team puts every individual's life at risk. Having said that, I believe we have no choice but to carry out the raid. We have to get the codex back where it rightfully belongs. The group is well trained, and I have full confidence in the mission's success. When we get back to Inverness, I'll instruct the squad to proceed with the operation."

The hall again broke out in applause, the islanders having bonded behind one vision. They had tremendous faith in the Guardians' ability to recover the codex. And not knowing the world, none of them could envision any form of failure. As everyone filed out of the hall and began walking toward their homes, Andrew came over to Sean.

"You chaired a good meeting," said the usually reticent Guardian, surprising Sean at the praise. "While I don't necessarily agree with the full result, we are united in getting the Word of Janus back and that's what is important."

With that, the men shook hands, and Andrew slipped out a side door with Leyland at his side.

*****

"It was a difficult session," said Sean as he walked along the Ring Road with Diane and Elijah. They were going home, and although Sean felt weary, there was a satisfaction in knowing the islanders had come through a challenging session with their collective commitment to peace intact. He had a new-found respect for the islanders' resilience in the face of an issue that had tested their values.

"Although we are dedicated to living apart from the world, this issue with the order has brought the globe to our shores," noted Elijah. "It has been an uncomfortable reality, and if this debate has shown me anything it is that we cannot take our principles for granted. Andrew may have meant well, but he demonstrated how we must always strive to preserve and continually reinforce our commitment to understanding and peace."

It was a sobering realization, and the three of them walked in virtual silence as they passed several houses until arriving at the Prophet's home. As they were saying good night, Diane asked, "When does *Journey* leave for Inverness?"

"Andrew is taking her out midmorning," responded Elijah. "He's anxious to return and get the recovery mission under way. I'm planning on going to Inverness. This is one of the most critical undertakings we've ever attempted, and I want to be there for the entire operation. It would be a good idea if the two of you came along."

"What would we do?" questioned Sean, puzzled by the suggestion.

"It will give you both an excellent opportunity to learn the Guardians' inner workings. None of us know what the coming years will hold, but if things work out the way I hope, you'll be playing an important role in the island's future. And understanding the Guardians' function is a vital part of that process."

"How long do you expect we'll be gone?" wondered Diane. "We have the farm and harvesting to consider."

"From the way Andrew was talking, I expect we'll be away from four to six weeks. *Journey* is being placed in dry dock for her annual overhaul. In addition, work is needed on one of the engines, which is why the ship will be out of commission for such a lengthy time."

"But that should still get us back with about a week to spare for bringing in the crops."

"Well what do you think?" Sean asked Diane. "A trip to Inverness sounds like fun. Can we spare the time away from the farm?"

Diane hesitated for just a moment before saying, "Since we'll be back before the harvesting, I think we should go. I'll ask the neighbor's kids to take care of the animals. They always do a great job, so I have no worries in that regard. And it would be useful to learn more about the Guardians."

"Great," said Sean, the night's weariness lifted from his shoulders at the thought of exploring Inverness and northern Scotland with Diane. "We can treat it as a working vacation."

"Excellent," said Elijah. "Let's meet on board *Journey*. I'll get there early and let Andrew know you'll be coming along."

Chapter Twenty-Five

Sean looked over the conference room table at Ray Shepherd. The affable former British commando had flown into Inverness from Zaragoza to brief the Guardians on how his team was going to recover the codex.

Dressed in a form-fitting black T-shirt, jeans, and soft-soled shoes, Shepherd had a casual yet professional air that Sean could sense immediately instilled confidence with everyone in the room. He stood well over six feet and was lightly but firmly muscled. Pale blond hair cut drill-sergeant short sat atop a tanned, angular face with pronounced cheekbones and a firm jawline. With piercing, sea-blue eyes set on either side of a straight nose that ended in a gentle hook, Shepherd could have been sent from central casting.

He was a well-trained soldier who had stayed in excellent shape and now plied his craft for causes he believed made the world a better place. During the last few years, most of his assignments had involved operating undercover with the British security forces, MI5 and MI6, working to thwart terrorist attacks throughout Britain. However, he was not a wide-eyed idealist. He demanded and received large amounts of money for his services. Shepherd was good at what he did and expected to be compensated in direct proportion for the risks he took. That meant anywhere from $100,000 to $250,000 per mission.

Sean had seen the report from the three families of the Janus diaspora who had recommended him. Shepherd came with a reputation as a highly principled person, whose greatest asset was his commitment to carrying out the assignment while staying within the agreed parameters. "He is not a cowboy and relies on skill, technique, and brains, rather than brute force to get the job done," read one line in the dossier. Noted another, "Shepherd is expensive, but he gets the required results, and his word can be taken at face value."

There was another point that played in his favor. Sean read that, two years previously, the former soldier had spent seven months in Spain on an assignment. Although the details were classified, it was noted that he had become proficient in Spanish.

It was an impressive résumé, and Sean's only concern was how Shepherd would react to the admittedly idealistic plan to recover the codex without the use of weapons. Joining them at the table were Bella, Olga, Andrew, Leyland, and Elijah, who was sitting beside Diane.

The session had started on a tense note when Shepherd declared, "Andrew told me about the mandate of going in without firearms, not even a Taser. That doesn't make sense to me, and it's a foolish restriction to put on a team about to undertake a dangerous assignment. I won't pretend to understand why you're asking us to make the commitment, but we'll be going into a site that has armed guards. If things go sideways, we could be captured at best, or killed in the worst-case scenario."

"The reason we contracted for your services," answered Bella, "is to ensure the operation is completed without anything going wrong. According to our information, you have a reputation for getting assignments done effectively and efficiently. That's what we're looking for here. Are you telling us the assignment can't be carried out unless everyone is armed?"

Shepherd ran a right hand over his chin. "Every op is different, with one common element. You go in trusting there won't be a confrontation but well prepared with sufficient firepower if there is one. From what we've determined about this job, the risk of a skirmish is low, but it still exists.

"When I was first contacted by Andrew, we agreed on a fee of $150,000. That was based on my belief that I'd be running the show without any interference. And up until now, you've stuck to that understanding. But I never agreed to go in without weapons.

"You've given me four good people, and I've trained them well. They're bright, athletic, and understand how to follow orders. I don't know what you're paying them, but it isn't enough if we are unarmed. Then again, what you pay them is your business. In my case, the fee will be $50,000 more if you want me to stay."

Having learned as part of his review that Bella was the Guardians' financial director Sean looked over to see her reaction. She was staring at Shepherd, eyes rapidly blinking, but otherwise showing no outward appearance how she viewed the demand or what impact it would have on the Guardians' financial operations. Looking quickly around the room, Sean saw that everyone had their eyes fixed on Bella, expecting her to say something about the newly disclosed addition to Shepherd's fee.

When she didn't say anything, Andrew asked, "How do we know you'll keep your end of the bargain?"

Sean thought Shepherd would be offended. Instead, the former soldier leaned back in his chair and casually said, "I know you've checked me out and have a report on my activities over the last few years. If I say something is going to be done a certain way, then that's how the mission is carried out. Pay me the money, and no one will be armed.

"This plan was put together with a focus on using the skills and techniques I taught your team and was designed to recover your codex without any confrontation with the guards. It's what I came here to show you, but that should be done after you've discussed my new fee. I'll wait outside while you take a few minutes to consider if you'll meet my price."

Before anyone could respond, Shepherd uncoiled from his chair and walked out into the hallway, closing the door behind him.

The room's momentary silence was broken when Bella said, "This is blackmail. That puts Shepherd's cost at $200,000. Once you factor in all the other expenses, like hotel rooms, the leased private plane, rental cars, and whatever else he needs, the bill for this exercise is going to come in at close to a million dollars. We should let him walk away and save ourselves the extra money. Our team in Zaragoza is well trained. They can do this job without him."

"That isn't the issue," responded Diane. "The Guardians have a mandate from the islanders to recover the codex. The question is do we have the funds to cover this operation? I agree it's a lot of money, but we all know the codex's value to Janus. I don't believe we can put a price on its recovery."

"That's not what I'm doing," countered Bella. "I'm just saying that Shepherd has brought the team to where I believe it can operate without him. We don't need to spend the money for him to babysit the squad."

For the next ten minutes, the conversation revolved around whether Shepherd should be cut loose from the project. It soon became apparent that it wasn't a question of whether the Guardians could afford the extra cost. The monthly tithe collected from the diaspora's members, along with the yearly large grants from its many wealthy adherents, ensured the Guardians' operation was well funded. Andrew led the move for paying Shepherd and going ahead with the briefing and the retrieval.

"It doesn't make sense for us to let him go," argued the senior Guardian. "We want the codex back, and none of us has any understanding of the mission's complexity or how dangerous it could be. To suggest our team could handle the recovery without him is to put the operation at too great a risk. And it's not blackmail. We were the ones that changed the rules of engagement. He has every right to ask for more money."

Bella remained adamant in her belief that Shepherd wasn't needed for the project's final phase.

Not surprisingly, it was Leyland who ultimately persuaded Bella by adding a much-needed perspective to the situation. "The reason we exist is because of Janus and our diaspora," he began, talking directly to her. "We have a mandate from the islanders to recover the codex. That is the mission with which we have been entrusted. Nothing else matters. We are expected to spend the money wisely on their behalf."

"That's because they have no concept of money," retorted Bella.

"Exactly my point," offered Leyland. "The only reason you're taking the position that Shepherd should be pulled from the project is because of the extra fee he has requested. It has nothing to do with his capability or his expertise. If he hadn't asked for the additional funds, you would support his retaining leadership of the recovery team.

"This isn't about money. It is about commitment and the fact, as Andrew has noted, that we changed the rules of the game. One of the major aspects of being part of Janus is that we honor our obligations. Throughout our history, when islanders say they are going to do something, we all know it will be done.

"This is what we must do with Shepherd. We made an agreement with him, and that guarantee must be honored. Not only that, but how will the team feel if we choose to have them operate without the person who has trained and prepared them for this mission? And we took the decision because of money. The Janus way must be respected. In this case, it applies to Shepherd, along with the team."

"When you put it that way," Bella said, "it starts to make a lot of sense. We can't lose sight that this exercise's primary goal is to recover the codex."

Andrew, seizing the moment, asked if everyone was in favor of retaining Shepherd as the group's leader. Each person nodded their agreement.

"Excellent," said Andrew. "Let's bring Shepherd back in the room and get his briefing underway. The quicker we get him back to Zaragoza, the faster we can begin liberating our codex."

Olga walked to the door, opened it, and invited Shepherd into the room. The soldier entered and took his seat. Without wasting any words, Andrew told the soldier his terms for continuing with the mission were acceptable and that the operation should proceed as planned.

The former commando nodded his head and gave Andrew a brief salute. Shepherd then thanked everyone for their confidence, concluding with, "I'm glad we've come to an arrangement. So, let's get on with the briefing."

Chapter Twenty-Six

Shepherd had plugged the thumb drive into the conference room's presentation computer. He was now standing at the front of the room off to the left side of a large whiteboard. A remote control was in his right hand and a laser pointer in his left.

"As some of you know," he began, "Olga and her technology department have been invaluable in working with me to create the plan I'm about to present. I'll be calling on her later to detail the aspects of her group's participation."

Sean hadn't been aware of Olga's involvement but wondered if that's why she had been silent during the discussion about Shepherd's fee.

Using the remote, the former soldier brought up the first photo. It was a group shot of three men and two women. Everyone was clad in black and wearing balaclavas that covered most of their faces. Only Shepherd was recognizable to Sean.

"Our team is comprised of four Guardians and me. We have been in Zaragoza for two weeks and, during that time, have reconnoitered the site on a continuing twenty-four-hour basis. Our plan is to launch the mission in three days."

The remote clicked, and a second photo appeared.

"The target is located within a six-foot-high stone-and-brick-wall compound. There are three guard-patrolled entrances and fifteen buildings. Four are embassies; three are top security NATO complexes; two house European government departments; and the rest range from office towers to two- and three-story, upscale office blocks. The wall was built during the sixteenth century to delineate the boundaries of a land baron's property. The city has preserved it, and the wall is now used as a perimeter for security purposes."

Bringing up the third photo, he said, "As you can see, our target looks like a prestigious low-rise structure, which helps it blend in with the area buildings. It's not a museum in the true sense of the word. Rather, the facility is used for the storage and restoration of precious Vatican pieces of art."

The next slide showed one of the compound entrances, taken with a telephoto lens. The focus was on an automated sensor pad.

"This is an electronically gated complex. Unrestricted access through the gates is only by employee and embassy staff key cards. The armed guards are on duty to check the credentials of anyone else seeking to enter the grounds. A visitor must give the telephone number of the person they came to see, and that is checked out by the guard. Only once the visitor has been confirmed can they move through the gates and onto the compound.

"Although the sensor pads are electronic, they are controlled through part of the overall computer network. Disable the program, and the electricity cuts out. If that happens, the gates can only be operated manually until the system is back online.

"There are advantages and disadvantages to the compound," continued Shepherd, speaking briskly and with authority as he indicated a fifth photograph, taken at night. "Because of its location, there aren't any tourists or office workers wandering around the complex after dark. And obviously, there are no visitors. The area is generally deserted, except for the occasional embassy personnel or company staff cars. Leaving the compound isn't a problem. For cars, there is an automatic electronic eye, and if someone is walking, there is an interior sensor pad. Both methods slide the gate open.

"For these reasons, the perimeter entrances have no guards on duty from 10:00 p.m. to 6:00 a.m. That's the positive.

"Now, we have a couple of negatives. First, all the area buildings are linked through an off-site security firm, Cerrajeros Zaragoza. Among the services it provides is a patrol car with two armed personnel that take over once the entrance guards go off duty.

"They patrol the perimeter and the remainder of the compound in a thirty-minute rotation through to 6:00 a.m. The second is that the place is lousy with infrared cameras, which are constantly monitored. If a person scaled the wall or a vehicle crashed through the gate, it would immediately trigger an alarm at the Cerrajeros control desk, and the patrol car would be dispatched via an onboard computer to check out the intrusion. We tested the response time at night by pretending two members of our team were drunken English tourists pounding on the gate to be let in. It took less than three minutes for the security car to reach the gate.

"That takes care of the external issues."

The next photo showed three different angles of the museum. Using his pointer, Shepherd illustrated each one while talking. "The target has three entrances. Besides the front, it has a loading dock and a back door with an internal metal staircase to be used in case of emergencies.

"Two armed guards equipped with radio transmitters are located in the front entranceway. There are three eight-hour shifts, seven days a week. During the day, both guards generally remain at the desk. There is a walk through the building by one of them around noon that takes about fifty minutes. Other than that, their responsibilities include accompanying any visitors or tradespeople, such as plumbers and electricians. No outsider is permitted to go through the building unaccompanied. One guard must always remain at the front.

"Starting at 7:00 p.m. and continuing until the day shift comes on at 8:00 a.m., the routine changes. One guard does the fifty-minute patrol every hour on the hour. There are various check-in stations around the building where they have to use an identifying key card, so there is no slacking off. They also report to the guard manning the front desk.

"But that's not all. Through a sophisticated security system, the roof, walls, windows, and doors are protected with laser systems, motion detector sensors, sound alarms, and closed-circuit television cameras that reveal exactly where a break-in is occurring.

"It's a complete network system designed so that both external and internal grids feed through the Cerrajeros control center.

"Should an intruder somehow manage to climb the wall and cross the compound without being discovered, the moment they attempted a break-in at our target, the system would immediately detect and register the intrusion with the security company and at the building guards' desk. At the same time, the Cerrajeros patrol car sentries would be notified of the location and drive directly to the breach. Simultaneously, the guard on patrol would head toward the intrusion area. He is considered the second line of defense behind the security apparatus and has explicit instructions to engage the intruders.

"Every guard is armed with a Taurus PT-100. The weapons have a ten-round capacity and are lethal when fired at short range. If something goes wrong, that's what we're up against."

An uncomfortable silence briefly settled over the room until Andrew asked how the information had been obtained and whether Shepherd was positive of its accuracy.

The former soldier gave a wide smile. "It's amazing the freedom a baggy blue jumpsuit, a hard hat, a clipboard, and a security inspector's badge will get you," he said.

"Where'd you get the badge?" wondered Bella. "And how did you get past the guard at the gate?"

"One of my Madrid contacts did a pile of research online and produced most of the required documents for two of us. Along with the badge, the paperwork included an authorization form with a bogus phone number for the inspection department under the Cerrajeros corporate logo.

"At this point of the operation, the most difficult aspect would be getting into the compound. For that, we needed a key card. That was when I first contacted Olga.

"I'm now going to ask her to take you through the next part of my presentation."

The Guardians' technology director got up and walked to the front. She moved to the right of the whiteboard while Shepherd remained on the left side.

Glancing at her iPad, Olga looked over at Shepherd and nodded her head. He pulled up a photo taken with a telephoto lens showing a woman accessing the sensor pad with a card. The name of the pad's manufacturer, Toujour Industrie, was clearly visible.

"Regardless of how tight and complex a security apparatus may be, there is always a weak point," she began. "In this case, the vulnerable point is the cards. They operate through a coded metallic strip that is swiped along the sensor pad.

"The pads are manufactured by a company based in France. It took a couple of days, but we were eventually able to break through their security firewall. Once that was accomplished, we accessed the company's files and found the codes accepted by the sensor pad Cerrajeros uses at the compound's gates. Each company and embassy has a different code. We just selected one and moved on from there.

"After that, we purchased a number of blank cards from a Dutch company that supplies the type of cards used by Cerrajeros, programmed the code, and sent them off to Ray."

"The cards worked perfectly," continued Shepherd. "They gave us access to the compound, and from there, it was an uneventful drive to the target.

"Once we got inside the building, the desk guard phoned the number to check us out. It led straight to a burn phone that was manned by one of our squad in the hotel. I had taught her enough Spanish to act like a typical surly clerk who wasn't big on conversation. She confirmed we were there to inspect the building and ensure it still complied with Cerrajeros's security equipment and protocols, before quickly disconnecting.

"That was good enough for the guards. As per their procedure, one of them accompanied us, but basically we had the run of the place for a couple of hours. The guy shadowing us wasn't that interested, and I was able to take whatever photos I wanted. It also gave me a chance to speak casually with the guard. It's a boring job, and he was glad to talk. He was happy to boast about the building's security. The questions I asked were relatively innocuous. But by asking enough of them, I was able to gather all the information I needed."

Shepherd clicked the remote, and a full frontal shot of the facility appeared.

"Most of the building is comprised of two floors. It is here that the offices and some labs are located. We went through every lab in this area, but there were no parchments. One lab is two stories high. The guard told me this was to allow space for some of the equipment used in restoring various art pieces, especially large sculptures.

"Employees reach it through a door on the second story with interior stairs leading to the ground floor. This was the one area we were not permitted to inspect. When I asked the guard why we couldn't enter the room, he told me they were working on a special project, and the lab was sealed against dust. Everyone has to wear lab coats, along with hairnets, cotton gloves, and shoe coverings.

"We were, however, allowed to look through a viewing window on the second floor. Armand, the Guardian who was with me, confirmed they were working on parchments. I asked the guard what project was underway. He didn't know but said it had only recently been brought in and had something to do with the pope's abdication. We determined that this is where the Word of Janus is being restored."

Shepherd paused for a moment and then continued. "Before getting into the details of how we're going to physically recover the codex, Olga will review the security network. It's the most critical obstacle to retrieving the parchments."

Looking at the technology director, Shepherd said, "As you'll see, the Cerrajeros operation presents a unique challenge. I've encountered something like it before, but not this sophisticated. The expertise displayed by their tech operators is impressive. This is a security system with several moving but coordinated parts."

"After Ray contacted me," Olga said, "I immediately instructed my team to conduct a covert cyber reconnaissance on Cerrajeros and determine how to disable the security network that's in place for the compound and the buildings. The more our technicians probed the system, the more they saw the handiwork of the order's technology division. It has created an almost impenetrable wall around the target. The problem is not insolvable, but it does increase the mission's risks."

"What sort of threats are we talking about?" asked Andrew.

"The kind that could get us captured or killed," answered Shepherd quietly but with a ribbon of steel running though his voice. "I'm not trying to be dramatic, but this will not be easy. We are dealing with a highly sophisticated and lethal defense network. Defeating it will require a tightly coordinated liaison between Olga's group and my team when we go in."

"And that's what we've been working on," said the head of technology. "But first, some aspects of the system and what we've accomplished. Knowing Dante as we do, it shouldn't be a surprise that he would want to control everything impacting security around one of the order's holdings. He has involved every building within the compound. Cerrajeros is a state-of-the-art operation, and it's obvious that substantial financial and technical resources are committed to safeguarding its security apparatus.

"Cerrajeros constantly upgrades or changes its firewalls, routers, and modems. In order to combat this, we scanned the system's ports and determined a weakness that is created through this constant upgrading. Once that was established, we built a program that will allow us to get into the network without constructing files that can be detected. We probed the system, learned all we could, and then built a backdoor that will give us an entry point.

"We have created an invasive program, or Trojan horse, that will be introduced through our backdoor within the next two days. It will be activated by a routine e-mail that will be a dummy of one they frequently receive from their clients.

"The Trojan horse will be dormant until we trigger it the moment Ray's team goes through the gate. The main system will crash and be inoperable for the entire time of our mission."

"So far, it all sounds good," said Andrew, cutting into Olga's presentation. "But doesn't it mean that, when the team leaves, they'll have to manually slide the gate back. Ray has already said that, once the computer goes off-line, the electricity is cut, forcing the gate to be opened manually. Won't that delay them in the event there's a problem?"

"You're right," said Olga, "but we've solved that issue. The gate should still be open when they leave. Unfortunately, this is also where the mission gets complicated.

"I have major concerns with their backup system. It could take weeks, even months to discover how it comes online once the primary network goes down. And even then, there's no guarantee we'd have it completely figured out. We can write a program that will temporarily fool the backup into believing that the main system is still functioning, but I don't know how long it will hold."

"How will that impact your mission?" Andrew asked Shepherd.

"Ideally, we need both to be offline for twenty minutes," stated the former soldier. "But there is some room to maneuver. I learned from the guard that the backup system takes about eight minutes to be fully operational. So, we need the backup coming online to be delayed for a minimum of twelve minutes before it's functional. Olga and I have built that into the plan."

"What happens if the alarm goes off?" asked Sean.

Shepherd was silent for a moment. "Both guards and the security car rush to the breach, which has been identified by the computer program. The gate also locks into a closed position. I estimate we'd have less than a couple of minutes to get off the compound. So long as we can get to our car, we'll stand a chance. If not, we will be captured. What happens then is anybody's guess."

Once again, a somber silence enveloped the room until Andrew looked at Olga and asked, "Is the time frame Ray's indicated for the backup program doable? Twelve minutes doesn't seem that long."

"That isn't the point," said Olga. "As I explained, they're constantly rotating the systems and introducing new programs. We'll keep working on a better solution until the mission is operational. But if they decide to introduce a new firewall, for example, between the primary and backup systems on that day, we'll have a problem. Perhaps we could delay the mission until I have a firmer handle on the backup network."

"That's not possible," responded Andrew. "Not knowing what Dante wants with the codex should have all of us nervous. He's obviously planning to do something with it, or he wouldn't have people working over the parchments. And I don't want to take a chance on it being moved to a place we can't find. You and your group will be working for the next three days to give Ray what he needs. Use the time to also work on the backup system. That's about as far out as I believe we should go."

"I'd like to hear what Ray has to say," offered Sean. "The risk will be borne entirely by him and his team."

"When putting the plan together, I knew the backup could be problematic," replied Shepherd. "It's impossible to plan for a perfect mission, and I've been on many with far less probabilities of success. The backup will be taken out. The only question is, will it remain down? I wouldn't be here if I didn't like the odds. My people are well trained. We'll work with what Olga gives us."

"Excellent," said Andrew. "Does anyone else have a concern?"

"We've come this far, and if Ray is fine with it, I don't see a reason to hold back," said Bella.

"I have faith in Ray," said Olga, looking over at the former soldier. "Let's go for it."

Sean, Elijah, and Diane nodded their heads in agreement. Andrew shifted his attention to Leyland, who gave a right thumbs-up sign.

"Everyone's on board," said the senior guardian enthusiastically. "Now let's hear the rest of the presentation."

Chapter Twenty-Seven

Shepherd clicked the remote, and a slide of the Guardians' glass-walled central control room slid up on the whiteboard. Sean knew it was the hub for both the Inverness and Edinburgh technology operations used to keep in touch through computer and telephone contact with Janus's worldwide diaspora and to monitor the order.

"We'll be in constant communication through my mission coordinator from the moment the team leaves the hotel," began Shepherd. "I'll be wired with a headset to stay in contact with Sharon, who will be at the hotel monitoring our progress. She'll maintain the relay between our op and this control room. You'll be able to hear me, but if there's a need for voice contact from you to me, it will be through Sharon. Olga and Sharon have already established the coordinates and conducted several procedural tests. The bugs have been ironed out, and we're ready to go."

A photo of the compound shot from inside and showing the security car passing by a gate was next up on board.

"Now we move to the raid," said Shepherd. "We have rented three vehicles. The cars have been regularly wiped down and vacuumed. There will be no trace of us once the assignment is completed. One car will be for the job, one will be for our backup plan, and the third will be used for our drive to the airport. Four of us will take part in the raid. One will be the driver and remain with the car. Three of us will go into the building. We'll be wearing cotton gloves, rubber-soled shoes, and black pants and shirts, along with balaclavas. The fifth member, as we've reviewed, will synchronize with you from the hotel room.

"There is a coordinated watch schedule between the building's guards and the security car," continued Shepherd. "The interior guard's patrol route brings him to the laboratory at five minutes past the half hour. There is a keypad check-in station by the door, which ensures he validates his patrol. Fifteen minutes later, he is back at the front desk. The security car passes by our target every thirty minutes, on the quarter hour. Its route swings past the perimeter gate we'll be using about six minutes before that.

"Our departure from the hotel will be at 1:50 a.m. From that moment, I'll synchronize our movements through my stopwatch, while Sharon will immediately lock our coordinates with Olga. The drive has been taken each night for a week, and we'll now continue running through it until the mission date. With the lack of traffic and adjusting our timing for such things as streetlights and maintaining the speed limit, we'll hit the perimeter entrance at precisely 2:12 a.m., three minutes after the patrol car has passed."

On the whiteboard was a photo of the wall's front section showing the three entrances. Over the one on the extreme left, an arrow had been superimposed. "This is where we go in," said Shepherd, using his pointer to highlight the entrance. "We will use the key card to gain access to the compound. But we will not enter until the computer has been taken out. That will happen when I give the all-clear signal, which will be thirty-one seconds after we use the key card. That's how long it takes for the gate to slide open. With the computer down, the power will be cut to the gate, leaving it open.

"Our twenty-minute countdown starts at 2:13, which means we're out of the compound by 2:33. We'll be at the gate six minutes before the patrol car makes its next pass at 2:39.

"It lets us leave the gate open, meaning we can get off the compound without having to stop.

"I'll be in constant contact, but if for any reason the feed is interrupted before the computer can be brought down, we will abort. There will be no evidence of our presence, so we'll retreat, regroup, and reengage the following night."

Shepherd brought up the next photo. It was an overview of the area, and he pointed to the target. "We'll get onto the compound, into the lab, and out of the building before the guard comes to check the lab door at 2:35.

"Our drive to the target will take two minutes. We are going in through the back door." Here Shepherd indicated the photo that he'd just pulled up. "It is steel plated, with hinges that are located on the inside, so we have no access there. The lock is a German Bond industrial with two dead bolts that feed into the door's steel frame. We will use a small amount of C-4 to blow the locks. That puts us in the building by 2:19. It gives us twelve minutes to get up the stairs, through the laboratory door, into the room and grab the parchments, while still leaving us enough time to be out of the building and headed toward the entrance before the interior guard's arrival."

The former commando brought up a photo of a wide interior door with a large keypad clearly visible. "This is what stands between us and the parchments," said Shepherd, pointing to the security pad. "This requires a pass card and a combination. This door also has two dead bolts. We'll attach another amount of C-4 to the pad and blow the locks."

"Aren't you concerned the C-4 explosions will alert the guards at the front?" asked Andrew.

The Hope of Janus

"No," responded Shepherd. "The noise on the exterior steel door will blow out, not inward. And the amount of explosive we'll use for the inner door will ensure the noise won't be heard throughout the building.

"Once we blow the door," continued Shepherd, "we'll take four minutes to go through the room and scoop up everything that looks even remotely like the parchments. I'm also assuming the Hebrew translation is there, and we'll take that as well.

"After that, we're up the stairs and out into the car a minute later. Two minutes after that, we're through the perimeter wall and on our way back to the hotel."

"What's your backup plan?" asked Sean.

"I was just getting to that," replied Shepherd.

He clicked the remote, and a road map of the area appeared on the board. On a point where the streets C.D. Jaime and Coso intersected, a circle had been superimposed.

"Our backup car will be stationed here," Shepherd said, indicating the circle. "If anything goes wrong, we'll immediately head for the vehicle parked outside our target. I'm assuming that, at this point, we'll have the security car after us. I've trained our driver in evasive tactics. I don't suspect the guy driving the security vehicle has had much training in following an escaping car. But anything is possible; that's why we've parked the escape car here. We also have to be aware that the police will have been alerted to the break-in and a vehicle description sent out.

"The moment we're through the perimeter wall, we'll head toward the second car, using these streets," Shepherd guided the pointer's beam along a number of roads leading to the circle. "Just as with the route from the hotel to the compound, we've driven these streets each night for the past week. We know every laneway, narrow street, boulevard, and intersection. Losing a chase car won't be that difficult.

"When we get to the second vehicle, we'll switch cars. We've rehearsed the manoeuver and have it down to less than thirty seconds. There'll be no fingerprints or anything else that can tie us to the abandoned car. After that, we'll drive carefully back to the hotel.

"Once there, we'll wipe clean the two rooms we've been using and parcel up our communication equipment. The rest of our gear, except for the equipment, will have been packed before we leave for the mission. Then it's downstairs to the parking lot. Just in case someone spotted our car, we'll wipe everything clean and leave it. That's where the third vehicle comes in.

"The Zaragoza Airport is located ten miles west of the city and operates round the clock. We'll use the third vehicle for the trip to leave town. A private plane has been contracted for the mission. Once we're onboard, it's wheels up and a flight back to Inverness, where we'll hand over the codex to you.

"The pilot is a member of your diaspora so we'll be able to maintain security from takeoff to arrival," concluded the former commando.

"How are you going to transport the parchments?" asked Elijah. "As I'm sure you're aware, they need to be handled carefully."

"We'll be using a large briefcase with a padded interior that's been handmade according to dimensions given to us by Leyland."

Sean nodded his head and said, "From beginning to end, it all sounds like a well-thought-out plan, except for one thing.

You haven't mentioned custom papers and bills of lading for the briefcase. How will you clear security when you land?"

"I've coordinated those details through Andrew," responded Shepherd. "I'll let him answer."

"With the amount of Guardians we have working at the airport, it won't be a problem," said Andrew. "Now that I know the team's approximate arrival time, I'll have a couple of our customs officers assigned to the flight. There won't be an inspection of the briefcase.

"We'll also have the plane taxi into a hangar. A car will be waiting for Ray and a van for the crew. Ray will be driven here, while the crew will be dropped off at their homes. They'll have some well-deserved time for rest and recreation. After that, they will be reassigned."

"What happens then?" Diane asked Andrew.

"Once we determine the parchments are all there, Bella will make the necessary arrangements to have Ray's fee deposited in a Cayman Islands bank account that he's provided us. At that point, our business is concluded. The car will be waiting downstairs to take him to the airport. There'll be instructions at the British Airways counter to provide him with a first-class ticket to whatever destination he wishes."

Shepherd nodded his head and said, "That's exactly as we agreed. Now, all that's left is for me to deliver the goods."

"That's right," said Andrew. "Leyland will now take you to the airport," which brought Shepherd's participation in the meeting to a close. He picked up his overnight satchel, slipped into a light jacket and departed the room with the Guardian.

Olga turned to Elijah and said, "Dante will know we have the codex. He came after it once. What's to stop him from trying to steal it back?"

"Nothing," interrupted Andrew, his expression grim. "But this time, we'll make sure our security is airtight. Dante will never again have the codex in his hands. He beat me once. There won't be a second time."

Chapter Twenty-Eight

✣

"The gate is open. Cut the computer feed."

The reception was patchy, but Shepherd's voice was confident and calm as it fed through the conference speakerphone into the Guardians' Inverness control room. Olga quietly issued instructions through her headphone connecting her to the waiting tech operator.

The room went silent as everyone waited for word that the team was on the compound. Sean watched the digital clock on the far wall. It had been set one hour ahead to reflect the time in Zaragoza. The readout was in hours, minutes, and seconds. The team had arrived at the gate precisely on time. Now as the Inverness group waited for word from Shepherd that the squad was through the gate, the time stretched into thirty seconds, fifty seconds, and then fifty-five.

"The perimeter has been breached, and we're heading toward the target," came Shepherd's words. "We'll be on-site in one minute."

A collective sigh of relief overtook the room. There were tight smiles, but no one relaxed.

Sean took a moment to take in the scene. At the far end of the large table, closest to the speakerphone, Andrew and Olga were seated. Leyland and Bella occupied chairs on opposite sides of the table near the phone. Joining Sean were Diane and Elijah. The three had gathered around one of the table's corners—opposite the door.

"We've reached the target and are on sched," rasped through the speakerphone. "So far everything is quiet. We're going to blow the door."

They had a four-minute window to wait for Shepherd and his crew to decommission the locks. Andrew was staring intently at the speakerphone, as if willing it to emit Shepherd's voice. Leyland leaned over and whispered something to him. The senior Guardian merely nodded his head. Leyland got up and walked to the coffee trolley that had been brought in at Elijah's suggestion.

"It's going to be a long night," the Prophet had noted. "We'll need something to keep us going."

The hissing of coffee escaping the urn's spigot as Leyland filled two cups was the room's only sound. The Guardian carried the cups back to where he'd been sitting and handed one to Andrew, who immediately took a long drink.

By this time, everyone was staring at the clock. The seconds spun slowly into minutes. Finally, the clock revealed thirty seconds to the C-4 blast detonation. Sean counted the seconds down with the clock. Four minutes—nothing from Shepherd. Five minutes since the former soldier's last report, and the speaker stayed quiet. Six minutes, and still no word.

The waiting was intolerable. Everyone was shifting in their seat. A leaden feeling was quickly developing in the pit of Sean's stomach.

Static was emitted by the speaker, but no report from Shepherd. Further static, and then, in what seemed to Sean a surreal moment, a composed female voice came over the speaker. "This is Sharon. We have lost contact with the squad."

Andrew's hand shot across the table and punched the phone button. "What do you mean we've lost the connection?" he shouted.

"I can't communicate with my team," Sharon calmly said.

"Isn't there anything you can do?" asked Andrew.

There were several seconds of silence, followed by, "No there isn't. I'm signing off. The channel needs to be kept open for the squad's next transmission."

Sean saw that the thought something had gone terribly wrong was etched on the faces of those around the table.

"The crew has been well trained, and Shepherd is an expert," said Sean, hoping his words didn't betray the doubt he was feeling. "I'm sure we'll hear from the team in a matter of moments."

Andrew leaned forward and was about to respond, when there was a crackling over the speakerphone, followed by nothing but silence.

"This is becoming unbearable," Diane whispered to Sean.

Static again, and then, "We've encountered a problem." It was Shepherd's voice. "There must have been a change to the timing of the interior guard's rounds. He was close to the back entrance when we were attaching the C-4. He opened the door, saw us, and slammed it shut again. The guard couldn't engage the steel rods to lock the door fast enough, so I was able to go in after him. He's alive and has been physically neutralized, but it won't be long before he's missed. The other guard will come looking for him."

Shepherd made it sound as though the hiccup was a routine event that often happened on a mission. And perhaps it was. But for everyone in the room, the stress had reached close to breaking point.

"What's your next move and does your planned departure time remain a go?" asked Sharon.

"Negative," replied Shepherd. "We still have to blow the interior door. We're running four minutes behind schedule. I also expect we'll soon have to deal with the other guard. That could delay us another three to four minutes."

"You're still within the window for getting off the compound before the security patrol passes by the building," confirmed Sharon.

"That's what we're working toward," Shepherd calmly responded. "We're going to take care of the keypad. I'll report back once that's done."

The conference room's auxiliary telephone unexpectedly rang. The shrill jangle startled everybody. Olga opened the line and spoke into her headset. Everyone's eyes turned toward the technology director. She listened for a few seconds and then asked, "Is there anything we can do?"

After a momentary pause, she said, "We don't have that amount of time. See what you can do without having it traced back to us."

Closing the line, Olga looked around the room. "They discovered our Trojan horse and sealed us out," she half-whispered. "The backup system should be online within the next eight minutes."

"Shepherd has to know," said Sean. He walked the length of the table, leaned over the communication console and pushed

The Hope of Janus

the open button. "The security system will be operational in eight minutes," he told Sharon.

The words were greeted by momentary silence. Then, "Say again," echoed around the conference room.

"Tell Shepherd he has less than eight minutes to complete the mission," said Sean. "Security will be up and running. Do you copy?"

Instead of a response, the room heard Sharon desperately trying to raise Shepherd through his earpiece.

The seconds turned into a minute and then sprinted to the three-minute mark.

"I can't reach him," said Sharon, her voice betraying the stress that everyone was feeling.

Seconds later, Shepherd's voice blasted through the room saying they'd blown the security pad on the lab door. Sharon relayed Sean's news, and after a momentary delay, the former soldier came back with a composed, "How much time do we have?"

"What's the answer?" demanded Sharon, her voice containing an edgy tone of rebuke.

Everyone looked at Sean, who did a quick calculation and said, "They have about four minutes."

Sharon relayed the news, which was met with, "The team is already going through the lab. I'm staying by the door in case the guard comes looking for his buddy. Since there isn't the time we planned for, I've instructed the guys not to be gentle. They're grabbing every piece of parchment we came for and stuffing them in the briefcase. How much longer do we have?"

"Your window for getting off the compound closes in three minutes and twenty-seven seconds," responded Sharon, her voice surprisingly calm.

"I'm going down to help gather the material," said Shepherd. "That's a better option than waiting for a guard who may never show. I'll sign off and report back once we're finished here."

Silence filled the conference room.

Olga turned and looked at the clock. "They're running out of time," she said. "The system should come on line in about two minutes."

"And there's nothing your people can do?" questioned Andrew.

"If there was, I would have heard long before now," snapped Olga, her face turning crimson, eyes stretched wide with anger.

"Let's stay calm," said Elijah quietly who, up until this point, hadn't uttered a word. "This is a very difficult time, and we need to remind ourselves that recovering the codex is the point of this mission. We have all done what we can from here. It's now in the hands of Shepherd and his team."

Sean could sense how the Prophet's words had defused the situation. There was still an immense amount of stress, but it was directed at what was happening in Zaragoza, not at each other. Everyone's eyes were focused on the clock. The longer there was no communication from Shepherd, the faster the seconds and then the minutes seemed to race by.

Two minutes of silence came and went.

"The backup system has probably kicked in," said Andrew to no one in particular. "Even if they get out of the building, there isn't enough time for them to cross the compound without being seen or the gate closing."

Sean was about to say that they should let everything unfold before jumping to conclusions when the speakerphone crackled into life. Immediately everybody's attention was riveted toward the unit.

"We have everything including the Hebrew version." Shepherd's calm voice poured into the room. "So far no guard and no sign of the security system going live. We're heading toward the back door. All we need is another couple of minutes, and we'll be home free."

The booming sound of a Klaxon reverberated throughout the room. Everyone knew the squad had run straight into the security network that was now online and protecting the back door. Even if the team made it to the car, they'd be intercepted by the patrol vehicle before getting off the compound. And the guards were armed.

Chapter Twenty-Nine

❖

Shepherd's mike was open, and apart from his heavy breathing, the first sound the group in the conference room heard was a loud crack, followed by a string of curses.

"They've shot out the rear window," yelled the former soldier. "No one's hurt, and we're out of the compound. But the gate was closed, and we had to crash through it. The car's radiator and front end are damaged. The engine is starting to overheat. And the security car is following. We're going to the backup plan."

Sean could feel the room's collective stress. He wondered what it must be like in the car.

Sharon's voice came over the speaker, asking Shepherd for a report.

"We're several streets south of where the backup car is parked," he replied. "The security team is about a block behind. They're better than I expected. There are sirens in the distance, closing fast. Cerrajeros must be radioing our position. It looks as though the security team is hanging back but keeping us in sight until the police arrive. I don't think the car can last much longer. The engine heat gauge is in the red zone.

"There's a plaza about a mile ahead. We'll cut through that, hopefully lose our followers, and then double back to the escape car. I'll report in once we know what we're doing."

"Roger that," said Sharon, and the speakerphone went quiet.

Several minutes passed. No one spoke as the seconds sped off the clock. The silence hung heavy, and Sean knew his face mirrored the grim expressions around the table.

And then Shepherd's voice filled the room. "We've made it through the plaza and doubled back," he reported. "But the security car stayed with us. The sirens are getting closer. There's a small laneway that we're planning to duck into and hopefully lose the chase car. That's all I have for now."

The speakerphone went silent as the tension in the anxiety-ridden room continued to climb.

Sean looked at the clock and saw that about thirty minutes had elapsed since the team left the compound. "What's the status with the plane?" he asked Andrew.

"It's ready to go," replied the Guardian. "A flight plan has been filed with the tower and with the airport's operation center. The team is running late, but that shouldn't impact take-off."

"This waiting around is worse than being there," said Bella testily. "I wish we'd hear from Shepherd more often."

"I believe he's a bit busy at the moment," said Elijah quietly.

Andrew looked over at Bella and was about to say something when the speaker came to life. "We made it," said Shepherd, his calm voice barely audible through the speaker. "We're in the escape car and headed back to the hotel."

Sharon's voice cut into the transmission. "I expect them in about twenty minutes. We'll contact you when we're leaving for the airport."

There was static on the line for several seconds and then a loud click, signifying Sharon had cut the connection. The news had been so sudden that, for a few moments, there was nothing but stunned silence in the room.

Then all the initial anger at having the codex stolen by the order, and the joy that it was now virtually on its way back to Inverness, coalesced into an emotional explosion throughout the room. The generally stoic Andrew cheered loudly while Leyland let loose with a deep and carefree laugh. Sean and Diane stood as one and hugged each other. Olga opened the auxiliary line and gleefully relayed the news to her tech department, while Bella rhythmically clapped her hands as though she was at a concert. Even the usually composed Elijah participated in the room's passionate display by shaking his fists in the air.

It was a moment they'd all remember for, as sometimes happens to a group united in a cause, there was a collective feeling of having shared something special. Their mission had succeeded, and regardless of what happened in the future, Sean knew they'd be forever linked by this one unique experience. The bond would live eternally in their memories.

*****

The wonderful group dynamic had been put aside. There had been repeated hugs and many handshakes. But now everybody was again nervously waiting. Shepherd had been the one to tell them the team was vacating the hotel and would shortly be on its way to the airport. While everyone was taking turns showering him with congratulations, the former soldier had seemed remote. He quickly sobered the room by reminding them, "The job isn't over. It won't be completed until we land in Inverness and I hand you the codex. We don't know what's between us and the airport. No point in celebrating too early."

Sharon had then taken over the call and said the next communication would come once they were in the air. That had been more than ninety minutes ago, and anxiety had again slithered its way into the room.

Sean looked at the wall clock and was amazed to see that it was coming up on 9:15 a.m. They had been gathered in the room for more than eleven hours as the mission unfolded. And it still wasn't over. The coffee urn was empty. A general sense of weariness pervaded the group. The adrenalin that had been created through being a tangential part of the break-in and codex recovery had now faded. Everyone was nervously waiting confirmation that the plane had successfully lifted off and the team was headed to Inverness.

Shepherd's voice suddenly spilled out of the speaker. "The pilot tells me we're about two hours from landing. We'll see you shortly after that. Roger out."

Stress and fatigue fled the room. A muted cheer swept through the group. The mission was just about over. In a few hours the parchments would be back where they rightfully belonged—with the people of Janus.

Andrew looked around the room, a large smile splitting his face. "It's over. We have battled the order and won, while staying true to our values."

It was a singular moment, and Sean reflected on the range of emotions he'd experienced over the past hours. He had shared them with people he respected and with the woman he loved. Dante's reaction when he discovered the loss didn't matter. Decisions about the order could wait for the future— which would come soon enough. For now, it was time to enjoy the wonderful feeling of accomplishment. He leaned over and squeezed Diane's hand. She returned the gesture before saying, "It's finally over with Dante Sabatini."

Sean could only hope that was true.

Chapter Thirty

✣

The call had come on Andrew's personal cell phone. From the expression on his face, it was obvious to everyone in the room that Shepherd and his crew had landed. After saying his thanks, the Guardian closed the phone and looked around the room.

"That was one of our people at the airport. Shepherd is on his way with the codex. He should be here by noon."

The group had returned to their regular conference room. Earlier, Andrew had ordered breakfast from a small restaurant about three blocks north of the office. Frequented by the headquarters' staff and owned by a couple who were members of the Janus diaspora, the staff was familiar with the Guardians. The delivery included heated trays of scrambled eggs, sliced ham, and breakfast rolls along with two urns of hot, strong coffee. Although the group was weary, they were well fed.

The minutes passed slowly as everyone kept an eye on the clock. There was little conversation. What talking there was focused mostly on the new security procedures Andrew planned to put in place around the lab. It was a topic that interested Leyland, but no one else joined the two Guardians as they discussed an electrified fence, more guards, a reinforced front gate, and concrete barriers. The buzzing of the conference room phone, when it came, grabbed everyone's attention.

Andrew quickly opened the speaker. A disembodied male voice told them Shepherd had arrived at the reception desk and was on his way to meet the group. Andrew quickly walked to the front of the conference room and opened the door. Moments later, the soldier walked in and was greeted by a handshake from the Guardian.

"Welcome back," said Andrew. "It's good to have you safely in Inverness."

Everyone in the room voiced their congratulations, followed by a spontaneous round of applause.

"Glad to be here," responded Shepherd, smiling broadly and raising his left hand, which held a large briefcase. "I believe this is what you've been waiting for. As you know, it was a bit rushed, but I'm sure we got all the folios, along with the Hebrew book."

Shepherd handed the case to Andrew, who placed it on the conference table. Everyone instinctively looked at Elijah. The Prophet quickly got to his feet and walked the room's length to stand in front of Shepherd.

"You and your squad have returned our island's most meaningful piece of history, and on behalf of everyone associated with Janus, thank you," said Elijah, his voice filled with emotion.

Seemingly taken aback by the Prophet's reaction, Shepherd responded with a simple, "Glad we could get it done."

"How's the team?" asked Sean.

"They're in good shape and looking forward to seeing their families," answered Shepherd. "It was a difficult mission, but they carried out their assignments like true professionals. I enjoyed working with them."

"We'll meet with the crew in a few days and have a quiet ceremony," added Andrew.

Sean nodded his head and said, "That's a great idea. Each of them deserves our congratulations."

In the meantime, Elijah had turned and opened the briefcase. The parchments were neatly stacked with the book containing the Hebrew translation sitting on top. Everybody was standing around the table with anticipation. Elijah turned to Sean and asked, "Would you help me lay out the pieces of parchment so we can know that everything is here?"

Sean was mildly surprised. He thought that, if Elijah was looking for someone to assist, it should be Andrew. However the Prophet had already handed him the briefcase. Sean's task was to take the folios out one at a time and hand them to Elijah. He removed the Hebrew version and placed it to one side on the table.

As he reached into the case and carefully withdrew each folio, Sean, for the first time, felt a sense of familiarity with the parchments that he hadn't previously experienced.

He realized intellectually that the more he became familiar with Janus and the island's people, along with the role he was expected to play, this would naturally happen. Nevertheless, he was surprised at how emotionally comfortable he was beginning to feel about staying on Janus. Living with Diane had a lot to do with it, but he also sensed a willingness to participate in the island's future. What this meant for his relationship with the Spirit, Sean still didn't know. But he accepted that his involvement in a future where Janus played a role on the world's stage was no longer the non-starter he had once believed it to be.

Sean understood that a turning point in his life had come through the *hope of Janus*. His birthmark and the words found in the parchments had meant something, but they were voices calling to him from the past. The ring, however, was different. It possessed the one element that had been missing from the other two. While both assumed peace would naturally occur if the world could only realize that its survival depended on it, the ring symbolized that nothing would be achieved without a firm grasp on the hope and on the optimism that it could be realized.

For Sean, that was important. The Spirit had worked with Elijah's great-grandfather to have the band crafted. Therefore, it understood that the essence of peace—the optimism that peace could be achieved—had to precede every discussion about the practical aspects of bringing the world to a less violent state. With that in mind, Sean was beginning to believe he and the Spirit might have a common ground on which to continue their discussions.

Everyone watched carefully as Elijah pieced together the parchments. It was similar to putting together a large jigsaw puzzle. The pieces were of varying widths and lengths. The words were in Aramaic, and only Elijah, with his knowledge of the language, was capable of correctly positioning them.

A silence had enveloped the room as the story of Jesus surviving his time on the cross was slowly revealed.

The group focused its collective attention on the table and counted the pieces as Sean withdrew them and Elijah placed each one in its correct order. When all nineteen folios were properly aligned, Sean picked up the Hebrew translation and gave it to the Prophet. Elijah looked through it and announced that all the pages were intact. Everyone shared laughs filled more with relief than happiness.

"It looks as though I'm done here," said Shepherd. "If you ever need my services again, Andrew knows how to get in touch."

With that, the soldier gave a quick salute and walked out of the room. Everyone assumed it would be the last the Guardians would see of the man, but life does not always go as planned.

As the door closed, Andrew voiced the thought that was now on everyone's mind when he asked, "What sort of damage was done to the folios during the theft and then getting them back?"

"All of them seem fine," answered Elijah in a puzzled tone. "In fact, there are a couple of areas where it appears some restorative work was started. I was confused when we found that Dante hadn't ordered the parchments destroyed, but I really don't understand why he would have the codex restored. It is such a dangerous document for the Church, yet he obviously wanted it preserved."

"Dante's intentions don't really matter," said Andrew dismissively. "What's important is that we have everything back. As Leyland and I were discussing, we're strengthening the lab's security. There'll be no theft by the order this time."

That's probably what Dante believed about the Guardians when he placed the parchments in Zaragoza, thought Sean. However, he wasn't about to detract from the collective buoyant mood. The group had been in the building for eighteen hours, and he was looking forward to getting some sleep. He looked over at Diane and suggested they leave for the bed-and-breakfast inn where they were staying.

"Before you go, I have some news regarding *Journey's* retrofit," said Andrew. "We had some difficulty getting a couple of parts for the engine we're overhauling. It means the ship will be in dry dock for a couple more weeks than expected."

"That will make me late for harvesting," worried Diane.

"You won't be alone," reminded Sean. "This year, there'll be two of us. That should help."

"It will," said Diane. "With both of us working the fields, we should be fine as long as the weather holds."

"Then that's what we'll hope for," declared Sean. "In the meantime, what about my suggestion of getting some sleep?"

Diane agreed, and within a few minutes, they were walking outside the building. The afternoon sun was bathing the city in its light from a pale blue, cloudless sky. The temperature was warm by Inverness standards. Cars trailed each other up and down the street, and the sidewalk was crowded with the first rush of office workers hurrying home.

Sean couldn't help but think of how conventional it all seemed, compared to what had happened with the codex since they'd entered the Guardians' headquarters. His life had changed so much since arriving on Janus.

What it all meant for the future, he didn't know. But with the Spirit in his life and the *hope of Janus* on his finger he realized that he was venturing down a road that held more questions than answers.

Chapter Thirty-One

✤

Dante watched as the TV camera panned its way to the top of the Sistine Chapel. The white smoke emanating from the chimney indicated that a minimum two-thirds majority of the Roman Catholic College of Cardinals gathered in a conclave to elect a new pope had chosen the one who would represent the Church throughout the globe. It was, as Dante expected, a first ballot choice. Although it was not yet known to the world, the prelate also knew the cardinals had designated Charles Emile Ambrosia as the next pope.

The selection of a pope represents a momentous occasion for Roman Catholics. It signifies rebirth and, for many, a validation of the sanctity of God's blessing on the Church, beginning with its first Bishop of Rome, Saint Peter in 67 AD. It was a rarity for the college to elect a pope on the first ballot. One benefit was that it appeared the cardinals were decidedly in favor of Ambrosia. This could only be positive for the Church, as it presented a unified front to its followers.

For Dante, it signified something entirely different. Of the college's 126 members, 115 had been qualified to vote. Eleven cardinals did not participate because they were older than the eligible age of eighty. Through his campaign of blackmail and intimidation, along with promises of future senior and influential positions within the Church for a number of the cardinals, Dante had ensured that Ambrosia had at least 54 votes. That left him 24 short to be safely within the two-thirds majority.

The fact Ambrosia had been blessed by Pope Paul to succeed him easily carried the remaining votes needed and another five, giving him a comfortable margin of victory. Although voting within the conclave was one of the most closely guarded Church procedures, Dante had easily circumvented the process. He was not concerned with the vote count. Rather, he was deeply interested in determining whether the cardinals under his control had lobbied for Ambrosia. If anyone had broken ranks and gone against Dante's explicit instructions to support Ambrosia, the prelate wanted to know.

If that had happened, he would release the file on the offending cardinals. The prelate would make the information public for two reasons. First, in a paradoxical form of logic, given how he had obtained the information, Dante's view was that, if the cardinals did not assist Ambrosia, they had betrayed the order. And that must be met with swift and brutal justice. Second, it would serve as an example to the other cardinals whose files he maintained the dire cost of not complying with the prelate's demands journeying into the future.

The man chosen by Dante to supply him this information was Cardinal Pierre LaGrange. The cardinal had embezzled more than $350,000 from one of the largest churches in France, where he was the resident archbishop. The money had been used over several years to pay for the company of young men and girls. His sexual tastes ran to the extreme, and Dante had threatened him with exposure if he didn't relay, once the conclave was completed, how the lobbying among the cardinals had transpired. After viewing the contents of Dante's file containing film, audio, and photographic examples of his indiscretions, LaGrange was more than willing to carry out the prelate's instructions.

Although LaGrange didn't know the names of the cardinals under Dante's control, his assignment was to report those who had voiced opposition to Ambrosia becoming pope.

The call from LaGrange had come within minutes of the white plume of smoke rising from the Sistine Chapel's chimney. The timing surprised Dante. He had told the cardinal that a delay of several days would be sufficient. Dante had no intention of ruining one of the Church's most joyous occasions by immediately publicly shaming any cardinal under his control who had not voted for Ambrosia. That would happen in the coming months. However, LaGrange's reasoning was soon apparent.

First, the cardinal reported that only nine cardinals had indicated especially fierce opposition to Ambrosia taking the throne of Saint Peter. Dante asked for their names and recognized that none of those who opposed Ambrosia were within his grasp. This was a good sign, for it meant his hold was firm on those whose indiscretions had brought them under his power.

"I have done what you asked and more quickly than you expected," said LaGrange, once he had finished relaying the information. "In view of my faithful service, will you give me my dossier? I believe this cancels my debt to you."

But Dante was unyielding. There was no quid pro quo when it came to the prelate's hold over any cardinal—regardless of how quickly Dante's demands were carried out.

"You are in a trap of your own making," responded the prelate, his voice cold and unemotional. "Go back to your parish and live whatever life you want. But know that, when I request your assistance, you will do my bidding. There will be no returning of your file."

"That means I'll never escape the purgatory you have consigned me to," wailed the cardinal.

"And that's how it should be," said the prelate, before cutting the connection.

Dante's eyes went back to the TV screen, the camera focused on the St. Peter's Basilica balcony that was empty now but would soon be the setting of great glory for the Church. It heralded a return to stability following the confused and troubled final year of Pope Paul's tenure. The event was equally significant for Dante. It marked a milestone in his mission. With the election of Ambrosia, Dante was about to put into motion a vision for the Church's future that he believed would create a dynamic and forward-thinking institution, which would once again become a truly relevant and influential global force. The prelate would bring in people who would work to implement that vision.

Having successfully gained control of the papacy, the appointment of men and women to head every major department within the Church could begin. These would be cardinals, archbishops, bishops, and even some from outside the Church whose ties to the order were unquestioned. For some, it was simply an unshakeable belief in Dante's vision. For others, it was a reward for a lifetime of devoted service to the Church and to the order. All appointments would be based on merit, and those chosen to lead a section—whether men or women—would have years of experience in that particular field.

Dante realized that having women department heads within the Vatican would initially shake the Church to its foundation. But he was a fervent believer in the best person for the job. And what better way to demonstrate how forward-thinking the Church was becoming.

No longer would the order be an adjunct to the Church. In Dante's concept, the Church was to become a subsidiary within

The Hope of Janus

the order's already massive and diverse international holdings. The order's companies manufactured and sold products that ranged from steel to fast foods and from computers to automobiles. In Dante's mind the Church was also selling a product—faith in a divine being. That's what he would be promoting.

At the same time, Dante's belief that Christianity was the one true faith remained fundamental to his vision. He foresaw a world where through the order's commercial concentration on the Church, Roman Catholicism would become the world's paramount religion, with a membership easily surpassing the combined totals of all other faiths.

But Dante's vision did not just encompass the Church's religious side. The order would control the Church's vast land, buildings, investments, and art holdings throughout the globe, worth billions of dollars. However, of even greater importance to Dante was the more than one-seventh of the world's population who identified as Roman Catholic. They were consumers. And as he grew the Church's membership, he believed they provided a captive audience for the order's many companies and their products. Entire advertising campaigns and marketing promotions would be directed to Roman Catholics. With the aid of the order's vast technology division, this would become a profitable reality.

All this passed through Dante's mind as he stared at the screen while the cardinal protodeacon, the senior Cardinal Deacon, declared from the balcony of the Basilica, "I announce with great joy, we have a pope." The Deacon then proclaimed that Ambrosia had taken the name of Alexander, the ninth pope to bear the name and the first since 1691. At that point, the Deacon vacated the balcony. And Ambrosia, or as he was now known, Alexander IX, emerged to the cheers and clapping of a rapturous crowd while a brass band in the forecourt played the *Pontifical Anthem*.

The man Dante had put on the Vatican throne led the crowd in prayers for the health of his predecessor and then blessed the gathering before retreating into the Basilica. There was much more news commentary to follow about what the new pope would mean for the Church's future direction, but Dante had seen enough. He pushed the remote, and the screen went dark.

He had purposely stayed away from the proceedings for a number of reasons. Chief among them was the prelate enjoyed operating in isolation. The order's secrecy within the Church suited Dante and he favored wielding his immense power far from public scrutiny. He also had a couple of issues related to Janus that required his immediate attention.

Dante got up from the dark brown leather couch and walked across the room to behind his desk. Sitting down, he let the chair's plush leather envelop him. His mind coolly and calmly assessed the fallout from an issue that not even the successful completion of having Ambrosia ascend the papal throne could vanquish from his thoughts.

Dante was a pragmatist who evaluated facts in the cold, hard light of reality. And while his thoughts were now focused on the stolen parchments from his Zaragoza fortress, there were no feelings of being violated or of anger that might haunt others in his situation. The prelate clinically assessed what had happened and how he would proceed. He viewed the problem from a business perspective and allowed his vast experience to guide his thoughts.

His commercial ventures over the years had been carefully evaluated moves, building on one business after another. Although it was rare, he had known the occasional failure. However, rather than succumb to feelings of frustration or defeat, he had used the order's vast resources to correct course. Dante was able to bide his time with a patience few people possessed. And when the moment was right, he corrected the setback with a surgeon's precision. His actions were emotionless; ruthless; and, above all, highly successful.

Business was an arena where leveraged takeovers, stock manipulation, corporate espionage, and the occasional assassination were familiar ground for the prelate. In the years he had spent building the order's corporate empire, Dante had beaten back every assault. He had never viewed any move by a competitor as personal. The corporate world was about striving to be the best, regardless of how that was accomplished.

However, Dante had to admit this was different. It didn't emotionally impact his planning. But it made him realize he had underestimated the Guardians' capability. This was a stunning admission for a man who prided himself on being able to correctly assess any possible threat.

The prelate often told himself that he had taken the Word of Janus to protect his religion, rather than to gain a stranglehold on the papacy. If there was one thing Dante valued more than his business accomplishments, it was his relationship with his Supreme Being.

The Guardians, acting no doubt on instructions from Elijah and Brennan, had struck at the heart of Dante's justification for everything he did. He would visit the chapel later and confer with his god. But the prelate believed whatever action he took to correct the wrong the Guardians had visited upon the order and his Church would be blessed. Through the order, he was the defender of Roman Catholicism, and the codex was a corrosive and deadly threat to his faith.

There was no doubt in Dante's mind the Guardians had engineered the theft. The only items taken had been the parchments and the Hebrew translation. If the heist had been orchestrated by any other group, there were too many pieces of art and paintings that would be far more valuable on the black market than a codex that no one but the few inside the Church and the Guardians knew existed.

In the past, Dante had been willing to be a keenly interested but passive observer of the Guardians' cyberwar with the order. He believed, along with his head of technology and her division, that the Janus group posed no threat. But they had obviously found a chink in the order's technological armor. How else could they have known about Zaragoza? His first step had been twofold.

Summoning Anna, he had instructed her to revamp all of their firewalls and update every piece of defensive technology possessed by the order. If the Guardians could hack the system, there were vulnerabilities. Dante wanted every resource, including technicians, software, and financing, available to his technology department. The mission was straightforward—create an airtight perimeter.

He next dispatched a four-person team of watchers to determine whether Brennan was in Inverness and to establish whether the codex had been taken to the same Guardians' location where it was previously being restored. He wanted the Word of Janus back, and it was past time for Brennan to be eliminated.

Both moves had produced results. Anna had informed him yesterday that the order's firewalls and technology defenses now exceeded even that of the Chinese, Russian, and American governments. Just as important, his head of technology had established a counter-espionage section staffed with expert hackers whose mandate was to continually test the order's network.

The watchers' report had been relayed earlier that morning. It confirmed what Dante suspected. The security at the Inverness site had been substantially upgraded. Just as important, it indicated Brennan and Elijah were in Inverness.

The Hope of Janus

The prelate re-read the document. He slowly rolled the pages on his computer screen. The Guardians had obviously learned their lesson.

The gate had been fortified with steel pillars, concrete barriers blocked the entrance, and an electric current now ran through the fence. More infrared cameras surveyed the property. The door to the lab was newly strengthened with reinforced steel, along with a Weiser triple locking mechanism. Entry was through a palm-reading system. And a backup gas-powered generator had been installed. The watchers had cut the power to the site, and the report noted that it had taken exactly three minutes for the generator to bring the electricity grid back online.

There were at least three sentries on duty at all times over a twenty-four-hour period. While two rotated throughout the property, one remained in the guardhouse. One positive aspect was that they were unarmed. The prelate was baffled that there would be guards without weapons. However, he was glad for the apparent weakness in the property's otherwise tightened security measures.

The watchers noted that some personnel were wearing lab coats, cotton gloves, hairnets, and shoe covers. Reading that last bit of information, the prelate allowed himself a brief smile. The codex was definitely at the site, and work was progressing.

The report also indicated that *Journey*, the Guardians' ship, was undergoing its annual retrofit, including an engine overhaul. After speaking to one of the men involved with the work, his lead watcher was able to determine that *Journey* would be dry-docked for the next five weeks. This was of great interest to Dante.

It meant Brennan was confined to Inverness. What Dante now required was a complete breakdown of Brennan's movements. He needed a pattern to be determined by his watchers, and it had to be on his desk within a week. That would provide his assassin and her team enough time to track and eliminate Brennan.

He also wanted a clear review of the guards' schedules at the Guardians' compound. That would be important for both his assassin and his retrieval team.

It would be a staggered campaign meant to completely destabilize Elijah and the Guardians. He would have Brennan killed, and then within two days—while everyone was reeling from the impact of Brennan's death—the compound would be attacked and the parchments retrieved.

Dante leaned forward and habitually rested his elbows on the desk while clasping his hands. Brennan and the parchments were problems that had eluded solutions for too long. Not only were they posing a complication for the order and for his Church, but Dante was also feeling personal pressure to retrieve the parchments as quickly as possible.

He knew that Salazar had undoubtedly informed Ambrosia of the theft. The newly elected pope would have quickly relayed the information to Reinhart. The prelate recognized that, with all the ceremonies surrounding the installation of a new pope, both Ambrosia and Reinhart would initially be too busy to pay the Fraternity much attention. However, it wouldn't be long before Ambrosia, feeling emboldened by Dante's loss of the parchments, challenged the prelate's plan for controlling the Vatican.

Without the codex, Dante was missing an integral tool in his drive to manage Ambrosia. It would lead, Dante knew, to a showdown over whether the prelate was willing to expose Ambrosia's past misdeeds and throw the Church into disarray.

It was a gamble the prelate wasn't prepared to take.

The Hope of Janus

Dante reached for the computer keyboard. He typed a coded message to his lead watcher, detailing her instructions.

It was time to bring the Janus chapter to a close.

Chapter Thirty-Two

The report had come back from the watchers. Reading through the account, Dante was surprised at how much time Elijah and Brennan spent together. Although Elijah had moved from the guesthouse to the home on the property shared by two of the Guardians, the watchers reported it had not changed anything regarding the time the men shared. While Brennan and his girlfriend remained in the city, he arrived at the house by taxi every morning, before leaving with Elijah and the Guardians for the Janus headquarters.

Their departure was always between 8:05 and 8:15. The two only left the building for lunch, which they had together at a local pub. They regularly went for coffee at about 3:00 in the afternoon at a small café and generally stayed for about forty-five minutes. After that, Brennan's movements were too random for planning an assassination.

The watchers recommended the best time for taking out Brennan was the morning, when the group left the house. They had scouted a location where the sun would be at the sniper's back and in the target's eyes. In the confusion, the shooter could easily escape through the underbrush that surrounded the land and out to the country road, which passed by the property where a pick-up car would be waiting.

It was time to contact his assassin, Angelica. More than any other person, even Anna who he worked with on a daily basis, Angelica represented someone special for Dante. She had been brought to the chateau as an infant from one of the Palestinian refugee camps. Dante had overseen every aspect of her life, from her meals to her sleeping hours and from her education to her gradually acquired killing techniques. She had emerged as a lethal assassin. There was no sexual tension between them. Dante's incapability of physical desire or emotional need meant such thoughts did not exist for the prelate.

Over the past fifteen years, she had been responsible for thirty-six kills. Her targets were assigned by Dante and included whomever he believed was a threat to the order or to the Church. The range of assassinations ran from corporate leaders to politicians to labor bosses and, in one rare instance, a Church bishop whose sexual deviancy was about to be made public by *The New York Times*. The threat died with him, when none of his victims would go public with their horrific experiences.

Brennan had already been assigned to Angelica. However, killing him on Janus was proving difficult to arrange. Everyone knew each other, and Brennan was the first stranger in many years. It would be impossible for Angelica to arrive on the island without being noticed. And being invisible was the fundamental lesson Angelica's instructors had taught her. Also, Angelica was a long-range sniper, not a close-in killer.

But with Brennan confined to Inverness, the mission could be completed. Dante reached out and pulled his computer keyboard close. The prelate typed the one-word code, *Avenger*, that would bring Angelica to the chateau. He leaned back and smiled. Soon Brennan would no longer be a problem.

However, there was something that was troubling Dante. He reviewed the report's section devoted to Brennan and Elijah. Gradually his belief intensified that he had another issue besides the threat of Brennan taking the Janus message about peace, diversity, and inclusion worldwide. And that was what to do with Elijah. The prelate believed that Brennan would not be in a position to spread the island's mantra without the support of Elijah. Dante had previously thought the Janus problem would be solved by eliminating Brennan. However, there was a deepening sense that more needed to be done.

While it was true Brennan seemed to be Elijah's protégé, what was to stop the Prophet from taking over the mission after Brennan's death? Having Brennan killed was a necessary reality, but what about the Prophet? Dante realized that he might nullify one problem while creating another.

The threat posed by Brennan and his mark of Janus, signifying he was the Spirit's messenger, would be over. But that still left Elijah as the Janus spiritual leader. Over the years of hacked e-mails and intercepted phone calls between Guardians, Dante had come to realize that everyone associated with Janus appeared to have an equal relationship with their Spirit.

However, in a culture deeply committed to this association, it seemed that Elijah, along with Brennan, had built a unique bond based on taking the Janus message global. As a result, Dante had grown increasingly wary of the Prophet. The prelate believed Elijah wielded immense influence over the islanders, the Guardians, and the Janus diaspora.

In Dante's mind, that had proven correct with the codex's theft from Zaragoza. He believed it could not have been undertaken without Elijah's approval, and for the prelate, that made the Prophet a dangerous adversary.

If Elijah could oversee something as dramatic as the parchments' retrieval, would he also consider working with the Spirit and the islanders to take the Janus message global? It would be a dramatic reversal for a man who was committed to the island's anonymity. However, Brennan's death might be the catalyst to change the course of Janus's self-imposed exile from the world. And even if the Prophet chose not to embark on the mission himself, could he not mentor someone else to replace Brennan?

For the prelate, who strived to ensure a corporate culture where there was a minimum of surprises, the Janus situation posed too many questions.

Dante had long felt he was building a new Garden of Eden for his Church. The analogy was not based on ego. Rather, as a devout student of the Bible, Dante believed he was creating a new world for the Church. It was a place where all those who accepted the tenets of faith as spelled out by the Vatican would have a place under its figurative roof. It would be a time of peace and goodwill within his Church. He saw no conflict with his vision of Eden as a place where the order, by his manipulative planning, would control every facet of the Vatican. He was, after all, carrying out God's mission.

But there was a threat to Dante's vision, and it was posed by Janus. The Satanic cult, as he viewed the islanders, was similar to the snake that had poisoned the biblical Eden. In the prelate's version, Janus was indeed a snake for the way it was threatening to bring down everything that was sacred in his life—the order and the Church. If it was known that the islanders could speak directly with the Supreme Being, what need would there be for a Church? The prelate mentally recoiled at the thought. Why would anyone depend upon a priest or even the pope if they could communicate directly with God? The island would become a mecca, the holiest place on earth, making the Vatican an anachronistic symbol of a bygone and disgraced era.

Forty years of planning would be wasted if the Church were no longer relevant. The order would survive, but every company he had built, every bank he had acquired, and every government he had corrupted was done with one thing in mind—to take advantage of the followers that called the Church their religious home.

Brennan posed a very real threat, but Dante was slowly coming to the conclusion that so did Elijah. The prelate couldn't escape his analogy of a snake. Leaning over the keyboard, he pulled up two photos the watchers had sent him, identifying the subjects as Brennan and Elijah from intel they had gleaned through their daily watch of the Guardians' headquarters. Previous photos were on file, but Dante was a stickler for the most current. He had learned that the growth of a beard and even a change of hair color or styling could dramatically alter a person's appearance. He stared at the picture of Elijah, honing his thoughts, focusing on the issues that confronted him.

This is the head of the snake, thought Dante. Brennan is your acolyte.

An idea began to take shape. It was audacious, but so was taking over the Church. What do you do with a snake if you want to kill it, Dante asked himself. The answer was self-evident—you cut off its head.

Like bouncing a rubber ball against a brick wall and catching it when the sphere returned, Dante slowly tossed the idea back and forth in his mind. It wasn't a question of eliminating one over the other. He would instruct Angelica to focus on the house, take out the first target that was available, and then shoot the other designate in the ensuing confusion.

It would mean a lengthier stay at the hide nest, but when would such an opportunity again present itself?

Dante's exhaustive research conducted on Brennan when he first arrived on the island had indicated the man had no children. That meant the mark of Janus, which had been passed from generation to generation since the son of Jesus, would die with Brennan. And from the hacked e-mails of the past couple of years, Dante knew that Elijah had no living relatives. The killings would destroy the Janus threat. It would drive the islanders deeper into their self-imposed isolation. He would prove to them what they already assumed—that the world was a dark and dangerous place.

The scenario was perfect. In one operation, he would eliminate the threat to his Garden of Eden. The fact he was going to kill two men who had a unique relationship with the God he daily prayed to did not bother the prelate. He would review the plan with God in the chapel that evening. Dante knew he would receive the Supreme Being's blessing. After all, Dante was defending the order and the Church, which were extensions of God's will on earth. As a man who had engineered the current pope's election, Dante fervently believed this action would also be sanctioned by his god.

He opened the site Anna had created for his classified e-mails. Angelica had written that she'd be at the chateau early the following day. Dante was looking forward to her arrival with an anticipation that he reserved for no one else. She was his creation, and he marveled at how she had blossomed into the perfect assassin.

*****

Convinced he had solved one issue, Dante turned his attention to the report's other section—the Guardians' compound and recovering the codex. Apart from the requested details about the guards' watch schedules, there was little new in the document that impacted Benita, his extraction team leader. Dante was satisfied he had what was required for her team. He immediately sent a coded e-mail releasing the watchers from Inverness.

Dante planned to give Angelica two weeks to complete her mission. That involved bringing her team together; establishing a base in Inverness; acquiring the necessary transportation; reconnoitering the kill zone; and, finally, carrying out the assignment.

The prelate didn't believe Benita and her unit required the same preparation time as Angelica's squad. They had already stolen the codex once and were familiar with Inverness and the Guardians' property. Additionally, the watchers had provided information that, when combined with what Benita and her team knew about the Guardians' compound, meant there was not the same need for reconnaissance.

Dante knew that, with the heightened security, the Guardians believed they had done everything possible to prevent a repeat of what had happened. They would suspect the order would come after the codex and be ready for an attack.

But they weren't prepared for the coordinated assault Dante had planned. And the assassination of both Brennan and Elijah made attacking the compound forty-eight hours after the killings even more viable. There would be rampant confusion, and no one would be thinking of a raid to steal the codex.

Benita's crew had never failed to deliver on an assignment. Dante had used them often in the past, whether it was stealing state secrets to facilitate one of his companies bypassing national regulations, ransacking corporate records to enable a hostile takeover, or robbing various museums to acquire pieces of art he believed belonged to the Vatican. Although the prelate took nothing for granted, he was confident Benita would succeed.

Dante pulled up Benita's imbedded e-mail address and attached the relevant pages from the watchers' dossier. He composed a short note detailing that he wanted her at the chateau with a preliminary status report within three days. He closed by writing that Juan would contact her with the travel specifications.

Dante considered the ramifications of having two crews focused on the Guardians' property at the same time. However, they were professionals, and he would advise the team leaders to coordinate their operations.

The prelate tapped the intercom, and when Juan's whispered voice answered, Dante told the assistant his instructions. Juan said he'd report back in thirty minutes with Benita's arrival day and time. Dante closed the intercom and settled back in his chair.

Within a few weeks, his operatives, along with their teams, would bring an end to the Janus threat. The deaths of at least two people did not concern him. All that mattered was the execution of his missions. The plans had been set in motion. What remained was to ensure the expectations were met.

Chapter Thirty-Three

Dante had spent some time putting together a file for his session with Angelica. It contained material from the watchers, including the updated photos of Brennan and Elijah, frontal shots of the gate and house that encompassed newly installed concrete barriers blocking the entranceway, photos of the country road that ran by the site, and shots of the electrified fence.

There were diagrams of proposed kill zones and timetables showing when the targets, along with the accompanying Guardians, left the property and what time they returned. Security schedules, along with an aerial view of the grounds and surrounding area obtained by a high-altitude whisper drone, rounded out the information.

Dante had downloaded the material from the chateau's hard drive onto a memory stick. The file would be closely reviewed with Angelica. She would take the "stick" with her when leaving the chateau. It would be up to Angelica and her team to decide the logistics of handling Brennan and Elijah.

The prelate had mentally put the Janus dossier aside and was reviewing a large financial transaction by one of the order's American firms when Juan told Dante over the intercom that Angelica was waiting to see him. Seconds after he'd told his assistant to send her in, Angelica glided through the open doorway and into the room.

"Hello, Dante," she said quietly.

As always, Dante's world became a little brighter, the load he carried slightly less heavy.

He studied her as she walked toward the desk. Her coal black hair flowed in soft ringlets to well below her shoulders. She had on a greenish-tinged shadow that emphasized the darkness of her eyes. In a departure from past visits, Angelica was wearing blush that highlighted her prominent cheekbones. A natural tan, accompanied by a subtle pink lipstick, a shade he'd never seen her wear, lent a gentle contrast to the hair and makeup. She was wearing a black silk blouse with the top two buttons undone and gray pants tucked into black knee-high boots. Hanging from her shoulder was a thin, black handbag.

"Why don't we sit in the Queen Anne chairs," Dante said as he came out from behind his desk.

There was no kiss on the cheek, no hug, not even a soft clasping of hands. The experiences they had in common were all related to the order. Whatever secrets each possessed were not shared. He never wondered about her life. The thought she might have someone to love and to hold was so foreign to him that he was incapable of imagining that kind of life for her.

And yet, as she sat across from him, he felt a genuine pleasure at her presence. It was a feeling no other human brought him. He never examined the experience, merely acknowledged it and then let it slide from his subconscious.

For her part, Angelica would have preferred more of a connection. When she was with him, there was a sense of well-being. It was always good to see Dante, and she would have liked him to know that. Yet, expressing such feelings was beyond the horizon of their relationship. The bond that held them together had been forged when she was young and being trained to become his assassin. So, as always happened, she stayed quiet and waited for him to begin.

Interestingly, while Dante always offered coffee to his guests, Juan was never summoned when Angelica came to the chateau. Through the prelate's training, she eschewed any beverage with caffeine, believing it was not good for one who relied on steady nerves to complete an assignment. However, such was the nature of their association that it never occurred to either of them to have water or juice brought in.

There was no preamble. Dante explained about the house in Inverness and what he now wanted. He focused solely on her assignment, revealing nothing about the thought process that had gone into the change and why Elijah had now become a designate, along with Brennan. Using a laptop, he scrolled through each piece of information from the file, and Angelica studied them as he spoke. She would later share the dossier with her team leader.

As always, their voices were hushed, almost intimate. She received the news of Dante's changes to her assignment with the usual calmness that governed every aspect of their relationship. Nothing surprised her when it involved Dante. It wasn't that she anticipated the unexpected from him. Rather, her lack of reaction was a part of the detached serenity that came with her training and when she was with the prelate. Angelica was not surprised that her mission had been expanded and was more complex. She accepted the news about Elijah with the unemotional professionalism she brought to every task Dante assigned her. The playing field might change, but the match always ended the same way—she completed the mission.

This was the first time she had been asked to take out two targets in one assignment. The danger inherent in the operation was uppermost in Angelica's mind. The time required at the hide nest would rise dramatically, thus exponentially increasing the odds of being caught or killed. But Dante had given her the assignment, and she would carry it out because that was what she did.

This was her life. Dante was the master; she was his disciple. It was not her mission, but his. And she would assist him in the way she'd been trained. If anyone had ever asked why it was she only felt truly alive when lining up a kill, her answer would have been straightforward.

"I'm carrying out God's will."

That was the mantra Dante had repeated every day of her training. He was head of the order. The Fraternity was there to protect the Church. The Church did God's work on earth. Therefore, as an agent of the order, her missions naturally came from Dante and were ultimately blessed by God.

She was one of God's angels, hence the name Angelica. It was a philosophy that left no room for confusion or doubt. But in Dante's mind, she was more. He thought of her as his Azrael, known as the Angel of Death in some mid eastern religions. Several years ago, he had shared this with her. She coveted the name, for in her mind it not only brought her closer to Dante but was also further justification that her assignments were spiritually guided. Known throughout the chateau and among her team as Angelica, when she and Dante planned their assignments, he always called her Azrael.

Finishing his talk, Dante detailed her flight arrangement to Inverness and that she was booked into the Glenmoriston Hotel. He then asked if she had any questions.

"It's all very clear to me," Angelica noted, without emotion. "You want this carried out over the next two weeks, before the targets return to Janus. I'll gather the team. We will complete the mission within the required time frame."

Dante nodded his satisfaction. He withdrew the memory stick from the laptop and handed it to Angelica. She opened her purse, slid the device into a tiny interior pocket, and closed the small shoulder bag. It was the signal that the session was over. They stood in unison.

There was no emotion on either side, no acknowledgement that Angelica was about to embark on her most dangerous mission since she had begun serving Dante. For both of them, it was an assignment.

"Go with God, my Azrael," said Dante.

"I will do as you command," she responded.

Angelica turned and walked toward the office entrance. Without looking back, she pulled on the handle, opening the door, and slid gracefully into the hallway. Dante took the several steps that would bring him to behind his desk, his mind already on Ambrosia and Rome.

And yet, as the door closed and Dante sat down, there was, for a few moments, an emptiness about the office that he couldn't intellectually understand but emotionally sensed. The prelate experienced the briefest feeling of regret. His Azrael was gone. The impression was so unfamiliar that it was lost in less time than it takes for a bird to flutter its wings. The prelate pulled the keyboard toward him and was soon lost in his plan to remake the Vatican in the order's image.

As Angelica walked toward the parking lot and her leased luxury Volvo, she was already planning her next steps. When she got back to her room at the AC Hotel Valencia, she would contact her squad leader, Jose. Angelica would give no details over the phone, only that she would meet her team in two days at the Glenmoriston.

The Hope of Janus

Angelica left that afternoon on a British Airways flight to Inverness. She always spent a day alone in the place where the killing was assigned. It was a time to walk the streets, to feel the rhythm and pulse of the people and the locale. She cherished the anonymity and drew power from it. She was Azrael, carrying out a sacred mission. Nothing could defeat her.

Chapter Thirty-Four

✣

Angelica's all-male team, chosen by Dante, had been assigned to the assassin for her first kill. With the exception of Angelica, all were third- or fourth-generation members of the order. The squad had been together for every murder, and each member was vital to the operation. Although Angelica was the shooter, she was one part of a team whose function was to not only stage a successful mission but also to ensure no trace could be tied to the order.

As the team leader, Jose was the gatekeeper. A perfectionist when it came to planning, he acted as the banker and was the manager and the scheduler for all on-site information required by the crew and by Angelica. At fifty-six, he was the oldest in the group and the only team member, besides Angelica, to have direct and ongoing contact with Dante. Built low to the ground, Jose had thinning, white hair and was barrel-chested with heavily muscled arms, powerful hands, and tree trunks for legs.

It was the gatekeeper's responsibility to acquire false identification papers, including passports, for use during the mission and for after the assassination had been completed. He was also charged with finding accommodations and having the team there well enough ahead of time to have conducted an in-depth review of the area where the planned shooting was to take place. Most importantly, he was accountable for ensuring that each crew member got safely away.

His direct responsibility was Angelica. Whatever she required and however the job was to be carried out, it was his function to ensure her operational needs were met.

Angelica's spotter was Bill, a short, compact man with prematurely gray hair that was in stark contrast to the deep brown of his full beard. Quiet and soft-spoken, Bill's initial responsibility was to tour the kill zone with Angelica. He took all the required measurements, including footage from Angelica's location to the target area, wind speed, and atmospheric conditions, and ensured the hide nest met Angelica's specifications. His primary function, however, was to be with her during the assassination, updating information on what was happening around the death site while Angelica concentrated on one thing alone—ensuring the kill shot was accurate.

The mechanic and driver was Frank, a tall, forty-something American. During the first couple of days, he was especially busy. After meeting with everyone at the Glenmoriston, he journeyed back to Inverness Airport. While there, he visited three car rental companies, Alamo, Avis, and Budget. He leased three vehicles—a Toyota Corolla for general use, a Chrysler van able to transport the entire team, and a Chevrolet Aveo that would function as a backup and getaway vehicle.

Once that was completed, he went to Halfords Auto Parts Store on Harbour Road and purchased the required tools and auto supplies to ensure that the vehicles were tuned and, if necessary, the engines modified so that nothing failed during the mission.

Tom, a thin, balding man, with bad teeth and a pockmarked complexion was the gunsmith and sweeper. An American as well, he was a former Marine, where he'd served with distinction.

He obtained Angelica's rifles for whatever country she was working in.

She preferred to use and was equally adept with any one of three weapons, either the Remington 700 rifle, equipped to fire .308 rounds; the M16 that fired .223 Remington rounds; or the British manufactured Enfield Enforcer, firing .308 rounds. Tom would strip, clean, and test fire the weapons before Angelica used them. He personalized the stock and, if necessary, re-bored the barrel so that Angelica was always handling a weapon that was familiar in weight, sighting, and velocity. He also supplied her with the shells she required.

Tom's secondary role was to wipe down whatever location the team was using as a staging point, ensure the vehicles had no traces of the occupants, and clean any tools or utensils used by the crew members.

When the team met in Angelica's hotel room, she handed over to Jose the memory stick given to her by Dante. Jose plugged it into the port of a laptop. The crew's initial reaction to assassinating two targets was surprise and concern. There were too many variables. Both shots had to be fired quickly and accurately. Angelica's breathing would have to be regulated far longer. The spacing of the two men could pose problems. Angelica's time on the kill zone's periphery would be extended, thereby compounding the risk of discovery. The guards would have time to react, possibly compromising the escape route, placing her and the support team in danger.

However, this was also a seasoned group of professionals. Led by Jose and Angelica, the squad's other members soon began to focus on the mission's logistics. It was a routine they had followed many times, and the assignment's tasks were soon all that mattered. They would successfully complete the mission, and it would rank as one of their finer accomplishments. Another incentive was that Dante had doubled their usual payment.

The Hope of Janus

Only Angelica believed she was doing God's work. The rest of the team was under no such illusions. They worked for money and for the Fraternity—in that order. The fact Dante had recognized the danger with the only compensation they truly understood made up for whatever concerns they might have.

As the meeting came to a close, Jose handed each person a carry bag that held a forged European Union passport, a doctored international driver's license, an envelope containing five thousand euros in used bills, three credit cards bearing the name on the passport, and airline tickets, along with a burner phone.

It was also decided that Angelica would remain at the Glenmoriston. The rest of the squad, as per standard procedure, would spread themselves throughout the various Inverness hotels until Jose found a permanent address. It was always best to minimize the chances of being seen together.

While the gatekeeper was finalizing a house rental, the group was busy. Angelica and Bill began their survey of the Guardians' property. Frank was test-driving the cars. And Tom had journeyed to London, where he met a member of the order who supplied him with the necessary weapons. The serial numbers had been filed off and the barrels rebored, making them untraceable. The contact also supplied ammunition.

By the third day, Jose had a place for them to operate from. It was a furnished three-bedroom house on the city's outskirts. The owners, several days into a ten-week second honeymoon in Hawaii, were overjoyed to learn their home had been leased for a month.

The rental check had been written on one of several shell companies owned by the order and located in Bermuda. A post office box served as the address for the recently formed company. Established only for this job, it would be dissolved when Angelica had completed her work. Because of the order's labyrinth of shell corporations, it would be impossible to trace ownership.

Chapter Thirty-Five

Angelica and Bill had been scouting the location on a daily basis for the past week. On every occasion they'd arrived precisely at 7:00 a.m., having been dropped off about half a mile from the Guardians' home by Frank in the Corolla. They'd fade into the trees and make their way toward the home. It was a round-about route that would be turned into a straight line between the pick-up point and the hide nest on the day of the assassinations. In the meantime, they were taking every precaution by staying away from the property until they were within a short distance of where Angelica and Bill had decided the fatal shots would be fired.

After leaving the couple, Frank traveled about six miles along the unpaved country road in the opposite direction of the route the Guardians used on the daily journey to the Inverness city center. Arriving at a fork, he turned west, joining a paved road. Following several more turns, he guided the car to the home base. It was one of several houses in the area. All were located a fair distance from each other, affording a great deal of privacy.

Through a careful watch of the Guardians' house, it had not taken more than three days for Angelica and Bill to determine that the home's occupants never deviated from the departure pattern described in Dante's notes.

The four-man group left in a Chevrolet SUV between 8:05 and 8:15 every weekday morning. This consistency, along with the unarmed guards and the property's surrounding forestry were considered positives. On the negative side were the electrified fence, the security patrols, and the other defensive systems, including the entranceway barriers. A major issue was the distance from the hide nest to the road and the get-away car's location.

These problems, though, were not for Angelica to solve. Her sole function in this preparatory stage was to determine the logistics of applying the kill shots.

Having identified the targets from photos she'd placed on her cell phone, Angelica analyzed how the killings would take place. Both targets always climbed into the back of the SUV that was parked several yards from the home's front gallery. Angelica had committed to memory a kill zone that led from the front door, along the porch, to beside the Chevrolet.

While the driver and the other Guardian entered the SUV from different sides, the targets followed a different pattern. The younger man held the right-side back door open for his companion. Only after the old man climbed in did the younger subject travel around the back of the vehicle and get in on the left side. Bill had meticulously timed the trip from when the targets emerged together through the front door to when they arrived at the SUV. There would be between 90 and 125 seconds to take out both men.

Apart from identifying the kill zone and monitoring the inhabitants' movements, Angelica and Bill were there to determine everything from the varying wind direction and velocity and the terrain to the sun's angle, its affect on sight lines, and how everything appeared on a cloudy day to primary and secondary locations for the assassin's positioning and escape routes. The assassin had already decided she would take out both targets as they approached the edge of the porch before descending the three steps to the stone-encrusted courtyard.

As described by the watchers, the two Guardians always went first. This meant they would be on the steps or ground level, providing the assassin with a clear line of sight for the required kill shots. If, for some reason, the routine varied, she would wait until they got to the side of the SUV. The porch was the primary option because it offered direct shots. The Chevrolet, while presenting a viable option, offered less of a frontal shot for the targets. Its one advantage was that the Guardians would already be in the vehicle, thereby delaying their reaction time.

Following much discussion between Bill, Jose, and Angelica, it had been decided that the only way to handle the fence was for Bill to use bolt cutters to create a large enough hole to offer an unimpeded sight line. At that point, Angelica left the discussion. How that would be accomplished was not within her area of expertise.

Fortunately, the solution had already been handed to the squad. When the watchers had cut the electricity to the Guardians' property as a test to determine when the power generator would engage, the team had sliced the line in an empty field midway between the Guardians' house and the Inverness city limits. In bringing the grid back online, the watchers had bypassed the main power cable with a triage of wiring, deceiving the computer at Scottish and Southern Electricity into believing that the line was sound. Since there was no permanent interruption in the power grid, crews were not sent out to troubleshoot the problem.

Another break in the line could be achieved by taking apart the triaged wires with a strong two-handed pull. The watchers had reburied the compromised wiring a couple of inches below the ground's surface and denoted the spot with a red post marker that was easily visible from the road.

Jose would drive Tom to the site in the Corolla. Once the Guardians' power was out, the two squad members would proceed to a designated spot in front of the Guardians' property and serve as backup in case the plan unraveled. No one expected a problem, but Jose was meticulous in his planning.

Chapter Thirty-Six

Jose and Benita met in a small pastry shop on Inglis Street. After picking up their coffees and a carrot muffin for Benita, they secluded themselves around a small table at the back. The café boasted Internet capability, and they were the only ones with heads not buried in laptops. No one took the slightest interest in their presence.

Benita, small and lithe with sandy brown hair cut pageboy style, nevertheless quickly surveyed the room with clear, almond-colored eyes before saying, "Dante told me your team would be here. Following normal protocol, he didn't share any of the details, only that we have the same target. All I know is that my operation is to take place a couple of days after your unit pulls out.

"As always, we have excellent intel from the watchers, and my team knows the target from a past operation," continued Benita. "We won't need much time to recon the site. So I'm here with just Aldo. He'll serve as my advance scout. The full squad will arrive in three days. That will give us four days to mount our operation. There isn't much overlap, so we'll be able to stay out of your way."

Jose acknowledged the professional approach with a nod of his head. He liked knowing Benita was handling the concurrent assignment. Through the years, they had coordinated on several operations.

He admired her expertise and dedication to completing a mission, regardless of how difficult. He saw many parallels with Angelica, including the Svengali-like commitment to Dante. And like Angelica, she had killed for the order's greater good. Jose did not envy anyone who stood in her way of retrieving the parchments, for they would, without doubt, experience an untimely death.

"Since you don't have your full team here, I'll have Tom coordinate our movements directly with you," said Jose. "We can follow the same routine we used in Caracas."

"That worked well," offered Benita, referring to the assassination by Angelica of a senior Venezuelan politician, which was used to distract the police from a museum robbery led by Benita that took place the following day.

She reached into her backpack and pulled out a small pad of paper, along with a pen. After scribbling two sets of numbers on a sheet, she handed it over to Jose. "The first one is for the burner I'll use until my team gets here. After that, I can be reached on the second one. Ditch the number you used to contact me for this meeting. I've already switched phones."

"This should do it for now," said Jose, while putting the paper in his shirt pocket. "Why don't you leave first. I'll follow in a couple of minutes."

Benita reached across the table and took hold of Jose's right hand with her own. "Good luck, my friend," she said, surprising him with the unusual display of camaraderie. "If all goes well, we'll meet again on the other side."

"That we will," responded Jose as Benita slipped out of her chair, walked the length of the café, and headed out the door.

Several minutes later, Jose exited the coffee shop.

The coffees and muffin lay untouched on the table.

Chapter Thirty-Seven

It was a cloudy and rain-filled evening. They had gathered in the living room. A strong coal-fed fire was blazing, the flames captured by the screen of an open laptop on the large coffee table. The room's chairs had been re-arranged, and the group was gathered around a portable whiteboard. Standing to one side was Jose, with a laser pointer and a remote control for the computer. He had spent the last three hours programming and diagramming how the operation would unfold.

Most of the procedures were already known to the group. But the countdown had begun to the following morning.

Jose handed each person, with the exception of Angelica, a headset and battery pack. The range was approximately five miles. It was standard operational equipment for the team, and every unit had been tested several times that morning by Frank and Tom. Angelica was never given a headset. Her focus was the kill zone, and any instructions were relayed directly by Bill.

"Before we begin," opened the gatekeeper, "there is some news that impacts our mission. Dante contacted me a couple of hours ago. The chateau's technology department intercepted a phone call between two Guardians earlier today. The Janus ship is out of dry dock and in the water. She will be sailing to the island with our targets the day after tomorrow.

"This doesn't change our operation. We were always planning to complete the mission in the morning. But it does mean that we have no room for aborting the assignment. Dante doesn't want either target back on Janus."

The group accepted the news with the type of professional calmness that comes after thirty-six successful missions. This would be no different. All the planning and scouting ensured success.

Frank inserted a memory stick into the computer's USB port. Jose pulled up an overhead shot of the property, taken by the watchers' drone. The gatekeeper had circled the kill zone, including the area marked in blue twenty feet outside the electrified fence where Bill and Angelica would be positioned.

With his pointer, he highlighted the colored area. "Angelica and Bill have chosen this location as the hide nest. The spot is well hidden, with tall vegetation and perfect sight lines. It also features several large rocks, which Bill has moved into place. One of them will provide a platform for the gun's bipod."

Jose engaged the remote control, and the next photo to appear was a cropped picture showing just the house and the hide nest. A black line linking the two points with the notation "224 yards" was superimposed over the photo. The yardage had been obtained by Bill using a distance gauge.

"This is what Angelica will be working with."

Jose next brought up a photo of the hide nest and the road that ran past the property. A wooden post with orange paint across the top—the type used by Inverness road crews—had been planted by Bill. It was situated on the roadside approximately 100 yards from the fence bordering the east side of the property.

"Using the van, Frank will drop Angelica and Bill by their usual spot at 6:50." Jose fixed his pointer's beam several inches to the right of the orange-topped post. "They will be at the nest by 6:52. Frank will then return to the house with a departure at 7:35, to arrive back here at 7:50."

Jose moved the pointer's beam over to rest on top of the orange-topped post. "He will be here to pick up Angelica and Bill once the mission is completed."

The next photo to appear was of the road and the red marker in the field that indicated where the cable supplying electricity to the Guardians' property had been rigged by the watchers. Jose, always precise, had written the distance between the road and the marker at twenty-three yards.

"Tom and I will arrive here in the Corolla at 7:45." The pointer's beam played over the roadside directly opposite the red marker. "Once Tom is in position and the cable has been exposed, he will notify Bill. When the four men appear on the gallery, Bill will give the go-ahead, and Tom will pull apart the triaged wiring.

"That gives us a three-minute window before the backup generator comes on and the fence is again electrified. Using bolt cutters, Bill will cut a hole providing Angelica with a clear sight line. The angle has been determined, and paint has been applied to the strands that must be cut.

"In the meantime, we will have moved the Corolla to behind the van, in case there is a problem."

Jose next brought up a cropped shot of the Guardians' house, with the gallery and the top of the SUV highlighted in white.

"The targets will appear on the gallery between 8:05 and 8:15," he said. "They will be accompanied by two Guardians.

Angelica and Bill, along with the watchers, have determined this is their consistent pattern, and there's no reason to assume it will change tomorrow."

Jose then pointed to the Chevrolet. "The SUV is generally parked about forty feet from the house. This is their destination."

The gatekeeper swung the pointer back to the gallery. "The two Guardians descend the steps first, followed by the targets. Bill has timed out that there is a twenty- to twenty-five-second window when the targets are on the gallery and the view is not obscured by the Guardians. That is when the kill shots will take place. The spacing between Angelica's first shot and her second will be no more than four seconds.

"Once the targets are eliminated, Angelica and Bill will move directly to Frank, using the fence as their guide. It will take them two minutes. That's longer than I'd like, but it's an operational reality we can't change.

"Now, we have two related issues," said Jose as he brought up the aerial shot of the full property. "We have three minutes to get the job done. A battery-powered alarm will sound across the property when the power is cut. But that's not our problem. The issue is that once the backup generator begins supplying electricity to the property, a monitor will activate in the guardhouse, pinpointing where the break in the fence has occurred. Angelica and Bill, you have to be gone by then.

"Bill will have sixty seconds to cut the required strands. That leaves Angelica with two minutes to carry out the assignment.

"This brings us to the two external guards. They patrol the property on a constant basis. While they have specific routes, there are no set times that they have to be at a given point. Bill has estimated that the one who patrols the perimeter could be as far away as six minutes or right on top of the spot where he will be cutting the fence.

Although the guards are unarmed, this one could provide enough interference that the targets will become aware of Bill and Angelica. That obviously can't be allowed to happen. If this guard does get in the way, Bill will be responsible for terminating him before he can sound an alarm."

At this point, Tom got up and left the room. He returned a minute later with a large satchel. Reaching in, he handed out Smith & Wesson handguns, along with two modified, ten-round magazines to each person. Angelica was the lone exception.

The men clinically studied their weapons. They loaded and unloaded the magazines. Everything was in perfect working order. Each man inserted one of the clips into his weapon. The guns, along with the spare magazines, were then placed on the coffee table.

"What about the lab workers?" Frank asked.

"They start arriving around 8:45, so it won't be a factor," responded Bill.

"What's the weather for tomorrow?" asked Tom, looking out the window, where drops of rain ran down the panes of glass.

"I checked the meteorological website," said the gatekeeper, indicating the laptop. "This rain is supposed to end sometime tonight. They're calling for cool, dry weather, with sunlight beginning in the morning."

Jose manipulated the remote and brought up the photo of the orange-topped post.

"Bill and Angelica should be in the van no later than 8:17. We'll all then come back here to change clothes for traveling.

"The weapons, remaining ammunition, and clothing for Bill and Angelica will be dumped in the Corolla's trunk. Tom will have swept the house before we leave in the morning. Once we arrive back, he will do a final sweep and clean off the weapons, along with the vehicles. Tom will take the van to Gatwick, where you'll board a British Airways flight to Paris.

"Angelica and Bill will take the Aveo. You'll drive to Edinburgh, where you're booked on an afternoon KLM flight to New York. After that, each of you will make your own arrangements for getting back to your home bases.

"Frank and I will drive to Glasgow in the Corolla. We'll leave the weapons and extra rounds in the trunk. Without serial numbers, all the weapons are orphans, so nothing can be traced back to us. From there, we'll fly to Heathrow, where we'll pick up an Air Canada evening flight to Toronto. We will then split up and make our way out of the city.

"The cars will be left in the parking lots. It'll be days before they're found. By then, we'll all be safely home. As per our standard precaution, everyone will wear gloves while in the vehicles.

"Payment will be delivered in the usual way through a deposit in our Barbados accounts," concluded Jose.

Looking around the room, the gatekeeper asked if there were any questions. He expected none. Everyone knew their respective role. The format had been followed often enough. It was now time to execute the plan. No one had a question.

"Fine," said Jose. "That's it for this evening."

Angelica went to her room. She was in bed and asleep within minutes. The others played cards for a couple of hours. There was, as usual, no talk of the mission. Soon, everyone was bunked down for the night.

Chapter Thirty-Eight

✥

Frank had dropped Angelica and Bill off at the designated spot. They'd arrived at the hide nest a couple of minutes later than planned due to the underbrush having been made slippery by the night's rain. However, neither of them was concerned. This was the reason you left time for contingencies.

Angelica and Bill were wearing British Special Forces camouflage-colored, close-fitting, woolen toques; gun gloves; and reconnaissance jackets. Their camouflage pants were US Army issue, as were the knee pads. Each was wearing a pair of black Iranian killing shoes—very much like the North American Indian moccasin. Their faces were blackened. Bill had a small backpack filled with several bottles of water, the bolt cutters, a Leupold Mark 4 spotting scope, and the spare ten-round clip. His loaded Smith & Wesson was holstered on his hip.

Angelica was armed with the Remington 700 bolt-action rifle. It was her favorite weapon. Tom, as usual, had made two adjustments to the gun. The stock had been reworked to where it felt familiar and comfortable for Angelica. He had also reconfigured the weapon to use a Leupold sight, instead of the one that was stock issue from the manufacturer. He favored the compact scope's optical quality, precision accuracy, and fast target acquisition. Angelica had used the scope on her last six missions and had a high level of confidence with it.

They settled down to wait.

The eastern sky behind them was aflame with the rays of a slowly rising sun. Its warmth hadn't yet found a way through the brush and forest. The moisture from the night's rain hung close to the ground, and tiny droplets of water fell from tree leaves every time a slight breeze disturbed the stillness.

They were lying flat on their stomachs, hidden behind the grouping of four rocks that Bill had painstakingly moved into place. He had situated the rocks so that the flattest one provided an ideal level site for the Remington's bipod and gave Angelica an excellent line of sight to the gallery.

Bill was keeping watch. He'd alert her when it was time to begin the final preparation or if anything changed. They had worked together for so long that she had an inherent trust in his ability to keep her safe.

Angelica retreated to the place she always visited before it was time for her to work. It was her calming mechanism and was part of the pre-killing ritual—as important as checking her weapon and visualizing the kill shot.

She thought of Dante. The motivation for Angelica's life was the pleasure she experienced from carrying out the kills he assigned her. She took enormous pride in never having failed. That's what kept her going from one job to the next. She accepted every mission's inherent danger because of the pathological need to please Dante.

He had brought her from the poverty of the Palestinian refugee camp to the chateau. She owed her life to him. Everything she had was because of the man's generosity and kindness.

There were no men in her life, other than the prelate and the team. Her beauty often attracted strangers, but after a few moments, they saw the cold disinterest in her eyes and stopped the pursuit. She had never failed Dante and knew to the very core of her being that she would rather die than disappoint him.

The moment passed, and Angelica folded the thoughts, placing them again in the farthest drawer of her memory. She instinctively knew it would very shortly be time for her to become Dante's Azrael.

"It's 7:30," Bill whispered.

"What is the wind speed?" she asked.

From one of the inside pockets of his reconnaissance jacket, Bill pulled out a small anemometer. It read 2.1 mph, slightly under the 2.4 mph that Angelica, playing a game with herself, had guessed.

Angelica quietly went through the detachable box magazine. It held eight rounds, more than enough for two kill shots. She knew this, but experience had taught her to be prepared for any eventuality. She then checked the padded Leupold sight and slightly adjusted it.

Chapter Thirty-Nine

Sean decided to have the taxi let him off at the fortified entrance. It was a comfortable walk to the house, and the driver didn't have to negotiate the newly installed four concrete barriers that had been placed in front of the gate at angles preventing a straight drive through to the property's entry point.

The feeling that Andrew was turning the place into a fortified camp crossed Sean's mind as he paid the driver and climbed out of the cab. Putting the car in gear, the driver headed the vehicle back to Inverness. The sentry had seen Sean coming and the steel-reinforced gate slowly slid open. Walking past the guardhouse, Sean smiled and gave a casual wave. The guard returned the gesture. Sean knew that two more sentries were patrolling the property.

He was feeling relatively happy about life. Yesterday, he'd been told that *Journey* was out of dry dock. The Guardians would be preparing her today for sailing to Janus. It meant he and Diane, along with Elijah, would be leaving for the island tomorrow morning.

Inverness was a nice city, but after more than a month in a guesthouse, it would be good to be home.

Since this was their last day before returning to Janus, Sean and Diane had decided on a trip to Nairn, a small seaside town located on the Moray Firth. It was about a thirty-minute drive from Inverness. They planned to spend the morning on the beach, have a late and long lunch in one of the village restaurants, and then return in time to pack.

Diane was picking up the rental car and would meet Sean on the street outside the Guardians' headquarters at 9:15. Traffic was heavy at that hour, and stopping was always a hazard, so he was committed to being there on time. That wouldn't be a problem, since he was part of the group that included Elijah, Andrew, and Leyland, which always left for town by 8:15.

With these thoughts accompanying him, Sean continued down the path toward the house, passing the laboratory where the Word of Janus was being restored. Arriving at the home, he climbed the steps to the gallery, strode across the hardwood planking, and entered through the open front door. As Sean continued down the hallway, he could smell the enticing aroma of eggs, ham, toast, and coffee intermingled in the air. Leyland, as usual, was preparing breakfast, and Sean approached the kitchen with anticipation.

He arrived just as the Guardian was readying the plates. Sean took his accustomed place opposite Elijah, while Andrew and Leyland sat across from each other. There was little talk as the men ate. The plates had been wiped clean with the few remaining pieces of toast, and everyone was relaxing over coffee when Andrew's phone rang.

After answering, he listened for about a minute before agreeing with the caller. Closing the phone, Andrew turned to Elijah and said, "That was our friend Ray Shepherd."

"And why is he calling?" asked the Prophet, matching Sean's thought.

"I contacted him a few days ago to see if he could review what we've done to keep the codex safe," said the Guardian. "He'll be here in about thirty minutes."

Sean immediately looked at his watch. It was just past 7:00. *No worries about meeting Diane on time,* he thought.

"What's he doing in this part of the world?" wondered Elijah.

"I don't know," responded Andrew. "When I e-mailed him, it was more with the thought of sending him diagrams about what we're doing with the property. But Ray phoned back; said he'd be in the area this week and would be glad to drop by. I immediately took him up on his offer."

"It will be interesting to hear his views on your security system," said the Prophet.

"I'm looking forward to it," answered the Guardian as Leyland and Sean stood to begin clearing the table and washing the meal's dishes.

Chapter Forty

✤

Sean was putting the last of the breakfast plates away when Leyland called from the front door that Shepherd had arrived. Looking at the wall clock, Sean noted the time was 7:40. He glanced over at Andrew, who was eyeing a fresh pot of coffee made by Elijah before he'd gone outside to meet the retired soldier.

"I suppose my cup of java will have to wait," said the Guardian, looking wistfully at his empty mug. "Never mind, I'll have some before we leave for town. Let's go and see what Shepherd thinks about our upgraded defenses."

"Good idea," responded Sean. "I'm meeting Diane in front of headquarters at 9:15, so I'd like to be on our way with enough time to make sure she's not waiting."

"That shouldn't be a problem," said Andrew. "I'll make sure we leave no later than 8:30."

"Thanks," responded Sean as the two men walked down the hallway to the front door and outside. A black Volkswagen Transporter was parked close to the bottom of the steps, forcing the men to walk around the vehicle's front end before entering the courtyard.

Andrew's new vehicle, the Chevrolet SUV was on the left side of the driveway, about midway between the home and the guardhouse.

Standing next to Elijah, Leyland, and Shepherd were two men who seemed to have been cut from the same mold. Like Shepherd, both were wearing loose-fitting British army fatigues and combat boots. Both were tall and bulky and had hair cut razor close to the scalp, deep tans, and eyes hidden behind dark aviator glasses.

Shepherd did a quick introduction, revealing the men's names were Cooper and Holt. Each nodded as his name was called and then turned back to Shepherd for instructions about reviewing the security system. No handshakes were offered, and it didn't seem to be needed, as the encounter between the Janus group and Shepherd's team would be brief.

Sean turned toward Andrew and was about to suggest they should get the review under way when he noticed the bottom of a holster poking out from underneath Cooper's shirt. Sean looked more closely at Holt, along with Shepherd, and saw they also were armed.

Surprised at the sight of firearms, he said to Shepherd, "A concealed weapon is illegal in Scotland. Why are you and your team carrying so much firepower?"

"What do you have?" asked Andrew, the curiosity obvious in his voice. "My men are unarmed."

"We're each carrying the Ruger P90," said Shepherd with obvious pleasure. "It gives us eight shots with .45 auto-loading rounds. And there's an AK-47 in the Transporter. We have a special dispensation from the office of the Chief Constable of Scottish Police.

"I picked up an assignment guarding a prince from the Saudi Arabian royal family. He has this thing for old castles and is touring the country seeing what his money can buy. We're in Inverness because there seem to be a lot of castles around here, and it's close to Loch Ness. I don't suppose any of them are for sale, but one never knows how loud those petro dollars can talk."

"So why are you here and not guarding him?" asked Sean.

"It's a twenty-four-hour detail. Three of my men are with him now. I'm only here because Andrew contacted me, and I knew we were coming to the city. We'll do a walk around, make any suggestions that could help tighten your security, and then be on our way."

"Do you need a guide?" offered Andrew.

"No thanks," responded Shepherd. "I like to approach these assignments with fresh eyes. Cooper will check out the perimeter. Holt will survey the lab and look over what you've done with the cement barricades and the gate. I'll spend my time in the guardhouse going over your procedures in case of an attack. It should take us a couple of hours. We can meet back in the house."

As the armed contingent moved off, Andrew looked over at Elijah and said, "There isn't much we can do here. Leyland can take you and Sean into town. I'll stay in case Shepherd needs anything."

"I made some coffee a few minutes ago," noted Elijah. "I'd like a cup before we go. What about the rest of you?" he said, looking at Andrew.

"Sounds like a plan," responded the Guardian.

With that, the group cut back in front of the Volkswagen, climbed the stairs, and walked single file into the house. Sean looked at his watch. It read 7:59. He still had plenty of time to meet Diane.

Chapter Forty-One

✣

The arrival of the black Volkswagen Transporter was a variable that surprised Angelica and Bill. The driver parked it sideways to the hide nest. What shocked the couple was when they saw the three men in army fatigues climb out of the vehicle. Both noted the walk, the erect carriage, and the way each man surveyed the surroundings as they disembarked. These weren't security guards; they were professional soldiers.

"Are they armed?" Angelica hissed.

Bill put the Leupold scope to his eye. Slowly and with patient precision, he began scanning the men. He soon spotted the bulges along the side of their waistbands.

"They're carrying. But I can't tell what they have."

"Well this group will certainly know how to use them," said Angelica.

"They've parked the car in front of the gallery," whispered Bill. "What's your sight line?"

Angelica nestled the Remington against her shoulder and looked through the Leupold. "If we shift my platform to the right about a foot, I'll be fine."

The pair quietly slid the rock over. Angelica rested the bipod on the base and again sighted. "I have a clear shot," she announced.

Because the distance was the length of almost two football fields, it was impossible to hear what the men were saying. The couple watched as Elijah came out with one of the Guardians and joined the newly arrived squad. A few minutes later, Brennan and the other Guardian left the house and became part of the group.

"Do you have a shot?" Bill, from force of habit, whispered the question.

Angelica had been scoping both her targets. However, the group was a constantly shifting montage of bodies. She could put a bullet through one of the natural spaces in the chain-link fence. It meant she could take out one of the subjects, but she knew that, in the confusion to follow, it would be impossible to guarantee a kill shot on the second target.

She explained that to Bill, who wondered if the targets were going to leave after conferring with the soldiers. "They might not go back in the house," Bill noted.

"Then I'll take them out as they walk across the yard," said Angelica with an icy calmness. The assassin's entire focus was on the targets. The only sound she heard was Bill's voice; her only view was what she was seeing through the Leupold.

"But you won't have a clear shot at both through the fence," Bill said. "Not only that, but we have a group of armed soldiers within the zone."

Incredibly, there was no tension between the two. The conversation was remarkably calm as they discussed the problem.

"What do you recommend?" asked Angelica.

Bill checked his watch. The time was 7:56. It meant Frank was at the pickup point, and Jose and Tom were positioned to take out the electrical cable.

"I'm going to contact Jose," he told her.

He opened the headset and relayed the situation to the gatekeeper. Jose's initial response was to request Frank confirm he was in place. When the driver came back with, "Affirmative," Jose instructed Bill to hold the position.

"What happens if they start moving toward the SUV?"

"Then we scrub the mission," came the instant answer. "Tell Angelica that she is not to deviate from the plan. The risk under any other scenario is too great."

Bill was about to sign off and tell his shooter what Jose had said, when he saw the soldiers heading toward the far edge of the property and the targets along with the Guardians walking into the house.

"We're still a go," said Bill, his voice calm and emotionless. He detailed what had happened. Jose told him to keep the communication open.

Angelica raised her head from the sight as the four men disappeared into the house. There was no need to discuss the conversation between Bill and Jose. It was extraneous to the situation. However, she did want to know the time.

Bill checked his watch and told her it was 8:01. Slowly, she pulled the Remington up, nestled the stock against her right shoulder, and gently placed her right eye against the padded Leupold sight. The time was near.

Chapter Forty-Two

✥

It was 8:04. The spotter gave Angelica the wind direction; it was coming out of the southwest at 2.3 mph. He pulled the bolt cutters out of the backpack and laid the tool within easy reach on one of the rocks.

Focusing through his spotting scope, Bill gauged there was little heat rising off the ground. No corrections for wind or heat needed to be made by Angelica. Although they'd done it several times before, he gave her the distance reading to the top of the steps—240 yards. She didn't need to adjust her scope, but there was comfort for both of them in doing what had become routine through so many kills.

Angelica continued breathing through her nose, using her diaphragm, not the chest. This brought air down to the lower portion of her lungs, where the oxygen exchange was most efficient. She could feel her heart rate slow, the muscles relax. The natural tension she had felt earlier faded into the background.

*****

Bill relayed that it was 8:15. The targets weren't out yet. Bill had taken note of how the soldiers had dispersed around the property. He and Angelica had been on difficult assignments before, but the spotter was feeling increasingly uneasy about the mission. One of the soldiers had met up with the perimeter guard, and they were gradually coming closer to the hide nest.

Bill looked at his watch—8:17 and still no sight of the targets. He could feel the sweat collecting on the back of his neck and along his forehead.

*****

Elijah, Andrew, and Leyland didn't seem to be in a hurry. The conversation was focused on the codex and how pleased the Prophet was about getting it back. Finally, Leyland stood up and said, "I suppose we should be getting into town."

"That's a great idea," Sean almost shouted. The wall clock showed 8:20.

"I'll come out with you," offered Andrew. "I'd like to see how Shepherd and his men are doing."

The four of them walked down the hall, with Andrew and Leyland, as was habit, in the lead. The two Guardians opened the door and stepped out onto the porch. Elijah and Sean followed.

A siren sounded across the courtyard. The power had gone out.

"That's the second, time this month," said Andrew as he trod on the first step. "I'll have to contact the electrical …"

*****

As Tom, following Bill's command pulled the triaged cable, the alarm blared, and the spotter leaped forward. With the bolt cutters, Bill hacked away part of the fence, exposing the gallery to Angelica's unobstructed view.

The Guardians stepped onto the porch, followed by the targets. Everyone was walking outside the house. The Guardians were blocking her line of sight, but that had been expected.

For a brief moment, she settled her vision through the scope. Now, there was no more thought. She cradled the stock into her shoulder. The index finger of her right hand rested alongside the weapon's trigger.

Her mind had locked itself away, allowing her physical training to focus entirely on the task. The moments ticked by.

Chapter Forty-Three

The Guardians in unison climbed down to the bottom step. Angelica followed the line of sight from the scope. Her breathing was slow and measured. The targets were at the top of the porch. Angelica brought the sight's red laser up to the man's chest. She caressingly squeezed the trigger. The bullet tore out of the barrel at a velocity of more than 2,500 feet per second.

It struck the target in the chest, creating a splash of red as it drove into the heart and exploded. The man was driven backward, splayed across the porch.

The weapon jolted back onto Angelica's shoulder. She quickly and smoothly swung the Remington's barrel over to the second man while reloading the breech and prepared to shoot. But instead of seeing a standing target, she saw that he'd been knocked off balance by one of the Guardians. She fired, not sure whether she'd hit him or he'd stumbled. He was on his back.

Bill had instinctively picked up the cartridges and was telling her it was time to leave. Heavy fire was being directed into the trees from two soldiers—one who was on the perimeter and one who had been looking at the lab. They only had a general idea where the kill shot had come from but were pouring enough rounds into the area that it wasn't safe for Angelica and Bill to remain.

The soldier who had been in the lab began running toward the Transporter, laying down a ribbon of bullets as he ran. Covering fire was coming from the soldier in the guardhouse. Bill sighted the Smith & Wesson and fired several rounds at the running soldier but missed. Angelica ran forward and crouched at the fence opening. She sighted at the soldier who had been firing at them from the perimeter. He was less than fifteen feet away, with the guard behind him.

She put one shot into the soldier's forehead. When he fell, she reloaded the breech and fired a shot into the guard's chest. Retreating back to the hide nest, Angelica crouched with Bill behind the rocks.

"I can hear shooting," said Jose over Bill's headset. "What's going on?"

"We have one target down, the other wounded," replied Bill. "But we're taking fire."

"Then get out of there," commanded Jose.

Suddenly, the unmistakable sound of an AK-47 discharging could be heard behind the Transporter. The noise was intense. Bullets were ripping into the forest, tearing at tree trunks and leaves. They careened off the rocks protecting Angelica and Bill and dug into the ground.

The spotter cut the conversation. Abandoning their position was uppermost in his mind.

"Time to go," said Bill. "When I begin firing, start running. I'll follow."

"I need to finish the mission," Angelica screamed. All her feelings for the prelate had overwhelmed her. He was her life. She was his creation. How could she go back to Dante, knowing she'd failed him?

"No, we have to leave," Bill beseeched her.

"You go," she yelled over the ever-closing gunfire. "I'm staying until I eliminate the second target. They leave tomorrow. I won't have another chance."

"It can't be done," screamed Bill. "The mission is blown. We can't match their firepower."

Just then, another series of rounds from the AK-47 poured into the rocks. The bullets tore gaping holes in the fence, glanced off the rocks, and decimated small trees behind them.

A shard of stone flew into Angelica's face, opening a large gash on her cheek. Blood began to trickle down her face and seeped onto her jacket. She nestled further down behind the granite wall.

Bill did a quick calculation. Angelica had fired four rounds; that left her with four. He had used six rounds in a futile effort to stop the soldier from running across the courtyard, which meant he had four bullets remaining in the clip of his Smith & Wesson and a ten-round magazine in his backpack. Eighteen rounds between them.

An eerie silence had settled over the kill zone. It didn't last long. From the guardhouse door came five evenly spaced shots. Bill instinctively ducked lower behind the rocks. The firing stopped, and he saw a soldier dart out from the guardhouse and head toward the Transporter. The AK-47 immediately started up, giving the runner powerful and deadly cover by pinning down Angelica and Bill. There was no opportunity to fire at the swiftly moving target.

As the running soldier ducked behind the Transporter, the shots from the AK-47 became evenly spaced. No longer was it a swath of fire, but instead there was a volley of eight to nine

The Hope of Janus

shots at a time, fired at the hide nest in what seemed like five- to ten-second intervals.

"This is bad," Bill said. "They have us trapped here. We can't move without being hit."

As if to reaffirm Bill's words, another burst from the AK-47 tore at the fence and the underbrush. Since the Transporter was sideways to the hide nest, it meant there was ample protection for those behind it. The soldier was leaning across the hood, using the vehicle's body as protection while he continued to unleash volley after volley.

Bill and Angelica buried themselves behind the rocks. The sound was unlike anything either of them had ever known. It was loud, powerful, and unrelenting.

Suddenly it stopped, to be replaced by deadly accurate handgun fire. Bill knew the AK-47 shooter was putting in a new magazine and the small arms fire was designed to keep him and Angelica immobilized in the hide nest. For some reason, Bill found peace in not hearing the hellish lash of AK-47 bullets pouring in at them. The quiet lasted mere seconds.

Once again, the AK-47 rounds were coming after them, searching the ground, the rocks, and the brush as they sought out a human target.

Jose's voice came over Bill's headphone. "We've just pulled up behind Frank's van. What's your status?"

Bill, remembering the briefing, was shocked that only about four minutes had elapsed since Tom had pulled the power line. It seemed a lifetime had passed from when Angelica fired her first kill shot. "We're pinned down with heavy fire from an AK-47," replied the spotter. "We've got eighteen rounds between us."

"What about enemy manpower?"

"Two soldiers," replied the spotter. "They're the only ones doing the firing. There has been nothing from the Guardians."

And then Bill heard the words he'd been desperate to hear. "Tom and I will be with you in a couple of minutes," said Jose. "Use just enough ammo to hold them off. We're going to need every round we have to get out of this mess. Frank, keep the engine running. We won't have any time to spare."

"I'm at the post and ready to haul ass out of here," declared the driver.

Almost as an afterthought, the gatekeeper asked if the other target had been eliminated.

"That's a negative."

There was a slight pause, and then Jose replied, "Okay. We'll regroup at the house and see what Dante wants done."

Dante was the least of Bill's concerns. His only objective was to get Angelica and himself away from what had become pure survival.

Angelica was sighting along the Remington. "I can get the shooter," she said. "I just need a better angle." Before the spotter could stop her, Angelica got to one knee and sighted on the soldier. Bill grabbed at her back. He was pulling Angelica back down when the spotter felt her body shudder and heard a scream escape her lips. She fell backward, writhing in pain. The bullet had torn apart her left knee. Bone and cartilage were poking through her pant leg. Blood was pumping out, staining the ground around her.

Angelica's face had gone a pasty white. She had bitten through her lip, and there was blood on her chin, joining the ribbon of red from where the rock chip had wounded her cheek. For Bill, an already terrible situation had just become a lot worse. If they were going to get Angelica out alive, it meant she would have to be carried. She couldn't walk and was losing a lot of blood. Several seconds later Jose and Tom belly crawled into the hide nest. No explanation about what had happened was needed.

If they can get in, we can all get out, thought Bill.

The Transporter's engine started. The vehicle turned and began coming directly at the hide nest. Hugging the Transporter's right side rear was a soldier with the AK-47. He had the weapon nestled in the crook of his arm and was carpeting the hide nest. No longer were the shots being spaced. This was a full-on deadly barrage of bullets.

The vehicle inched closer. The soldier was firing low, the bullets piercing the ground and kicking up earth. Chips of rock were flying in all directions.

"Grab Angelica by the shoulders," Jose commanded Bill and Tom. "We're going to crawl our way out of here, and we'll drag her with us." Bill slithered over and grabbed Angelica's left armpit. Tom, who'd taken refuge behind the largest rock, crawled his way from the shelter. He lifted up slightly reaching for Angelica. The bullets quickly found him, tearing at his flesh, ripping apart his back, and turning his head into a pulpy mass. The slugs drove Tom's body several feet over the ground, and Bill retched at the sight of his head.

And still the Transporter moved relentlessly forward. In another minute, it would be at the destroyed fence—twenty feet from the hide-nest. There was a pause. Someone was yelling at them to surrender.

Bill looked at Jose, who shook his head. Surrender was not a consideration. It wasn't in their DNA. They were fourth-generation members of the order. The code was inbred—battle on or retreat to fight another day. Whatever the cost, the order's anonymity had to be protected.

Bill stood and emptied the Smith & Wesson at the vehicle, shattering the windscreen. But it was no use. Seeing Bill, the driver had ducked beneath the dashboard.

"We have to go!" screamed Jose.

"What about Angelica?" Bill yelled.

The soldier with the AK-47 had started up again. Jose never got to answer the question. The bullet that found him was a ricochet off one of the hide nest rocks. It dug deep into his right side, snapping rib bones and ligaments. Blood started to flow in an ever-increasing stream. He screamed and passed out from the pain.

Bill knew he had a decision to make and only seconds to carry it out. He could stay, which meant certain death. Or he could unleash a barrage of rounds using Jose's fully loaded Smith & Wesson, hoping the distraction would allow him to run toward the road and the waiting Frank.

Bill was afraid but resolute.

Tossing his empty gun, he reached for Jose's weapon and was staggered by the amount of blood that had flooded the ground around the gatekeeper. The gun was slippery with blood and gore. Bill didn't have the time or the inclination to check Jose's pulse. He knew the man was dead. That left him and Angelica, who was moaning with the pain.

He realized it would be difficult, but fifteen years of being together for so many missions bred a loyalty that few people would understand. Bill grabbed her right arm and positioned it over his shoulders. She instinctively wrapped the arm around his neck. He didn't recognize that the AK-47 had gone quiet. He just knew there was only one way out.

Bill was terrified of dying, and was confused by all the noise that had pummeled him and the carnage he'd seen. He was used to death but at a distance, where it never truly impacted him. This was so different, and it sickened him. There was just one thought in his mind. Fire the weapon and get safely to the road with Angelica. Frank would take them away from this place that had become such a frenzied nightmare.

The Transporter was still rolling. It was within ten feet of the fence. The AK-47 had remained silent. There was yelling from behind the vehicle, but Bill's mind had left him and gone to a place far beyond his reach. He didn't understand what was being said.

He knew only that he had to escape. Bill stood, grabbed Angelica's arm with his left hand, and hoisted the assassin to her feet. With the right hand, he unleashed a volley from the Smith & Wesson, emptying the chamber.

The rapid-fire rounds from the AK-47 found them before they'd gone five feet. Bill felt a searing pain in his back. He was knocked down, bringing Angelica with him. They lay on the ground, face-to-face, like two lovers in a macabre play. He reached out and grabbed her hand. Angelica was spitting blood.

The final words he heard her say were, "I failed him."

Bill felt infinitely sad and afraid. He didn't want to die. Another volley of bullets pummeled the ground close to him. He screamed as one of them tore out his stomach. It was the last sound he made.

Chapter Forty-Four

Elijah was talking to Sean about his excitement at returning to Janus in the morning. They stepped out onto the gallery and walked a couple of steps. Sean asked what time they would be meeting aboard *Journey*.

The siren from the guardhouse sounded, meaning the electrical power was out. Andrew turned and was saying something when the Prophet suddenly fell backward. Sean felt a pair of hands pulling his legs out from under him. He stumbled and experienced a burning sensation in his right thigh. He fell heavily on the gallery. Andrew and Leyland were yelling for him to stay down. They were crouched behind the Transporter.

Sean looked over at Elijah and gaped. Where the chest had been was torn and mutilated flesh mixed with the remains of his jacket and shirt. The glasses lying beside his body, one of the lenses missing, were a poignant testament to a life ended. Blood was spilling along the porch.

The lifeless eyes told Sean all he needed to know. There is no prolonged dying when a bullet rips apart the heart. Elijah probably only had several seconds to process the shock of what had happened and that sickened Sean. For a few moments there was life and then there was nothing. The Prophet was dead. Overcome by shock, horror, and disbelief, coupled with frantic confusion, Sean could only stare at what, seconds ago, had been the embodiment of everything Janus represented.

Someone was pulling him off the balcony. Andrew and Leyland half-carried him behind the Transporter. He slumped down onto the ground, his back against the vehicle. The pain was excruciating. It felt as though someone had thrust a hot poker into his leg. Yet he was losing the feeling in his foot.

The sound of gunfire from the soldiers echoed across the yard. Sean couldn't be sure, but he thought the shots were coming from two locations.

To be under fire, to see Elijah killed, was traumatizing and frightening. Sean could feel his heart racing, and his body felt clammy. He wasn't sure if what he was experiencing was from shock, from the wound, or from fear.

Sean was pulled out of his thoughts by the sound of heavy gunfire heading toward the Transporter. One of the soldiers— Sean remembered his name was Holt and that he'd been inspecting the lab—dove headfirst behind the Transporter.

The courtyard lapsed into a bizarre silence.

"How many are out there?" asked Andrew, his breath coming in short, rasping gasps.

"Probably two," replied Holt. "It looks to me like one's a sniper, while the other's a spotter. I saw plenty of these teams in Afghanistan. From the sound, I'd say the spotter has some kind of handgun."

"What about the other one?"

"It has to be a sniper rifle, but I can't tell the make."

"What else could they have?" asked Sean.

"If they had something more powerful, it would have been used by now," responded Holt.

"Then we have them outmanned and outgunned," said Leyland. "Does anyone have a fix on the location?"

Holt got into a crouch and looked over the Transporter's hood. He beckoned for Andrew and Leyland to do the same. "When I was running across the courtyard, the shots came from behind that clump of trees," he said, pointing to a spot about two hundred yards from the vehicle. "I fired in that direction and heard a couple of rounds bounce off some rocks. It seems they've built a hide nest."

Just as the men lowered themselves back down, two shots in rapid succession broke the stillness. Holt again raised himself into a crouch and looked over the Transporter's hood. When he came back down, his face was grim.

"What's going on out there?" asked Andrew.

"They got Cooper and one of your guards," Holt replied. "I'm pretty sure they're both dead. I see they got the old guy and wounded you," he said, looking at Sean.

"The old guy's name was Elijah," Andrew stated quietly. "He was a very special person—a man of peace."

Holt nodded. "Yeah, well that's too bad. But right now I have a job to do." He reached up and opened the back door of the Transporter. Shimmying across the seat and partway in, he came out with the AK-47. Holt checked the magazine and put his finger on the trigger. He crawled over to the vehicle's front, stood, and began firing.

Sean heard shots coming from the guardhouse. Holt laid down a heavy carpet of rounds. Shepherd arrived on the run, ducking behind the Transporter. Holt stopped firing and dropped down beside Andrew.

"I've lost a good man," Shepherd said before anyone could say anything. "Cooper has been with me a long time."

"He was a great friend," responded Holt. "It's time to finish this thing."

He got up, leaned over the Transporter's hood, and began a systematic firing of eight to nine shots at a time, evenly spaced. "This will keep them pinned down," he yelled at Shepherd.

The intensity was deafening, and Sean sat, stunned at the brutality of the punishing noise.

"I'm getting low on rounds," said Holt.

Shepherd reached inside the Transporter and handed another magazine to Holt. As Holt switched the cartridge clips, Shepherd emptied the magazine of his Ruger P90 in the direction of the hide nest.

Holt tossed his Ruger to Shepherd, crouched over the Transporter's hood, and began firing. Once again, he fired in short, evenly spaced bursts.

Shepherd kept low behind the Transporter and moved over to where Holt was keeping up the spaced barrage. The two soldiers huddled at the Transporter's front end, discussing their next move.

Andrew duck-walked over and looked at Sean's thigh. He pulled out a Swiss Army knife and cut away the pant leg above the laceration.

"You're lucky," he said. "It's a flesh wound. There's still plenty of blood, though. I'll put a tourniquet on it. That should help until we get you to the hospital."

Ripping the pant leg into two strips, Andrew used one to tie the tourniquet. He balled up the other strip and handed it to Sean.

"Put this over the wound and keep pressure on it," advised the Guardian. "Are you able to walk?"

"The leg feels a bit stiff," responded Sean. "But I shouldn't have any trouble getting around. The tourniquet seems to be working. There's little bleeding now."

"That's good," said Andrew, just as Leyland scuttled over, asking if there was anything he could do to help.

Before Sean could answer, Shepherd knelt down beside the three men. They paid close attention as the soldier spoke rapidly and quietly.

"Holt and I have put together a plan. We're going to use this thing here," he said, slapping the side of the Transporter, "like an armored truck to overrun their position."

Sean listened carefully as Shepherd laid out the operation's details.

Chapter Forty-Five

A volley of bullets was the assailant's response to Shepherd's call for them to surrender.

The Transporter's windscreen had been shot out, but that didn't stop Holt from ensuring the vehicle continued its relentless move forward. He was hunched down behind the dashboard, occasionally peering out to see that he was keeping the Transporter heading straight at the target. Huddled behind the vehicle were Sean, Andrew, and Leyland. On the right side was Shepherd laying down another deadly barrage from the AK-47.

He stopped firing, and for Sean, the silence was profound and strangely comforting. Shepherd again called for the assailants to put their weapons down and come out. The Transporter continued on and was within ten feet of the shattered fence.

"Maybe they're all dead or have escaped," said Leyland as the vehicle came to a halt.

"Someone is in there," responded Shepherd. "I hear movement."

The soldier again yelled for the attackers to surrender.

It happened so quickly that all Shepherd could do was react instinctively. A fusillade of bullets poured out of the hide nest. Shepherd fired a steady stream of rounds.

He stopped firing, and the silence echoed in Sean's ears. Shepherd unleashed another volley. There was a terrifying scream and then silence.

Shepherd told Holt to drive the vehicle into the fence. The soldier slowly drove forward until the Transporter had brought down a portion of the barrier. He then backed the vehicle up about fifteen feet and brought it to a grinding halt. Several bullets had pierced the radiator and torn into the engine block. Steam was hissing from the front end, and oil was pooling underneath.

Shepherd inched toward the vehicle's front. He held the AK-47 at waist level and fired in a sweep, with the hide nest as the middle point. Holt opened the Transporter's door and joined his colleague. Shepherd beckoned for the two Guardians along with Sean to join him.

The five of them walked over the downed portion of the fence and the twenty feet to the hide nest. There were the remains of three men and a woman. It was a mess. Human flesh and bones were not made to withstand the destructive power of multiple bullets entering the body. All were on their backs, except for the woman, who was in a fetal position.

Shepherd walked forward several steps and kicked/rolled the woman onto her back. For a moment, Sean was stunned. He took an involuntary gulp of air, and his eyes widened. Even in death, her beauty was mesmerizing.

"Recognize anybody?" asked the soldier.

Andrew and Leyland shook their heads, silently surveying the destruction.

The quiet was overwhelming. The only sound Sean could hear was a ringing in his ears. Adrenalin was pumping through his body. His leg had gone stiff, but he didn't feel any pain. He wasn't sure whether he was going to laugh in relief or vomit at the carnage. He forced himself to do neither.

Instead, he looked at his watch. The battery-powered numbers told him it was 8:35. But that was impossible. He was sure the firefight had lasted for at least an hour. It couldn't be just a few minutes since he and Elijah had left the house.

Elijah. The Prophet was dead. A profound sadness overcame Sean, almost pushing him to his knees. His eyes filled with tears. The droplets ran down his cheeks, giving bleak evidence to his distress. He wiped a dirty hand across his face. This was not a time to show grief. That could come later. Right now, he needed to work with the others in determining what came next.

The sun, seemingly too sickened to witness the destruction, had retreated behind a high bank of clouds. A lone bird began to chirp. It was soon joined by others. A squirrel ran up one of the trees bordering the driveway. Balancing on a limb, it sat and stared at the scene below before retreating to the ground and disappearing into the forest.

*****

The men had left the hide nest and were gathered in the courtyard's center.

For a few moments, there was quiet until Andrew said, "This has to be the work of the Praetorian Order. Only Sabatini would mount something like this against us."

"We can leave that for your intelligence and tech ops people to figure out," said Shepherd, his tone abrupt and coldly deliberate. "Right now, we have to get this cleaned up. I know you have a lot of influence in Inverness. Is there a way you can keep the local police away from here?"

Andrew nodded his head. "The chief constable is one of us. I'll call him now. There'll be no interference."

The Guardian pulled a cell phone from his back pocket, walked several feet away from the group, and punched in a number.

While Andrew was on the phone, Shepherd turned to Leyland. "Do you have people who can handle what we've got here?"

Leyland was silent for several seconds. "There are a number of ambulance crews we can call in. That will allow us to bypass the coroner. And there's a funeral home that will allow us to have the bodies cremated. It can all be done quite quickly."

"Is everyone in Inverness part of your organization?" wondered Shepherd, clearly impressed at the Guardians' reach.

"Not everyone," said Leyland quietly. "But we have enough spread throughout the city and the council area that we can handle most situations—even this one."

Andrew returned to the group. "It's done," he said. "We'll be left alone."

When Leyland told his partner about the plan for handling the situation, Andrew responded, "Everything is good with one exception. Elijah will be taken to Janus. I'll take care of the details."

Sean knew the Guardians were operating on adrenalin generated by the firefight. Andrew and Leyland would need time to grieve Elijah's loss, but for now action had to take the place of anguish.

"I'll work with you," he told the Guardian.

The relief spreading across Andrew's face like high tide on a beach told Sean all he needed to know. Grief and tears were close to the surface, testing the Guardian's stoic nature.

Leyland had taken a seat in the SUV and was on the phone. Shepherd and Holt were with him. The two remaining sentries were in the guardhouse. It reminded Sean that the lab workers would soon be arriving.

"This place needs to be closed down for the day," he said. "We should position one of our guards at the gate. The lab people can be told something's happened with the electricity, and there'll be no work for today."

"Good idea," replied Andrew. "I'll get that organized."

As the Guardian headed to the guardhouse, Sean was left alone in the middle of the courtyard. He limped over to the gallery and hobbled up the steps to where Elijah was lying.

The pool of blood had already started to congeal into a sticky testimonial to death. He picked up the broken glasses and put them in his pocket. The sightless brown eyes without the protection of glasses made the body seem small and intensely vulnerable. Careful not to step in the blood, Sean leaned in close. He reached out and ran a hand over the Prophet's eyes, pulling the eyelids down. It made him feel better for Elijah—as though he was restoring some measure of deserved dignity to the corpse.

As Sean straightened up, he felt a tap on his shoulder. It was Andrew.

"We have three ambulances on the way," he said. "They should start arriving in about ten minutes. Leyland has arranged for Elijah to be taken to the funeral home along with the rest of the bodies. Shepherd and Holt will ride with their man."

"I'll go with Elijah," said Sean. "That way, you and Leyland can handle the situation here."

"Of course," responded the Guardian. "How's your leg?"

In all the turmoil and aftermath, Sean had forgotten about his wound. He looked at his leg and was surprised that the tourniquet was holding. "After I make the arrangements for Elijah, I'll ask Diane to drive me to one of our doctors."

"We have a number at Raigmore that will take care of you without asking any questions," said Andrew. "Diane will know what to do."

"We'll probably have to delay our sailing by a couple of days while everything is prepared for Elijah," noted Sean.

"I'll handle that," stated the Guardian.

An ambulance with the markings of the Scottish Ambulance Service emblazoned across its side slowly trundled into the yard. There were no flashing lights or siren, and as the attendants stepped from the cab, Leyland pointed them in the direction of the gallery.

Sean limped down the steps. His right leg felt stiff and sore. He'd call Diane when he got to the funeral home. For now, his focus was on the Prophet.

"It's time we got Elijah ready for going home to Janus," he said.

Andrew nodded his head, tears carving rivulets in the dirt and grime that covered his face.

Chapter Forty-Six

✣

Frank yelled into his headset mike. There was no response. Fear was consuming him and churning his stomach. He tasted the bile as it rose in his throat. He had heard the rapid rounds of gunfire and knew his team wasn't equipped with anything capable of unleashing that kind of firepower.

And then there was nothing but silence. Frank's nerves jangled as if they were sparking electrical wires. How long should he wait? He glanced up and saw the Corolla framed in the van's rearview mirror. He opened the Chrysler's door and climbed out. Feeling nervous and exposed, Frank walked several yards into the underbrush bordering the Guardians' property. He found the fence, walked several more yards, and looked along its length. What he saw turned his legs weak and set his bowels rumbling.

From the group of men standing in the courtyard, the only one he recognized should have been dead. That was the young guy whose picture he'd seen during Jose's briefing. He looked to the gallery and saw the old man's splayed figure. Again, from the briefing he knew that the porch was where both targets were to be taken out. Angelica had eliminated only one.

No one was holding a gun, which meant they were confident the danger had passed. With the insight that came from being together for fifteen years, Frank instinctively knew his team members were dead. The commitment to the order was too strong. Each of them would rather die than be taken prisoner. Not only that, but if there were captives, they'd be undergoing interrogation. Nothing like that was happening.

There was a momentary feeling of remorse, but Frank's overpowering urge was to escape. He turned and charged to the van, not caring how much noise he made. Getting into the Chrysler, his heart was beating a rapid tattoo, and his hands were shaking so badly he had difficulty closing the door.

He'd done as Jose had instructed and had left the engine running. But it sounded so loud that Frank's fear of discovery caused him to almost have an anxiety attack. He took several deep breaths, then slammed the shift into gear and stepped on the gas too hard. The vehicle nearly plowed into the underbrush before he yanked the wheel to his left and the Chrysler skidded its way onto the road.

His only thoughts were on getting back to the house, picking up his carry bag, and leaving Inverness. The Corolla would have to stay where it was. For the moment, Frank was intent on one thing—survival.

He focused on driving, trying to calm himself. It wasn't working. The panic rattling his body wouldn't be stilled.

Like a power drill ripping into his brain, the morning's events tore at him. Angelica, Bill, Jose, and Tom were dead. They'd never prepared for anything going this wrong. In the time they'd been together, there'd been a few scrapes and bruises, but this was as bad as it could get. He pulled the van into the driveway beside the Aveo.

Frank knew one thing—he had to get out of Inverness. And the quicker the better. He went through the back door into the kitchen. Sitting at the table, Frank struggled to organize his thoughts. Jose had always made the decisions, but now Frank was on his own.

His first inclination was to grab his carry bag and drive to Glasgow as originally planned. But that would leave two cars and a house full of evidence for the authorities to sift through. Tom always did the final sweep. And after fifteen years of working with the gatekeeper, Frank knew one of the primary rules was to never leave anything behind that could be traced to the order.

There was also the matter of payment. Jose had always let Dante know when a job was completed, and that triggered the deposit of $100,000 into Frank's Barbados account. The amount had been doubled for this job. He could get on the plane and disappear, but there weren't many job opportunities for the driver of a hit squad. He needed the money, and $200,000 would keep him comfortable for a while. The other alternative was to fly into Heathrow and contact Dante from the airport. But that still left a scene full of evidence.

Frank had just experienced the killing of his unit and had enough self-awareness to know he wasn't thinking straight. He needed help making a decision. There was only one person he could call, and that was Dante. The prelate would give him instructions, and Frank desperately wanted someone to tell him what to do now that Jose was gone.

Frank had never spoken with Dante. That was always handled by Angelica and Jose. But there was a first time for everything, and this certainly qualified. Getting up from the table, he went into the bedroom that had been shared by Bill and Jose. He reached into Jose's bag and suddenly had a feeling of such intense remorse that he had to sit on the bed to compose himself.

Three hours ago, they'd shared breakfast, and now everyone was dead. It was almost impossible to process.

He pulled out the cell, opened the phone and scrolled through the numbers, until he found one labeled simply "Valencia." That had to be the one. He hit the readout, put the phone to his ear, and waited.

Chapter Forty-Seven

Dante stood by the window. Dark gray clouds rolled across the morning sky. A wind stirred the leaves of several pine trees located along the western edge of the chateau's gardens.

This was the worst time—the hours when Angelica was in the gravest danger. Restless, Dante moved from the window to behind his desk. He had financial reports to review, but for once, they couldn't hold his attention. Every mission was different, and this was no exception.

Although he never doubted his decisions once made, Dante was fully aware of the danger Angelica faced in eliminating two targets. That it was the first time he'd ever asked her to carry out such an assignment only heightened the concern he always felt. He had justified the need for the two terminations by convincing himself this was the best way to remove a major threat to the Church.

The phone rang on the direct line assigned to Jose. With an overriding sense of relief, Dante picked up the instrument and jammed it against his ear. Instead of Jose's confident voice telling him the mission had been completed, a stranger was asking if he was Mr. Sabatini.

"Who's this?" demanded the prelate. "Where's Jose?"

"It's Frank," the voice replied. "I'm the driver, and I am at the house."

A small worm of doubt began to grow in Dante's stomach. Something obviously had happened to Jose. But what?

"I know who you are," said the prelate, fully familiar with every aspect of Angelica's operations and team. "Why am I talking to you? Where's Jose?"

"We ran into trouble, and he didn't make it. Jose's dead."

While the words were filled with emotion, the impact on Dante was to immediately begin calculating what this meant for the operation. Losing Jose was catastrophic. But if the mission was successful, then the gatekeeper's death was the cost of doing business. There was much the prelate needed to know.

"What happened with the mission?" he demanded.

In a halting voice, Frank told him the old man was dead, but the other target was only wounded, and the injury didn't appear serious.

Dante took a deep breath. This was worse than he thought. Only Elijah was confirmed. Brennan hadn't been eliminated. It meant Angelica had failed. He demanded to know more details. Just as important, Dante needed to hear that Angelica was safe.

"There was a firefight," Frank continued, so quietly that Dante strained to hear. "They're all gone. I'm the only one left."

"Did you see it? Are you sure?"

"I checked the situation. I'm positive they're dead."

"How did you escape?"

"I'm the driver," Frank said, defensively. "The shooting took place at the hide nest. That's not my responsibility."

For a few moments, there was silence on the connection as the prelate struggled with the impact of what he'd heard. It was a testament to Dante's unwavering commitment to the order and his remarkable self-control that, at the same time he was processing Angelica's death, he was also factoring how to end a mission that had failed so badly.

First, he had to ensure the driver remained at the house. Frank had to believe he was going to take care of him.

"You're right, the hide nest wasn't your responsibility," said Dante, allaying any concerns Frank had about recriminations. "We need to get you out of Inverness. Give me the address of where you're staying."

Frank dutifully gave the information.

"I'm sending a team over to clear any evidence and handle getting you away from the city."

Fortunately, thought Dante, Benita and her team were in Inverness. "Is there anything more I should know? Did anyone see you?"

"No one knows I'm here. But a car has been left at the site, and there's two here at the house. None have been cleaned, so I don't know what evidence they contain."

"So there are the cars and the house that have to be swept. What else needs to be done?"

Dante's calmness might have surprised some. But since the mission had failed and Angelica, along with three of her companions, was dead, the cars and house were insignificant. The prelate had previously assumed the Guardians would easily come to the conclusion the order had orchestrated the killings. He was prepared for the backlash, just as those associated with Janus should have expected some sort of reprisal for stealing the codex.

"That's about it," came the reply.

"I'm going to make some arrangements," said a composed-sounding Dante. "As soon as the details are worked out, I'll call on Jose's phone. In the meantime, stay put. We'll get this wrapped up quickly."

The prelate knew these were words Frank wanted to hear. It would keep him at the house until Benita's squad could implement Dante's plan.

"Thank you," said Frank, the relief evident in his voice.

But Dante had already cut the connection.

Focusing on what needed to be done, the prelate knew there was only one answer. Frank was expendable. Without Angelica, what use was the driver? He may be a loyal soldier, but Dante had to cut his losses. It was a decision devoid of emotion. Every aspect of Angelica's operation including forgers, bank accounts, and weapon suppliers had to be shut down. A new squad needed to be formed. Frank represented a liability and was no longer required.

The order had to be protected. Nothing else mattered. Dante hit the intercom and told Juan to book four seats on the last flight that day from Inverness to anywhere outside Britain. Several minutes later, Juan phoned back with the flight number and departure time for a flight to Amsterdam.

Dante closed the intercom, grabbed his cell, and punched in a series of numbers.

Chapter Forty-Eight

✤

The first hint Benita had that her mission was about to change came when she was meeting with her squad for a preliminary review of the operation. It was midmorning, and the team had collected in her suite at the Culloden House Hotel before the mission's final run-through slated for the next evening.

The recon had gone well, and the four-member team was confident of the operation's success. They were armed with AK-47's, Walther P-99s, and concussion grenades. It was going to be a full frontal attack. They didn't expect much resistance but were experienced enough to know that killing might be necessary. It had happened before on other missions, and no one, including Benita, ever shied away from taking a life.

Based on the timetable Dante had given her, Benita knew this was the day Jose's team was to carry out its assignment. Not knowing the time for the attack, she assumed, when the phone rang, it was Jose with a last-minute update. Benita believed the worst news she'd hear was that the operation had been scrubbed.

Putting the phone to her ear, the team leader was shocked to hear Dante's voice.

"We've encountered a problem," the prelate said without preamble and with no emotion. "Jose's mission has failed.

There's only one survivor. Your team has to clean up some loose ends."

"What do you need?" asked Benita, wondering if this would impact her operation.

Dante initially described the house, which needed scrubbing, and explained that two cars were to be wiped clean and dumped. There might also be weapons at the house that must be removed. Benita quickly catalogued the assignment. The process was routine for completing a mission.

"Is that it?" she asked.

Dante didn't pause and immediately responded with, "There's a man at the house. I need him terminated. The body is to be left someplace where it won't be found. He will be waiting for you, so there's no need for a surprise entrance.

"The mission is to be completed within the next two hours. Juan has texted you the address and directions for getting there."

Benita was a child of the order. She had grown up and matured, like Angelica, under the guidance of Dante. And similar to Angelica's team, her squad was comprised of multi-generational members of the Fraternity.

Unlike Angelica, however, she had no illusions about the need for a god in her life. She and every member of her squad worked for Dante, the order, and money. Dante and the Fraternity made the money possible.

Instinct told her the man she was to eliminate was the lone remaining member of what had been Jose's team. She had a brief, hesitant thought about assassinating another member of the order, but then easily rationalized that it was Dante's issue. He was the prelate, and from everything known in her world, his commands were the ones she followed. It had been that way since she was young. The one intense and overriding need that Benita shared with Angelica was the desire to make the prelate proud of her.

She would carry out the mission because it was a command from Dante. And, as always, he would reward her in the only way she fundamentally understood—with funds deposited in her Monaco bank account. It would confirm for Benita, as it did after every mission, the prelate's pride in her accomplishment. There were never any words of praise from Dante. But the cash transfer was all she needed.

"Has our original mission been canceled?" she asked calmly.

"That's affirmative."

"What's our exit strategy?"

"Once the assignment is completed, you and the crew are to immediately implement your departure protocol. I want you out of the hotel, cars returned, and weapons dumped so you can be on a plane out of Inverness this evening.

"Juan has booked all of you on a KLM flight to Amsterdam that leaves at 7:35. He will send the details to your phone. Tickets will be available at the airline counter.

"I'll expect a text from you confirming completion before you board the plane. Once that is received, a payment for you and each member of your team will be deposited in your bank accounts. I am tripling the amount you were each to receive for the original mission."

Benita didn't need a calculator to know her take would be US$225,000. Each member of her team would receive $150,000. Jose was the only member of his team she had ever dealt with. Dante hadn't said who was to be killed, and she was experienced enough not to ask. She hoped the gatekeeper wasn't at the house. But if he was, $225,000 would go a long way toward easing her conscience.

"We'll handle it immediately, and I'll confirm by text," said Benita.

The prelate cut the connection without replying.

*****

Dante picked up the phone and hit the number for Jose's phone. Frank's nervous voice floated over the miles.

"Stay where you are. I'm sending a team. They'll soon be there."

"What about the vehicles?"

"That'll be taken care of. Don't worry."

"What should I do?"

"Wait until the team gets there. After that, follow the new plans we've laid out for you. You'll be contacted in the future."

"Thank you," was all Frank could think of to say.

Dante closed the phone.

It was only then that Dante allowed himself the briefest passage of time to mourn the loss of his Azrael. But for the prelate it was a wake based on thoughts and recollections, not emotions.

He recalled a young girl, full of life, who grew into womanhood before his eyes. Now that she was gone, the only keepsakes he had to remember her by were his memories. There were no photos, letters, or mementos. She had come into his life with nothing and, in leaving, had left him with only delicate wisps of thoughts. They had spent more than half her life apart, yet the prelate had always felt a tangible connection. That had disappeared.

He grieved her loss in the only way he knew—alone and with nothing but his thoughts for solace. But Dante was also faced with the moment's reality. He had a problem in Inverness. So he took his thin book of memories about Azrael and placed them in his mind's strongbox. The book was closed. It would never again be opened to re-read the pages.

*****

Several weeks later, a Chrysler van and a Chevrolet Aveo were discovered abandoned in the Old Town Rose Street multi-level car park. The vehicles had no plates, and their identification tags had been removed. The mystery was solved when the police, looking at their reports on stolen cars, noted that Avis and Budget had, through their rental agencies in Inverness, reported a van and an Aveo long past overdue in being returned. Through their contacts, the Guardians had already returned the Toyota Corolla to the Alamo rental agency at the airport.

When the home's owners arrived from their Hawaii vacation, they were pleased to see the house had been left in excellent condition.

It was the following spring when a farmer walking through an unused portion of his property with his favorite hunting dog came upon a makeshift grave. It contained a decomposing body. The local constabulary was called, and it was determined by the coroner that the man had died from a single .45-caliber gunshot to the head. The police later determined the gun in question was a Glock semiautomatic. There was no identification with the body, and the murder would forever remain an open case.

Chapter Forty-Nine

✣

Journey had been taken out of Inverness harbor and through the Inner Moray firth close to five hours earlier. As usual, Andrew and Leyland, along with Malcolm and Joseph, comprised the crew.

For Sean, the new reality was staggering. Elijah was dead. The Prophet was returning home in a coffin. The casket was in the cargo hold, and the twins were taking turns sitting vigil. Elijah's body would be prepared for burial once they returned to Janus.

Sean was fighting a deep feeling of guilt. Elijah had been killed, yet he was alive. Apart from six stitches in his right thigh and stiffness in his leg, he was relatively unscathed. If Andrew hadn't pulled him down, his body would also be in the cargo hold. The questions reverberated through his mind. Why had he escaped death while the Prophet had not? Was Elijah the intended target and he was just collateral damage? Had the Spirit broken its primary rule and intervened to have him spared?

He'd spoken to Diane, telling her everything about his feelings.

As always, she was eminently practical. "Elijah's death had nothing to do with you," she rationalized. "It was entirely at the shooter's discretion. What's important is the future. You wear the *hope of Janus*, and your thoughts should be focused on what you're going to do now that Elijah is gone."

It was sound advice, and Sean appreciated the logic. There were decisions to make regarding his future on Janus and with the Spirit. But he still required time to process Elijah's death. He needed to settle the many ramifications for both himself and the islanders now that the Prophet was gone. Sean didn't want to reach any impulsive conclusions.

Diane had brewed a full pot of coffee and was pouring some for Sean when Andrew came down from the bridge and asked if the three of them could talk. Leyland was behind the wheel and piloting *Journey.* Malcolm was with Elijah's casket, and Joseph was asleep in his portside bunk.

Sean suggested they wait a couple of minutes while he delivered a coffee for Leyland and one for Malcolm. When he returned, Diane and Andrew were seated in the ship's well-appointed sitting room. Diane had taken the couch, while Andrew was in one of the plush armchairs. Both had steaming mugs of java on the table in front of them. Sean picked up his coffee from the galley counter and joined Diane on the couch.

"We have to think of the future," Andrew began. "Although the car left behind by the killers didn't yield any clues, what happened at the house was obviously the work of the order. A plan for an armed retaliation has to be put in place."

"Before we start talking about retribution," offered Sean, "there has to be an understanding of what it means to us as a society if we allow violence to become part of how we look at the world. Any form of armed reprisal would destroy our society's commitment to peace."

"There's also another issue that must be resolved before we decide on what to do going forward," said Diane. "How do we reconcile the bloodshed that happened at the house with our values?"

"Not one shot was fired by anyone associated with Janus," responded Andrew. "And we did not initiate the violence."

"We can't absolve ourselves because we didn't participate," said Diane. "Shepherd and his men protected you and took lives on our behalf. More than that, lives were lost in defense of Janus. As a society dedicated to peace, how can we ignore what happened? It is counter to everything we believe."

"We don't disregard anything," said Sean. "Instead we must use it as a way to strengthen and build on our commitment to peace. It will take time for the islanders to heal after the loss of Elijah. That process, though, should not involve plotting comparable revenge.

"It is difficult to reconcile what happened in Inverness with what we believe as a society. We will best honor Elijah by living life as he did; at peace with each other and separate from the world. That won't change what happened, but it will keep us true to our basic tenets. And that is what's most important."

"We can't stay cosseted on our small, peaceful island forever," claimed Andrew. "Sometimes violence must be met with violence in order to preserve peace."

"That's where we disagree," countered Sean. "In this case, maintaining peace does not mean attacking the order. Your argument has been used since the first tribes roamed the earth. And all it has brought is continuing war. Aggression met with more aggression only creates a never-ending spiral of ongoing bloodshed.

"I believe any form of armed retaliation is the worst decision the islanders could make. It will not bring Elijah back."

"You seem to be forgetting that we used violence to beat back the attack in Inverness," said the Guardian.

"I'm not forgetting anything," said Sean. "None of us who were there can escape the reality that people on both sides died a brutal death. But the answer does not lie in seeking retribution. It does us no good to use it as a basis for declaring war on the order."

"What you don't seem to understand is that we are definitely at war with the order," responded Andrew with emphasis. "First they hack our systems. Next it was the codex. Now it is Elijah. We can't just sit around and wait for Dante's next move."

"We are also successfully hacking them, and we have the codex back," countered Sean. "None of our responses has involved violence. As for Elijah's death, I believe we should stay true to the Prophet's beliefs and find a way to confront the order that does not run the risk of more bloodshed."

"You're being unrealistic," argued Andrew. "We live in a world committed to armed conflict as the ultimate way of resolving disputes."

"But it doesn't have to be that way for Janus," responded Sean. "For two thousand years, we have lived at peace. Does the death of one man justify losing the essence that is Janus?"

"If we don't, it will prove that Janus is weak," countered Andrew. "What's to stop Dante from coming after the codex if he knows we won't respond?"

"I believe we have a strong security system in place," said Sean. "We know what to expect, and we're well prepared."

"What if he comes after you? Obviously Dante understands what you could mean to the island's future."

The Hope of Janus

"Has he hacked our systems to that extent?" questioned Diane, her voice a mixture of shock and fear.

Andrew paused long enough to take a deep drink of coffee.

"Elijah was targeted. That means the order knows a great deal about our operations. Sean wasn't wounded by accident. He was also supposed to be killed. Although I believe the threat isn't imminent, it hasn't passed."

"What makes you think Sean isn't in imminent danger?" challenged Diane, her eyes unusually wide.

"We learned from a hacked phone call between Dante and someone called Benita that he has only one assassin. It was the woman killed at the site. Given that the order is such a clandestine organization, I can't see Dante hiring an external crew. It will take time for him to put together another team. Now that we know how he operates, we can ensure you remain safe."

"And how are you going to do that?" asked Sean.

"Initially, it means you living on Janus. I don't believe Dante would be foolish enough to put a stranger on our shores and think the move would succeed. You wear the *hope of Janus* and are integral to our future. Every islander will be looking out for your welfare. You'll be safe on Janus."

For Sean, Andrew's clinical assessment of the situation took the sting out of his words. Although the prospect of being in danger was mind-numbing, Sean wasn't prepared to let it dominate his thoughts. Instead, he was going to focus on how to destroy Dante's organization. The threat had to be ended, not only for him, but also for the islanders.

"That's fine for the short term, but we have to come up with a plan to dismantle the order," said Sean.

"And how do you plan on accomplishing that?" responded Andrew. "It's a global conglomerate with tremendous resources."

"This is why violence isn't the answer. Every organization has a weakness. We just have to find the order's Achilles' heel. But it can only be done in a business context. The way we'll defeat Dante is by crippling his organization."

"That's obviously easier said than done," said Andrew.

"I know. But there must be a way. Leave it with me. Once I have a plan, I'll bring it to Inverness, and we can work through the details with your management team."

"What should we do in the meantime?"

"As you said, it will take Dante some time to regroup," noted Sean. "Olga's tech ops people continue to monitor the order. You never know. A mistake may be unearthed that might help us bring Dante down."

Sean picked up his cup and took a drink of coffee. It was lukewarm but not yet bitter. He took another sip and looked at Andrew, who seemed to have drifted away into his own thoughts.

"There's something else on your mind," Sean said to the Guardian. "Why don't we get it out of the way and clear the air."

"I've been wondering why the Spirit didn't protect Elijah." The words came in a rush, and it was easy to detect the immense frustration behind them.

"And how it is that Sean was saved," added Diane.

"I have no problem with that," said the Guardian, frowning. "It's not a question of why Sean was spared. I was the one who knocked him down, and I would do it again in a heartbeat.

The Hope of Janus

No, this is simply about Elijah and his relationship with the Spirit. You'd think because of their closeness, it would have intervened."

"We have lost fishing crews at sea and farmers have been killed on their land," began Diane. "Both have been through accidents of nature. We have never questioned the Spirit's rationale for what happened because it was irrelevant. Every islander acknowledges that the Spirit chooses not to influence an islander's life. Why do you believe this should have been different?"

"Because it was Elijah," said Andrew quietly. "He should have died peacefully in his bed, surrounded by all of us who loved him—not by a bullet that tore apart his chest."

"It's not the Spirit who chooses how we die," said Diane. "That is part of the universe's natural cycle."

The Guardian nodded his head. "You're right of course. It's just that I miss him so much. Janus won't be the same without our Prophet."

"We all miss him," said Sean, reaching over and placing his right hand on the Guardian's forearm.

The light from one of the bulkhead lamps caught the ring and was strikingly reflected across the room.

Andrew pursed his lips and slowly nodded his head. "The *hope of Janus*," said the Guardian, staring at the band. "I think hope could be the watchword for our future."

"Hope and optimism," said Diane, looking first at Andrew and then at Sean. "We are entering a new era for Janus. There will be challenges. But we're islanders, and we'll see them through the way it has always been done—with a commitment to understanding and peace."

That signaled the end of the conversation. As everyone got up from seats, Sean was thinking that, while Andrew and Diane might have resolved their feelings about the Spirit's inaction with Elijah, he wasn't satisfied. The next time he was at the cave, it was something he planned to raise directly with the Spirit. Elijah should not have died the way he had.

CHAPTER FIFTY

✤

Dante was leaning forward, elbows resting on his desk. The prelate was contemplating a problem that he thought would be solved by now. While Elijah was dead, Brennan had survived.

Elijah's death, although useful, in no way diminished the danger Brennan still posed for the Church. And while the order had a brutal assassination team presently operating in the South American drug wars, the prelate was not willing to consider using what he viewed as mercenaries for the task of killing Brennan. He wanted a surgeon's blade, not a sledgehammer. Also, the assassin needed to have a commitment to the order and to God.

At no time during his considerations did Dante feel a sense of loss or sadness over Angelica's demise. He viewed her death as an inconvenience and was focused on how to solve his issue. His Azrael was the emotional past, and that was an uninhabited foreign land for the prelate.

Dante had not built his strong and expanding empire without putting in place a series of fallback operations. Internally, this applied primarily to such corporate areas as financial administration, including tax evasion and money laundering, along with executive management succession planning. Externally, the order was well prepared for cyber-attacks or a competitor's thrust into a Fraternity firm's market. There was always a strategy in place to handle any situation.

Although Angelica and her team had possessed a highly specialized expertise, Dante had several candidates who were undergoing the same rigorous training that his assassin had completed. One, a young woman, was fairly advanced but still did not possess the necessary skill set required by Dante. After learning of Angelica's death, the prelate had immediately visited the facility where his assassins were in training.

Each had been chosen from the select group that was destined to play an integral role within the Fraternity's operations—whether as the president of a company, a chief financial officer, or a trained killer. Recruited, as usual, from Palestinian refugee camps, the youth were kept together until they were twelve years old. At that time their future course was decided and the separation of studies began.

The assassination preparation was a highly sophisticated operation and involved every aspect of a trainee's life from a conventional education to religious knowledge and from personal grooming to psychological indoctrination. Executing without thought for the victim is a specialized talent and involved a mindset virtually devoid of feeling. Many never graduated to this level of capability. While Zelda, as she had been named at the chateau, had shown all the mental, emotional, and physical attributes of a trained killer, the school's instructors estimated she was still four to six months away from going on an assignment.

A new team needed to be recruited from among the order's families. They would be brought to Valencia and, along with Zelda, welded into a closely knit squad. Under normal circumstances, the timetable would have suited Dante.

The prelate believed he had a six- to eight-month window for devising a plan to handle Brennan. Dante felt the islanders, along with Brennan and the Guardians would take at least that long to recover from the Prophet's death. Dante didn't expect any major moves from Brennan in the short term and would mount a new campaign to have him eliminated with the coming spring.

However, while time was a friend in the case of Brennan, it was a foe when it came to the codex. And that brought him to three issues—retrieving the parchments; Reinhart and Ambrosia; and the traitor at Zaragoza, Alberto Salazar.

If this had been an issue with one of the order's companies, Dante would have Salazar fired. However, the man was in possession of a secret that, if revealed, would doom Christianity. The prelate had no doubt about what needed to be done. Salazar had to be eliminated. Dante felt no remorse or even the necessity to personally justify Salazar's planned death by rationalizing that he'd betrayed the order. Instead, he viewed the man's elimination as a necessary element of the Fraternity's mandate to protect the Church regardless of the action required.

As Dante thought about the Salazar issue, he came to the conclusion that it would be an excellent first mission for Zelda and the squad soon to be formed around her. Her training results were extraordinary and merited the live test. The target was low risk. It would provide an opportunity to determine how she functioned in an operational situation, and would establish whether she and her team were ready for the Brennan assignment.

He would talk to the handlers and have her training regimen intensified. He wanted Zelda to be ready within the time frame he had given himself to resolve the issue of Ambrosia and Reinhart. He knew it would be a tightly condensed schedule. Several weeks had passed since Ambrosia had become pope. Dante's estimation of three months for Ambrosia to settle into his duties as the pontiff now stood at only slightly more than eight weeks. After that, a portion of Ambrosia's attention, spurred on by Reinhart, would surely be taken up with the codex. Dante didn't want a loose end like Salazar when the prelate began his battle for ownership of the Janus parchments.

And that brought him to re-acquiring the codex. What he didn't know was how the attack in Inverness had impacted the Guardians' view of security for the lab. For example, were the guards now armed? However, the groundwork had been done. There was no need for a report from the watchers, which would cut down on the time needed for an assault.

Dante usually liked to give his teams some downtime after an assignment. He realized the missions were intense and stressful. And to have them performing at peak efficiency for a new operation required they have time away to decompress.

However, the prelate estimated he had from five to six weeks in which to retrieve the codex. It would take at least a couple of days for Benita and her longtime scout and driver, Aldo, to be located and brought to the chateau. They would have to be briefed. Items such as passports and drivers' licenses needed to be produced and burner phones obtained. Hotel accommodations required booking. Weapons needed to be sourced in Britain. The prelate was already committed to providing the squad with whatever equipment and arms they believed were needed for an assault on the property.

Dante estimated that Benita, based on his past experience, would need a week to ten days for pulling all the various elements together. After that, she and Aldo would fly to Inverness and meet with the rest of the crew that had already been contacted. And despite her familiarity with the Guardians' compound, Dante estimated a one-week property reconnaissance before the team went in.

The prelate believed the operation could be completed and the codex back at the chateau within four to five weeks.

The Hope of Janus

The only issue was Reinhart. Ambrosia would be busy settling in as the pope, but a great deal depended on how much the new pontiff would assign to Reinhart during this transition period.

If Reinhart did suddenly demand the parchments be delivered to Rome, holding him off before the parchments were in Valencia would be difficult, but Dante felt fully confident he could keep the cardinal at bay—so long as the mission in Inverness went as planned.

The prelate's thoughts were interrupted by the hum of his intercom. Opening the speaker, Dante listened as his assistant told him that Monte was on the line and needed to urgently speak with the prelate.

"What's the crisis?" asked Dante.

"Reinhart is at Zaragoza," responded Juan.

That could mean only one thing, reasoned the prelate. The cardinal was looking for the codex.

"Fine, I'll take the call," he told his assistant.

Dante slipped on his wireless headset and tapped the flashing button on his phone.

He was only able to say, "Hello," before Monte uttered, "We have a major problem."

"I know," said Dante. "Reinhart is with you. I assume he wants the parchments."

"The cardinal says the pope has given him instructions to oversee their immediate delivery to the Vatican. What am I going to do?"

Dante had already decided that the only answer was to directly confront the situation and buy time.

"What have you told him?"

"Absolutely nothing about the codex," answered Monte. "I explained that you have taken charge of all matters relating to the parchments. But Salazar must have told him about the theft."

"Where is Reinhart now?"

"He's in the outer office looking through our inventory catalogue. The pope wants some paintings to hang in his office and apartment."

"Put him on the phone."

"But what are you going to tell him?"

"That there was no theft and the codex is here at the chateau for safekeeping."

There was a momentary silence, and then the director whispered, "But the Guardians have it. What if Reinhart wants to meet with you at the chateau?"

"One problem at a time," growled Dante, a sign to Monte that he was severely testing the prelate's patience.

"I'll tell the cardinal you want to speak with him," Monte said, rushing through the words.

There was a brief silence, and then Dante heard Reinhart's heavily accented English saying, "Good morning."

After Dante returned the salutation, he said, "The codex is not in Zaragoza. I've had it brought to the chateau. Given the story they tell, the safest thing is to have the parchments here. I can provide tighter security than at the museum."

"So, I'm to believe the codex has been transferred to your chateau for reasons of safekeeping." The tone of Reinhart's voice indicated a knowing disbelief in what he'd been told. "Still, it doesn't matter," the cardinal continued. "I have instructions from our Holy Father to have the codex immediately delivered to the Vatican.

"I'll be at the chateau tomorrow to manage the operation. I'd appreciate if one of your cars could meet me at the airport. My assistant will be in touch once the flight details are known.

"If the codex is at the chateau as you claim, I want to see it."

Salazar had obviously told Reinhart about the theft. What neither of them knew for certain was whether the parchments had been recovered. This was an instance where knowledge of the order's ruthless efficiency was a distinct advantage for Dante.

While the prelate expected Reinhart would try to box him in with an ultimatum, Dante had years of experience dealing with people like the cardinal. The situation was difficult, and the prelate knew he could only hold off the inevitable for so long. But all he needed was five weeks. There was one card he could play, and now was the time to lay it on the table.

"Did you hear what I said?" Reinhart brusquely stated, his accent even more pronounced. "I will be at the chateau tomorrow."

"That won't be possible," said Dante. "I am Prelate of the Praetorian Order. A visit to the Chateau Valencia only happens if I offer an invitation. That is not being extended to you, Cardinal Reinhart. As you know, the one person who can see me without my approval is our Holy Father. It is a right guaranteed the order by Gregory XIII's written declaration of 1583."

Silence momentarily captured the connection between the two men.

"I am aware of the Vatican's history," said Reinhart, his voice low and ragged with rage. "Are you arrogant enough to forbid a cardinal deacon of the Roman Catholic Church from visiting the chateau?"

Dante allowed himself a brief smile at the word *arrogant* and then calmly said, "Nothing is being forbidden. I am merely not extending an invitation. This is a busy period for the order's companies, and I don't have time to be involved with the codex."

"You're playing a dangerous game," fumed Reinhart. "I will personally see to it that our Holy Father visits the chateau. He will strip you of the codex, if you have it. And I'll be there to watch it done. Should you not have the parchments, I'll gladly watch your power crumble. For you see, either way, without the codex you have no power over the Vatican."

Dante had received far worse threats during his years of extending the order's influence and power. It was obvious Ambrosia had not told Reinhart about the Vienna tape. However, for now, Dante was only concerned with keeping Ambrosia and Reinhart away from the chateau long enough so he could regain the codex and also to permanently silence Salazar.

Chapter Fifty-One

Journey would be arriving at the Janus pier in a little over four hours. Leyland was on the bridge. Malcolm and Joseph were in the cargo hold watching over Elijah's coffin.

Diane, Andrew, and Sean were seated at the galley's small table, lingering over their after-breakfast coffees. Talk was initially sparse, until Andrew raised the subject that Sean had only briefly thought about.

"This is a critical time for Janus," said the Guardian. "With Elijah's death and our ongoing battle with the order, strong leadership is needed."

One aspect of Andrew's personality that Sean admired was the Guardian's desire to meet every situation head-on. He never sugarcoated his opinions and would rather confront a problem than let others handle the details. That's what he was doing now.

Andrew leveled his gaze at Sean. "You bear the mark of Janus, you're a direct descendent of Jesus, and you've been given the *hope of Janus*. More than anyone associated with the island, you are destined to become our guide and mentor."

"But it's too soon to raise it with everyone," responded Sean. "Some time must be allowed to pass. People will only be finding out when we land what has happened to Elijah. They'll need time to process that the Prophet is gone."

"That's true," acknowledged Andrew. "But for most islanders, Elijah is the only leader they've known. There will be a vacuum, along with confusion about the future. You need to fill that void. The island's regular fall meeting is in two weeks. That's when we should put your name forward."

"Andrew is right," voiced Diane. "We need strong leadership. And while you haven't been on the island that long, your ties to the Spirit and to our past that Andrew just mentioned, means you're the one to provide it."

But Sean wasn't convinced. "It's fine to sit here and talk about my becoming leader, but Elijah has only been gone for four days. I've thought about the question of leadership but never considered becoming the islanders' guide. What about Elijah's relatives? Wouldn't one of them be more suited for the role?"

"The question of leadership will be a first for the island," explained Diane. "Throughout our history there was always someone in Elijah's family who would be the next natural guide and mentor. But Elijah is the last person in his line. There are no relatives, even in our diaspora. Andrew's right. Our fall meeting is an excellent way to decide who should succeed the Prophet. All our major decisions are made through assemblies. And I can't think of any issue more important than this one."

Turning to face Sean, she said, "In this way, you'll have time to decide whether the responsibility is what you want. We'll also see if anyone else would like to succeed Elijah."

Sean nodded his head in agreement. "It sounds like a good idea."

"So how do we go about making it happen?" asked Diane.

"It's not really something either of you can bring up," offered Andrew in his usual preemptory manner. "I'll take care of deciding when to make the suggestion. And that leaves us with just a couple of other things to settle."

"What else do we have?" Diane asked.

"Elijah has always led the funeral services. We need someone to take care of it for the Prophet. Would you be willing to handle the service?" he asked, looking over at Sean. "Your relationship with him was special. I know everybody would be comfortable if you managed our farewell to Elijah."

Sean knew from Diane that island funerals were a celebration of life and involved people sharing their memories and thoughts about the deceased. There was considerable laughter, some outrageous stories, and much reminiscing. It was a special time. The islanders came together not only to comfort one another but also to share in the joy of life, rather than to unite in sadness at end of the deceased's journey.

"I'd be honored," said Sean.

"What was the other point you wanted to discuss?" Diane queried the guardian.

"I think Sean should tell everyone about Elijah's death," said Andrew. "You're the one they'd expect to hear the news from."

Sean thought about it for a few moments and then nodded his head in agreement. He really didn't want to do it, but Andrew was right. Of everyone on board *Journey*, his relationship with Elijah dictated that he be the one to convey the news.

"I think the best way to handle things when we dock," said Sean, "is for Andrew and me to get off first, while everyone else stays aboard. It's not much, but I'm hoping not to emphasize Elijah's absence until I've told them what has occurred."

"It makes sense," stated Diane. "People will immediately wonder what's happened to Elijah. This way buys us some time for Sean to make the announcement."

Sean thought about the Prophet's body lying in a casket below deck and wondered, not for the first time since the shooting, how long it would take for things to really make sense again.

Chapter Fifty-Two

※

When *Journey* docked it was met by the usual gathering of excited and expectant islanders. Janus's supply of fresh produce and meat was about to be replenished. There would be news from relatives in Inverness and throughout the diaspora. And most importantly, they would learn if the codex had been recovered.

Low, gray clouds, like tanks on parade, rolled through the morning sky. There was a cold wind blowing in from the north. Sean couldn't help but feel that the day's bleakness was appropriate for the news he was about to convey.

Descending the gangplank with Andrew, Sean detected a hint of confusion sweeping through the crowd. It was usual for Elijah to be first off the ship. When they stepped on the dock and Andrew put up his hands, signaling for quiet, the islanders obliged, but a restive feeling hung over the harbor.

"Sean has something important to share with you," said the Guardian before stepping to one side.

"I hope you're going to tell us the Word of Janus has been retrieved from the order," shouted Daniel Haas, a farmer from the island's eastern flank.

The interruption caught Sean by surprise. He had been so focused on talking about Elijah that he'd forgotten the islanders' only frame of reference when *Journey* last departed Janus, was the Guardians' mission to retrieve the codex.

He looked over at Andrew, whose coal-black eyes were staring back at him.

"It's time to be a leader," said the Guardian, his voice so low it was impossible for even those in front to hear the words.

"I have two things to tell you," Sean began hesitantly, feeling uncertain about how to proceed. He stopped for a couple of moments, hoping something illuminating would come to him. It didn't, and he could feel the crowd growing restless. Deciding to plunge ahead he said, "We have recovered the codex, and it is back at the lab in Inverness."

A loud cheer rose from the crowd. There were hugs and handshakes throughout the gathering, and some islanders started moving forward ready to congratulate Andrew.

Sean quickly shouted, "I have something else you need to know."

Sean sensed every pair of eyes focusing on him. Despite the day's chill, he felt the sweat beginning to form on the back of his neck. He looked skyward and then back at the crowd and said as calmly as he could, "There was a major attack by the order at the compound. Several people were killed."

Pausing for a long moment, Sean took a deep breath. "I don't know how to say this any other way. Elijah was among the casualties. Our Prophet is dead."

In the moments immediately following his words, the gathering was so profoundly silent that Sean could hear a seagull calling to its mate and the waves washing up against the dock. He knew there would always be memories of the wind's chill on his back.

And then came the explosion of noise that sounded almost guttural. People demanded to know what had happened. Some began to cry; others stared straight ahead in disbelief. The crowd milled about, directionless amid an avalanche of dismay, noise, and confusion. Lost was the joy at having the codex retrieved.

Once again, Andrew asked for silence. Sean took the cue and explained what had taken place. He left almost nothing out, including that he'd been standing beside Elijah when the fatal shot had hammered into the Prophet's chest. He told them that *Journey* had brought the Prophet home. The only thing he elected not to mention was his wound. It seemed inconsequential when everyone was trying to emotionally process Elijah's death.

He wasn't sure how long he spoke for, but the crowd gradually quieted. Shock and disbelief were replaced with a stoic sorrow. With the islanders' deep-seated resilience came acceptance of the situation's reality.

"We have to plan a funeral," said Ian McKenzie, the island's doctor.

The words again reminded Sean of the islanders' practical nature. They would grieve, and there would be intense sadness. But death, once it came, was a truth that could not be denied. Elijah would always remain a treasured memory, and stories would be told about him in the coming years. But for now, there were rational decisions to be made.

"I'll need to prepare Elijah's body for the ceremony," continued Ian. "The casket should be taken straight to my office."

As was traditional on the island, the service would be held that evening in the Community Center. Andrew suggested that Sean lead the service, and everyone voiced their approval.

By this time, Diane and Leyland had joined Andrew and Sean. "There's a lot of confusion and sadness," Diane said to Sean. "Your offer to lead the funeral has taken care of one concern. It's obvious the islanders are comfortable with you. The fact you wear the *hope of Janus* and what that signifies means a lot to our people."

Diane had barely finished speaking when Andrew shouted that he wanted everyone's attention. In his usual straightforward style, the Guardian said, "This is the first time in our history that we've been without a guide. And since Elijah has no relatives to follow him, I am proposing that we have a vote to elect a successor. Our regular fall meeting is in two weeks. That would be a good time."

Sean felt a sense of wariness running through the crowd. The islanders had received two major pieces of information in such a short space of time that there was almost a reluctance to be told anything for a while—at least until everything could be emotionally absorbed.

Sean also questioned the Guardian's timing. The Prophet's funeral hadn't taken place, and Andrew was already calling for a leadership vote. He recognized that the islanders were a tough and practical group but wondered if Andrew had given everyone enough time to grieve before making his announcement.

However, Sean was in for a surprise.

"Two weeks makes sense," said Maria Garcia, a sheepherder from the valley. It will give us time to send Elijah on his way and to properly mourn him. But death, like birth, is no stranger to our shores. We must now carry on without our Prophet. He was a mentor, a friend, and a guide through some of life's more difficult times. I believe his advice would be to quickly settle who will lead us."

The crowd had grown surprisingly quiet. It was hard for Sean to determine what everyone was thinking about Maria's words. There was the rustle of hushed conversations as people spoke to one another. But there seemed no consensus about having a vote in a couple of weeks. The islanders appeared lost without someone to guide them through this difficult time.

Diane took Sean's arm and walked him several yards down the dock, away from the crowd. "These people need you," she said. "They have to know someone is there for them. Elijah's death has shocked everyone. They're looking for a direction, and that's what you can provide.

"This is your time. The vote may be in two weeks, but now is when everyone needs to hear words that will comfort them. I believe Elijah would have wanted you to be strong in his place. The Prophet was thinking of the future when he gave you the *hope of Janus.*"

The words had been spoken with an intensity that captured Sean's thoughts. For the first time, he felt a desire from deep within to lead the islanders. He wanted to be the one they'd come to for advice. It had nothing to do with his history or even the ring. He truly liked these people. They were good, kind, and willing to do anything for each other. Living in peace was not an aspiration for them; it was a reality they cherished and worked hard to maintain. They truly lived their mantra of understanding, tolerance, equality, and forgiveness.

Diane was looking closely at him. "What are you going to do?" she asked.

As an answer, Sean took her hand and walked to the center of the dock so he was standing in front of the islanders. He asked for everyone's attention, and in a few moments, the crowd had quieted.

"I know how terrible losing Elijah is for each of us," he began. "We all cared deeply for him, and we know how much he loved Janus. There aren't any words that can convey the depth of this tragedy, but we also know that our Prophet would have wanted us to move forward with our lives. He believed in not looking back with regret but always living in the moment and having a passion for life.

"So that is what I'm calling on you to do. We will celebrate his life this evening. After that, we will take time to mourn our loss and then vote for someone to be the island's next guide. No one will ever replace Elijah. But whoever succeeds him will carve a new path. And together we will walk the journey with that person."

For a few moments, there was silence, and then the clapping began. Soon, everyone had joined in, and more importantly for Sean, there were smiles beginning to dot the crowd.

A noise from behind them momentarily startled him—until he turned and realized it was Malcolm and Joseph opening *Journey*'s cargo hatches. They looked at Andrew, who directed them to prepare Elijah's coffin for lifting out of the ship's hold.

The four Guardians, along with Sean and Ian, took the coffin out of the cargo hold and began the slow walk to the doctor's office. Everyone from the quay followed in a slow procession, marking the Prophet's few remaining hours on Janus.

Chapter Fifty-Three

✢

On an island with a limited landmass, setting aside property for a cemetery was impractical. There was a crematorium the islanders often used, but Elijah had always indicated a preference for a sea burial. And that's what everyone wanted for their beloved Prophet.

The heavy, gray clouds of morning had haunted Janus all day, and as people began to gather in the evening at the Community Center a light rain began to fall.

Every islander was present as the four Guardians—Andrew, Leyland, Malcolm, and Joseph—along with Ian and Sean, brought Elijah's casket to the hall's door. The silence that greeted the group as they carried the coffin up to the front was a profound reminder of how much the Prophet had meant to Janus.

Once again, the island's customs were followed, and that meant a closed coffin. The islanders believed people should be remembered as they lived, not how they appeared in death. The casket was placed on a wooden platform that stood on pillars about four feet above the floor.

What followed was an opportunity for any islander to stand beside the coffin and reminisce about an event or story they had shared with the Prophet. Sean's role was merely to ask who wanted to talk next and, when hands were raised, choose the subsequent speaker. It was a time of caring and laughter, as everyone was taken through Elijah's life with a reverence for a man who had devoted his time to the needs and wants of every islander.

His link with the Spirit and the importance it played for islanders seeking advice was a prevailing theme. It reminded Sean that, if he chose to run and was elected as Elijah's successor, this relationship with the Spirit would be a vital role in his life going forward.

Sometime during the evening, Sean realized that, while this was a tribute to Elijah's impact on Janus, it was also a celebration of life in general. No one discussed what Elijah's absence would mean. What came through with every speaker was how much life should be treasured and the importance of living each day with no regrets. The islanders were using the occasion to affirm their joy at being able to wake up each morning and know that a full day of possibilities lay ahead. That was the way Elijah had lived, and everyone knew he would have wanted the stories about him to reflect that belief.

And while there were difficulties and hardships that overcame everyone, Janus was a society based on the premise that being a part of humanity was a gift to be treasured. There was the acknowledgement that, through respect for the island's diversity and equality, along with a deep and abiding commitment to inclusiveness, the joy of life could truly be appreciated.

These were not mere words. They were beliefs that infused every facet of life on the island and had been passed from generation to generation. This desire for a life well lived was, in part, based on the understanding that a progressive society allowed for the full expression of individual and collective strengths. Along with that came a responsibility to ensure everyone an equal opportunity and rights in every societal facet, including education, chosen occupation, or choice of partner.

One other aspect of the ceremony Sean noted was the absence of any talk about a violent retribution against Dante and the order. The commitment to peace was unwavering. Every story reflected Elijah's dedication to harmony, and the islanders seemed determined to honor his memory by staying true to this conviction.

As the service drew to a close, everyone walked past Elijah's coffin and said a brief farewell to their Prophet. Soon the only ones left in the hall were the four Guardians, Ian, Sean, and Diane, along with a fishing boat captain, Selma Richards.

Journey and the Guardians would not be involved in the sea burial. The island's centuries-old practice called for the fishing fleet's newest captain to handle the function for all sea burials. Taking someone on their final voyage was viewed as an honor, and Selma had been performing the ritual for slightly more than two years.

Only Selma and her crew—two brothers, Kyle and Bruce—would be aboard the ship, the *Ocean Friend*. Everyone knew how much Elijah enjoyed the start of a new day. The fishing boat was to leave before dawn, and just as the sun was cresting the horizon, Elijah would be delivered to the sea. Following another tradition, the coffin would be weighted with six large rocks gathered from the island's quarry by direct descendants of the four families that were the first to set foot on its shores. Along with the three holes drilled on each side of the coffin, the rocks would ensure the casket sank rapidly.

Although the rain had stopped, the cold northerly wind was still blowing across the island as the casket was taken out of the center. Led by the Guardians, along with Sean and Ian, the coffin was carried slowly along the Ring Road, which was lined with islanders. Diane and Selma had left earlier for the *Ocean Friend*. Selma wanted to check on the work Kyle and Bruce had done in readying the ramp that would be used to slide Elijah's coffin into the North Sea's frigid waters.

Arriving at the dock, the contingent climbed the gangplank and placed the coffin onboard the *Ocean Friend*. After the casket was lashed to the front deck, Sean felt an overwhelming sense of sadness. Throughout the trip back to Janus and during the service, he had intellectualized Elijah's death and kept his emotions closely guarded.

However, watching the brothers secure the casket to the deck had unleashed a deep feeling for the friend he had lost. This was the man who had brought him to Janus. He thought of their talks and the wisdom he had gained. Sean remembered the Prophet's commitment to convince the Spirit that only by working directly with Sean and the islanders would its goal of bringing peace to the globe be realized. Elijah's excitement at being involved in such an epic adventure played across Sean's mind and found a permanent place in his heart.

But now he was gone. Sean reached out for Diane and brought her close. She noticed the tears forming in his eyes and held him in a tight embrace. The Guardians, along with Ian, walked slowly off the vessel and headed in the direction of *Journey*, which was tied up farther down the wharf. Selma and the brothers retreated from the cold into the *Ocean Friend*'s small cabin, where they would spend the night.

Sean and Diane were left alone with the casket. Gradually, Sean brought his emotions under a fragile control. But the sadness would not leave him. He had lost not only a mentor but also a unique ally in understanding the ways of the Spirit. Diane pulled back and wiped the tears from his face.

"We should be getting home," she said quietly. "It's time for Selma and the brothers to begin their vigil. The crew will stay awake to keep the Prophet company before he makes the final journey as part of the Janus family."

"Where do you imagine he's going?" Sean wondered.

"We believe that Elijah is traveling on the long trek to join his family. It exists in another dimension, as does everyone who dies. The soul is shared with the Spirit, but Elijah's essence will travel through eternity with his ancestors. Death represents the end of one life, but there is another universe where his existence will continue. What shape or form that takes we don't understand, but it is reassuring to know we will all meet again."

Even among a population that claimed no religious affiliation, there was still a need to believe in another life beyond this one, reflected Sean. It was an interesting human dynamic that applied to many cultures, and although Sean had not given the afterlife much thought, he found himself wondering if it was true.

The older I get, the more I am willing to consider such possibilities, he thought somewhat ruefully.

Sean stared at the casket and remembered that it was time to leave. Placing his right hand on the coffin, he whispered, "Farewell, dear friend. May your travels be always peaceful and every day filled with a shining sun. Your life was one of goodwill for all those you met. Know that you were loved by all and will be sadly missed. I know there will be days when I will long for your words, your inspiration, and your company. But I also know that memories of our times together will keep my thoughts grounded and focused on living life as best I can."

He turned away and looked for Diane. She was waiting for him on the dock. Sean knew she had given him privacy to say his final good-bye, and he was grateful for her understanding. It was just one of the many reasons he loved her. The future would be different without Elijah, but he knew that, together, he and Diane could handle whatever came their way.

Sean strode down the gangplank and joined Diane on the dock. They proceeded to walk up the path to the Road and toward home.

Chapter Fifty-Four

Dante had just finished a call with the president of the order's bank in Antigua and was about to remove his headset when he noticed one of the buttons on his external phone pad was flashing. Moments later, the prelate's intercom sounded, and Juan's voice whispered in his ear that the pope's executive assistant was waiting to place a call from the Holy Father.

The prelate thanked Juan and tapped the button, opening the line. On the other end, as he expected, was the Franciscan monk, Georgio Casavante. Papal protocol dictated that the pope would only pick up his phone after the person was put through by his assistant.

Although this marked the first time Dante and the pontiff would be in contact since Ambrosia had ascended the papal throne, the prelate had already started moving the order's personnel into the pope's inner circle. Casavante, while a relatively minor figure, was indicative of how fast Dante was proceeding to seize control of the Vatican. He had replaced the head of the Vatican bank and was in the process of completing the roster of cardinals who would be Ambrosia's closest advisors.

The assistant shared with Dante that Reinhart had just left the papal office. "He was complaining about your conceit and that you were refusing to give up something called the Word of

Janus. Strangely, though, they seemed to agree you might not have it—that it may have been stolen. The meeting didn't last long, and that was all they discussed. The Holy Father seemed upset with the news and immediately asked me to contact you."

After Dante thanked Casavante for the advance notice, the assistant put him on hold while he put the call through to Ambrosia.

Dante wasn't surprised to be kept waiting for a couple of minutes before the newly elected pope picked up his phone. The prelate surmised that Ambrosia was demonstrating not only the power of the papal office but also his frustration at Dante's rejection of Reinhart's demand to hand over the codex.

When Ambrosia—Dante refused to think of him as Pope Alexander—did come on the line, he immediately launched a verbal volley at the prelate.

"You have no right to keep the codex," he said, his voice loud and aggressive. "You forget the order reports to my office. Cardinal Reinhart was acting on my behalf, and when I ask for something, it should be delivered. He will be at the chateau tomorrow as my emissary, and I expect he'll return to Rome with the codex—that is, if you have it. I understand the parchments might have been stolen. Is that why you're refusing a visit from Cardinal Reinhart?

"Now before you say anything, I'm fully aware of the edict of 1583. However, as my envoy, Cardinal Reinhart has every right to visit the chateau without your permission."

Dante knew Ambrosia had studied the Vatican's history when first being appointed a cardinal. However, the prelate didn't realize the new pope had been such a keen student of the order's relationship with the papacy. But as usual, Ambrosia had misinterpreted the facts.

Dante waited several seconds before responding. "There is nothing about emissaries in the decree," he said calmly. "I suggest you go back through our history. It is very specific. Only the pope has the right to visit my chateau without an invitation."

Ambrosia's labored breathing bore into Dante's ear.

"Then that is what I'll do," the pontiff declared triumphantly. "I'm going to make a secret visit to your chateau. If the codex is in Valencia, you will have to give it to me. And if you don't, I'll know you're a fraud for claiming to have something that is not in your possession."

Dante involuntarily shook his head. Ambrosia, as he always did when faced with an obstacle, offered the most implausible solution. "You're forgetting that you are no longer a cardinal. The pope can't disappear from Rome. What about your security detail, your assistants, and the press?

"You could plan a trip to Valencia, but that would take months to organize, given your schedule. Our prime minister, Valencia's mayor, and various government officials would have to know. You're viewed as a head of state and can't travel to another country unannounced."

There was quiet on the line as Ambrosia struggled with the reality of Dante's observation. One route remained for the new pope to follow, and the prelate wondered if Ambrosia was astute enough or a capable enough student of papal history to understand the full breadth of his power. However, Dante felt well prepared.

"From the moment you initiated your campaign of blackmail and threats about exposing the minor and forgivable sins in my past, I have studied every aspect of the relationship between the Vatican and the order," began Ambrosia. "In some ways, it became an obsession as I sought ways to escape your satanic grasp."

Ambrosia was speaking fast, seemingly emboldened by Dante's silence. "Up until you became prelate, the order's head was summoned to Rome on a monthly basis to report on the Fraternity's activities. That was part of the prelate's original mission when the order was formed. This element of your mandate has never been withdrawn. You simply chose to ignore it, and none of the Holy Fathers who preceded me elected to enforce the requirement.

"You will be receiving from me a letter that requires your presence at the Vatican on a monthly basis beginning next week. And as part of our first meeting, I want to have the codex delivered to me. You may wield a great deal of power, but not even Dante Sabatini can ignore a papal order."

The prelate leaned back and smiled to himself. He had already planned on being in Rome for a couple of days a month as part of his campaign to take over the Vatican. It was difficult to effect the changes he wanted from Valencia. He needed to be onsite and meeting with the people he was appointing to the various departments and those who would form a cloak of steel around Ambrosia.

"I will be there," said Dante. He paused for several seconds. "But I will not have the codex with me."

The silence that flowed over the line was taut with tension. Ambrosia was testing his new power, and Dante understood the pope was searching for a response that would demonstrate his control over the order. Despite what the pontiff, might say, Dante had history as a bulwark against anything Ambrosia could attempt.

Ambrosia cleared his throat, bringing to life the dead line. "You are going to disobey me," said the pope, his voice steely with menace. "Do you realize the consequences? I could have you removed as head of the order. I could have you excommunicated."

"You will do neither of those things because I am within my rights to refuse your order about the codex."

"Cardinal Reinhart warned me you might try something like this. What arcane judgment are you claiming overrides a papal decree?"

"I'm referring to the 1920 ruling by our Holy Father Benedict XV, in which it is stated that all artifacts and documents can only be removed from the chateau with the prelate's permission. It is neither arcane, nor is it a ruling. It's part of Vatican law, and until such time as you reverse the codicil, everything within the chateau's walls stays in Valencia. And we both know that, given the Vatican's bureaucracy, any change could take months, if not years.

"Not only that, but by the time you have such a document drafted, I will have people in place that will effectively bury your proclamation in so much paperwork that it will never be put into force."

"Everything you say is true," replied Ambrosia, "but the codex will one day be mine. I don't care how long it takes, I will overturn Benedict's ruling because leaving the parchments in your hands will only jeopardize everything concerning our Church. You have no interest other than controlling every decision I make.

"I am not doing this for me but for those who follow in my footsteps. The order must be stopped."

"All I want is what's best for the Church," said Dante.

"You want only what will benefit you and the order," retorted Ambrosia, anger lacing every word. "The Church is just a way for you to achieve that goal."

"And suppose that's true," answered Dante. "A strong order benefits the Church. That doesn't happen if the positions are reversed. For that reason, the codex and your files will only be exposed if you make it necessary."

"In other words, if I don't acquiesce to your commands, you will ruin me and my Church."

"I know you too well, my dear pontiff." Cynicism tinged every one of Dante's words. "You will do nothing to endanger your lofty position."

Once again, there was a strained silence between the men. Dante soon became impatient and was about to ask if there was anything else Ambrosia wanted to discuss, when the pontiff surprised him with a question.

"Why can't we work together?" he asked. "We both want a strong and united Church. So much could be accomplished through a partnership between us."

Many people might have been tempted by the offer of unity. After all, working with a former adversary can sometimes be quite successful at achieving common objectives. But Dante was not among those who believed in associations. He was singularly successful and believed completely in his abilities.

In the prelate's view, Ambrosia had neither the aptitude nor the intelligence to take the Church where Dante intended—as the dominant religion throughout the world. Ambrosia had been installed as pope for the sole purpose of advancing the Fraternity's control over the Vatican. Dante had his files and would soon have the codex. With the files, he could intimidate Ambrosia. With the codex, he could threaten Christianity's foundation. Dante was not about to yield any form of power through a coalition.

"I have no interest in an alliance," Dante said, his voice cold and distant. "Continue to follow my directives, and all will be well. Do we understand each other?"

Several seconds of quiet were followed by the tone of a closed line. Ambrosia had hung up.

Dante took off the headset. He was not offended by Ambrosia's move. His points about control had been made. The phone call's other important aspect was that his bluff about possessing the codex had worked. He had bought the time needed to retrieve it from the Guardians. Benita would not fail him.

And within six months, both Salazar and Brennan would be eliminated by his new assassin. There would be no breakdown this time. Having moved on from Angelica, Dante thought only of Zelda. Sadly, he was incapable of reflecting on Angelica's death or what had happened to her body.

The prelate turned his attention to the computer screen. He pulled up his schedule for the next thirty days. Dante needed to have Juan make arrangements for his first monthly visit with the pope. The prelate would propose several dates and allow Ambrosia the belief that he had some semblance of control within their relationship by deciding on which date he would see him.

Dante pressed the intercom button. When Juan answered, the prelate gave the dates he was available and told his assistant to make the arrangements with Casavante. He then focused his attention on a detailed plan that involved many pages of diagrams, graphs, financial reports, tech ops, product projections—in short, everything needed to ensure that the order was positioned to take advantage of his takeover of the

Church. It was proceeding ahead of plan. Within a couple of years, the Roman Catholic Church and its followers would be at the mercy of the order's dynamic marketing and sales initiative.

With the review completed, the prelate pulled up the membership list for the College of Cardinals. It was time to finalize who he would select as Ambrosia's advisors. The primary criterion was a simple one—complete and unbending loyalty to the order.

Chapter Fifty-Five

The two weeks following Elijah's funeral had gone quickly for Sean and Diane. It was harvest time on Janus, and everyone had spent the days late into the evenings bringing in the crops. It had been a good year, with adequate rain and long days of sunshine. Throughout the island, farmers were talking about having one of the best yields in years. Diane's fields of wheat, barley, and corn had fared well during the summer and early fall.

The couple had passed long days toiling under the weak, late September sun. It was backbreaking work, but for Sean, the satisfaction he got from seeing the harvested crops fill the barn and silo was unlike anything he'd experienced. There was a tremendous feeling of accomplishment that came with the steadily growing supplies being laid in for the winter.

Diane's farm was among the last to be harvested. They had started later than the other famers because of the time spent in Inverness. However, the weather was holding, and Diane believed they'd be completed in a couple of days. She made the observation to Sean while they were having an early morning breakfast before heading out to the fields.

Sean raised his coffee mug in a mock salute and said, "It will be good to get it finished. Our meeting at the Community

Center is tomorrow evening. That means we'll be able to attend without worrying about having crops in the field."

Diane absently nodded her head, and it was obvious to Sean that she now had something else on her mind.

"What are you thinking about?" he asked.

"Have you given any thought to visiting the Spirit?" she responded.

"Not really," Sean answered. "We've been so busy with the harvest that it didn't seem that important. There'll be plenty of time once we bring everything in."

"Normally I'd agree," said Diane. "But we have the meeting at the center. I don't believe there'll be an issue about you becoming the island's leader. With the *hope of Janus*, Elijah put his faith in you to take us into the future.

"But I think you have to get settled in your mind and with the Spirit what sort of a relationship the two of you are going to have. Because you wear the ring, everyone will want to know how you and the Spirit are going to work together in guiding Janus, now that Elijah is gone."

Sean took several long sips of coffee. Putting the cup down, he looked across the table. "I've agreed to succeed Elijah if the islanders want me. Shouldn't that be enough? You know how complicated my relationship is with the Spirit. We still have a long way to go before settling on how I'll work with it in this quixotic venture of leading the world toward peace. It will take time to establish parameters that satisfy both of us."

"You don't have that luxury," answered Diane. "Elijah's death has changed everything. You know how integral the Spirit is to our lives. I'm not saying you have to work out a complete peace plan with it, but if your destiny of leading us is going to be realized, you'll have to arrive at an arrangement with the Spirit."

Sean thought about Diane's position. He knew it made sense. Sean had no plans to take on Elijah's role as the island's spiritual advisor. He would serve as a mentor and as a guide through his understanding of the world. It was real-time experience, and he believed the islanders could benefit from his knowledge. However, Sean knew he didn't have the Prophet's qualifications to decipher what the Spirit sometimes meant in its discussions with the islanders.

But the islanders had every right to know what sort of a relationship he had with the Spirit. And given that he didn't really have one, he needed to establish a firm understanding with it. Once again, Sean found himself wondering at the situation's bizarre implications. He was planning on negotiating with the Supreme Being. It would be his free will as a human seeking to find common ground with an entity whose power was beyond a person's comprehension. But he would approach it with an open mind. Surely a compromise could be reached.

"That's true," he finally said. "In the past I would have balked at the thought of becoming a leader for the island. But through you, Janus has become incredibly important to me. The order is a real enemy for us. Neither the islanders nor the Guardians are equipped with the ability to deal with the threat while maintaining our commitment to peace. I believe there is a role I can play in working with the Guardians to negate Dante's impact.

"I also realized the other day that I'm looking forward to the meeting and hope the islanders want me. It would be a massive responsibility but also a great honor. And you're right. It does mean, among other things, stabilizing my relationship with the Spirit.

"There's also a proposal I'm going to put before the assembly that involves you."

Diane gave him a puzzled look, a frown creasing her forehead. "We haven't discussed anything that would cause you to bring up my name."

"That's right," responded Sean. "It's why I want to explain what I'm going to say now so you'll have time to think about what it means to you and to us."

"Go on. I'm intrigued."

"We're a partnership, equal in everything we do. According to the Word of Janus, we'll work together in implementing the Spirit's message."

Diane nodded her head. "We've already been over this. How does this impact what's going to happen tomorrow night?"

"I'm going to propose that we both lead the islanders," said Sean. "I know it has always been the first born son in Elijah's family that has held the position. A male has always been the guide. But these are different times. The islanders believe fundamentally in equal rights for everyone. I want us to bring equality to the Janus leadership."

Diane's expression was thoughtful. "There's equality of opportunity on Janus," she said slowly, clearly thinking aloud. "And now that Elijah's family is no longer a part of the island, things will change. That's obvious with you being considered as our leader. Tomorrow night, anyone who wants to take over from Elijah will have the option of putting their name forward. And race, occupation or gender will not be a factor. The islanders will vote for the person, whether a man or woman, who we believe is the best person to take us into the future. I don't see why I have to be involved to indicate equality."

"Yes, everyone is equal," Sean agreed. "But that's not the point. Through the Word of Janus, it's already understood that, if I can establish an understanding with the Spirit, you and I will work with it in convincing the islanders to lead the globe toward peace. It only flows naturally that we serve together as guides for the island, if that's what everyone wants.

"It's a perfect match. I bring experience from the world. You have your history with Janus. These are new times, and the islanders, including you and me, have to adapt."

Diane picked up her cup and took several sips of coffee. Placing her mug carefully on the table she said, "I have a suggestion. Why don't we see what you arrive at with the Spirit? If you are going to be involved with it, then that means I'm part of whatever happens going forward. In that case, it makes sense that I also work with you on shepherding the islanders through the future."

Nodding his head, Sean said, "That sounds like a fair arrangement. I'll visit the cave tomorrow afternoon and be back in time for us to review what we want to do before leaving for the meeting."

"The timing is good," responded Diane. "The harvesting will be just about completed, and whatever is left we can finish the next day. Have you decided how you're going to approach the Spirit?"

"Not really. It will obviously know about Elijah and why I'm at the cave. That will be my starting point, and I'll just let things flow from there. But I won't leave until we have some sort of understanding."

CHAPTER FIFTY-SIX

✣

Sean was sitting on one of the benches that surrounded the cave's fire pit. He was staring into the flames of a fire he'd built to ward off the cavern's slight chill. But he wasn't thinking of his upcoming talk with the Spirit. Instead he was filled with a deep sadness at the memories looping through his mind.

He shifted his gaze and looked at the band on his finger. He thought of the words Elijah had used about hope and peace. The Prophet's commitment personified the island's dedication to living lives of non-violence. Not for the first time since Elijah's death, Sean wondered how he could ever succeed his departed friend.

Sean thought of talks they'd had in the cave, on the Prophet's gallery, and while traveling aboard *Journey*. He slowly got to his feet and walked to the back of the cave. Finding the cavity where the Word of Janus was usually kept, he stopped. From his shirt pocket he took out Elijah's glasses that he'd brought with him from Inverness. Sean held them in his right hand for just a moment, before placing the glasses deep into the hollowed out portion of the wall.

In the realm of life it was a small gesture. But for Sean it was his way of ensuring there would always be a physical reminder of Elijah resting alongside the island's most treasured document when it was returned from the Guardians. He realized, with a sudden burst of self-awareness, that this deeply personal tribute was his way of continuing the journey of taking the mantle of leadership from the fallen Prophet. Somehow, the possibility of being a guide for the islanders now seemed a little less intimidating.

With this thought in mind Sean slowly walked back to the bench. Sitting down, he began to wait. Soon, his birthmark started to throb. It had been months since he'd experienced the ache, and on this occasion, he sensed it meant the Spirit was near.

Moments later, an aura of tranquility cocooned Sean. He was no longer captured by negative thoughts. His mind and body were acting in consort, and it felt like a willowy breeze was caressing him. There was an awareness about him that heightened his senses. He vividly felt the cave's permanence and was conscious of the calm this brought him. It wasn't as though his mind was filled with good thoughts. Rather, the feeling of ease was an end in itself. All that existed was an acceptance of complete peace.

"Hello, Sean," said a voice that floated lazily through his subconscious, like billowy, rich, white clouds drifting in a sapphire-blue sky on a warm summer day.

The Spirit had arrived. But this was unique from Sean's past experiences with it. There was no distinct difference between him and the Spirit. His mind was not being stretched to comprehend its power. Instead, he felt as one with the Spirit and appreciated the universe's majesty in a way that left him marveling at the grandeur of the billions of galaxies comprising the Spirit's realm.

He understood it was presenting a shared experience that revealed the Spirit's desire to work with him in having the Janus concept of peace brought to the world. But despite the tranquility, there was something stirring in Sean that he knew had to be discussed before there could be any talk of peace.

"Why did you allow Elijah to be murdered?" he began. "The Prophet was a true messenger of harmony between all people and yet you permitted him to be destroyed with violence. Elijah was a kind and gentle person whose life was dedicated to helping others. Yet you allowed him to be killed by a bullet. I don't understand how you could abandon someone who had so much faith in you."

Sean suddenly realized he was breathing heavily and taking gulps of air. The feeling of tranquility was gone, lost in the vapors of his anger and the resentment he felt toward the Spirit. He wanted to lash out, and for the moment, Elijah's death represented all that was wrong with the world.

"You claim to provide humans with the gift of life yet have no interest in what happens to them. What is the point of humanity if so much of the globe is marked by hatred and unrest because of religion, skin color, or race? It doesn't have to be this way. We are all part of the human family, yet people focus on our differences rather than our similarities. People take advantage of one another, there is rampant poverty throughout the globe, and violence continues unabated.

"Why are you allowing this to happen?"

Sean had been so intent on his tirade that only when he stopped talking did he realize how profoundly silent the cave had become. It was as though all sound had been driven from the cavern to be replaced with a nothingness that reached deep into his soul. He never realized silence could be a force unto itself, yet he felt the overwhelming power of a stillness that was almost physically and mentally crushing.

No sound was escaping from the fire. The flames were flashing in an ever-arching dance, but they were performing with the silence of a mime. Sean shuffled his feet and heard the welcome rustle of shoes on sand-covered stone. He snapped the middle finger and thumb of his right hand and was comforted by the noise. However, when he stopped all movement, nature's stillness again overwhelmed him. He was caught in the vortex of a void and instinctively knew the Spirit had withdrawn its essence from the cave, causing a vacuum of silence to remain.

Sean tried to focus on the discussion he would have about the Spirit working with him and the islanders. But his thoughts seemed untethered and disjointed. He found it difficult to concentrate in the silence.

He knew the Spirit professed to be devoid of emotions. The universe was its domain, and the force inherent in the constant ebb and flow of more than one billion galaxies with their planets, stars, and moons provided the Spirit's energy. It claimed to have no need of simple human feelings for motivation. And yet it had retreated from the cave when criticized.

Sean was puzzled by the seeming contradiction. Did the Spirit possibly possess a grain of human emotion? Was that why it was so interested in what happened to humanity and to earth? This was something Sean had never thought to consider. It had previously been beyond the realm of his consciousness. What was the Spirit but a force of the cosmos? It had repeatedly claimed that fact in their previous conversations. He chased through his mind for several seconds the concept of the Spirit possibly having some form of human feelings, but no satisfactory conclusion would come.

He was frustrated the Spirit had left without engaging him in conversation. It didn't auger well for their future relationship. Was the Spirit so autocratic that any criticism was met with a refusal to discuss the subject? If he did decide to work with it, there'd be times when disagreements would occur.

Sean accepted that it obviously could not be a partnership of equals.

But he would be adamant that, in every discussion, his opinion was to be considered before arriving at a mutually agreed upon conclusion. That was the way of Janus. If the island's message of peace was going to be conveyed to the world, then it had to be reflected in not only Sean's arrangement with the Spirit, but also its relationship with the islanders.

The Spirit believed that, eventually, every citizen of Janus would be an active advocate for world peace. However, before any of that could happen, Sean knew he had to arrive at an understanding with it. That was supposed to be the purpose of today's session. The longer Sean sat, there was a growing awareness that he shouldn't have allowed his anger at Elijah's death to govern his first words with the Spirit.

It was not so much an acknowledgement of the Spirit's ultimate power. Rather, it was an acceptance that, in any relationship, condemnation should be tempered with understanding. And a fair part of that consideration should begin with trying to determine why the action was or wasn't taken. Only then should there be criticism, and it should be constructive.

Easier thought than done, reflected Sean. But it was a valuable lesson for the future—not only in his dealings with the Spirit, but also in all his relationships. It was something the islanders had practiced for generations and was part of the foundation that enabled them to live in harmony.

The silence continued its relentless attack on his nerves. Sean considered leaving. But with the community meeting set for that evening, Sean knew he had to have what he was going to do settled in his mind before facing the islanders. And the only way that could be accomplished was by coming to terms with the Spirit.

But what if it didn't return? However, Sean had an instinctive feeling that the Spirit would revisit the cave. Through the *hope of Janus*, he had been chosen by the Spirit to lead the islanders in bringing some semblance of peace to the world. Would it let a momentary tirade derail that mission?

Sean waited. And then he noticed that the fire was crackling and hissing. He didn't know how long it had been making noise, but he welcomed the sound, with anticipation that it meant the Spirit was close by. But the time passed, and there was no sense it had arrived. The fire was burning low, and Sean felt a chill throughout the cave. He got up and placed more coal and peat on the flames. Fueled by this rebirth, they were soon cavorting and frolicking, bringing heat to the area around the benches.

The warmth was comforting. And then Sean realized that it was not only coming from the fire, but that the Spirit was also infusing the cave with its presence. He could feel the entity within the beating of his heart. His life force had melded with the Spirit, and Sean wasn't sure where the essence of each began or ended. But this time, there were no secrets about the universe being revealed. The Spirit was focused on what it wanted to discuss with Sean.

"You're back," he quietly observed.

"I have returned to continue our discussion. But first there is something you must understand."

There was a pause, and Sean had a unique sensation of traveling deeply back through an unfolding universe. It was illusion rather than reality, but for him it contained all the characteristics of a journey. He had lost track of time and space.

And then it stopped. He had no understanding of where he was. Sean puzzled at the sensory experience and wondered what it meant. The question was soon answered.

"I am giving you a tangible and personal demonstration of how deeply what I am about to say is embedded within the human psyche. From the beginning, I have given every human the most precious element I can bestow—free will. How can I provide this ultimate liberty and then interfere with the way it is used? Free will is the essence of humanity. With it, humans have progressed through the centuries to an era of relative self-awareness. Up until this point, I have chosen to let humanity walk a variety of paths to where earth now finds itself.

"But much of the world has lost its way. There are inequalities of wealth, destruction of the globe's ecology, and escalating violence both individually and collectively. I watch all this and know I cannot interfere. For if I begin, where do I stop? More importantly, how can people exist in a world where there would be no consequences? All concept of reality would be lost. And if I save one individual or a thousand from an untimely death, what about the millions of other people? I possess neither the desire nor the willingness to intervene. It is also not in the best interest of humanity if I were to do so."

"Is that what happened with Elijah? You chose not to interfere because you have never become involved."

"I did not allow Elijah to be killed."

The words were spoken with an intensity that surprised Sean. Obviously, Elijah's death had stirred something within the Spirit. Sean wondered if his earlier thought about it possessing even a small particle of humanity was accurate in some way.

"His death was a premeditated human act," continued the Spirit in the same passionate voice. "It did not involve any other aspect of your world, such as a natural occurrence like an earthquake. The subtlety may be difficult for you to comprehend, but it is nevertheless real. Just because I do not interfere in the events of your world does not mean I permit events to take place.

"It is true that I am omniscient, to use a unique human word that is applied to me. But that does not mean I bear a responsibility for what humans do to each other. And this is the case whether the actions are positive or negative. Once again, we are talking about free will. The affairs of humanity are like the waters of a river flowing to an ever-shifting sea. It is not for me to interfere with their eventual destination."

"So, why have you chosen this time to take a direct interest in what happens on earth?"

"Do not mistake my calling on you to lead a movement for peace as a sign that I am becoming intimately involved in your world's affairs. The need for a dedication to peace, an understanding of earth's environment, and a commitment to equality has never been more important than at this time in your globe's history.

"But all of these can only be accomplished through human endeavor. I will guide only you and you alone, for ultimately it must be the will of each and every person to make the world better than it is now. Every individual has the ability to reach out to another person and build an earth that is hospitable to all humans.

"That is what I am calling on you to start. Begin with the people of Janus. They must learn to appreciate that their island is unique in that, on it, there is peace, equality, and a devotion to enhancing the environment. This is the true meaning of wealth, for it is a commitment to the present and to the future. But it is uncommon in the world. And, through you, I am calling on them to move beyond Janus and to demonstrate that a cooperative peace between nations, societies, and cultures is the only way forward for your world."

Sean sensed something he had felt before about the Spirit's interest in earth. It radiated through the Spirit's words that, while it claimed to be devoid of feeling, there was the hint of something deeper—an emotion of caring. It surprised Sean and made him curious.

"Why are you so interested in earth?" he asked. "Your domain is massive, filled with billions of stars and planets, yet my world seems to hold your attention. Why is that?"

"Earth is not unique within my universe," began the Spirit. "There are many planets with life—some humanoid, others whose appearance would shock you. All are in various stages of physical, emotional, and psychological development. Some are behind earth, while others are light-years ahead in their contemplation of what constitutes life and their place in the galaxy they inhabit.

"But of all my planets, earth, I believe, is at the most critical point in its history. People have become corrupted by wealth and power. Technology has become a tool to enhance the lives of a few, while many others are left behind. The growth of weapons continues to escalate. However, it is the ongoing degradation of the environment that poses the largest threat, and little is being done to reverse the destruction humans are imposing on the ecology.

"Progress at this point does not mean more weapons or continuing advancements in self-serving technology. Rather, it rests with the development of humanity's awareness about the planet you all inhabit. And that can only truly take form with a commitment to peace. The problems over the ecology cannot be solved until all nations band together in a responsible manner with an understanding that commitments have to be honored. There has to be a greater distribution of resources, and once again, that can only result through a harmonious understanding that global sharing is the answer.

"Just as important, the task will not be completed until there is equality and understanding between all peoples, regardless of race, color, or belief. It becomes most important where men and women are concerned. No person—and just as truly, no religion, society, or culture—is superior to another. All form the human family, and it is time people recognized the humanity in each other."

The words had been spoken without a hint of passion. It had been a cold catalogue of the world's ills, prompting Sean to feel emboldened about defending his planet.

"Much of what you say is true," he began. "But there is an awareness about the problems facing earth, and I believe we are willing to confront the issues, especially as it relates to the ecology."

"Confronting is not solving," said the Spirit, its tone clipped and without emotion. "There is only one solution, and that lies in a concerted drive toward global harmony."

Sean believed he knew what was coming next. It was time to make a decision he had resisted for more than two years. "I suppose this is where you and I discuss working together as we turn the islanders into ambassadors of peace."

"No one is asking you to be another Elijah," responded the Spirit. "The role I envision for you is very different. It speaks to a new global order—one where peace and security replace war and unrest."

"I don't know if you understand the enormity of what it will take to stabilize the world," said Sean. "It will require time and a unique foresight among people who choose to join our movement. By its very nature, it must begin small—in communities, then cities, then nations, and then regions—before the world can truly be called a place of peace and enlightenment. It will take several generations of hard and committed work to make the world a place where everyone has a future they can truly believe in against the background of a sane and progressive globe.

"We can only trust it will occur before time runs out, especially for the environment. But I agree with you on one important point. It must begin now."

"That is truly what the *hope of Janus* signifies," said the Spirit. "People will need the optimism that Janus can provide. If close to two thousand people can live in peace for two millennia, what is to stop the world from venturing down the same path."

"I will lead the islanders," said Sean. "But I will not be the emissary of peace for the globe. I believe a group of true leaders will emerge from among those on Janus. They will reach out and create more trailblazers, who will eventually span the world. Diane will be involved with me. It must be understood that we are equal partners in this mission. Whatever pertains to me applies to her. If you want equality throughout the world, then you must recognize the equality within our relationship."

"I never viewed that as an issue," responded a seemingly perplexed Spirit. "Equality extends to all humans, regardless of sexual orientation, race, gender, or color."

Sean couldn't help but notice that the Spirit no longer conveyed the cold and distant attitude it had at the beginning of their conversation. The Spirit seemed warmer and more willing to discuss rather than dictate. He wondered if this was the relationship Elijah had had with it. If that were the case, it would explain why the Prophet was so anxious and positive about Sean working with the Spirit.

"I think it's too early to tell the islanders about your plan for the world," said Sean. "They are just coming to terms with Elijah's death. I will explain that we are working toward an understanding, and while Diane and I are not yet in a position to be their spiritual leaders, it is a role we will gradually assume over time. For the present and the immediate future, do we have your approval to be their guides and mentors?"

"You have grasped some of what I was saying, but in essence you have missed the most important point," said the Spirit. "You don't need my approval, and I am not giving it. Rather, we have an understanding that the island needs leadership, and along with Diane, you are going to provide it. This is the same for the world. Moving it back from the brink of destruction will be the task of those who are willing to take responsibility. It all rests with the Janus principles of understanding and peace. Every person, in their own way, has to adopt these tenets and take it upon themselves to make your world a better place.

"This is how we'll work in the future. I will offer guidance, but as free-thinking beings, you and Diane will have a choice about whether you follow my words. The result will be what you create. I will not be a part of the result. Remember, I do not interfere or participate in your world. Many may believe differently, but this is my reality."

Sean was about to say he'd try his best to fulfill the Spirit's faith in him, when he noticed a void where his mind had linked with the Spirit. It had left, and there would be no further conversation for this day. Sean sat and was suddenly overwhelmed with the commitment he'd made. He was about to go before the islanders and pledge that he and Diane would become their guides and mentors. And after that was the momentous task of convincing everyone on Janus to be global ambassadors for peace. But the more he thought about it, the more he experienced a feeling of pure joy.

Sean looked around the cave. He was surprised at how intimate it felt. No longer was it a cavern of jagged and impersonal rock with a smooth, sand-covered granite base. He now realized why Elijah had felt so at home here. In many ways, Sean had come to terms with himself. He had defined a purpose for his life, which he believed was what the pursuit of happiness was about. He had a goal he truly believed in—leading the islanders on a march toward universal peace.

And he realized with a sudden clarity that having a purpose, so long as it didn't hurt or hinder anyone and regardless of what it encompassed, was the essence of being fulfilled with life. He had spent his life going from one project to another, without really defining what he wanted to accomplish. Always there was the feeling that he should be happy, but the emotion seemed just out of reach. He knew there would be difficult days ahead and that not everything would fall into place as he hoped. But there was now a line, a backstop that he could always come back to—his purpose.

And he also realized something else. It was not his talk with the Spirit that had defined his focus. He had come to it on his own, following conversations with Elijah and Diane. Similar to how individuals would make the world realize that change was needed; people had reached out to him and helped him find a goal.

Sean got up and trod slowly over to the stream that trickled along the cave's eastern wall. He took the metal bucket, filled it with water, walked back to the fire, and emptied the contents over the flames. The fire hissed and threw off some sparks. Sean waited a few minutes to make sure it was out. Walking to the cave's mouth and out into the day's fading light, he proceeded up the path that would take him to the Ring Road and then the house and the future shared with Diane.

Chapter Fifty-Seven

Sean, seated next to Diane, glanced around the Community Center. Every seat but one was filled. This would be the first general session in more than half a century not led by Elijah. For many islanders, he was the only spiritual leader they had known. As a matter of respect, his usual chair in the assembly's front row had been left vacant. It was not an orchestrated tribute, but rather a sense throughout the gathering that their former Prophet deserved the honor—at least until a new mentor was chosen.

Journey had come in that morning. Andrew and Leyland were seated in the front row. A number of Guardians, including Bella and Olga were also in the hall but seated farther back.

A quiet air of expectation permeated the center. Choosing someone as a guide would be a new and unique process. It marked a dramatic change from more than two thousand years of history, and there was a recognition the islanders were participating in a momentous event.

The towering, white-haired figure of Ian McKenzie strode to the hall's front. "I have been asked by several of you to chair this gathering," he began. "But as we do with all collective decisions, there should be a vote to determine if that meets with everyone's approval."

Sean looked back across the hall and saw that everybody had put up a hand signifying their agreement.

"Excellent," said Ian. "Let's get started. It's difficult for all of us, but our task this evening is choosing a successor to Elijah.

"Before his death, the Prophet indicated that Sean should be our next guide. This was revealed when the Spirit agreed he should wear the *hope of Janus*. As we know, this signifies a defining and crucial bond with the Spirit. The union is also shown through Sean's triangular birthmark and his direct link to Jesus as written in our codex. We should also remember that, while Sean's family has not lived on the island for more than a century, it originally came here with the first settlers. So he is definitely one of us."

As Sean listened to Ian describe his ties to the Spirit, he couldn't help but marvel that a door was opening to a completely new phase in his life. His existence would be fundamentally influenced through a direct connection to the Spirit. And there was his relationship with Diane. Her involvement in not only working with him as they mentored the islanders but also with her equal role in the Spirit's movement for peace, meant their lives would be virtually consumed with the island's future.

Once again Sean experienced the satisfaction of having a purpose to his life. The prospect of joining with Diane and the Spirit in working with the islanders had a calming effect that he was glad to be experiencing and that had previously eluded him.

When Ian asked if he'd agree to being nominated for election, Sean immediately replied in a voice that carried throughout the hall that he would gladly accept becoming the Janus guide if that's what everyone wanted.

Ian beckoned Sean to join him. As Sean was walking to the front, the doctor looked out over the crowd and said, "Is there anyone else who would like to be considered as a successor to Elijah?"

From the back, a hand was raised. Sean recognized that it belonged to Lucy Colberra, manager of the fish sorting plant at the harbor. "I believe Sean is an excellent choice as our next guide," she said. "But before there's a final decision, I believe we'd all like to know about your relationship with the Spirit. Elijah was our spiritual mentor, and while I recognize you'll not be immediately fulfilling the role, it's important to know about your future plans to accept that responsibility."

Sean waited a moment before answering. Following his conversation with Diane, he had given the subject much thought.

He began in a clear, strong voice. "As you know, my association with the Spirit is relatively new. When it comes to determining the relationship's boundaries, we are still learning our expectations of each other. I believe this is only natural. We have discussed what my future role will be here on Janus, and those talks will continue.

"But I commit to each of you that I will work with the Spirit in ensuring it remains integral to every islander's life. In that way, there will be no difference between my role and the one Elijah fulfilled. You also have my pledge that I am dedicated to making certain the ideals of tolerance, understanding, and peace remain a vital and living part of our culture as they have for two thousand years.

"There will be challenges in the years ahead, just as there have always been. I will stand with you in confronting them, and together we will continue building a tomorrow that provides all islanders the opportunity to realize their hopes and aspirations."

Sean brought his talk to a close by telling everyone that he would always be available to counsel, while at the same time more than willing to take advice in helping him be a better guide and mentor.

A tide of applause swept through the hall. Sean believed he had been honest and straightforward about his relationship with the Spirit and was glad the islanders appreciated his candor.

Once the clapping stopped, Ian again asked if anyone wanted to join Sean as a candidate to succeed Elijah. No one put up their hand.

Sean looked at Diane who nodded her head. This was the time to put forth a sharing of responsibility.

"Before there's a vote," said Sean, "I'd like to propose a change to how the leadership function will be handled."

It was obvious from the undercurrent of voices and the confused looks that the islanders had assumed the next order of business would be to confirm Sean.

Ian quickly turned to him and asked, "What are you suggesting?"

Sean felt every pair of eyes swivel from Ian to his direction and knew he had the hall's complete attention. "As you know, it's dictated in the Word of Janus that I will have an equal partner in all respects. That person is Diane. What I would like to see happen this evening is that we carry the message contained in the codex through to having Diane share the island's leadership role with me."

The room reacted with stunned silence. Janus had never been guided by two people. Not only had the islanders lost Elijah, but now they were also being asked to break with a centuries-old tradition. Sean watched as everyone quietly processed his request.

Finally, Marcus Burne, owner of the Knob, the island's general store, stood. "You wear the *hope of Janus*," he began. "That, more than anything, tells me that you are viewed as a confidant by the Spirit. And now you're proposing that Diane join you. I'm wondering if this is an indication that the Spirit intends on bringing the Word of Janus to life. As we know, the codex states that the two of you will one day work with all of us in showing the world the true meaning of peace.

"Is there more to your proposal than just having you and Diane lead us? Are we going to wake up one day soon and find that the Spirit has enlisted us in its plan? Does it mean we are on the verge of losing our anonymity by becoming some form of global ambassadors? We haven't been consulted about participating in such a movement. And if we were, I doubt many of us would want to go along with it."

As was the case with everything on Janus, the words were spoken quietly and with no sign of an argument. Marcus was merely stating facts that he wanted clarified. And from the nodding of heads in the hall, it was easy for Sean to understand that everyone agreed with the Knob's owner. Despite Janus's non-confrontational way of life, the islanders, as Sean had warned the Spirit, would resist becoming involved in any movement that threatened to destroy their separation from the world.

Sean hadn't wanted this discussion to happen at the meeting. He still believed it was too soon after Elijah's death for it to be debated. But the subject had been raised, and Sean decided to directly confront the issue. He knew that discussing the Spirit's involvement in a global peace movement would alarm many islanders. However, he wasn't going to share their lives and ask them to accept Diane's involvement by hiding the truth.

"I have had some talks with the Spirit about a global initiative for peace," he said, to a stone-silent hall. "But there are a number of things you should know. The discussions are still extremely preliminary. I have yet to determine my role. No decision has been made about how deeply Janus will be involved. And participation by any of you will only come through the island's collective agreement to move forward on this project."

From the far right corner of the hall a woman immediately stood. It was Loretta Heine, who captained a fishing boat. "What are we to make of all this?" she asked. "I came here this evening to vote for a guide and mentor. And somehow we're also discussing our involvement in an idea the Spirit has for world peace. As you know, I've lived out beyond our shores. The reality of global peace is that it will never materialize unless the Spirit gets involved. And I can't see that happening.

"I believe we all want Sean to be our leader. So that just leaves two things to decide. Should Diane be involved in guiding us? And do we want to work with the Spirit? I say let's discuss Diane's participation and have Sean tell the Spirit we're not interested in its plan."

A blast of applause rocketed around the hall. The clapping was loud and sustained. Finally, Ian raised his arms, and the center became quiet.

"The first thing we'll do is vote on Sean and Diane becoming our guides," said Ian, his voice loud and authoritative. "After that, we'll discuss Loretta's motion to have Sean tell the Spirit we won't participate in whatever it is proposing for us."

Looking over at Sean, Ian declared, "The floor is yours."

An expectant quiet had overtaken the hall. Sean took several moments to look around the center. He realized with startling clarity how important Janus had become to him. There was confusion about the Spirit's plans for the island, but he knew with a deep certainty that he and Diane could guide everyone through whatever the future might hold. He was ready to lead.

"The proposal that Diane and I share the role of mentor is, in many ways, a recognition that, with Elijah's passing, change has come to Janus," Sean said. "As islanders, we have always been progressive and enlightened about our belief that there are no boundaries between cultures, races, or sexes. Each of us contributes equally and in our own way to the benefit of everyone.

I believe that our society can truly gain by having a man and a woman as guides. We will bring different perspectives to the various issues that confront us, both individually and collectively. And that is important. This is not a criticism of Elijah and his family. It is, however, an acknowledgement that the principles governing our society evolve over time, without a change to their fundamental purpose. My request provides us another opportunity to continue enhancing our tenets of understanding, forgiveness, tolerance, equality, and peace.

"And while they ensure every islander enjoys the same rights and freedoms, there should be no room for complacency. With this change comes the opportunity to review and strengthen our society. Our basic beliefs have and will continue to be the bedrock for how we live. They have evolved with time because it has always been accepted and understood that the task of enshrining them into the way we live is a continuing responsibility we all share.

"That is what Diane and I are placing before you this evening."

Sean paused. It seemed as though everyone had been holding their breath, for there appeared to be a collective exhaling of air.

However, Sean wasn't finished. He looked over at Diane. She nodded her head, got up from her chair, and joined him and Ian.

"This is a vital position within our community," she said. "And by combining my knowledge of the island and our history along with Sean's experience in the world, I believe we can truly extend the work Elijah has done. While we can't ever hope to replace him, we will both put our heart and soul into ensuring the gift of friendship and understanding Elijah brought to everyone lives on in the work we do.

"As your nurse, I have treated and helped Ian mend your bodies. During those times, I have had many talks with you about what is happening in your lives. We have shared our hopes, dreams, and sometimes the difficulties. This won't be much different, except I can now guide you about the Spirit, which was always Elijah's role. I truly believe that what Sean and I can offer would be a true benefit to the island."

Diane stopped and took a long look around the hall. Sean knew from experience that she was carefully considering her next words.

"I also realize that what we have discussed about the Spirit becoming directly involved in our lives is deeply unsettling," Diane said. "This proposed intrusion is unprecedented. I understand that many of you feel that just because we speak with the Spirit does not mean it can dictate to us. And I agree. But we also have to recognize that, while Janus is separate from the world, what happens beyond our border—whether it has to do with the environment or the globe's social order—will eventually impact us and, more importantly, impact our diaspora."

Diane paused for several moments, before saying, "The justification for giving up our anonymity and peaceful lives in the Spirit's pursuit of global harmony is something we need to discuss. It is a decision we will make as individuals, for we all have the right to choose our society's destiny. However, there is the consideration that, as our principles evolve, so should how we view our position as it relates to the globe's reality."

Having concluded what she wanted to say, Diane said, "I'll now hand the meeting back to Ian."

Before Ian could utter a word, Loretta stood again and declared, "Diane is right. We have always controlled our lives, and that must not be allowed to change. Let's have the vote about Diane and Sean as our guides. After that, we can decide what to do about the Spirit's proposal."

Sean noticed that a majority of islanders were nodding their heads in agreement. He knew it wasn't about the vote but had everything to do with rebuking the Spirit. Since the first settlers, Janus had been isolated from the world, and that had served the islanders well. The thought of giving up their peace and security held no appeal for them.

This placed Sean in a difficult position. As he had discussed with the Spirit, he believed that, given time, the islanders would eventually support its initiative. However, Loretta had just moved the issue to the present and made any future negotiations with the islanders incredibly challenging. How was he going to reconcile his role as a mentor who believed in the Spirit's proposition with the islanders who seemed ready to reject the plan?

It was a problem that needed to be resolved before Sean could begin determining his future relationship with the Spirit.

Ian cut into Sean's thoughts by loudly proclaiming, "I think we're ready to vote on Diane and Sean becoming our guides. Are there any questions before we proceed?"

No one put up a hand or stood.

Sean realized this was a defining moment in his life. The implications of the journey on which he was about to embark were staggering. Along with Diane, he would oversee the well-being of close to twenty-two thousand people when the

The Hope of Janus

Guardians and the island's diaspora were added to the Janus population. His conversations with the Spirit would take on a new dimension in the search for global peace. The life he was living with Diane would move to a higher level of commitment. The challenges and the possibilities of what the future could hold were intriguing.

But am I ready? Sean wondered. He reflected on his deliberations about a purpose for his life and the responsibility inherent in the *hope of Janus*. And then he realized that this was his opportunity to make a positive difference—regardless of how large or small—in the lives of those around him. And in that instant Sean knew he was eager to walk a new path.

Sean was so caught up in his thoughts that he almost missed Ian's call for a vote. The consensus was unanimous. The doctor turned, grasped Sean's right hand in his, and shook it with enthusiasm. He repeated the action with Diane.

"Elijah's legacy now rests with you," said the doctor. "The Prophet's work was the essence of what it means to be an islander. You will be our guides with the Spirit and become mentors to us all. I know you appreciate this is a heavy responsibility, but it's obvious everyone believes the two of you will continue the Prophet's philosophy of compassion and understanding."

Sean was momentarily stunned at how humbled he felt that the islanders had so much faith in him and Diane. This was a new beginning for Janus, and he was immensely proud of the islanders. Ian asked if either of them had anything to say, and Sean indicated he did.

Ian moved to one side and beckoned for Sean to move forward.

Sean looked out over the gathering. Collecting his thoughts, he said, "It is a privilege to know you believe we can continue

Elijah's work. Once again you have stayed true to the Janus vision of being open-minded and forward-thinking when it comes to human values. It would have been simple to dismiss our request to have Diane join me as one of your guides. You could have chosen to reject our proposal for several reasons, including it had never been done, we'd always had a man, and how this might impact Elijah's legacy. Yet you looked past all that—not because Diane is a woman but because you knew she is qualified for the work.

"We are all part of the human family. There is no reason our lives should not be lived with equal opportunities for all persons. Diversity, inclusiveness, and equality have marked the Janus story through the centuries. Based on your decision tonight, I can see these principles will be with us well into the future."

Sean wasn't sure what he expected to happen after his words, but the silence that greeted his brief talk left him wondering what the islanders were thinking. The answer was provided by Agnes Palmerston, a sheepherder who stood and said, "Thank you for the kind words. But this is the way we are. There is no need to congratulate ourselves. No one thinks specifically about equality. We simply believe all people should have a fair opportunity, regardless of the task.

"As I'm sure you have discovered, Janus is more than just our home. We have built a society based on the words you used not because we had to for survival but because our ancestors realized that here was an opportunity to create a culture based on the best of human principles. It is true that our continued existence has come through adhering to these tenets, but we follow them because we genuinely believe that the common thread among us is our desire to live in harmony with one another and provide ourselves with a future we can all believe in.

"I know you bring experience from the world, and that will add to our knowledge of different ways to do things. But I also trust you'll allow us to share with you what we have learned over the centuries. In that way, hopefully we can learn from each other."

Agnes sat down, and Sean smiled. The response was typical of the islanders' mind-set. They were kind and thoughtful people whose lives of understanding and tolerance were not forced or mandated but, rather, a simple recognition that living in peace is to be enjoyed and treasured.

"I'll probably learn a lot more from all of you than you'll learn from me," said Sean to comfortable laughter around the hall.

Chapter Fifty-Eight

✥

After the laughter had subsided, Ian glanced quickly at Sean before saying, "This is the first any of us, with the exception of Sean and Diane, have heard about the Spirit's project. I believe that, as Loretta stated, we have no desire to be a part of the Spirit's plan for some form of global peace. It is, or should be, quite capable of doing that without destroying our way of life. We want to continue living separate from the world."

Sean understood. Peace was fragile. It had to be worked at and respected. The islanders were not only justifiably afraid of losing a culture anchored in collective harmony, they were also confused by the enormity of what the Spirit was asking.

Susan Minor, the island's botanist and part of a farming family from the northern peninsula, rose from her chair and, looking at Sean, said, "During your talks with the Spirit, what exactly did it say about this peace project?"

Sean took a minute to frame his thoughts. "We spoke about the Spirit's overriding concern for earth's future. It is deeply troubled by the human inequalities that exist, along with an ongoing lack of concern for the environment and the continuing wars between cultures and societies. The Spirit believes that, with Janus's deep commitment to societal peace, coupled with our respect for earth's ecosystem, we can show the world what can be accomplished by recognizing the importance of committing to a stable future."

"So, we are expected to instantly give up everything that has sustained us for two thousand years because the Spirit has decided that humanity now needs to be saved from itself?" asked Susan, frustration clearly evident in her voice.

"In defense of the Spirit, there was never the intention that we would immediately begin working with it," Sean answered. "The Spirit realizes just how important our anonymity is to every islander. It is prepared to work with each of us in determining how best to convey what has been accomplished on Janus."

"We are slightly less than two thousand people," said Marcus. "How can we ever hope to change the world? My issue is that we will be giving up so much for what I believe is a project destined to fail, unless the Spirit is directly involved. And if it does participate, why does it need us?"

"That's exactly my point," added Loretta. "If the Spirit wants things to change, it certainly has the power to make that happen. Perhaps it's time the Spirit looked at who's causing the problems and deal directly with them, instead of calling on us."

An enthusiastic burst of applause followed Loretta's words.

Although Sean had expected there would be opposition, he was surprised that it encompassed so many residents. Since he hadn't intended to have this discussion for some time Sean felt woefully unprepared. But here it was. Somehow the project needed to be salvaged, at least until he could speak with the Spirit.

"Humanity has been given the gift of free will," began Sean. "But with that comes the need to accept responsibility for our words and actions. If the world is to arrive at some semblance of peace, it has to come from a willingness of people to acknowledge that solutions to the world's problems will only come about if individuals take it upon themselves to work and cooperate with each other.

"At the same time, it cannot be mandated that vast groups of individuals seek collaborative solutions to the world's problems. There are no simplistic answers. The Spirit isn't compelling us to become involved. But it is asking us to be a force for good. And we wouldn't be alone. There are many enlightened groups, nations, and societies that are striving to make this world a better place for all inhabitants. We could enlist them in our cause. The difference between us and them is that we would be guided by the Spirit. It would assist but not interfere."

Sean held up his right hand and pointed to the ring. "The *hope of Janus* represents an aspirational belief that we can be a vital part of leading the world toward peace. The Spirit is thinking of earth in its totality. I realize that the island's harmony is to be treasured. But peace is not ours to own, and our good fortune should be shared. As islanders, we have a responsibility not only to ourselves, but also to the world. We are rich in many ways. Shouldn't we be prepared to use that wealth of knowledge and cooperation to help others who are striving for the same thing we have?

"We have people from throughout the world on our island and within our diaspora. We believe passionately in the equality of every human being. With the Spirit's assistance, we have the opportunity to take this message beyond the island. We can reach past our every day lives and show people that cultural and societal harmony can be a reality.

"All I am asking is that you allow me the opportunity to talk with the Spirit and understand what it envisions our role will be. Most people want a safe and sane world. What's needed is a vehicle to galvanize these individuals into working together and learning how to build the foundation that enables peace. It is more than good intentions. It means equal opportunities for education, jobs, and housing and, most importantly, respect for one another. But it has to start somewhere, and the Spirit is telling us that, given our history, we can be leaders."

Sean stopped talking. He had brought passion and, he hoped, logic to his belief that the islanders should at least meet with the Spirit before categorically dismissing its plan. The hall was quiet as each person pondered what Sean had said. He felt weary, his emotions spent. Sean hadn't realized until this moment how much, both physically and mentally, he had invested in defending the Spirit's plan.

He wondered who would speak and hoped it would be someone who shared his view. However, Sean wasn't surprised when Loretta stood. He was prepared to have her recommend a vote to decline working with the Spirit. Sean was already deliberating about what he would tell it during his next visit to the cave.

"You still haven't convinced me that we should participate," said Loretta. "But you made some good points about a responsibility to reach out and share what we have. I'm willing to propose that each of us discuss this peace concept with the Spirit and then hold a vote to decide whether we'll be involved."

Sean let out an involuntary sigh of relief. Given that the idea of working for peace had been a surprise to the islanders, Sean knew Loretta's proposition was the best he could hope for. Now, he waited to see how everyone would react.

Ian asked if anyone was opposed to Loretta's proposal. There was a general rustling among the gathering, but no one put up a hand to vote it down.

"We have a unanimous agreement," said Ian. "Given Sean's relationship with the Spirit and since he and Diane are our counselors, the next meeting on this subject should be called by them. Does everyone agree?"

It seemed to Sean that every hand reached upward.

Finally, it was over. Sean looked at Diane and returned her smile. Knowing that he'd soon be home with Diane lightened his mood.

"Is there anything else? Or can I close the meeting?" asked Ian.

"Before we adjourn, I'd like to know what plans Sean and Diane have regarding Dante Sabatini and the Praetorian Order?" asked Andrew from his chair in the front row. "I believe this is an ongoing threat to Janus. The order has stolen the Word of Janus; attacked our compound; and killed Elijah, along with two other men."

Sean could sense the hall's renewed interest. This was something that struck deeply at the island's core.

"I am not asking for physical retribution," continued Andrew. "What I want to know—and I'm sure everyone here has the same question—is how are we going to protect ourselves in the future?"

Given the Guardian's temperament, Sean had expected the question from Andrew and was prepared.

"I believe there is a way to fundamentally cripple the order without the need for placing any of our people in physical danger," he said. "It will involve engaging the order through non-violent actions. We will stay true to the Janus principles."

"So you have a plan," voiced Andrew.

"The beginning of one," cautioned Sean. "Our strength and the order's weakness in this conflict is that, apart from the highest reaches of the Church, we are the only ones in the world who know it exists. More importantly, we have been engaged in a cyberwar with it for years. This gives us extraordinary knowledge that I believe we can expand on and exploit."

"You believe we can attack the order through its computer network?" There was no mistaking the surprise in Andrew's voice.

"If what I'm thinking can be done, we'll be able to cripple Sabatini and the order. But before we go any farther, I need to meet with Olga, Bella, Leyland, and you in Inverness."

"When will that be? From my perspective, and for the safety of Janus, it can't be soon enough."

"I have some things to take care of here on the island. You'll be returning in six weeks with our fall supplies. I'll travel back with you then."

Andrew nodded his head in agreement. "I wish it could be sooner, but I suppose that will have to do."

"We'll discuss everything when I'm in Inverness," said Sean, who turned to Ian and suggested the doctor bring the meeting to a close.

Ian, who, like the rest of the islanders, had been listening with rapt attention to the conversation, asked if there was anyone who had something to say. When no one responded, the doctor declared the session over.

As the center was emptying, Diane joined Sean and the couple made their way slowly out the door and on to the Road. They walked arm-in-arm toward home. Little conversation passed between the two, and what talk there was focused on the farmwork that needed to be done in the morning. There was a slight wind. No clouds obscured the moon and stars. The sea was calm, giving off a rhythmic chant as its waves washed up against the island's rocky shoreline, before retreating in an ongoing symphony of motion as old as time.

It was peaceful, and Sean knew he could never leave Janus. The commitment to Diane and to the island had brought a feeling of inner peace to his life. He was embarking on a new journey and looked forward to the future with anticipation.

Arriving at the house, the couple strode passed the front gate, up the steps onto the gallery, and through the always unlocked front door. After they had taken off their boots and while they were still standing in the front hallway, Diane made her only reference to the meeting.

"A lot happened tonight," she said. "There's our new responsibility as counselors; the islanders discovering the Spirit's plan; and, oh yes, your idea of taking down Dante by getting into a cyberwar with the order. How will that even be possible? What were you thinking?"

Sean reached out and took Diane in his arms. He could feel her body pressing into his, and he savored the physical and emotional energy it gave him. "It's been a long night," he whispered. "We can talk about how we'll face the future in the morning. Right now, I just want to get some sleep."

"That sounds like a good idea," said Diane.

With that, she stepped back and took Sean's hand. Together the two walked slowly down the hallway to the bedroom.

An excerpt from *The Time of Janus*, the final book in the four-novel Janus Chronicles

Cardinal Reinhart turned to the pope and said, "We don't have a choice. Sabatini is a threat that can no longer be tolerated. He is a cancer that will destroy our Church. If we don't do something, he will soon have complete control of the Vatican."

"That can't be allowed to happen," whispered Ambrosia. "But he has so much power. There are the incriminating files and the codex. The Praetorian Order has such incredible wealth it is beyond our influence. I feel his tentacles slowly choking me, and yet there is nothing I can do."

Reinhart didn't say anything for several moments. "I have a plan," he finally said. "It is dangerous, but there are times when one must walk through the valley of death. We have reached that point."

"What do you have in mind?" asked the pope, his voice slightly quavering.

"It is best you don't know the details, old friend. All I ask is that you bless my mission. The only way to deal with a cancer is to cut it out. And that's what I will do. Sabatini cannot be allowed to continue his stranglehold over us."

Ambrosia caught Reinhart's eyes with his own. The men stared at each other for several seconds before the pope looked away.

"There is no chance your actions will come back to haunt us?" asked Ambrosia.

"Absolutely none. Within a month, Dante Sabatini will no longer be a problem, and we will have gained control of the order."

The *Time of Janus* will be published during late Spring, 2019.

CPSIA information can be obtained
at www.ICGtesting.com
Printed in the USA
LVHW092247210420
654253LV00001B/12